FIRE
WITH
FIRE

FIRE
WITH
FIRE

ALLAN KAHANE

Pyro Publishing

Published by Pyro Publishing, LLC
191 Post Road West
Westport, CT 06880
www.pyropublishing.com
www.firewithfire.info

For ordering information or special discounts for bulk purchases, please contact
Greenleaf Book Group LP at: 4425 South Mo Pac Expwy, Suite 600,
Austin, TX 78735, (512) 891-6100.

Design and composition by Greenleaf Book Group LP

Library of Congress Control Number: 2006903670

ISBN 10: 0-9785202-0-3
ISBN 13: 978-0-9785202-0-5

Printed in the United States of America on acid-free paper

09 08 07 06   10 9 8 7 6 5 4 3 2 1

First Edition

For Patricia

PROLOGUE

———————◆●◆———————

After burying their lethal cargo in the island of Qeshm they moved away from the other boats and sailed the 55-foot Ferretti past the smaller barren island of Hormuz at a steady thirty knots.

Hormuz and Qeshm stood like bodyguards around Bandar Abbas, one of Iran's major cities and its biggest port. The crew intended to dock there and make their way to the next target, the 232,000 barrel-a-day refinery at the outskirts of town.

The deep blue waters, so tranquil beneath the surface, were swarming with military vessels. Iran was preparing to block the Strait of Hormuz, which would cut off the export route of most of the oil from Kuwait, the Emirates, and Saudi Arabia.

The Israeli cocked his head and scanned the horizon. Theirs was the only leisure boat in the area. "You'd better be sure about our security clearance," he said, straining to be heard against the pulsating drone of the boat's engine.

"I'm sure. Relax," the Frenchman answered, his deeply wrinkled face contrasting sharply with a youthful smile. "How are you doing there?"

"Almost ready," the Israeli replied, testing the remote-controlled detonator. Its LED lights were flashing red.

New York City

He smiles as he enters the toy store with his wife and daughter. As always, FAO Schwarz on Fifth Avenue and 58th Street is crowded with shoppers and children. A doll catches little Claire's eye. She dashes across the slippery floor to look closer, a single brick in a looming wall of pink and lavender.

It is then that he sees the clean-shaven man with the bulky trench coat descending the escalator and striding purposefully toward the middle of the store, past pyramids of stuffed animals and action figures in cardboard-and-cellophane boxes.

He grabs his wife and daughter, tries to protect them by pulling them deeper into the store. A small clown with huge red lips mouths the crazy cute FAO Schwarz theme-song: Welcome to the world of . . .

He registers the flash, then the oddly metallic roar, as he and Stephanie and Claire are sent flying, pushed through the air as if by huge hands.

A brief silence. Then the shriek and rumble of the escalator's slow collapse. The musical tinkling of broken glass. The bite of cordite in the nostrils. Broken toys are everywhere—he will never forget the image of the gigantic Steiff giraffe, its neck torn in two—amid the smoke and dust and unidentifiable building materials.

And blood. Everywhere.

His wife's motionless eyes are open. She lies to his right, looks almost natural. It's her head, resting against a pillar at an impossible angle, that gives her away. Then, amidst the cries and moans of the hundreds injured in the blast, he hears a soft gurgling behind him. He turns and finds his daughter. Her chest is covered with blood, which is spurting rhythmically from her mouth. Her eyes are on him, crying, "Daddy it hurts get me out of here Daddy please it hurts I can't breathe Daddy please Daddy Daddy."

Only then does he release the howl he had choked back when he had first sensed the danger, when doing what he'd always done. Handled things. Solved problems. Stayed cool.

He can do nothing now, pinned under a collapsed beam. During the eternity until he faints, he cries out to God as he totters between despair and madness.

BOOK I

CHAPTER ONE

Jake Burke had always taken the engineer's approach to odds. If the chances of something happening were minute, that thing wouldn't happen. All the telecommunications networks that he'd been an early investor in were engineered like that. The famous "four nines": 99.99 percent reliability equals 100 percent reliability. This was how Jake had become a rich man. It was his strength and the secret of his success.

And yet probability was just that: probability. It wasn't certainty. And so, on the day that Jake's life was torn apart, what had once been a small risk—so tiny as to be negligible—became reality.

Afterwards, he couldn't stop thinking about the odds. Since the start of the latest wave of terrorist attacks almost six thousand Americans had been killed—one in every fifty thousand. One chance in fifty thousand of it happening to Stephanie or Claire. One chance in 2.5 *billion* of it happening to both, if they had been strangers. But they weren't. So the odds of his family being killed were one in one hundred thousand, he had decided in his pointless calculations. *Five* nines—a 99.999 percent certainty that they would be safe. Jake had taken risks so much bigger.

Jake buried his wife and daughter side by side in Stephanie's family plot in Wisconsin. He hadn't cried yet. He couldn't. Something that happened during the explosion evaded his memory, gnawed at his sanity, denying him the finality and release of unrestrained grief. The events of that day were still replaying in his mind's eye, an ever-repeating, silent horror film.

From the moment he sighted the suicide bomber to his loss of consciousness a short time later, everything was in super-slow motion and total silence.

Something was missing, though. Something he couldn't reach. Like those forms inside the eyes, little snakes and dots that flee when you try to focus on them. It was torture.

A week after the attack, when Jake returned to the hospital to have his bandages removed, the attending physician advised him to seek a psychiatrist's help, warning him about the long-term effects of untreated trauma.

"I know your type," the doctor said, a beautifully groomed man of sixty or so who appeared to have come to New York Presbyterian straight from his barber's. "Stubborn. You think you're okay, that you can handle this on your own."

"You're right, I do."

"It doesn't work that way. The main cause of trauma is powerlessness, helplessness. It's the feeling the rape victim gets when she's being assaulted—that there's nothing she can do to stop it. Reminders of this powerlessness, or moments of stress, can cause involuntary reenactments of the traumatic event in the victim's mind."

"And . . ."

"Your chart says that you lost consciousness after the bombing, even though you were only slightly hurt."

Jake shrugged. "So what?"

"Imagine if the same thing happened in an emergency, when you needed your wits about you."

"I passed out because of the bombing. Why would it happen again?" A gurney rattled past the open door of Jake's private room, guided by two burly orderlies.

The doctor nodded. "Fainting was your reaction to the trauma. You felt powerless during the bombing, so your system went into a state of surrender. If you're reminded of that feeling and can't control it, it could happen again."

"If it happens, I'll control it. I'll just . . . focus on other things."

"Actually, that's exactly what you should do. But the hard part is remembering to do that."

Standing beside the I.V. pole on the side of the bed, the doctor turned over Jake's chart. With a slim gold ballpoint pen, he drew three circles on the back of the page. The smallest was less than an inch in diameter; the largest took over most of the page; the middle one was about three inches across.

"I've seen too many cases of untreated trauma," the doctor said. "Let me put it this way: If you don't address this, you'll have a problem this big in a very short while." He pointed to the largest circle with his pen. "You'll panic . . . I mean, *really* panic. At times you won't be able to function. You'll pray that treatment might be able to reduce the dimension of the problem to this size." Now he indicated the middle circle.

"Mm-hmm." Jake wasn't terribly engaged by the analogy. Circles: Who gave a damn? The spice-rack scent of the doctor's cologne filled his nostrils.

"The reality is that the problem's probably this big." The physician pointed to the smallest circle. "If you deal with it now, it need never grow any larger. See my point? Do *not* delay treatment."

Jake generally avoided doctors, and he'd always felt uncomfortable with the idea of seeing a shrink. Instead, soon after the bombing and the burial of his wife and daughter, he tried hard to resume his routine, beginning with exercise early each morning. One hour of cardio and one of weight-lifting six days a week. And the occasional run in Central Park. At six-foot-three, Jake weighed 180 pounds. No unnecessary fat to carry around. He had been thirty-eight when he married Stephanie. That same year he finished thirty-fourth in the New York City Marathon.

With his thick black hair, plus the recent dusting of white at the temples, the penetrating brown eyes and their playful expression, he had the looks of a movie star. At least that's what his wife had always said. A romantic lead in a 1940s black-and-white movie, to be exact.

None of it mattered now. Jake was profoundly depressed. He'd always been a morning person, but now getting out of bed each morning was a struggle—a colossal challenge, like lifting an SUV off the pavement. All Jake wanted at 5:00 A.M. was to sleep and sleep and sleep some more, as he'd done in the hospital. Consciousness meant that the bed was half-empty, that the bedroom down the hall was still. Even so, at the sound of his second alarm clock and the smell of brewing coffee, he forced himself upright and to the gym. His private trainer was waiting for him. After two grueling hours, he'd go back to the apartment, into the shower, out the door, and downtown. To work.

Jake was the founder, main shareholder and CEO of the country's third-largest hedge-fund management firm, the one that had shown the best performance in each of the last three years. Thanks to a combination of intelligence and energy, he'd already accumulated enormous wealth. Now the intelligence was dulled; Jake's head felt swaddled in bubble-wrap. He found his energy erratic, at best.

The only thing that broke through the fog of depression, though it did so only in fits and starts, was the hunch that he possessed important information. Deep within his mind and untapped as yet, that information could help him understand what had happened that fateful day, and perhaps even why.

Still, to most of the people left in his life, Jake appeared to be carrying on. Only his personal assistant, who in many ways was his closest confidante, sensed the depth of his inability to heal. Miranda saw the lingering hollowness in his gaze when they talked stocks or he gave instructions for a transaction. He had to commend her perceptiveness—she somehow knew that time alone wouldn't be enough to heal his wounds.

"Jake, I know it isn't really my place," Miranda said one evening after a long day at the office, "but have you considered grief counseling? It could ease some of the burden you're carrying."

He hesitated to reply. Though her normally cool gray eyes were warm, he could tell that she'd been working up the courage for some time. It was a difficult moment for them both. Though Miranda was almost twenty years his junior, they had an atypical employer/employee relationship. Beyond an informal tone, Jake encouraged Miranda to speak her mind and valued her input on any issue. A fellow Harvard grad, she was extremely bright and in three years had become expert in every aspect of the business. Jake was grooming her as his successor—if someone didn't steal her from him first.

But this was much more sensitive ground than they'd ever treaded before.

"I appreciate that," Jake said, finally. "But I'm not looking to manage this. I'm not sure what I need, but . . . it's not acceptance. Does that make sense?"

"Yes," Miranda said, and for a moment Jake thought she might be on the verge of tears. That was a first. She was as tough-minded as the most ruthless corporate raider. He'd had no idea that she even possessed a sensitive side.

"It's just that," she went on, "you're so . . . I can see that every day's a struggle."

Jake nodded, his dulled emotions suddenly flaring to life. He knew things could never be the same, but the bombing's catastrophic effect on his entire world view suddenly hit home for him. He no longer enjoyed his life. The business he'd always loved had become an exhausting chore. The agony of his loss might be receding in tiny increments, but he had lost interest in what was left.

"Thank you," he said, reaching over his desk to awkwardly touch Miranda's arm. She smiled sadly. Beneath conservatively coiffed dark hair were delicate facial features that belied her forthright personality. But in this moment, Jake's steely assistant seemed truly vulnerable.

"I'll be all right," he said stiffly, and changed the subject.

This exchange was too surreal to Jake, somehow beyond the condolences he'd become accustomed to—now something deeper and more uncomfortable.

In the days following the toy-store bombing, Jake had received several visits from law enforcement agents—New York City Police, FBI, a bumbling bureaucrat from the Department of Homeland Security. These died down quickly, leaving him feeling forgotten. But on May 15th—exactly two weeks after Stephanie and Claire's deaths and the day after Miranda's expression of concern—Jake had returned from work and was lying exhausted on the living room sofa, his face covered by his arm, when the phone rang.

"Mr. Burke?"

"Yes."

"Jake Burke?"

"Yes, who is this?" Jake's voice was still muffled by his arm. He felt too tired to move it.

"My name is Samuel Stone. I'm with the CIA."

Jake sat up, instantly alert. "What can I do for you?"

"I'd like to talk to you. When can we meet?"

"Has there been a break in the case?" Jake stood. He detected something urgent in the agent's tone.

"I'd rather talk in person," Stone said.

Jake agreed to meet Stone beneath the colossal Dubuffet sculpture on Chase Manhattan Plaza the following morning at eleven o'clock.

When he got there, Jake discovered that the broad sun-kissed area in front of the building had been roped off with yellow plastic police tape. A security guard said the plaza had been closed three times since 9/11. New York—the world—had changed in so many ways, big and small, since that fateful morning. As Jake stood on the sidewalk to the south of the plaza wondering what to do, a voice came from behind him.

"Hello, Mr. Burke."

Jake turned around. "Agent Stone?"

Jake remembered reading somewhere that the CIA had modeled itself after the British intelligence services, choosing upper-crust men to serve as spies, the kind who'd attended Ivy League universities and felt at home in gentlemen's clubs.

Jake had assumed that this stereotype was ancient history, long since eradicated by the egalitarian values of the '60s. But Samuel Stone epitomized the old image. Unlike the conspicuously coppish NYPD detectives and FBI agents, Stone could've passed for a partner at a white-shoe law firm—from his sandy hair and hornrimmed specs to the conservative navy-blue suit and slightly surprising Hermes tie.

Deciding that clients and associates wouldn't suspect anything out of the ordinary, Jake invited Stone back to the Burke and Partners headquarters.

Once settled in Jake's corner office, Stone began by asking if he remembered seeing anything unusual prior to or during the attack.

"You know," Jake said, surprised at the question, "I keep telling myself there *was* something. In fact, I know there was. Problem is, I can't remember."

"That's not unusual," Stone said. "Why don't you tell me exactly what you witnessed? From the moment you went into the store."

And so Jake described the silent film that was always running in his head. He didn't hold back any of the terrible details, and at Stone's request told his story more than once. Jake felt oddly encouraged: It seemed as if Stone suspected something that required Jake's confirmation.

"What is it that you know?" he finally asked. "If you give me something, maybe it'll jog my memory."

"Nothing I'm at liberty to discuss, Mr. Burke. I'm sorry." Stone seemed truly regretful, but it didn't dull the disappointment. "I promise we're doing everything we can to find the people responsible for the FAO Schwarz massacre."

"But you must be stretched so thin. I mean, with so many attacks around the world over such a short period of time." In the past month alone, in addition to the toy-store bombing, twenty-seven American civilians were killed in two attacks in Saudi Arabia and Qatar. A Continental Airlines plane had been hit with a rocket-propelled grenade as it approached Cairo's airport. Miraculously, only three people died during the emergency landing and ensuing fire. And closer to home, in Miami, an especially powerful bomb had ripped through the crowd during a Heat game at American Airlines Arena. Eighty-two people died and hundreds were wounded.

"You're right," Stone said. "It hasn't been easy. But . . ." The agent looked away, toward the memento-hung wall of Jake's office, grappling with a decision. Finally, Sam Stone's pale blue eyes met Jake's with a gaze so piercing that it all but bored through him. "The toy-store bombing was special, Mr. Burke. That's all I can say. Think hard. A lot depends on you. And give me a call if you remember anything. Anything at all."

The toy-store bombing was special.

As soon as Stone left his office, Jake phoned an old college buddy, now a bigwig on the City Council. Jake's friend promptly called One Police Plaza and twisted some arms. While Miranda was away at lunch, Jake stood hunched over the fax machine on her desk, watching the alarmingly short file on his case print out. It had been so easy to obtain the confidential file on a terrorist attack, Jake realized—a sobering thought in this time of supposedly heightened alertness.

Back in his own office, Jake dialed the police precinct mentioned in his file. He invited the detective in charge of his case—Johnson, William D., the report said—for a late supper at a pizzeria on Lexington Avenue around the corner from the station house. To his surprise, Johnson accepted.

Then Jake took a closer look at the file.

Scrawled in a compact script on the second page was a brief note that he had missed the first time. See attached memorandum on suspect Ismail, Ashraf, it read. But the memo it referred to seemed to be absent from the faxed file.

When he called back his contact, a little checking around revealed that the memo was also missing from the original file. Jake's friend promised that someone would have it looked into "as soon as possible." But Jake couldn't wait for the slow wheels of New York's bureaucracy to turn. He was counting on Detective Johnson to shed some light on the matter of Ashraf Ismail.

Abdel Aziz Rifaat woke with the heat of the midday sun on his face.

He could see the red of his flesh, of his eyelids. He could even see the tiny veins. Is it safe to open my eyes, Rifaat wondered. *Where am I?*

His mind drifted to the image of an obelisk: the Obelisk of Luxor, officially given by the viceroy of Egypt, Mohamed Ali, to France in the early 1800s. Only the French controlled Egypt, and Ali had been a mere servant of the colonizers. "Given," my ass, Rifaat thought—it was stolen, plain and simple. Perfect phallic symbol, the obelisk. Napoleon had been one more in a series of takers of Egypt's manhood.

Where am I, he asked himself again, trying to focus while keeping his eyes closed. It took him a while to find the answer.

Ah, Place de la Concorde. The obelisk at the Place de la Concorde. I'm at the Hotel de Crillon at the Place de la Concorde. Good, I have it now. What else? Shit, he thought as he remembered. *Shit, shit, shit. But who knows, maybe the problem disappeared by itself while I dozed,* he told himself before opening his eyes.

Rifaat lifted his head from the pillow and looked left. No, she was still there, fully awake, her nursing eyes bursting with warmth and mercy. Shit again.

He hated that. He hated these American bitches who couldn't leave things alone, who felt that it was somehow their fault, who felt that all that was needed was more feigned passion. More kissing. More desperate stroking of his penis, as if it were some kind of Arabian lamp like the ones these people fantasized about and some fucking genie would bring back the attractive, interesting, and acceptably hard Abdel Aziz Rifaat at the end of dinner at the Tour d'Argent—after the duck and the booze and before the first bout of sex.

He closed his eyes again. *What's with you, big man? Once was not enough? After the first you knew that was it. You knew that you had lost all interest in the slut, if you ever had any. You knew that the right thing to do was to call it a night, explain that you had work to do in a few hours and call a taxi like a gentleman and take her home. Not send her home like the others did. Take her home. Enough. That would've been more than enough.*

But instead of being happy that you were able to do it—something rare—you had to go for another one. Bad idea. At the second go, you had already lost the surprise, the look of fear when they get hurt without warning and feel a pain more brutal than they expected. And without that, the slim chance of an erection was totally gone.

Now, in the early hours of Wednesday afternoon, instead of dressing and getting down to work, Abdel Aziz had to deal with smudged make-up, cutesy purring—what the fuck was *that*—and stale breath that smelled of alcohol and cigarettes and made him want to offer her a toothbrush. A toothbrush with a half-pound of very minty paste on it.

As he counted his blessings—because that's what he was, an eternal optimist—he was happy that he suffered from nausea that was slight and a feeling of shame even slighter. Sex can be great, he tried to convince himself. The only problem is getting rid of the body. Okay, let's get going, he thought, his illusion of power now surrendered to abject humiliation.

So there, in his sumptuous suite at the Crillon, as he had done many mornings before, he decided that this was the last time he would have sex. He wasn't interested in women. He just wasn't. He hated their smell, that moist, slightly rotten smell. The supreme punishment when he couldn't perform, because he *had* to satisfy them, was to perform oral sex, to plunge into that slippery, hungry, ugly place. He definitely wouldn't miss that.

Rifaat's mother died when he was five years old. An unstable and delusional man who saw himself as a wronged landowner, Abdel Aziz's widowed father had spent all his energy and his life's savings in baseless lawsuits, trying to recover land that had left his family over a century before. The man would beat Rifaat frequently, for the slightest of reasons or no reason at all. While she was alive, his mother's protection was rare, but it at least had been there when Rifaat absolutely needed it. Now she was gone.

Before long Rifaat had become a strange combination of street-gang leader and small-time trader. And these were not the only contradictions that coexisted in the short—five feet, four inches—prematurely bald young man with the pouty lips and bulging eyes. He was capable of displaying both kindness and unbridled cruelty without hesitation.

He had joined the Egyptian army at the age of eighteen. His country was in a confused mood. Anwar Sadat had made peace with Israel. There were those who saw it as the Peace of the Brave, after their country's victory in the October War, the war the Jews called the Yom Kippur War. And there were others, like Rifaat, who saw it all as a sham. Israel, not Egypt, had won the October War, and Sadat was dishonoring the country by surrendering and making peace. Rifaat had few doubts as to how the defeat had come about. Despite being tens of times more numerous than the Jews, the Arabs were governed by corrupt politicians more interested in earning kickbacks in weapons deals than in making sure that those weapons were used as they should be.

While he was in the army, Rifaat met a young officer by the name of Hamza El Biali, a deeply religious member of the Al-Jihad al-Islami, the Popular Islamic Jihad, a group that traced its origins to the Muslim Brotherhood. The Brotherhood was an organization that promoted a single Islamic nation encompassing all Muslims, Arabs and non-Arabs, united under the precepts of the Shariah. Its first leader and guide had been Hassan Al-Banna, who believed in "gathering men over gathering information in books" and emphasized building the organization by choosing its future leaders and establishing its internal rules so that it would keep going unaffected in the absence of any single man. After Al-Banna's death, the Muslim Brotherhood became a multi-pronged organization, with a layer of highly dedicated and prepared leaders unequaled in the Arab world. Hamza El Biali would be one of those leaders, Rifaat was sure.

Over the first year that they'd known each other, Rifaat grew to love Hamza like a brother—the wise and gentle older brother he had wished for during the years when his mother's death had left him defenseless against his father. He loved Hamza more then he had ever loved anyone, male or female. As the second year of their friendship went by, he became jealous of Hamza's brothers, Mohand and Ashraf, because they carried Hamza's blood in their veins. Yet he loved them as if they were his own family.

One day, in a quiet voice, Hamza told him simply that he was going to kill Sadat, the traitor. Did Rifaat want to join? They planned the assassination together and made a pact that, should something go wrong, whoever escaped would take care of the other's family.

But on the day of the assassination, Rifaat and three other members of his army unit were ordered to beef up the security detachment outside the parade grounds at the entrance to the reviewing stand. He tried to get permission to patrol inside, in the hope of participating in the attack when the moment came, but was told in no uncertain terms that his orders were to guard the perimeter. He heard the shooting and the ensuing chaos. In desperation he tried to run inside, hoping to join the attack, to join his friend in glory, in danger, maybe in death. But he was blocked by the same sergeant who'd refused him access earlier. The man pointed his rifle at Rifaat and told him he would be shot if he didn't return to his position. Later on, Rifaat wondered if the sergeant had been in on the plot, his role to prevent help from reaching the victims.

When Rifaat heard that Hamza had succeeded in killing Sadat, he felt absolute joy. And when Hamza was sentenced to die, Rifaat sank into total despair. Witnesses reported that Hamza had cried, "Allah is Great!" when facing his executioners.

Rifaat left Egypt immediately after his discharge from the army. With the money he'd saved from his hustling days and his meager soldier's pay, he flew to the United States as a tourist.

He arrived on the last day of March, 1982, determined to forget his origins, to build a new life away from the mutual recriminations and the viscous feeling of defeat present in all aspects of Egyptian life—not to mention his own. He would live the American Dream.

And he went about it with the passion of someone who needs to forget a painful love affair. He tried to learn English as fast as he could. He married one of the maids at the cheap motel on Biscayne Boulevard in Miami where he'd stayed during his first days in America, and then left her once his visa was in place. He earned a high school equivalency diploma in one year and plunged with abandon into his engineering studies at the University of Miami. He set aside his Muslim precepts.

When he wasn't studying, Rifaat liked to ride the bus to Miami Beach, away from his fellow students. It had become a habit after the strange sensation—a tightening of his throat and a consciousness of his penis against his underwear—that he had felt while walking next to the water once, very late at night. He had seen two men sitting far away on the sands of the deserted beach, the arm of one around the shoulder of the other. Curious, Rifaat had sat down unobserved to watch them together. When they kissed each other on the mouth, Rifaat stood up and walked briskly away, clutching his crotch, willing the beginning of an erection away.

Disgusting, he would repeat to himself every time the vision invaded his mind.

For a month after the incident, he had studiously avoided returning. After a while, though, he began revisiting the same spot at least once a week, always late at night. Soon he knew the neighborhood as well as any local.

During the last week of his freshman year, a freckle-faced, very skinny sophomore from down the hall called Rifaat a "camel driver." He didn't react. Two days later the same student called him a "sand nigger" in front of the entire calculus class. Again Rifaat didn't react.

On the day after the second taunting, he took a long walk to clear his mind of the anger that was distracting him from his studies. Most of the buildings in the Miami neighborhood where he ended up were small houses made of wood or cinder block, and painted in pale tones of green and yellow, pink and blue. He saw a lizard basking in the sun. He passed a small church, the white paint on its walls peeling in the salt air, the sidewalk in front crowded with people milling around after services.

Immersed in disjointed thoughts, it took him a while to realize that he had stopped in the middle of the sidewalk to gaze at a very old man, who was slowly advancing in the opposite direction, toward him. The man was weakly pushing a walker away from himself and, shifting his weight to his arms, half walking, half dragging his feet forward, one of his eyes useless behind a black patch.

When he got closer, Rifaat looked at the old man's thin, deeply creased face. The white skin was matted with brown and red patches, the drooping eyelid leaving only half of the white-encircled iris visible; and a small tuft of gray hair emerged from his limp long nose, matched by similar ones sprouting from his wide ears. He was neatly dressed, and there was dignity in his decrepitude. Rifaat thought he detected a faint trace of hospital smell when the man stopped in front of him.

"What are you looking at?" the man asked.

"Are you talking to me?" Rifaat was surprised.

"What are you looking at?" The man was angry.

"Nothing. I'm not looking at anything."

"You don't like what you see? Look at yourself first, you good-for-nothing." The old man's face was burning with rage and contempt.

"I'm sorry."

"Now get out of my way." The man pushed Rifaat aside with his walker and shifted away.

Surrounded by the contented crowd of the church's parishioners, Rifaat stood motionless, open-mouthed and shivering, despite the searing Florida sun.

For anyone else, this would've been a chance encounter with a bitter, perhaps deranged, old man. But Rifaat knew better. He repeated the words to himself many times. He did look at himself, and what he saw he didn't like. He saw a lost Muslim in a Christian world trying too hard to please, and too scared to think, too afraid to react. He had heard the Truth and was indeed ashamed.

He was walking alone in the park that night, along the lake at the center of the University's Coral Gables campus, when his freckled tormentor surprised him as he came to a particularly dark stretch of the path.

"Hey, Riffraff!" The drunken boy was wobbling his way.

"My name's Rifaat. Abdel Aziz Rifaat."

"When are you going back to Arabia?"

"There's no Arabia. There's Saudi Arabia. I am from Egypt."

"Is that right?" the sophomore persisted. The "right" came out as a prolonged, sneering *raaaa*. "I just want you out of here. Go home, you fucking faggot."

Rifaat remained perfectly calm. He drew closer, smiling. "Come on, what's your problem?"

The other imitated him in highly accented English and laughed, a superior, humiliating laugh. Rifaat didn't feel anger, just cold hatred. In one swift movement he pushed the boy into the lake, and then without hesitation jumped in after him. He wrapped himself on the flailing boy's back, legs around his waist, both hands keeping the bony head down, underwater. The boy only managed to come up for air once. Rifaat didn't need much strength.

He waited for three minutes after there was no movement, all the while repeating quietly in English, "Who's the faggot now?" Then he pushed the floating body toward the center of the lake. That he had chosen to taunt Rifaat on the same day that Allah, disguised as an angry old man, had spoken directly to him was the skinny redhead's bad luck.

Rifaat waited until his clothes were almost dry and then returned to his single room. He showered, changed, and went back out to dispose of his pants and shirt, just in case there was any trace of his victim on them. He put them in a bag and put the bag in the trunk of his car, together with two heavy stones. He drove toward Miami Beach. Once there, he parked his car in an unlit alley.

It was now 3:00 A.M. on a Sunday and the beach was deserted. With the bag in his right hand, Rifaat dove into the warm waters of the Atlantic. He swam as far as he could, the weight of the stones and his clothes inside the bag making it all very difficult, almost impossible. He reached a point of such exhaustion that he started doubting whether he'd have the strength to swim back. Then he let go. The bag sank silently.

Rifaat slept that night without dreaming.

The floating body of his victim was discovered after sunrise the next morning. No signs of violence were evident. Friends testified that the boy had left a bar totally drunk. The death was ruled an accident and, with the exception of the bar's lost liquor license for having sold alcohol to a minor, there were no other consequences. Rifaat was sure that Allah was watching over him.

The time had come to leave this Godforsaken country that was destroying him, eating him alive. Enough sordidness. Time to go back home where he belonged, to a place where women were not loose, where they knew to show respect to a man. One day, because Allah was great, Rifaat would punish America. Now it was time to engage in the struggle at hand, the one he had run away from. Time to fight the corrupt Arab leaders and their Western patrons. Time to fight back, to be a man again. To atone for having stayed behind on the day when the person he loved most became a martyr.

In the years following his return to Egypt, Rifaat led a double life. Secretly, he rose in the ranks of the Popular Islamic Jihad. Meanwhile, Matarma Maintenance Services, the company he'd founded on his arrival, grew—thanks in no small measure to supporters of the Brotherhood inside the government, who got him important contracts. He became a very wealthy man when he branched out into construction, doing work mostly for French engineering and oil concerns. A convenient give and take. The first deal was a most promising oil field put up for international bids in Tunisia, close to British Gas's discovery in El Hajeb. Rifaat was able to pass on information about what all the other companies were bidding to one of the main French oil concerns. When that concern was awarded exclusive exploration of the field, Rifaat was given the job of building most of the infrastructure.

France was trying to recover its standing with the Arab countries, a standing that had been deeply damaged by the Algerian Independence War and the Suez Campaign. A lot of money went behind this effort, money that was used to provide generous grants and aggressive financing. It was also used to buy information. Whenever asked by the DGSE, France's intelligence service, for such information, Rifaat obliged. Why not? And the struggle needed the money.

In keeping with his promise to Hamza, Rifaat kept an eye out for Mohand, Ashraf, and their mother. Mohand worried him most. He had always been a fighter. In the early 1990s the secular government of Algeria had cancelled elections that would've brought an Islamic party to power for the first time. Immediately after that, Mohand had snuck into Algeria and spent years fighting a civil war against that government. After that he decided to join the ranks of Osama bin Laden's organization and leave for Afghanistan.

Rifaat saw him off in person. Their farewell was an emotional one, five blocks from the Fenwick Park mosque on the outskirts of London. Rifaat told Mohand to be careful. He told him that his brother, who was in Paradise, was certainly proud of him, but that he would be prouder if Mohand remained alive to care for his mother and to continue the struggle for a united Arab world under the Shariah.

Rifaat also told Mohand that, from what he had been hearing, his little brother Ashraf could not be counted on to be there for their mother. Like his brother, he had dreams of glory.

"No, my brother won't do it," Mohand had replied.

"How do you know?"

"I know."

Rifaat said the words both had been avoiding—there was no place for softness in the war they were waging. "You think he's a coward."

"It's not that, not that at all. My brother can be a hero." The words came out partly mumbled, the eyes looking away. Mohand knew that Ashraf wasn't up to it.

"It's all right, Mohand. Not everyone needs to be a Shaheed. I don't want you to be one either."

"Don't worry. I will take care of myself."

In 1996 Rifaat was approached by two of his contacts within French intelligence who told him that they represented a group interested in buying MMS, his maintenance company. At that time, MMS already had branches in all the countries where the Brotherhood had contacts. Rifaat asked an absurd sum for MMS. When the mysterious group paid his price without even haggling, Rifaat wondered what their real motivation was. It certainly looked as if they wanted the company for ulterior reasons. He didn't care. Let them do what they wanted. He wanted the cash. He was preparing his war chest.

The time finally came. In February, 1998, Rifaat heeded Osama bin Laden's *fatwa* and decided to give himself fully to the jihad against the Jews and Crusaders. He sold the rest of his companies and disappeared underground, fully dedicated to the Popular Islamic Jihad.

After the destruction of the two towers in New York, America invaded Afghanistan and Rifaat never heard from Mohand again. When the mother of Hamza and Mohand called to ask for his protection, for his assurance that Ashraf would be kept alive, Rifaat made her a solemn promise that her last son would be safe. By then he was able to make such a promise. He had become the head of the Popular Islamic Jihad.

A few years later, he was ready. It was time to launch his first campaign of suicide bombings against soft civilian objectives in America.

And one day, because Allah is great, I will punish America, he had thought when he left Miami. That day had come.

His memory of the Algerian War of Independence from the French inspired him. At its beginning in 1952, the struggle had appeared hopeless. But in less than a decade the FLN had emerged victorious. More than one million French nationals were expelled from Algeria. After 150 years—since Napoleon—France's presence was no more. Rifaat had no doubt: Against vastly superior power, terrorism works.

From the moment he began attacking the U.S., Rifaat benefited from quiet popular support in his country. Several spectacular bombings of Israeli public places also helped. Yet, although he could hide men and assets in the slums of Cairo and Alexandria, because of the efforts of the Egyptian secret service he couldn't organize there anymore.

Iran and Syria came to the rescue. And because of that, despite America's efforts, his organization became stronger by the day. Thanks to Syria and Iran, his base in Lebanon was solid, and the Iranian mullahs made sure he had no funding problems.

It was in this thought that Rifaat found the inspiration to face the day. His brightening spirits were dashed at the pitiful bleat of the American cow.

"Want to get some breakfast or something?"

Rifaat looked at her, willing her to disappear. "Get dressed."

He wouldn't extend this one the courtesy of accompanying her home. One of his bodyguards could see her there safely. Or not. Rifaat's mind had already moved on to more important things.

CHAPTER TWO

"Four minutes," Detective Johnson finally said. The wreckage of a large pie with sausage, peppers, and extra cheese lay on a dented pan between them. "That's all it took for me to reach the site of the explosion. By total coincidence, I was shopping for a pair of running shoes at the Niketown on 57th Street." Throughout the meal, Johnson had dodged Jake's many attempts to discuss the case in detail. He apparently felt that no major harm could be done in the last minutes of their meeting.

"What did you see when you arrived?"

"Are you sure you want to talk about this?"

"I'm okay now. I just need some answers. For, you know . . . closure."

The detective looked into his glass and sipped his drink, a seltzer. "Right. I gotta tell you, I felt horrible. It was really a horrible scene. Horrible. The way your daughter—" Covering his mouth with one hand, the detective belched loudly. "Pardon me."

Jake had decided not to ask him directly about Ashraf Ismail. Not yet. Instead he rephrased Agent Stone's question from earlier that day.

"Was there anything or anybody . . . I don't know, *strange* on the scene?"

"You know, your wife was already dead. Your daughter died like ten minutes after the paramedics got there. These guys really tried to save her, but—"

"Did you see anything *strange*," Jake repeated. He was trying to remain calm, but clearly Detective Johnson was unwilling or unable to help him. Still, it made no sense to confront the man and disclose that he had seen the file—or what was left of it.

The waiter arrived at their table. "Anything else, gentlemen?"

Jake looked at the detective, who shook his head. "Just the check, thanks."

The waiter ripped the top sheet off his pad and placed it on the table.

"Strange? Nah." Johnson sipped his drink. "What did you have in mind?"

Jake tried another tack. "How much time do you think you spent on this case?"

The cop shrugged. "Not much. The FBI took over within hours."

"And . . . you just dropped it?"

Johnson seemed to take offense. "That's the way it works."

Jake didn't doubt it. The toy-store bombing was a federal case; of course the FBI would swoop in. The CIA too, apparently. Stone and his fellow agents, heavy hitters, way out of this poor guy's league. No doubt it was the feds who'd removed the memo from the report, though why exactly, Jake had no idea.

Still, maybe he could extract a thing or two more from Johnson. The detective had been first on the scene, after all.

But Johnson sounded defensive. "They debriefed me, okay? Two of them, in the presence of my superior. They thanked me and that was it. Listen, I gotta go. It's crazy at the precinct. As it is, I'm working 'til four in the morning these days. Here's for my pizza."

"Don't worry about that. It's on me."

"Sorry, can't accept. Regulations." Johnson stood and turned to leave.

His voice too low for anyone but the detective to hear, Jake said simply, "Your memo—the one on Ashraf Ismail—is missing."

Johnson stopped in his tracks. "Say that again?"

"Your memo. It's gone."

Johnson sat back down, looked Jake sharply in the eye. "Talk to me."

"It's true," Jake said. "The memo's gone. Any idea who took it?"

Instead of answering Jake's question, Johnson asked one of his own. "Where do you get the muscle to examine confidential police files? Which, I'm sure you know, is in violation of the law."

Jake shrugged. "I'm a wealthy man. Very wealthy. Money equals access."

Johnson said nothing.

"I'm not looking to hurt you, Detective. I actually think you're in the same boat as me, wondering what the hell's going on with what should be a straightforward investigation."

"Just what are you claiming to have found?"

"Evidence of a cover-up." Jake kept his eyes firmly on Johnson.

"A cover-up," Johnson repeated. "And what makes you say that?"

"You tell me. What's the story with the memo? It got your attention, so clearly it's meaningful to you. But I don't understand: If you were relieved of duty in this matter, why did you investigate further? You did investigate further, didn't you?"

The detective didn't answer for a while. Finally, his voice even, he said, "I'll start with this: Fuck you. If you think I'm part of some cover-up, I say, fuck you, motherfucker. If you weren't already in such pain, I'd punch your ass right now. You can shove your money right up your ass, you arrogant bastard. Is that clear?"

Jake nodded.

The man sighed. "You want to know why I investigated further? Because the last time these bastards blew shit up in my hometown, buddies of mine died. And then—" Johnson's voice broke. He sat up straighter. "And then somebody let their terrorist friends and relatives fly home. You know what I'm talking about, right? I'll be fucked if that's going to happen again."

"I'm . . . sorry about the deaths of your colleagues," Jake said. "Your friends. And I understand, believe me." Jake looked deep into

Johnson's tired, blood-rimmed eyes. He thought he saw a glimmer of empathy. "You investigated Ashraf Ismail on your own time because you couldn't stand for injustice to be done—again. Well, my friend, the fruits of your labor, all the evidence of your hard work, have vanished. Without a trace."

"How do you know this for sure?"

"Money equals access, remember?" This time Johnson looked receptive. "Now," Jake went on, "from one bereaved survivor to another, I'm begging you to tell me what you found, off the clock. If you do, I'll be the only one who ever knows you helped me. And I'm promising you here that I'll take that information and put my money and my connections to work."

Somewhat to Jake's surprise, Johnson spoke. "Ashraf Ismail was walking around the carnage in a daze. He had a long deep cut under his right eye and nothing more." The policeman stroked his stubbly face. "Lucky sonofabitch. It was more like a gash, though. It'll definitely leave him with a scar."

As his memory stirred ever so slightly, Jake felt suddenly dizzy.

Johnson continued. The cop's account of the bombing's aftermath was all new information for Jake.

"After he was seen by a doctor in the emergency room, Ashraf Ismail was interrogated by the police. He gave his New York address as the Holiday Inn on 10th Avenue. He claimed that he was buying a gift for his nephew in Egypt when the blast occurred, a video game that had just come out and was already impossible to find. He'd been told that only FAO Schwarz still had them in inventory.

"At their crazy prices," Ashraf Ismail had added. Though Johnson hadn't conducted the interview, he'd reviewed the transcript afterwards. For some reason he distinctly remembered those particular words.

Ashraf had remained in the ER for another hour or so, after which he was signed out by the nurse on duty. Not long after that, the feds took over and Johnson was taken off the case.

Johnson followed up on his own in the days that followed. First he checked the Holiday Inn records, which included information on the man's passport and the address he'd declared. Ashraf was indeed a visitor on a tourist visa from Egypt. The detective also contacted the INS. He obtained Ashraf's date of entry through Boston's Logan Airport twenty days before the bombing, as well as established his departure via JFK the day after. When he found out that Ashraf Ismail had been allowed to leave the country, Johnson was furious. He went to his superior officer for permission to resume the investigation on the record.

Less than an hour later the phone on his desk rang and Johnson was told to drop the matter for good. Immediately. Otherwise he would face disciplinary action. For the record, and on the slim chance that the case might be reopened someday, Johnson summarized his findings in the now-missing memo and put it in the file, adding a note directing the reader to it.

"Strange, don't you think?" The cop sipped coffee from a blue and white cup proclaiming, *IT IS OUR PLEASURE TO SERVE YOU.* Jake's identical cup of decaf sat untouched on the pizzeria table between them.

"Even as he was being taken to the hospital in an ambulance with a police officer inside, he wouldn't talk to anybody. Suspicious, don't you think? The officer with him thought he was in shock because he was laughing and crying all at the same time."

"Laughing and crying." Jake's heart pounded. He rubbed his temples. He was growing dizzier by the minute.

"Then he started, like, mumbling to himself."

"Mumbling what? Did they say?"

"Something in some foreign language. Finally he blinks hard and looks at them almost like he's waking up. Weird, huh?"

"Anything else that you can remember?" Jake could hardly breathe.

"He was wearing jeans and a Washington Wizards T-shirt."

"I'm surprised you were able to make out the logo. Weren't his clothes as covered with dust as his face, like I was?"

"Not that I recall. Wait. Actually . . . Shit." His face blanching, Detective Johnson looked away, looked around. Everywhere but into Jake's eyes. "You know what? When he was walking out with the cop he had tons of dust in his hair, on his face and his hands. On his shoes and pants. But there wasn't any dust on that goddamned T-shirt. The logo was as vivid as could be. I totally forgot about that. He was probably wearing some sort of a coat when the explosion happened."

"Was it found?" Jake asked.

"No, but that doesn't mean much. The place was pretty chaotic. As you know."

"But they did find additional explosives, right?" In the days following the bombing, the *Times* had reported a second set of explosives discovered near the scene of the crime.

"Yeah, but the assumption was that it was the terrorist's back-up, in case the explosives he was wearing malfunctioned or whatever. Listen, I really gotta go."

"Sure," Jake said. "And thanks for all this." Then he said to himself as much as to Johnson, "Why the hell wouldn't the feds think Ashraf Ismail might've been the second bomber?"

Johnson stood. "Second bomber?" He squinted. "What would be the point?"

"To blow himself up when people came in to rescue the victims. They do it all the time in the Middle East."

"You know your stuff, pal," Johnson said, with a measure of respect. "Too bad you're not on the FBI's payroll." He pushed his chair beneath the table, preparing to leave. "Sorry, I'm out of here."

"Don't worry about it," Jake said quickly. "And thanks anyway. This was very helpful. Take care."

Johnson nodded and left the restaurant.

The waiter approached; the place was now full and he clearly wanted the table freed up. But Jake wasn't ready to leave yet. He was now very dizzy. He needed to go over what Johnson had told him yet was having trouble reasoning. He ordered a bottle of Perrier.

The waiter brought the small green bottle, a glass and a new check. Jake grabbed the water bottle to fill his glass. He was trembling.

He tried to steady his hands as the bottle tinkled against the rim of the glass. It irritated him that he couldn't make the sound stop. He pressed the bottle flush with the edge of the glass, his knuckles white against the smooth transparent surfaces. The ringing wouldn't quit.

The musical tinkling of broken glass.

He decided to leave the restaurant right away. Jake signaled the waiter. It took him a while to gather the focus to choose a credit card. Feeling very lightheaded, Jake was having trouble identifying the contents of his wallet.

As he slowly walked out of the restaurant, a bus passed by. On its side Jake saw an ad for the Imax Theater at the Museum of Natural History:

MYSTERIES OF EGYPT
WONDERS OF THE ANCIENT WORLD

Against the background of a pyramid illuminated by a setting sun was a gorgeous mask of brilliant hammered gold—a man's idealized face. Under the image in smaller type was written, "Akhenaten, the Heretic Pharaoh."

And in that moment it came to him, the memory of the day he'd lost his loved ones. This time the silent film was complete.

Shortly after entering the store with Stephanie and Claire, Jake had seen something that struck him as strange, an odd tableau performed in pantomime. Behind his wife, beyond his daughter, at the top of the store's escalators, perhaps thirty yards from where he stood, Jake had seen not one, but two figures. For that's what they were: *figures*—too distant for their features to be discerned. Figures in khaki trench coats.

It was May. It hadn't rained in days. So why trench coats, Jake had wondered idly at the time.

At the top of the escalators, one of the trench coated figures, clearly impatient, gestured repeatedly, pointing at the down escalator. The other figure shook his head. The first man—Jake assumed they were male—then pushed the other in the chest and the second man fell backward against the machine's crawling handrail of black rubber. Shoppers moved past them, staring, puzzled by the scene.

While the first man stayed on the second level, the second one stepped with considerable reluctance aboard the downward-moving stairs. Clean-shaven, eyes wild with intensity—his face was now visible, especially those eyes—he descended in slow motion.

Wearing a belted, bulky trench coat.

After the explosion, right before losing consciousness, Jake had seen the man who'd remained at the top of the escalator. The man who had pushed the bomber forward, ordering him to carry out his mission. The man whose will had caused the death of Jake's wife and daughter.

That man was still alive.

Jake remembered it all now. The man was covered from head to toe with pale-gray dust. His right cheek was gashed and bloody. He was unbuttoning his trench coat while staggering through the wreckage and repeating something, the English words hardly intelligible.

"Allah is great. I have killed Pharaoh. I have killed Pharaoh. Allah is great."

Standing outside the pizzeria, Jake's knees went weak.

"Hey, are you okay?" A man in the crowd was moving toward him, but his voice sounded strangely distant.

Jake tried to focus on the face before him. His heart was pounding impossibly loud, his breaths coming short and quick. Something in his ears sounded like jet engines revving just before takeoff; they grew louder and higher-pitched until the volume and pitch of the sound was all but unendurable. Then they grew louder still. Higher-pitched. Now the margins of his vision fuzzed and faded, dropped away. Jake was left looking down a tunnel. At its other end was the face of the man before him, the expression on the face changing before Jake's eyes: from concerned to puzzled to . . . astonished?

When Jake regained consciousness he was lying on his back inside an ambulance. They were taking him to the ER, they told him. He remembered the well-groomed doctor at the hospital. He had suffered a severe panic attack. He had passed out on a New York City sidewalk.

The oddest part of the memory came to him last, as the ambulance stuttered toward Lenox Hill Hospital, its siren intermittently whooping. The surviving terrorist had been crying and laughing at the same time. In Jake's mind's eye, tears trickled down a dusty face to a soundtrack of maniacal laughter and the words, repeated like a mantra, about Pharaoh being dead.

He had never seen anything so frightening in all his life.

Miranda drove Jake home from the hospital. He'd tried to insist on taking a cab, but the woman could be difficult to deny when she felt strongly about something.

"Jake," she began, piloting her Lexus hybrid down Park Avenue, "I'm your assistant. I know about all the phone calls you've been making, who you've been talking to. What's going on?"

"Don't worry about it," he said, somewhat brusquely. His bout with human frailty had left him in a dark mood and the last thing he wanted was to involve Miranda.

"I just think," she said, searching for the right words, "that whatever you're doing might have something to do with what happened today."

They had reached Jake's building and he was in a hurry to get out of the car. "What I'm doing is personal. It doesn't pertain to our business, or you. So let's please leave it at that."

She nodded, duly chastened. He felt bad about saying it so plainly, so he lingered before stepping out. "But thanks, Miranda. You've been a huge help to me. Now more than ever."

She smiled, but there was a trace of the trademark Miranda edge in her reply. "No sweat, boss. See you tomorrow?"

"No, I've decided to go to D.C. More personal business. Call you from the ground."

She nodded. She normally made his travel arrangements, so his secrecy was definitely out of the ordinary. But she didn't press.

"Sounds good. Take care, Jake."

He closed the door behind him and the black Lexus sped away. Miranda was as aggressive behind the wheel as she was in the board-room.

Early the following morning, Jake flew on the shuttle from LaGuardia to Reagan International Airport. He needed to get to Washington immediately and find some answers, before the terrible anxiety overwhelmed him again.

He bought a business magazine prior to boarding and held it open to the same page for the first half-hour after takeoff, reading without comprehending a word. Restless and on edge, he continuously massaged a neck that felt stiffer by the minute. He ordered a drink. Throughout the remainder of the flight he sat in silence, fingering the ice cubes in his scotch, still unable to think, his anxiety mounting.

His mind flitted back to his favorite mental image of Stephanie. His wife had been a lover of all things beautiful—he could see the bliss in her face when she listened to Debussy's "Clair de Lune." She had adored the way the pure and elegant melody evoked a serene, moonlit night. She used to say that "Clair de Lune" was the final proof that only absolute simplicity could bring absolute perfection. Choosing Claire as the name for their daughter had been an easy decision.

He remembered the three of them awake in bed, early—usually too early, thanks to little Claire—on a Sunday morning. Their daughter between them, full of energy, happy that they were finally up. Stephanie's hair undone, her cheeks as rosy as their daughter's. He closed his eyes and was able to relive, if only for a few seconds, the warmth and the laughter of those moments. When Jake opened his eyes and saw the back of the broad first-class seat in front of him, a reminder of where he was going and why, the agony was almost unbearable.

He spent the better part of the day in the nation's capital, being stonewalled by his contacts.

Despite political connections achieved by means of sizeable campaign contributions throughout the years, Jake got nothing from the FBI. The toy-store bombing was being investigated under a complete information blackout instituted by the attorney general, they said again and again.

A meeting with one of the members of the Senate Select Committee on Intelligence followed. This too proved unsuccessful.

Back in New York late that evening, Jake sat by his computer, the senator's last words, "*I'm sorry, but my hands are tied,*" still ringing in his ears. Idly, he typed, "I have killed Pharaoh" on his computer's search engine.

To his surprise, an account of the assassination of Egypt's President Anwar Sadat came up. "The annual parade was in commemoration of the eighth anniversary of the 1973 war," stated the article, which had been written by Isabelle Said, a journalist working for the Egyptian newspaper *Al Ahram*.

Around President Sadat was a varied group of dignitaries, including several American diplomats. The Egyptian president was saluting the troops when a military vehicle lurched toward the reviewing stand. The assassin and three other men jumped out and threw grenades at the officials.

After riddling the president's body with bullets, the assassin cried, "I am Hamza El Biali! Allah is great! I have killed Pharaoh! I have killed Pharaoh!"

CHAPTER THREE

At 8:00 A.M. in New York, Theodore Suter, Jake's private banker, was at his desk at the New York office of Société de Banques Suisses—just as Jake knew he would be.

Suter was the quintessential Swiss banker. Once, during college, he had said to Jake, "I don't understand why you Americans made such a fuss about Watergate—no one lost any money in it."

Suter never gave Jake specific data about clients, but he was always ready with the necessary background information. And it went both ways. On many occasions Suter had benefited from Jake's knowledge.

Jake now told his friend that he needed information about an Egyptian: Hamza El Biali, one of Anwar Sadat's assassins.

"It may take a few hours for me to run this down. I'll get back to you before noon, though, I promise." No small talk. Suter had sensed Jake's anxiety.

Jake's cell phone rang an hour later. Suter told him that SBS had a stable of important Egyptian clients. Some, Suter said, were past members of Egypt's security apparatus.

Jake smiled. "Just past members?"

Suter didn't answer. Instead, he said that he could get the information Jake sought but that he felt extremely uncomfortable doing so. "My advice to you is to stop investigating. It doesn't smell right." Suter said that his source, a highly connected Egyptian official, had asked him if the person making the inquiry was a friend. "If so," said the man, "tell him to stop now and forget about it. Don't let anyone know about his interest in El Biali."

Jake could hardly believe what he was hearing. He tried to control his frustration as he asked again. "Let me tell you something. I *need* this information, and I'll get it. Either from you or from somebody else. Whatever it takes, I'll track this guy down. Even if I have to go to Egypt to get it." In truth, Jake had already decided to fly to Egypt, no matter how much information Suter yielded. "I need your help, Ted. I need it very badly. Can I count on it?"

"Okay," Suter said after a short pause.

"Good, I'll be at your office at . . ." Jake looked at his watch, "twelve. That gives you three hours to get the information."

"Very well," the banker said, after another, longer, pause.

As Jake hung up the phone, the intercom rang. The doorman told him that a Mr. Crowley was waiting for him downstairs. Jake knew who he was and didn't ask the doorman to send him up. He was rushing now. He had just a short time to prepare for the trip to the Middle East. Jake would see Crowley on his way out to work.

The enormous lobby dwarfed two sofas, two love seats and a coffee table. Crowley was seated on the sofa, his jacket fully buttoned, the collar standing oddly away from the neck.

Jake had met him before. Crew-cut and broad-shouldered—probably ex-military—he was one of the FBI agents who had been sent a week ago to tell Jake nothing. He had been evasive and obnoxious, and Jake had diplomatically but emphatically sent him packing.

"Mr. Burke, can we talk?"

"Sure." Jake sat down opposite the agent.

"I just came here to say once more that we're doing everything we can. It hasn't been easy. But everything that can be done is being done. So you can rest assured of that."

"Glad to hear it. Thanks." Jake began to get up.

"Don't go just yet, Mr. Burke," the man said, his words coming faster.

Jake sat down again, reluctantly.

"This is a very delicate operation." The federal agent shook his head. "We have enough trouble as it is with other agencies' interference."

"And?"

"And we don't need any help."

"Looks to me like you need all the help you can get. But what are you trying to say?"

"Just that." He looked at Jake for a long moment. "We don't need any more help. In fact, it would only cause trouble for everyone. Enough said?"

Leaning forward, Jake spoke quietly but with intensity. "Listen to me. I don't know what's going on, but something stinks. My wife and daughter have been killed and I will not, will *not*, be told to twiddle my thumbs while you decide whether this is a priority or something to be hushed up. As far as I know, you people don't even have a suspect in the case. And I know a thing or two about what's gone on in the matter of the bombing at FAO Schwarz. Enough *said?*"

The agent went red in the face. "If I were you, I'd give this some more thought. Before I did something I might regret. Have a good day, Mr. Burke."

Without waiting for Jake's reply, Crowley stood up, turned around stiffly, and walked away.

SBS's New York offices were located near the top of a modern skyscraper on Maiden Lane, in the Wall Street area. In fact, Jake noticed as he stepped into Suter's office, Ground Zero itself, construction underway, was plainly visible through the banker's floor-to-ceiling window.

Suter walked toward Jake from behind his desk. He was tall and thin, with skin the color of ash. A strip of scraggly blond hair wrapped his bald head, above alert grey eyes behind silver-framed glasses. Instead of shaking Jake's outstretched hand, Suter grasped it between both of his own. The banker smiled softly, and his voice showed concern.

"How are you, my friend?"

Jake liked Suter enormously. He had no time for the whole sympathy exercise, though, so got down to business before that routine had a chance to begin.

"I'm okay, thanks. But I need to deal with this."

"Of course." Suter motioned to a chair to Jake's right: an antique, of course—was it Georgian? Although the firm's headquarters occupied the 47th, 48th, and 49th floors of a glass-and-steel building constructed in the mid-80s, its furnishings were intentionally chosen to remind SBS's clients that the bank had been founded long ago and would be there forever. Lots of dark wood paneling and wingchairs covered in worn leather.

The only object on Suter's desk was a gold Waterman pen. Not a single piece of paper cluttered the polished wooden surface. Jake had always envied his friend's brutally efficient sense of organization.

"Would you like some coffee?"

Jake shook his head impatiently. He wasn't sure Suter understood the deadly urgency of his request. "Just give me everything you've got on El Biali."

Suter proceeded to tell Jake about Sadat's assassination. An extremely well-planned affair, he said, from the placement of a group of militants in a single army unit, to the flawless execution of their plan—in the presence of hundreds of soldiers, no less.

"That's all?" Jake asked, when Suter appeared to have finished. "I was expecting more. By the way, why do you call them militants?"

"I beg your pardon?"

"You Europeans are always calling these people militants. If they do the same thing inside the borders of your country, though, they're suddenly terrorists."

"Okay." Suter looked warily at Jake. "'Terrorists' it is."

Jake broke the uncomfortable silence that followed. "What else have you got?"

"I'm told that this could get dangerous. And to be honest, my friend, you're out of your depth. I'm not sure you have the cold blood necessary to navigate these waters."

Jake couldn't afford to turn Suter off. He feigned an easy laugh. "I'm not a commando, Ted. These are just questions I need answered. You know me—it's not like I'd do anything rash."

Suter relaxed. Evidently he remembered the old Jake, Mr. 99.99 percent. Jake was surprised he could still pass for that man. He no longer felt the presence inside him.

"All right. But just remember, getting yourself killed won't bring your family back."

Jake nodded curtly. "This isn't my idea of a suicide attempt, I assure you. So tell me more about El Biali. I'm very curious."

"He's dead."

"What?"

"Hamza El Biali is dead. After Sadat's assassination he was tried and executed."

"That's a downer." Jake meant it. "But wait a minute. If the guy's dead, why was your Egyptian contact warning me to stay clear of this?"

Suter sighed, started toying with his pen. "Okay. Hamza El Biali had two brothers. One of them, Mohand, is—or was—a close associate of Osama bin Laden. There's speculation that he was killed when the U.S. went into Afghanistan, but that has not been confirmed."

"I see. They're probably still chasing him. Is that why they don't want me to get involved?"

"Could be. I don't know."

"You said Hamza El Biali had two brothers . . ."

"Very little is known about the other brother, the youngest of the three. The family used to live in a very poor and crowded area of Cairo. It's called . . ." The banker pulled a tiny Hermes notebook from the breast pocket of his suit coat and opened it. "Darb al-Ahmar."

Jake wrote down the name. "How old's this living brother?"

The banker shook his head. "That's all I've got. I'm sure my contact has more, but he wouldn't give it to me. I tried. Believe me, I tried. But you were kidding when you said that you were going to Egypt, right?"

"Nope."

"But what will you do there?"

"I don't know." He really didn't. What would he do when he got to Cairo, to Darb al-Ahmar? What exactly would he do if he found Ashraf? "I'll figure it out when I get there," he continued, his determination unaffected by the uncertainty. "What I do know is that the investigation into the bombing is going nowhere and I won't accept that."

"This isn't smart. You know that. If you really want to investigate, why don't you hire the best people and let them take care of things?"

"I thought of that. But this isn't something I can delegate like a business chore. They killed my *family*."

Unable to dissuade Jake, Suter offered him the assistance of the man in charge of the bank's special operations in Cairo. Not a banker, but the local factotum—a Lebanese by the name of Jibril Malouf. "He's a tremendous problem solver. I'll tell him you're coming."

"That's great. I'll call you from Cairo if I need help. I leave tonight."

"You're not serious."

"If I leave now I can still make the 6:00 P.M. Air France to Paris, where I'll meet a connecting flight to Egypt. That'll get me into Cairo at 3:45 P.M., their time tomorrow. I'll still have the late afternoon to do some work there."

"You've already reserved these flights?" Jake had never seen Suter even slightly ruffled, but he looked positively astonished now.

Jake nodded. "It was great seeing you, Ted."

"Me, too. Remember Jibril Malouf. You're sure you don't need his number?"

"It's okay. I'll call you from there."

"You won't use him, I can see. And it's a shame. Malouf is good."

"It'll be okay," Jake said. "Don't worry. And thanks for the help. I'll see you soon."

As he waited for the valet to bring his car, Jake realized that he was hungry. He knew he couldn't eat, though; he was jittery from the four cups of coffee he'd already had and the excitement of the trip.

He looked at his watch. They were taking a long time to bring the car. Then he noticed a commotion at the payment booth. A man who looked to be the manager was rushing toward the exit to the stairs, two attendants in tow. One of the attendants snuck a look at Jake as the door swung shut behind all three. Jake walked to the booth. "What's going on? Where's my car?"

The man behind the glass motioned with his chin, to somewhere behind Jake's shoulder.

His Aston Martin was emerging from the elevator opening. Something was very wrong. The garage mechanism was dragging the car forward with difficulty. From where Jake stood it looked as if its windshield was broken.

As Jake started toward his car, a man, blond and blue-eyed with a day-old growth of beard on his face, approached him and spoke in a clear but slightly accented English. "This is for you, Mr. Burke." He handed Jake a FedEx envelope and turned to leave.

"Who are you?" Jake asked.

"It doesn't matter." The man walked swiftly away.

Still in shock, Jake put the envelope under his arm and walked to his car. He could now see that the four tires were slashed and all of the vehicle's windows were smashed in. Glinting pebbles of broken glass covered the leather seats. It looked worse than it was—the rest of the car was intact.

Jake looked around. The blond man was nowhere to be seen now. Jake hurriedly opened the FedEx envelope. In it was a sealed plastic pouch. With difficulty, he opened it and retrieved a manila envelope, also sealed. In it was another envelope, letter-sized and white. This clearly had been done to delay him, giving the messenger time to disappear. In the white envelope was a single sheet of paper, folded in three and typewritten. It said:

> Stay out of this. You won't get another warning. The next time we won't spare the body.
> *Your* body.

CHAPTER FOUR

———— • ◆ • ————

Ashraf Ismail Ibrahim El Biali walked slowly through the barren streets of Darb al-Ahmar. For as long as anyone could remember, Ashraf's family had lived here in the medieval quarter, the most densely populated area in all of the Middle East. Earthen houses lined narrow alleyways, which in turn were crowded with goats, donkeys and dogs. In addition to the pungent odors of these animals, each day the aromas of turmeric and cumin filled the air: the smell of home.

Ashraf loved dawn in springtime, when the air was still dry and fresh and the houses in his neighborhood were painted pink and then golden by the slanting light of early morning. He washed his face, hands and feet and slid quietly into the Blue Mosque.

Bluish on the outside, thanks to the distinctive color of its marble cladding, the mosque was even bluer within: Blue tiles brought from Istanbul and Damascus depicted azure plants and flowers. Square and octagonal pillars supported the mosque's elaborately painted arched ceiling. The *mihrab*, the niche closest to Mecca, was inlaid with marble of every color and an even more colorful mosaic in purple, pink, green and gray. And wonder followed wonder. The mosque's marble *minbar*, its pulpit, was inlaid with precious stones. Best of all, it was quiet within the Blue Mosque, a still refuge from the near-insanity of the neighborhood streets. An oasis.

Ashraf recited the Morning Prayer. He then pronounced the Five Pillars of Islam three times, prostrating himself forty times on his prayer rug—a dusty, somewhat threadbare carpet of wool woven for precisely this purpose by children in Harraneya.

When he left the mosque, the cool early morning had already turned into a brutally hot day. The merciless sunlight scorched the city of over ten million where automobiles competed for street space with donkey-drawn carts, where radios blasting disco music vied with the sound of the muezzins summoning the faithful to prayer. Houses built of mud-brick stood at the foot of steel-and-glass office towers. Cairo, *Al-Qahira*, was not merely one of the largest cities in the world, it was also—arguably—the most schizophrenic.

Outside the mosque, he put on his sandals, picked up his tool bag and started walking to work. Strapped for cash upon his return to Egypt from the U.S., Ashraf had begun looking for employment immediately, with little luck at first. All the while he waited for the knock on his door—the appearance of those who would call him to task for his abandonment of the cause.

Finally, a friend of a cousin told him about a shoemaking job that was available, mainly because the applicant had to provide his own tools, which were expensive. Despite handouts from the Islamic Jihad relief organization that his mother received monthly in honor of his martyred brother Hamza, there wasn't enough for both of them to live on. With the last of the money he'd been given for the trip to America, Ashraf bought himself a shoemaker's hammer.

It looked more or less like a regular hammer. The claws were narrower than most, though, and pointed—for piercing holes in tough leather.

Upon his arrival at the one-room factory every morning, he would survey his surroundings and ask himself what the brother of Hamza El Biali was doing in this place forsaken by Allah. Four men shared a fifty-square-foot space, a hole really. Filthy paint that may have once been light blue fell from the wall in hand-size chips, revealing here and there the brown tiles beneath it. Old shoes hung from pegs. Hundreds of scraps of leather littered the floor. Open containers of glue triggered his gag reflex, as did the odors of the men beside him. The heat was asphyxiating.

No question, Ashraf's new job was dirty, tedious and underpaid work—demeaning work for a man like him. And yet . . .

He loved it. He loved sitting at the table covered in worn copper, creating something out of nothing, usable shoes out of useless remnants of animal-hide. He loved repairing shoes—taking something that was broken and making it usable again. He loved the banter among the men, banter that eventually acknowledged him, included him, finally welcomed him. He was thankful that after the first week or so of cold stares, they had allowed him to become one of them.

This morning, he didn't make it to work. An old car appeared at his side a few blocks from the factory. A man pointed a gun at him from the back seat.

"In the car. Now."

Ashraf looked around. The area was deserted.

"Now!" the man shouted, apparently unafraid of being heard.

Ashraf sat next to the driver. He knew both men. The one holding the gun was Rashid, a cousin of his partner at the toy-store bombing—a cousin of the martyr who had actually summoned the nerve to blow himself up.

The second one, driving the old Renault, was Abdullah Ghorab. Like Ashraf, Abdullah lived in Darb al-Ahmar. Ashraf was sure that Ghorab didn't know him, but he knew Ghorab and his reputation. As a veteran of the war against the Russians in Afghanistan, where he had traveled after studying engineering in Germany, Ghorab was something of a celebrity in the neighborhood. His cruelty against enemies was legendary.

Rumor had it in Cairo's medieval district that Abdullah's group in Afghanistan had captured five Soviet soldiers and tied them up. With the men still alive, Abdullah sliced their skin at their waists, then pulled it over their heads and tied it. After the screaming stopped, their mutilated bodies were put in burlap bags and dropped next to a Soviet outpost.

Ashraf felt like vomiting. The stench of cigarettes and perspiration inside this car were causing it, he told himself.

I'm not afraid, he repeated to himself silently. *I'm not afraid.*

He was driven to an empty warehouse in Helwan half an hour south of Cairo.

In the sweltering heat, they entered the hulking brick building through a broken door atop a loading dock. Once inside, the martyr's cousin shoved Ashraf to the shattered concrete floor in the darkest corner of a cave-like room. Most of the windows high above were broken, and the rest were blackened with grime. Birds nested in the eaves of the building. Like frosting on some French pastry, their droppings caked every surface. Abdullah stood with his back to them, a small handgun—Ashraf recognized a Beretta .22—showing in the waist of his jeans.

The interrogation commenced without prelude. Rashid, the martyr's cousin, spoke first.

"The plan was for you to die at the toy store."

Careful not to meet the man's gaze directly, Ashraf spoke. "No, the plan was for me to supervise the fasting of the designated bombers, then preach to them of the glories of life in Paradise as well as reminding them of the obscenity that is the Great Satan. It was I who chose—"

Pain shot through Ashraf. He could feel it all the way up to the crown of his head, on the soles of his feet. Rashid had kicked him in the ribs, hard.

"You wriggled out of your sacred duty," the man said.

When he'd regained his breath, Ashraf tried to explain. "I wasn't even authorized to die. I was the one who decided to go against my orders. I felt that it would cement the commitment of the rest of the group if I were to sacrifice my own life during the first part of the mission—inspire them to do the same when they attacked the train station and the art museum." He was talking too fast—he could not, would not, show fear. He paused and breathed deeply, trying to regain his composure. "Still, I did not have orders to become a Shaheed yet."

"You did not have orders to become a Shaheed yet," Ashraf's interrogator repeated through his teeth.

"As mission operator," Ashraf went on, "it was up to me to decide who among my team would die and who would merely assist in the execution of our mission. I simply chose myself as one of the two bombers."

Abdullah turned briefly to face them. The logo on his T-shirt said, POLO JEANS.

"Then what happened in New York?" His voice echoed throughout the warehouse: *York. York. York.* "You announce to the rest of the group that you will see them in Heaven. Rashid's cousin dies and you show up in Cairo. Why are you alive, you worthless pig?"

Abdullah stepped across the cracked floor of the warehouse, pulling the Beretta from the waistband of his jeans as he did so. He pressed the gun's short muzzle against the side of Ashraf's head and cocked the hammer with a click that echoed through the cavernous space.

A dark stain spread across the front of Ashraf's pants. Lying on the floor of the deserted warehouse, he had wet himself. He struggled to find the words: "I . . ." he stammered, while his captors looked on impassively. "I . . ."

"You what?"

"I couldn't detonate the explosives. The force of the first bomb tore my detonator off."

Abdullah nodded, smiling ominously. He passed his gun to Rashid and reached into his shirt pocket for a box of cigarettes: Dunhill Reds. Despite his fear, Ashraf found himself wondering if perhaps the man had developed a taste for expensive tobacco as a student in Europe.

Abdullah struck a match on the wall behind him and lit up. Squinting into the smoke, he said, "That is not what the newspaper accounts said."

"Sorry?" Ashraf's pulse trilled in his chest, behind his eyes. Suddenly he couldn't swallow.

"The American newspapers said that a full set of explosives was found in a men's room stall at the toy store. The belt was still very much intact. So was the detonator. The bomb squad detonated the device days later, after examining it for fingerprints and the like."

The charade was over. Ashraf could see it in the man's eyes.

Everyone knew that he hadn't had the courage to pull that cord.

"Prepare to die." Abdullah dragged on the cigarette one final time and flicked it into the gloom, where the embers briefly flickered and then went out. He directed his attention to the far end of the abandoned warehouse, as if too disgusted to look upon his prisoner. Rashid lifted his gun.

"No! Please! I beg of you!" Ashraf rolled to a position of supplication on the ground in the corner of the deserted warehouse. "Listen to me. My brother killed Anwar Sadat. I am the brother of the Shaheed Hamza El Biali!"

Desperately, Ashraf turned and angled his head toward his back pocket, toward the piece of paper that he'd carried there for decades. If only his captors would look at it . . .

He'd been given the document at the age of fourteen, on a day that he'd spent like most days, playing football in the street with his friends. That particular day was like no other, though; it changed his life forever, starting with the cries that came spilling out of windows and doorways.

"Sadat is dead!"

"Sadat has been killed. Our Ras has been killed!"

Abandoning the ball in a gutter, Ashraf and his friends had dashed into a house and watched a small black-and-white television. Regular programming had been canceled. There were repeated announcements of Sadat's death amid readings from the Koran and film clips of the president's many so-called achievements: the 1973 war, which the government claimed had restored Egypt's dignity after its inglorious defeat in the Six Day War of 1967; the peace treaty with Begin; Sadat's Nobel Peace Prize—whatever that was. No film of the assassination itself was shown on Egyptian TV.

Late afternoon the following day, a man Ashraf didn't know appeared at the El Biali home, holding a large worn envelope the color of sand. Ashraf thanked the man and opened the envelope at the kitchen's rickety wooden table with his mother watching. A dish of *bil takhdi'a*, okra casserole, baked in the oven. Ashraf began to read aloud from the first page, a long message typewritten on brittle translucent paper.

To the honorable El Biali family:

May Allah Almighty be with you. This is an article from the American press, from their most important newspaper. The lackey of the Americans is dead and here is how they report it. Allah is great!

Ashraf laid the typed page on the tabletop and withdrew a newspaper clipping. "From *New York Times*," someone had written at the top. The little English that Ashraf had learned at school allowed him to understand that. It was an article in English.

CAIRO, Egypt, Oct. 6—President Anwar el-Sadat of Egypt was shot and killed today by a group of men in military uniforms who hurled hand grenades and fired rifles at him as he watched a military parade commemorating the 1973 war against Israel.

Regarded as an interim ruler when he came to power in 1970 upon the death of Gamal Abdel Nasser, Mr. Sadat forged his own regime and ran Egypt single-handedly. He was bent on moving this impoverished country into the late 20th century, a drive that led him to abandon an alliance with the Soviet Union and embrace the West.

That rule ended abruptly today. As jet fighters roared overhead, the killers sprayed the reviewing stand with bullets while thousands of horrified people—officials, diplomats and journalists, including this correspondent—looked on.

Within seconds of the attack, the reviewing stand was awash in blood. Bemedaled officials dove for cover. Screams and panic followed as guests tried to flee, toppling over chairs. Some were crushed underfoot. Others, shocked and stunned, stood riveted.

"It's about the assassination," Ashraf told his mother.
"I don't understand," she said. "What does it have to do with us?"
Ashraf shrugged and went on trying to read.

This correspondent saw one assailant, a stocky dark-haired man, crouching and firing a rifle into the stand used by Mr. Sadat.

"I am Hamza El-Biali!" the attacker shouted. "I killed Pharaoh. Allah is great!"

Ashraf repeated the last lines, "I am Hamza El-Biali. I killed Pharaoh. Allah is great."

"What?" his mother asked, panic in her voice. "Did Hamza kill our president?"

Ashraf wasn't sure, but he wasn't ready to show it. He nodded.

Ashraf's mother fainted, the tin top of a pot and her wooden spoon clattering across the kitchen floor as she fell.

Much later, having comforted his distraught mother, Ashraf withdrew the final sheet of paper from the envelope. It was printed in Arabic on the same paper as the first page with the message. It confirmed what he'd told his mother.

"*Your son Hamza is a Shaheed. He has sacrificed himself in the name of Allah. Keep this paper as your proof. With Allah's grace, you need not worry about money. We will protect your family forever. May Allah keep you in good health.*"

Ashraf sat on his own bed and started to laugh, his laughter turning to sobs almost instantly and then becoming laughter again. He wiped the tears from his eyes and laughed some more. It happened to him often, this simultaneous laughing and crying. Between the laughter and the tears he kept repeating in his primitive English, "I killed Pharaoh. Allah is great. Allah is great. I killed Pharaoh."

In the warehouse on the edge of the desert, Ashraf's voice grew stronger. "I have proof," he told Rashid, the cousin of the toy-store martyr. "In my back pocket. Take out my wallet."

Rashid hesitated, then belted his gun and pulled out Ashraf's wallet. He found the piece of paper inside and unfolded it for Abdullah.

Abdullah read the letter, then handed it back to Rashid, who also read it, eyes widening. The men looked at each other significantly. Then they tied Ashraf's legs, pulling them backwards and securing them to his bound arms—a reverse fetal position. Ashraf cried out in pain. Abdullah walked away. Ashraf heard the car's trunk being opened and closed. Abdullah came back with a dirty and foul-smelling rag and stuffed it in his mouth. Both attackers left without a word.

After hours in the same position, Ashraf's legs went into uncontrollable seizures. With each jerk, the knots on his wrists grew tighter, scraping away layers of skin. Both of his hands throbbed with pain from the lack of blood flow. As additional hours passed, the rest of his body started to ache. The rag seemed to be moving slowly down his throat. He was certain that it was only a matter of time before it would asphyxiate him.

Ashraf was sure that he had been left to die.

Hours later, their faces drained of color, Rashid and Abdullah rushed to Ashraf's side and, as if racing for their lives, struggled to untie him.

"Please forgive us," said Abdullah, his voice devoid of tone or emotion.

"Yes," said Rashid, with slightly more feeling. "Forgive us, please."

"We did not know," said Abdullah. "I never associated you with Hamza, your brother the great martyr. I should have. Please forgive me."

"We had no way of knowing."

Dazed and speechless, in such pain that he wondered if perhaps he'd been permanently crippled by the ordeal, Ashraf was driven back to Cairo and dropped at his mother's home.

Somehow he'd survived. Again.

CHAPTER FIVE

Jake was finishing things up at the office when Miranda appeared in the doorway.

"Your mechanic called," she said. "The estimate to fix the Aston Martin is $8500. He asked if you left it in the Bronx overnight or something."

"I told him to use my cell number," Jake said. *Damn.*

"Look, Jake, I know you're going to Egypt today. I don't know why, but I know it has to do with your family. And probably what happened to your car."

Jake shrugged. No point in lying to her. "All true. But this is my business."

Miranda came into the office and sat down on his desk. He noticed how good her legs looked as her skirt shifted around her thighs, and he instantly felt guilty for it.

It was clear that she'd given this some thought when she started to talk. "You've been a mentor to me and a friend. But you're only one man, and right now a man who isn't at his best. Let me in. You need the help."

"No," he said firmly. "But thanks anyway."

"I think I deserve more than a 'no' without an explanation."

Jake sighed. "As you might've guessed, what I'm involved in isn't exactly safe. I could never let you put yourself at risk for my personal crusade."

"With all that's going on in the world today, no one is safe. What happened to Steph and Claire is happening to people every day. If you're trying to do something about that . . . I'm in."

"I'm not. I just want to find the man who killed them."

"It's a start," she said softly.

"Forget it. You could get killed."

"I'm in, I said. I won't accept anything else. Don't try to stop me from being there when you need me." She would not be swayed.

So Jake bought Miranda a plane ticket to Egypt and, on their flight, told her everything he knew. If she was alarmed or regretted her decision, she didn't let on.

Deep down Jake was relieved not to be doing this alone. His panic attacks made him question his ability to act under pressure, something he'd never doubted before. He didn't doubt Miranda's problem-solving ability or mental fortitude, so there was every possibility he'd soon be grateful for her presence.

He just hoped he wouldn't get her killed.

A few hours later, Jake and Miranda sat in the lobby of the Semiramis Intercontinental Hotel, looking out at the Corniche el-Nil, the avenue bordering the Nile River. The hotel was almost thirty years old, but after extensive renovation, arguably the best in Cairo. Jake didn't care. He liked the fact that it wasn't far from Darb al-Ahmar, Hamza El Biali's neighborhood.

Sitting across from them was Isabelle Said, the *Al Ahram* journalist who'd written the article about Anwar Sadat's assassination. Said was also the author of two books on contemporary religious conflicts in the Middle East. She had agreed via email to meet Jake for a drink. She worked out of Cairo, so it wasn't an inconvenience, and Jake's message, which had revealed that he'd been a victim of a terror attack and had information possibly of value to her, had intrigued her.

Isabelle Said had arrived elegantly dressed in a beige Chanel-style suit and a strand of pearls. A sixty-ish woman, she had striking blue eyes, though a receding chin kept her from being beautiful. From his research on her, Jake knew that she'd actually been present at the 1981 ceremony and had witnessed the Sadat assassination firsthand.

Jake introduced Miranda as his assistant. He didn't know what else to call her, though this experience was far from a client meeting at the Four Seasons. "You speak English with a hint of a French accent," Jake said to Isabelle after the formalities were done. "Why is that?"

They'd sat in a quiet corner and had just ordered a bottle of sparkling water from the liveried waiter.

"I'm Lebanese. From Beirut. But I've been living in Egypt since the mid-seventies."

Jake already knew this from the short biography of her that he'd found on the Internet. And he was ready with a true story, which he hoped would quickly gain her empathy and assistance. "You know," he said, "a Lebanese friend told me a story thirty years ago that was pretty hard to believe at the time."

Mrs. Said smiled. "We are full of stories, we Lebanese."

"Please call me Jake, okay?"

"Okay. And call me Isabelle."

Jake took a sip of water and nodded. "My friend had an older cousin, a Lebanese Christian like him. He went with his parents to visit her one day in Paris. There was another man in her apartment, a Palestinian. A soft-spoken guy. His cousin was living with the Palestinian. They all talked pleasantly for a while, then the conversation turned to politics."

Isabelle set her glass down. "Hmm. Yes."

"Apparently the Palestinian went crazy. He started saying that the situation in Lebanon was unjust. That the Muslims were a majority in Lebanon and yet the Christians ran things. And—"

"When was this?" Isabelle cut in.

"Oh, maybe 1975?"

"Ah." She nodded.

"So this Palestinian says, 'Things will change. The Palestinians will start a revolution. We Muslims will blow up that country.' He said it twice. My friend remembered."

Isabelle nodded again.

"Literally a few months later, the civil war started," Jake went on. "Lebanon was destroyed. Well, you know that, of course. But it was incredible to me. The Palestinian guy knew it was coming. And that it wasn't some temporary thing. The destruction continued for . . . what? Years. Fifteen or more. I couldn't forget the story . . ."

"They never belonged there," said Isabelle, "the Palestinians, I mean. And their radical Muslim allies. I think we might have worked things out peacefully, if not for them. Lebanon was a place of peace, of tolerance. Everybody lived well together. Christians, Muslims, even Jews. It was the Switzerland of the Middle East. And Beirut was like Paris."

Jake saw a fleeting memory pass before her eyes. It was time to get back to the real topic, to his request. "Let me tell you the real reason we're here, Isabelle. I told you that I was a victim of terrorist violence. I lost my wife and daughter. But I didn't come here with a story for you."

Isabelle sat back, assessing him, curious but cautious.

"I mean, I don't mind if you write about this. You can write anything you want, and I'll help. But I'm here to ask a favor."

Isabelle signaled the waiter for the check. "Why don't you tell me what you want, Mr. Burke. Jake. I'm a big girl. I'm on your side. You don't have to win my sympathy. I know firsthand what these Muslim radicals, these Islamists, these *animals* are doing." She looked around and deliberately lowered her voice. "The world is like their Lebanon now. They are destroying everything."

Jake and Miranda exchanged glances. Isabelle was holding back a great deal of anger. If Jake had to guess, she felt angry for being made to fear.

Jake paid for the water but asked her to stay at the table a moment longer. He made his proposal: Help him find the youngest brother of Hamza El Biali; accompany Jake, translate for him; help him attempt to get to the murderer of his family and understand what drove such a man to kill innocent people without discrimination. Jake promised Isabelle that she could write whatever she wished afterwards. He also offered her a large, one-time cash payment for her services.

To his surprise, Isabelle agreed to help without further deliberation. She refused the money but at the same time offered to call her nephew.

He was, she said, a young, street-smart man who knew Cairo very well and could drive them. The nephew had paid for his college tuition working as a taxi driver, and he would gladly accept Jake's cash payment on her behalf.

"He's a great kid," she said as they stood and left their table. "And a devout Muslim, by the way. Not all Muslims are bad, you know," she added with a smile.

"Of course I do." Jake smiled back.

They were now waiting for Muhammad Iqbal, Isabelle Said's nephew. He had told them that he'd be at the hotel by 5:00 P.M. It was 5:35. Isabelle drank her water quietly while Jake watched the clock. Miranda gave him a look that meant, *Relax,* and he nodded.

Jake had read in *Frommer's* that the area between the Corniche el-Nil and the river was a park where people went for exercise and relaxation. He had visualized something like Riverside Park, its landscaping designed in such a way that cars went mostly unseen by promenading New Yorkers. Instead he was looking at a busy highway. The triangular sails of *feluccas*, the boats used on the Nile since antiquity, were visible to him—but only through a screen of cars and trucks, and beyond the cacophony of an infinite number of blowing horns. Jake was grateful for the thick glass doors that sheltered them from it.

He kept his other eye on the entrance to the hotel, trying to spot Muhammad, although he didn't have much to go on. Isabelle had described her nephew as a not-too-short, not-too-chubby man in his thirties, with curly black hair—an adequate description of half the men in Cairo. Most of those who stepped past the hotel doorman were clearly foreigners: businessmen, journalists, and tourists, their cameras, maps and idiotic grins giving them away. Muhammad was late and Jake was becoming annoyed with the delay, despite himself.

When at last a man approached them directly, Jake realized that Isabelle couldn't have described him any other way.

"Muhammad Ali Iqbal," he said. "Call me Mike." Somehow he managed a tone that was both businesslike and warm.

Jake stood up to shake hands. He was at least four inches taller than the Egyptian. "How are you, Mike? Muhammad Ali? Like the boxer?"

Mike smiled. "They say it's the most common name in the world. Almost one and a half billion Muslims, you know, and we all worship the Prophet Muhammad, so it makes sense. Sorry I'm late. Traffic here in Cairo is horrendous, impossible to plan for. I promise you, I left especially early for this meeting because I knew you would not expect my delay, and still—"

"Don't worry about it. I heard about the traffic," Jake found himself saying.

"And who is this?" Mike said, going into Lothario mode and taking Miranda's hand rather ostentatiously.

"Miranda Connelly. I'm Mr. Burke's assistant," she said with a smile that was broad but not at all coy. Her professional demeanor and Isabelle's disapproving glance ended Mike's courtly routine right there.

After the three of them had ordered and drank cups of the bland American-style coffee that the hotel offered in a misguided attempt at modernity, Mike led them outdoors. They stepped out of the air-conditioned lobby into the pandemonium of passersby, street vendors and beggars, their din drowned out by the insistent blare of truck and taxi horns. Upon his arrival in downtown Cairo, Jake had noticed the foul smell of exhaust fumes, but he was still taken aback by the noxious stench. In fact, his throat was somewhat raw already from breathing the polluted air.

Jake noticed a short, very dark-skinned man wearing a brown jacket and grey pants. Perhaps ten yards away from them, the man was lighting a cigarette intently. Jake turned his attention back to Isabelle and his guide.

"You're very close to the real center of Cairo," Mike was explaining. They had turned right upon leaving the hotel and now stood at the corner of Corniche el-Nil and a wide street called Sharia At-Tahrir. "*Sharia* means 'street.' If we walk two blocks on Sharia At-Tahrir, away from the river, we reach Midan Tahrir, which means 'Liberation Square.'"

"That's the epicenter of the city," Isabelle added. "Since many consider Cairo to be the capital of the Arab world, Midan Tahrir could be called the very center of the Arab world."

"Really?" Jake said.

"Not from the religious point of view, of course. That would be Mecca. But here," Isabelle pointed to a building to the left, "is where the leaders of the Arab world meet. The Arab League Building."

They had reached Liberation Square, actually a circular expanse of green.

Mike resumed the tour direction. "To the right is American University, the closest thing we have to an Ivory League University."

Jake smiled at the malapropism.

"It's very, very hard to get in. I did my undergraduate studies there," Mike said. He shot a look to Miranda, gauging her approval, but found only polite interest.

Impatient, Jake grunted.

"Well, then." Mike clapped his hands. "Now that we're oriented, Isabelle said that you wanted to visit Darb al-Ahmar, right?" Isabelle nodded. Jake felt his mouth go dry. "I parked my car a block from here," Mike continued. "The parking rates at the Semiramis are . . . what is the phrase? Highway robbery."

Jake was growing edgier by the minute. So as to conceal from their guide what felt like a nervous grimace, he turned as the four of them squeezed into Mike's Fiat to look in the direction from which they'd come. Following not ten yards behind them was the dark-skinned man in the brown jacket.

"Excuse me," he said to Mike, relieved in a way to break through the happy-talk. "But we have a problem."

"What problem?"

"Don't look back, but we're being followed."

"A car?"

"No, a man on foot."

"Okay, then let's go." Mike glanced into the mirror to make sure that Miranda had closed her door. Then he stepped on the gas and sped away. "That's it, he can't follow us now."

Jake looked back. The man in the brown jacket was entering a car on the passenger's side. "Not so fast. Do you see an old Mercedes, a blue one?"

Mike looked into his rearview mirror again. "Yes."

"That's him. They're at least two now. Maybe others in the back seat. I can't really see."

"Okay." Mike was driving fast in traffic that made doing so difficult. They were on the Corniche el-Nil, zigzagging between lanes as if no traffic regulations existed.

As Jake put his seat belt on and heard the ladies' click into place, he noticed that Mike didn't attach his. Mike glanced at Jake and saw his inquiring look. "I don't trust those things." The blue Mercedes maintained a constant distance between them.

"They're still behind us," Jake said, after they'd driven some two miles. Isabelle wasn't looking back. Her stare was determined, her jaw clenched.

Mike made an abrupt turn to the right, off the main road and onto a much smaller street, tires screeching. Jake felt the two wheels on his side leave the ground. For a moment he was sure they were going to roll over. His head hit the ceiling of the Fiat as the tires touched ground again and Mike floored the accelerator. The car bounced with each of the many potholes and bumps in the road.

Jake glanced at Miranda and saw that she was calm, even half-smiling. She noted his incredulous look and shrugged.

"Kinda exciting," she whispered.

He shook his head, wondering if he would've felt the same twenty years ago. He didn't think so.

They drove like that for what seemed like an eternity, in and out of narrow roads, some of them no more than paths in the mud, then onto a wide boulevard and back into the maze of one-way streets and alleyways. To his credit, Mike didn't seem especially worried about the state of his car. At one point Jake heard the car's chassis scrape against a hump on the road.

If he's trying to impress me, he's succeeding, Jake thought. The man was driving recklessly, with no sign of a preservation instinct. Jake looked back and didn't see the Mercedes anymore.

Mike made a hairpin turn and veered left. They sped down an alley so narrow, it hardly accommodated the car. By gluing her back to a wall, a black-clad woman barely escaped being crushed. Finally Mike turned into what looked like a small open market and brought the battered Fiat to a halt. Jake craned his neck back. There were no cars on the road. Mike was grinning at them. He winked at Miranda.

"Didn't I tell you? No problem."

Miranda rolled her eyes, but she was smiling with genuine respect. Jake looked at Isabelle. She was grinning too. He shook his head. "You guys are crazy," he said, allowing his head to roll back in relief and fatigue. They sat there in silence, the only sound the irregular beat of the car's tired engine.

"So," Mike asked Jake, "do we continue to Darb al-Ahmar?"

Jake nodded.

"We're actually very close," Mike said. And in less than five minutes, he announced, "Here we are." Mike tooled around for an additional fifteen minutes or so in search of a parking space. At last they climbed from the tinny car and set out on foot.

Jake was appalled by what he observed in the medieval district. The wretched mud-brick houses, the dirty alleyways and the putrid smell of animal waste—human waste, for all he knew—shocked him. Over the next half hour, Mike babbled gaily about the place and its origin in Saladin's time while Isabelle added tidbits on history, geography and religion. Jake's discomfort increased, the fetidness that filled his nostrils and mouth all but asphyxiating him while a shapeless dread expanded behind his ribs. Wherever he looked there were goats and donkeys. There were toothless men in filthy robes, smiling at them. Children ran after Jake and Isabelle and Miranda, touching them with their dirty little fingers, apparently asking for money. Jake cringed at every encounter. He began to feel dizzy. A young man passed by carrying a tray bearing a copper teapot and colorful glasses. Jake heard the glasses tinkle, their sound seemingly amplified. Now he wanted to push the children away, push the older men away, the miserable smiling toothless smiling ugly smiling masks that stared at him, hating him. A nightmarish mob made of filth and pestilence was trying to grab him, ravage him, transform him into one of them: a decayed version of humanity, living an eternal death.

And then Miranda caressed the face of one of the children. Jake couldn't believe his eyes. Squatting in the dust to tie his shoelace, he had fallen somewhat behind the others. Fifteen feet ahead of him in the crowded street, Miranda was talking to the boy, giving him money. Buying something from him.

Once again Jake's vision became obscured, limited, as if he were looking through a cardboard tube, or down a long tunnel. At the same time, the world seemed to expand and contract. To grow and shrink in time to his own short breaths. He was nearly overcome by nausea that snaked from the pit of his stomach to the back of his mouth. With a linen handkerchief pulled from his shirt pocket he mopped perspiration from his brow, his cheeks, his upper lip.

Jake's first thought was, *Have I come down with food poisoning? Or dysentery—maybe I drank some water that wasn't bottled, in the airport or at the hotel.* Mouth parched, he swallowed, and swallowed again.

And then he thought, *Of course. It's another panic attack.* While the others continued to interact at the end of his tunnel-vision, oblivious to him, he desperately reached for familiar thoughts.

What is my name? Jake Burke.

What is my favorite song? A tie: "While My Guitar Gently Weeps" by the Beatles, George Harrison; and Bob Dylan's "Like a Rolling Stone."

What do I like to eat? Sushi at Haru. The prime rib at Smith and Wollensky's. A Haagen-Dazs hot fudge sundae.

And to drink? Beck's dark beer. Finlandia straight up.

Slowly, as he answered the questions and breathed deeply, his nausea receded and his vision returned to normal. Good, Jake thought, I made it through. He was too tired to exult. In fact, he was exhausted. He could barely summon the strength to stand from his squatting position.

He'd been able to control a panic attack, rather than merely submitting to it. Would he be able to control all of them? Jake allowed himself to hope.

He nodded at Mike and smiled at Miranda, who had moved on. She held what looked from a distance like a blue bracelet. They didn't suspect anything, he thought. Great. The children nearest him were now keeping a respectful distance. They suspected something. He looked around. All was clear. He ran his fingers through his sweat-dampened hair and walked on.

An hour later, Jake sat with the others at a restaurant, all four posing as journalists.

Under the suspicious eyes of a waiter, the restaurant owner was answering the question Mike had put to him. Mike translated.

"There are three El Biali brothers: Hamza, who took part in Sadat's assassination; Mohand, who was with Al Qaeda somewhere in Pakistan since 2001; and one other, the youngest."

Jake could barely breathe. All he could do was repeat, "The youngest." Miranda looked at him with concern, eyes posing a question. Jake tried to respond that he was okay with his own. She nodded but kept sneaking glances at him.

The owner spoke further in Arabic. Mike relayed his remarks to Jake and Miranda. "Ashraf. He's back in Cairo after a few weeks away."

"Does this man know Ashraf?" Jake asked, hardly able to contain his anxiety.

Mike nodded. "He's a nice, quiet fellow, he says."

"What does he do?" Jake asked Mike.

"He's a cobbler. He's become even more withdrawn since the accident."

As Mike translated this last bit, the waiter interrupted. What was obviously an argument ensued.

"What's going on?" Miranda asked.

Mike explained. "The waiter is trying to stop the owner here from giving us information. He doesn't believe we are journalists." Mike paused, listened for a moment. "Now he's saying that he's going to get help. To protect the El Bialis. Let's get out of here. I'm afraid this is getting dangerous."

Isabelle nodded. "I think Mike's right."

"Now the owner's telling the waiter to shut up," Mike continued. "He knows I understand the language and doesn't want to show that he lacks authority in his own restaurant."

The owner turned back to them with an obsequious smile.

"We can't leave now," Jake said. "It'd look even more fishy. I don't think we'd make it out of the neighborhood alive. Let's push on. Ask him what accident."

Mike translated the reply. "A car accident. He's okay, but now he has a big scar on his face."

Bingo, Jake thought.

CHAPTER SIX

Fathma El Biali was preparing *fuul*—mashing fava beans with lemon juice, herbs and oil. Ashraf sat before a televised soccer game munching on *aish*, the Egyptian puffed pita bread dipped in olive oil. He was too hungry to wait for his mother to finish cooking.

His tool bag sat by the door where he'd left it when he entered the house.

Since his return to Cairo, Ashraf was thankful for every day that was given him, grateful to be alive in a way he'd never experienced before. He still saw himself as a Living Martyr—the "Shaheed al-Chai" Ashraf El Biali. But the al-Chai, the Living, was now everything. Slowly, he had started allowing himself to be happy, even to hope. And then, two weeks after his arrival back in Egypt, the encounter with Abdullah and Hafez had occurred.

That episode had concluded without undue harm to Ashraf, Allah be praised, though a day later he was still sore all over from his ordeal on the warehouse floor. Still, Ashraf knew that it was only a matter of time before someone else knocked on his door and picked him up. After all, famous brother or not, he had shirked his duty to the cause—his duty to Allah. Surely someone would demand retribution. And this time Ashraf would not be so lucky, he was certain of that.

His mother called him to the table. Ashraf switched off the television and joined her in the kitchen. Just as he sat down, he heard a knock.

He walked toward the door, opened it. Four figures stood in the street outside, three of them merely shadows behind the first in the early-evening darkness.

"Ashraf El Biali?"

"Yes." He felt his knees go weak.

"May we speak with you briefly?"

Ashraf feared these people with every fiber of his being, but it would desecrate the memory of his brothers to deny them hospitable welcome into the El Biali home. "I have to speak to my mother for only one minute. Can I do that?"

He ran toward the kitchen before the answer came. On the table, heaping helpings of food still obscured most of his plate, and his mother's.

"Mother, I want you to leave this house now."

"What? Why? Weren't you going out? Why are you holding me like that? You are hurting me."

"I said I want you out now. Go to Aunt Salma's. Don't come back until tomorrow."

His mother started moving toward the front of the house. Ashraf still held her. "There are some people out there. Walk straight out of the house and down the street without talking to them, do you hear? Even if they call you, keep going." He hugged his mother.

Tears glistened in her eyes. "I am frightened, my son."

"Go. Now. I love you." The old lady shuffled past the strangers and out of the house. Ashraf stood in the kitchen doorway and watched her leave.

"Thank you for waiting," he said to the figures outside his door.

"*As-salaam Alaykum*, may peace be with you, Ashraf El Biali."

"May peace be with you. Please come in." He welcomed his guests inside.

Now it was surprise and puzzlement, rather than fear, that Ashraf sought to hide. Before him stood the man who had addressed him a moment before: an Egyptian, probably in his late thirties. As expected. Beside him, though, was a Westerner: a tall man in casual but expensive-looking clothes. He looked oh-so-vaguely familiar, though Ashraf couldn't say why. His other visitors were, of all things, two *women*. One was Middle Eastern and the other an attractive white girl who looked like someone he'd seen in Hollywood movies.

"I'm sorry, who are you?"

"We're journalists. The man's name is John Harding and the ladies are Wafa Alahras and Susan Shepherd. They're reporters working for the Atlantic News Association, a company that sells news items to several newspapers. Syndication, they call it in America. The Americans don't speak Arabic. I am Abdullah Amarneh, and I'm helping them."

Now Ashraf was sure of it: He knew the second man, the silent Westerner. He had seen those hate-filled eyes before.

This was no team of journalists, though. No newspaperman bubbled over with the passion so clearly apparent on this man's face. Ashraf knew that look, for he had seen it in many of his comrades: a look of rage so black and towering that it practically cast a shadow.

"How do you know my name? How do you know where I live?"

"Actually, we had some trouble finding you. The El Biali name is famous, yet no one in the neighborhood seemed to know where your home was located." The Egyptian chuckled. "Their loyalty to the family was quite impressive, I must say. May we sit down?"

Behind the courteous tone Ashraf heard authority in the man's voice. Who *were* these people?

"Yes, of course. I will get you some tea with *nenah*; we have very fresh mint leaves."

"Don't worry, we're fine. My journalist friends here would like to ask you some questions."

"Of course."

The silent man slid his hand into his jacket. Ashraf leaped to his feet. Slowly, the man withdrew a pocket-size tape recorder and smiled at him. Ashraf saw irony in the smile. He sat down again.

"May we begin?" the Egyptian asked. "I will translate the questions."

For the first time, the formerly silent man spoke. Ashraf didn't recognize the voice. The Egyptian translated.

"You are Ashraf Ismail Ibrahim El Biali, is that correct?"

"Yes."

"And you are the brother of Hamza El Biali?"

"Yes."

Now the Arab woman spoke.

"The objective of this interview is to get to know you. To understand how it feels to be Hamza's brother. Westerners want very much to understand how radical Islamists such as Hamza think. Will you help us?"

What the woman said made sense. Hamza was a hero, after all, and it was right that the world would want to know him better—to know his family, even. For that matter, she seemed genuinely interested in hearing the answers to the questions she asked. Maybe these three *were* journalists after all. Ashraf glanced at the American man, still staring him down with unblinking eyes. No, he couldn't be a reporter. Still, what did Ashraf have to lose by talking? If a plot was afoot and a struggle ensued, he would be outnumbered anyway.

"Yes," he said.

"How does it feel to be the brother of a hero?"

"Hamza gave his life to establish an Islamic State in Egypt. I am proud to be his brother and the brother of Mohand, who was a fighter with Osama bin Laden. They say Mohand is dead, but he's alive."

"Why did you take part in the bombing at FAO Schwarz in New York?"

Ashraf started. Had American investigators traced the materials left in the men's room to him and reported their findings to the newspapers there? If so, it was time to go into hiding. Otherwise, not merely journalists would come knocking, along with his old colleagues from the Jihad, but the American C.I.A. as well.

The fear that Ashraf had been feeling dissipated in an instant. Pride surged through him. At last, after years of indirection and failed attempts, after years of anonymity, he was the focus of a worldwide manhunt by the most powerful country in the world, the Great Satan! Ashraf burned to tell his brothers.

He leaned forward and spoke proudly to his interrogators. "Following our destruction of their Towers of Evil, an attack justified by all the harm and corruption that they brought upon the Muslim world, the infidel countries were able to justify their dirty war against Muslims everywhere. They are at war with Islam and we are at war with them."

The tall American spoke, and the Egyptian translated his words. "This is the typical answer. Explain it better, please."

Ashraf knew from his brief stay in the U.S. that Westerners saw all Arabs, all Muslims, as backward and ignorant. He was not ignorant. He would show them. "The policies of the United States are supporting the corrupt regime of our country. They are supporting those thieves in Saudi Arabia, the United Arab Emirates and elsewhere. And of course they are supporting the Zionist entity in Palestine."

Now the pretty American woman spoke up. Ashraf waited patiently for the translation. "You say America is supporting the regime in Saudi Arabia. But Saudi Arabia is a strict Islamic State. So this can't be a war between the West and Islam, can it?"

I have to be careful here, Ashraf thought, they are trying to trap me. "Of course it is a war against Islam. They used us while it was convenient for them to do so, while we were fighting the Soviets for them in Afghanistan. And then they abandoned us, like they abandon all their former allies. They will do the same to Saudi Arabia. Which is just as well—the Saudi government is filled with tyrants, usurpers, illegitimate rulers."

The American man resumed his pointed questioning. "Is that why you went to New York to explode a bomb and kill women and children in a toy store?"

"Yes," Ashraf said, his chest quite literally puffing up with pride. "That's the only way it can be done. We have to go in there and kill their civilians, to frighten them into withdrawing from their colonies."

The American shook his head in frustration. Whoever he was, he seemed desperate to understand Ashraf's point of view—not just interested, as the women were, but truly needful of an explanation.

Just then someone pounded against the door from the outside.

Ashraf rose to open it. Outside, and clearly visible to his guests, stood a man Ashraf vaguely recognized: one of the waiters from the neighborhood café. With him was a group of threatening-looking men, some actually brandishing pipes and sticks, others likely holding more lethal weapons beneath their shirts.

"Is everything all right?" the waiter asked.

"Yes," Ashraf replied. He actually smiled with pride. "These good people are interviewing me for their newspaper." Or was it a magazine? Ashraf wasn't sure now.

"Are you certain?" The waiter leaned to one side so as to see past Ashraf into his mother's house.

"Don't worry, my friend, everything is fine," he said, in the dignified tone that he heard important people use when they were doing important things. "Thank you for your concern, though."

One of the other men, lip curled in a bellicose snarl, tried to slip past Ashraf for a look.

"They mean to cheat you, or worse," he growled, obviously thirsty for blood. Ashraf gently but firmly planted a hand in the man's chest.

"It is important that my words reach the world's ears," Ashraf said to the men as a group. "We must use the Western media to spread the word of Islam."

The waiter seemed satisfied with that and stepped back. The others withdrew more reluctantly. Before there could be further argument, Ashraf smiled beneficently and closed the door.

He returned to his guests and sat down to resume their discussion.

"So this is a war against America the colonial power, not a war for Islam," the Egyptian translated.

Ashraf slapped his forehead, bridling at the implication that faith was not paramount in his actions. "I already told you, this *is* a Holy War. A Holy War against America and the repressive, corrupt and un-Islamist regimes supported by America. It's the same as the Holy War against the Russians in Chechnya, against the regime in Western China or against the Crusaders in the past. The jihad never stops. It will only end once there is a just and pure regime anywhere there is a Muslim, under the dictates of the Shariah for all to obey and give homage to Allah."

Ashraf had just repeated the exact wording of the videotaped speech he had made at the end of his indoctrination course—all but the final phrase, that is. He remembered those words well: "For this I give my life. Allahu Akhbar, Allah is great!"

"So how come you didn't blow yourself up in the toy store? Why were you walking around saying, 'Pharaoh is dead'?"

The foreigner looked at Ashraf even more intently than before. In fact, the man's hands were shaking. Ashraf struggled to recall where he'd seen this man but came up with nothing.

"My brother shouted the same thing when he helped kill Sadat."

"That I understand. Sadat was the ruler of Egypt, just as the Pharaohs were. But how is bombing a toy store like killing Pharaoh?"

"To a Muslim, 'Pharaonic' means anything pagan, heathen. Sadat was a heathen. New York City is a city of heathens."

"Why didn't you blow yourself up at the toy store? Weren't you sent as a suicide bomber?"

"The detonator was torn off of me by the force of the blast." Ashraf had said this so many times, to himself as well as to others, that he was beginning to believe it was true.

"Will you try it again?"

"Of course," Ashraf snapped without thinking. After a beat, though, the truth revealed itself to him. The truth at the heart of his journey from disciple at the feet of his father to this very moment, with these strangers in this room in the house of his mother. *I am prepared to kill. But I am no longer prepared to die—if I ever was.*

He saw the Westerner speaking in a rapid impassioned voice. When the translation came, Ashraf wasn't surprised by its confrontational tone.

"How can you equate the murder of women and children with heroic resistance? Whatever your cause, the moment you take an action that is evil, you are no better than your enemies."

"I could say the same to you. By your logic, we are all evil. But it is the Christian, capitalist, colonial oppressors who do the most damage in the world. We would have to bomb every Starbucks in America to even come close!"

How the man responded must have been vitriolic, for it went un-translated. The American woman tried to calm him down with little success. Then the Arab quickly rose to his feet and said, "Thank you for your time. We should be going."

"Yes, perhaps you should," Ashraf said, full of righteous anger now. He opened the door to encourage their exit. "I suspect your friend will distort my comments anyway. But your audience will still hear truth in them."

"I'm sorry, but we won't be sharing your extremist rhetoric with anyone," the older woman said on her way out.

"I knew it! You are not with the media. Leave my house at once!"

The Western man understood the fury in Ashraf's eyes, and clearly wanted to stay to vent his own. But the Egyptian bodily removed him.

As soon as they were out the door, Ashraf slammed it but didn't bolt it. His mother, after all, was still outside.

It was back in the kitchen, as he picked at what was left of his dinner, that the identity of the angry American finally came to him, in images as clear as the faces of those that delivered the news each night on TV. Ashraf had seen the man twice. First, as he entered the toy store, in business clothes rather than the sneakers, blue jeans, and ridiculous baseball cap that he wore now. And later, under the rubble, a desperate look on his face.

Like Ashraf, this man was a survivor of the blast at the toy store in New York. Only this man was the enemy.

Wiping his mouth on the back of his hand, Ashraf stood and walked quickly toward the door.

CHAPTER SEVEN

After leaving Ashraf Ismail's house, Miranda stole worried glances at Jake, who hadn't uttered a word since they'd left. He stared straight ahead while they moved toward Mike's parked car.

Isabelle spoke first. "Well," she said to Jake, "do you feel that you understand this better?"

Jake was silent for a moment, his mind racing. "I'm parched," he managed to say. "Can we, uh, get something to drink?"

"There's this little café here. It should be clean, since it caters to the few tourists that come to the neighborhood," Mike said. A frown creased his forehead. "But we are still only two blocks away from the El Biali house. I don't feel totally safe. What if he has second thoughts about your being journalists and comes after us?"

"Let's drink fast, then. I . . . really need a drink."

But Jake got up as soon as they sat down.

"I'll be back in a minute," he said, offering no explanation. The masquerade, the role-playing, was over.

"Jake! Where are you going?" Miranda asked, trying to hold his sleeve. She had to know.

He shook her off. "I'll be back in a minute."

"Jake, don't be crazy!"

In seconds, Jake was running at a full sprint in the direction of Ashraf Ismail's house. Passersby got out of the way so as not be knocked down by the tourist who must have lost something. An expensive camera, perhaps, or a credit card. At the corner of Ashraf's street, Jake slowed so as not to call further attention to himself. He spotted the house: a filthy hovel like the rest, only a broom leaned against the doorframe.

He tried the doorknob. Open.

Jake stepped inside. As he did, he saw Ashraf moving toward him from the kitchen, green eyes alive with dread. They faced each other in silence, rivers of anger, fear and hatred flowing freely between them.

At the café, Mike and Isabelle tried to stop Miranda from going after Jake.

"You know where he went, goddamnit," Miranda said, gray eyes blazing. Isabelle nodded and released Miranda's arm. She rose to accompany the American, and Mike looked dismayed.

"Aunt Isabelle! It's not our business what he does."

"I have a feeling something terrible is happening," Isabelle said. "We've got to stop it." With that, she followed Miranda out the door.

With a sick feeling in his gut, Mike threw some money on the table and left. Miranda was half-running already. They seemed to cover the two blocks in a heartbeat.

The door to the Ismail house was open. Sounds of struggle—men grunting, furniture breaking—were audible from the street.

"Oh, my God," Miranda moaned, and rushed inside. Mike followed, steeling himself for the worst kind of trouble.

Blood was flowing from a cut above his eye as Jake grappled with the man who had killed his family. He was in a state of urgent hyperconsciousness, like an animal fighting for its life. They'd been at each other's throats only a minute at most, but it felt like an eternity. As Jake threw wild looping punches, he glimpsed Miranda in his peripheral vision.

She seized his arm and pulled, tears in her eyes. "Jake, don't do this! Let's get out of here!"

He blinked at her, hardly aware of what she was saying.

Ashraf now had the opportunity he needed. He snatched up a ceramic urn and smashed it into Jake's forehead. The urn shattered in Ashraf's hand. Jake stumbled back, skull ringing.

With innate dignity, Isabelle stepped in to separate the two men. "Stop this madness! We will leave your house—"

Ashraf grabbed Isabelle and pressed the shard he was left with against her throat. Battered and bloody, wild-eyed, he looked like an escaped mental patient.

"Let her go," Miranda demanded, outraged.

Mike also drew closer, extending an empty hand in supplication. Frozen with dread. "Please. I beg you."

Shaking with laughter, and yet emitting what sounded like a sob at the same time, Ashraf only held Isabelle tighter.

Then, to everyone's horror, he swiftly and silently slid the sharp edge across her throat. Half the width of the shard disappeared inside Isabelle's flesh. Jake heard the hissing sound of air escaping through the incision.

"NOOOO!" Mike screamed, rushing Ashraf.

Without thinking, Jake squatted to pick up the hammer that he had seen earlier in the tool bag on the floor.

Having let Isabelle's body slump to the living room floor, Ashraf fended off Mike, the bloody shard turned like a knife. There was no question about it now: He was laughing and crying at the same time. Just as he had been that day in the toy store.

As Ashraf jabbed his weapon at Mike, Jake withdrew the hammer and lashed upward with it. The heavy tool hit Ashraf hard on the side of the head, but Jake didn't feel the impact he was expecting, of metal against skin-covered skull. He felt a sort of wet yielding instead.

Ashraf slumped to the floor with the hammer embedded in his skull, the handle facing downward, his right eye lifeless above the long white scar from the toy-store bombing. The claw end of the tool, far sharper than most, had drilled deeply into his brain.

Jake looked at the dead terrorist. Blood pooled blackly on the house's floor of packed dirt. It was over.

Isabelle lay lifeless on the floor. His face contorted in shock and pain, Mike slumped beside her and cradled her head. Gently, he closed her eyes.

Jake stared, Isabelle's last cry ringing in his ears. Trying to save him.

As if reading his mind, Miranda slipped a trembling arm around him and spoke softly. "It wasn't your fault, Jake."

Jake didn't respond, eyes glazed in shock. He looked again at Ashraf Ismail. A flash of the last happy moment with Stephanie and Claire flooded his mind. They were entering FAO Schwarz, past the man dressed as a toy soldier. Claire smiled, then Stephanie . . .

Movement in the street shook Jake from the reverie. The waiter and his friends were approaching the open doorway at a dead run. Jake sprang into action, rushing to slam the door and flip the bolt closed. Seconds later the door shook with thunderous pounding. The men outside were shouting in Arabic.

"We're dead," Mike whispered. He was on the verge of falling apart.

"Any ideas?" Jake asked Miranda, desperately trying to think of one himself. He was keenly conscious of his ability to react, to overcome pain. That surprised him.

"Maybe there's a back door," she said hopefully, and rushed to see.

Sirens could be heard outside, and the squealing of automotive brakes. Now Jake heard the decisive thuds of car doors urgently shut. One man shouted what sounded like an exhortation. Many more voices responded, at first soft and tentative, then progressively louder and finally defiant. The banging on the little house's door resumed.

Miranda returned from checking the rooms. "No other way out," she murmured. "The courtyard in back is walled in."

Jake saw that Mike had snapped out of it and was listening to the voices outside. "What's happening? What are they saying?"

"It's the police telling the mob outside to disperse. They're refusing." Mike's voice trembled with fear. His stare ricocheted between the front door and his dead aunt.

To Jake, it seemed as if the police had blocked the entrance but were now being pushed against the house by the surging crowd. The muffled sounds and almost rhythmic thumping against the door and walls increased in volume and frequency, a tornado against the pathetic shack. It was hopeless. But then, as suddenly as it had started, the banging on the door stopped. Jake wondered if the police had succeeded in interposing themselves between the house and the attackers. The yelling continued.

"What're they saying?" Miranda asked Mike. She might be eternally undaunted in civilized life, but here her voice betrayed a tremor of fear.

Mike had no time to answer. The flimsy door flew open with a crash, the jamb splintered to pieces.

Someone stumbled into the living room brandishing a gun and shouting in Arabic. The dark short man with the brown jacket. Jake jumped at him, grasping awkwardly both the man's hand and his gun. He knew it was a mistake as soon as he did it; he heard a loud blast and saw flame burst from the handgun's muzzle. Miranda screamed.

Jake felt the heat from the shot but no sting. The bullet had missed him by a hair.

He held the man close while pushing his arm away. Now Jake felt a dizzying pain as his opponent smashed his forehead against his chin. Despite being smaller and weaker than Jake, the man was fighting mightily. Jake was at a loss as to what to do next—he was keeping the weapon pointed away but wasn't sure how long he could keep it up, how many more head-butts he could withstand. The man was shouting in Arabic, his spit and garlicky breath making Jake heave with nausea.

Mike yelled, "Let him go!"

Jake wouldn't. To do so, he knew, was certain death. Now he heard shots outside. At first just a few. More shouting.

"Let him go!" Mike yelled again. Miranda had picked up a chair, and he was holding her back.

Jake was suddenly blinded with pain. His opponent had kicked him in the groin.

Mike grabbed Jake from behind and pulled him to the ground. The man with the brown jacket turned to Jake, pointed the gun at him, said something in Arabic and, to Jake's dazed relief, spun around and surged away, shouting short commands. Jake heard more shots, many more. The pop-pop of automatic weapons. A full-scale shootout was in progress in the street. Mike was on him, holding him down, saying something he couldn't hear over the deafening fusillade.

Then, abruptly, the shooting stopped. Jake heard footsteps running away. He pushed Mike aside and ran out to the street.

Several men were lying on the ground. Jake counted five writhing and moaning in pain. Two others lay quiet and motionless, apparently dead. One of them, a hole where his nose should have been, wore the brown jacket—Jake's assailant. Jake walked toward him and looked down, relieved to see another enemy dead. Mike silently joined him and walked back inside.

Jake followed a short while later. "What were you doing?" he asked Mike, who was holding his aunt, tears running down his face. "This man almost killed me."

"Not really," Mike said, looking up. "He was the head of the police team that just saved our lives."

As if in answer, several men in plain-clothes but with smoking machine guns came back around the corner. They had evidently driven off the last of the mob.

The men, with a few harsh commands, directed them at gunpoint into the back of a police van. The door slammed shut, plunging them into darkness.

Abdel Aziz Rifaat put down the phone and gazed mournfully at the lights of Beirut. He had just learned that Ashraf Ismail, brother of his beloved Hamza El Biali, had been murdered by a Westerner. The suspect was being held in a Cairo jail.

A dark fury twisted Rifaat's guts that was stronger than his grief. He was not so much fond of Ashraf, who had undoubtedly been a disappointment, as he was humiliated that he'd broken his vow to keep Hamza's brother safe. He'd let his best friend down. And for that shame the Westerner would pay dearly.

Rifaat beckoned Khalil, the chief of his bodyguards, onto the terrace.

"We will need air transport to Cairo. At once."

Khalil nodded wordlessly and vanished inside. Rifaat picked up the phone again.

"Use your contact in the Cairo police," he told the man who'd shared the grim news. "This man will be released into our custody. It can look like an escape."

Jake sat at an interrogation table mottled with stains he'd rather not identify. Two Egyptian detectives stared at him from across the table. One, a small toad-like man, was seated and chain-smoked his hand-rolled cigarettes. The other was younger, lean and energetic. He leaned casually against the wall. Watching Jake intently.

"Why did you kill Ashraf Ismail?" he asked.

Jake groaned inwardly. Back to the simplest of questions. They'd been through all of this before; a dozen times, it seemed. The men spoke good enough English to understand him. There was another reason they were going over everything ad nauseam.

"Self-defense," Jake reiterated. "He'd just murdered Isabelle Said and was coming after us."

The young detective suddenly threw himself at Jake, glaring eye to eye. "We know you went there to kill him! Now tell us why."

Jake hadn't given them the incriminating truth about Ashraf's hand in the deaths of his family. It was clear there was no use cooperating with them further.

"Where's the American ambassador I asked you to call? Where's my lawyer?" he asked, keeping his cool. "If you've done anything to Miranda, you'll pay."

The cop spat on the floor in disgust, wheeling away. The other man shook his head, stubbing out a cigarette.

"Before your lawyer arrives, we'll have the truth. One way or another. Perhaps we've been too nice with you, Mr. Burke. We lost two good men at that house. We want to know why."

The door opened and an aide stuck his head into the room. He said something to the two cops, and what appeared to be a brief argument followed. The tall detective stormed out.

"Come with me," the other man said, giving Jake a hooded stare that Jake could only call menacing.

As he was roughly escorted out, he felt an icy tickle of mortal fear on his spine for the first time. But he was more afraid of what they might be doing to Miranda than he was for himself. He cursed himself for putting her in jeopardy as they loaded him into the back of the van.

This trip was longer, and Jake knew they were covering miles rather than blocks. When the van finally stopped and its doors opened, Jake saw what looked to be a private airfield in the desert. Then he recognized a carbon-copy of his own private jet. The G550 had a fully fueled range of almost seven thousand nautical miles—it could take them halfway around the world nonstop. They stood five yards from the plane's ladder. The policeman who'd opened the doors of the van used his gun to wave Jake up the steps and into the plane.

Once inside, he tried to get his bearings. The plane had the same surround-sound systems as his own aircraft, the same satellite phones. He even recognized the DirectTV feed on which he used to watch four news channels simultaneously. The rest, though, was radically different: the wood was inlaid with depictions of belly dancers; two small and very sensual Picasso paintings adorned the walls; the seat buckles were made of gold; and the seats themselves were upholstered in what appeared to be authentic tiger skin. Surreal.

As he made his way down the aisle, he came upon a seat with someone in it—Miranda. Dirty, unkempt, but alive and whole. She leapt up in relief and embraced him.

"Jake Burke, back in action!" she laughed, delighted.

"Thank God you're all right," he said, suddenly emotional.

"By the end of it they were afraid of me, not the other way around." Typical Miranda bravado. But Jake could see the echoes of strain shadowed beneath her eyes. He was certain her experience hadn't been any more pleasant than his.

Things only became more bizarre when a beautiful stewardess offered them expensive champagne. Jake sipped the drink without tasting it, wondering what could possibly happen next.

A cultured man about Jake's age sat down across from them. He had smooth well-cared-for skin and an expensive white suit. Belying the relaxed appearance were his steely eyes.

"Hello, Mr. Burke. Ms. Connelly. I am Jibril Malouf."

Though the man's English was accented but clear, it took an instant for Jake to process the name. When he did, a flood of relief told him how raw his nerves had been worn.

"Suter's friend," he murmured to Miranda. She relaxed visibly.

"Yes. And a good friend to have, as you've just discovered. You will be sent home. I would count yourselves very lucky."

Jake nodded. "What about Mike?"

"Your Egyptian friend was released. I have protected his identity, and yours, within the Cairo police department. Some very dangerous men were inquiring."

"Do you know who?"

"All I know, and all you need know, is that they are linked to international terrorist organizations."

As Jake considered this, Malouf rose from his seat. "I wish that you had sought my help upon your arrival. Things may have gone more smoothly. Have a good flight, Mr. Burke."

Jake shook his hand. "I don't know how to thank you."

"Thank Ted Suter when you return. And remember this experience. Luck, particularly the good variety, has a tendency to run out."

Rifaat sat patiently waiting in a rented car outside the police station. He was looking forward to spending some time with the Westerner. Quite a bit of time, in fact.

The sight of his agents returning alone nonplussed him. Rolling down his window, he scowled at the Cairo contact's glum expression.

"Your man has powerful friends," Rifaat's associate said. "Both he and his woman were given safe passage from the country two hours ago."

Rifaat glared into his driver's headrest. Thinking things through.

"I want a name."

"Sir?"

"His name! I want his fucking name! Can you do that?"

The man nodded quickly, made anxious by the flare of temper. Rifaat ordered the driver to leave. His trip had been wasted. Ashraf Ismail's killer had escaped Allah's justice. But Rifaat wasn't a man who was easily deterred. He began thinking of additional sufferings for the Westerner, and even found a smile. He would make that man wish he'd died today.

BOOK II

CHAPTER EIGHT

Jake was back in New York the following day, unable to rest, devastated at having caused Isabelle's death. His whole body hurt, and his arms and legs were made of lead. Crushing muscle pain and weakness—an adrenaline overdose like his last hours in Cairo would do that, he remembered reading somewhere.

Looking into his bathroom mirror, he saw a wretchedly tired man. Pale skin, eyes swollen and lips seared—a faded image of his old self—determinedly pulling sagging facial skin sideways, trying clumsily to shave.

For the first morning hours, he was in a sort of fever, unable to think and profoundly disoriented. On the one hand, he felt a sense of closure. In the matter of Stephanie and Claire's deaths things had finally been put right. It felt unsubstantial and illusory, though. Revenge was nothing more than a concept now, swallowed by the maelstrom of guilt and remorse at Isabelle's death.

Though it was Sunday, he drove downtown to the office. He needed to focus on something—anything. He found Miranda there, catching up on her own work.

"Why am I not surprised," Jake said dryly. "But you should be home recuperating from that disaster."

"No rest for the wicked," Miranda replied lightly, and he could tell she was trying to show him that she was fine.

"You're not wicked, far from it," he said, feeling new affection for her. She'd proven to be as resilient as he'd always suspected she was.

Jake spent the afternoon trying to re-establish some sense of normalcy but found himself unable to concentrate on anything beside his own emotions.

At four, Miranda walked in on him to find his head bowed over his desk, staring blankly into the tabletop. He glanced up, blinking with damp eyes, and forced a smile.

Before he could even muster some weak denial, she had hugged him. It felt all the more awkward in the office where they'd spent so many professional hours, but Jake took instant comfort in the human contact.

"It's okay to hurt," Miranda said softly. "Life isn't going to be the same. No use pretending it is."

Jake nodded, fighting the urge to shed tears he'd bottled since first hearing from the doctors that his wife and daughter were gone forever.

Instead, he said, "I'm sorry I got you into this."

She mock-slugged him. "Are you kidding? I practically put a gun to your head. Don't blame yourself for a second. Now, please. Go home. Get some rest."

"You go ahead. I've got too much to get done," he said, but it was a half-hearted protest. He'd been next to useless all day.

"Bullshit, Jake. There's nothing that can't wait until Monday morning. Let's get a drink. We could both use one." She bundled him out the door without further argument. They rode the elevator downstairs to the parking garage, discussing the best watering holes in the neighborhood.

Out of nowhere, a heavyset man approached them, weapon drawn. With him was a tanned clean-shaven man dressed elegantly in grey slacks and a blue blazer. This man's deeply wrinkled face contrasted sharply with his youthful gait and full head of salt-and-pepper hair.

"Mr. Burke?" said the man with the gun. Jake recognized a slight Hispanic accent. "I'm Agent Delgado of the Central Intelligence Agency. I want to talk to you about Ashraf El Biali."

"Sorry?" He tried not to betray any emotion. Miranda was silent, keeping an eye on the gun pointed at them.

"You know, our most promising lead into the higher echelons of Popular Islamic Jihad and the remnants of Al Qaeda?"

"What are you talking about?"

"Save it, Mr. Burke. Why do you think we let Ashraf Ismail leave the country after the bombing at FAO Schwarz?"

"What's that?" Now Jake wasn't acting. Had the Feds really *allowed* Ashraf to escape?

"*You. Arrogant. Bastard.*" Delgado shook with anger. "You actually believed that you and *only* you figured out the identity of the would-be bomber at the toy store that day? You thought he slipped through the NYPD's grasp, and the FBI's and the CIA's—and only you, Jake Burke and his intrepid assistant Miranda, could hunt him down and kill him?" Delgado laughed grimly. "Sure. We found a lunatic Arab repeating '*Allah is great*' in the rubble of a suicide bombing, and it never occurred to us he might be involved."

"Well . . ."

"Okay, now you shut up and listen," he said firmly. "I'll lay this out for you. We had Ashraf under surveillance from the time he left the U.S. all through his time back in Cairo. He was obviously a pawn in a bigger game. So, together with the Egyptian security services, we waited for a key figure in his organization to reveal himself. Then you came along and killed Ashraf. Just like that. Mr. Burke, you caused irreparable damage to the national security of the United States." Delgado seemed to look over Jake's shoulder for an instant. Then his eyes met Jake's again. "Now you're coming with me."

It was then that the second man, who had slid silently behind Jake, stabbed him with what felt like a very long needle. The last thing he heard was Miranda's scream before it was stifled.

When Jake came to, he was lying on a couch in what appeared to be the living room of an ordinary house. His hands and feet were tied. The shades were pulled. Across the room, a television with the sound muted was tuned to CNN.

Miranda was still out, slumped in an easy-chair. She too was bound. Though groggy from the drug that had knocked him unconscious, Jake tried to sort out what was happening.

He had been kidnapped. By two men. The thickset man—Delgado— had said he was part of some official agency. The CIA. But that made no sense.

Jake's mind was clearing fast. These people couldn't be CIA. The CIA would never do this and expose itself to the inevitable scandal and lawsuit. Not if Jake were going to be allowed to live.

His mind moved on to Ashraf and the bigger fish his kidnappers had mentioned. Even drugged, he knew he'd screwed up.

As his vision came into focus, he realized that there was something different about the look of the TV screen: A larger than usual ticker was running beneath the newscaster's talking head. It read: TERROR ALERT: HIGHEST. The Department of Homeland Security had dropped the color-coded alerts, just to replace it with this new, and still ineffective, system. It was essentially the same, and it still warned the public about any unspecified threats that arose.

"Our man's awake," he heard someone say.

It was Sam Stone, the CIA agent who had visited him originally. Stone untied Jake and led him to another room, where another man sat at a dining room table. The blinds had been drawn in this room too. Jake recognized the second man as the blond guy from the garage. He still wore a day's worth of stubble.

Jake felt too weak to get angry. Stone offered him a chair across from the blond man. Jake tried to sit straight, but he was sore all over from being tied up.

A moment later Miranda was led in, looking frightened and disoriented. Stone gently showed her to a chair.

"You owe me," Jake said to the man from the garage. "You wrecked my car."

"I'm sorry about that." Same clear voice from the blond guy. "I had to do it. Don't worry, I'll make it up to you. For now I need to ask a favor from you."

"What's that?"

"Suspend your anger for a moment and accept that we're on your side. You'll be convinced of that soon." Jake tried to place the faint accent in the man's speech. "Can you do that?"

What choice did he have? Jake looked around him, at the all-American interior of this small house. It looked like something straight out of the '50s, a little like the set of Neil Simon's *Brighton Beach Memoirs*, which Jake had seen with Stephanie some years before.

"Mr. Burke? Ms. Connelly?" Stone said, motioning to the blond man. "Allow me to introduce Danny Barzilai. Danny is with the Mossad—or was. They're the Israeli CIA."

Barzilai had to be in his early fifties; tall and athletic, he wore jeans and a faded black polo shirt. "Nice to meet you both."

"Israeli?" Jake asked.

"Danny was an important player," Stone said. "Pretty high up in the Mossad structure. He's done a lot. Ever hear of the raid on Entebbe?"

"You were at Entebbe?" The main thing Jake remembered about the event was that it involved a daring commando assault on some hostage-takers in . . . was it Uganda?

Barzilai nodded. "No big deal." He seemed to mean it.

"You'll have to tell me about it some time," Jake said, the words sounding absurd as he uttered them.

"Sure." Barzilai's upbeat tone sounded equally surreal. "My mother lived not ten blocks from here. I talked to her via long-distance before we took off."

"Anyway," Stone continued, "Danny's been retired for a while. The Mossad let him go after he did a few things outside the limits of his authority."

"I see."

"This isn't dinner at the club," Miranda burst out, lucid and angry. "Let's dispense with the chitchat and start talking about just who the hell you people think you are!"

The tense moment was interrupted when the front door opened and two more men entered.

"Ah," said Stone. "Gerard Duvivier and Ramon Delgado. To answer your question, Ms. Connelly, Gerard is with the DGSE—*Direction*

Générale de la Sécurité Extérieure. The French CIA, basically. Ramon Delgado is a colleague of mine in the Agency, a little higher up."

These were the two men who had abducted them. Both had dark complexions, one with Latino looks, the other of apparent Mediterranean descent. It all made sense now. The warnings and finally the kidnapping had a single source: this group. No, wait. The FBI agent was missing, the one who'd shown up in the lobby of Jake's building and told him that they needed no more help.

"No one from the FBI?" he probed.

Delgado smiled. "This doesn't concern them. Their only involvement was when we arranged for them to talk to you. To see if they could make you stop. Too bad it didn't work."

Miranda was far from placated. "Well, now we know who everybody is, but are you out of your minds? Have any of you ever heard of individual rights in this country?"

"Come now, you're unhurt, perhaps you can understand these are extraordinary circumstances," Barzilai said carefully.

Sam Stone interrupted. "None of us have the time for apologies. We've got business to discuss. Ramon?"

Delgado began what soon felt like an interrogation. "What do you know about Iran?"

Miranda shrugged, and Jake answered for both of them. "No more than most people. Why?"

"Because Iran is a good example of why we've brought you here today. Let me tell you a few things about it. First of all, orders of magnitude. Iran is a big country, five times the size of unified Germany in area. Actually, its population is almost as large as Germany's. You remember when they took the hostages in '79, don't you?"

"Who doesn't?" Jake wasn't sure he appreciated Delgado's didactic tone.

"Do you know why those hostages were released?"

"The way I remember it, they wanted to humiliate us. They especially wanted to humiliate Jimmy Carter, after he tried that rescue mission when the helicopters crashed in the desert."

"Well, the conditions that Iran presented to the U.S. were the following: the release of eight billion dollars in frozen Iranian assets, the return of assets held by the Shah's family, cancellation of our damage claims against them, an apology, and a guarantee by the U.S. not to interfere in Iran's affairs. Guess how many of these were met."

Miranda looked exasperated, and Jake was starting to feel the same way. "I have no idea."

"Pretty much all of them. Now this may not look so terrible, but it was the beginning of all the problems we're facing today."

This sounded to Jake like an overstatement. "What makes you say that?"

"The Islamic revolution in Iran was two things. It was the first time we were humiliated in the Middle East and didn't respond. It was also the beginning of an Islamic theocracy in Iran—and the birthplace, as such, of contemporary Islamic fundamentalism. It spread from there to the rest of the Muslim world, with no little help from Saudi petrodollars exporting Wahhabism, their own brand of strict Islam. And we didn't do anything to fight it."

"We thought it would soften with time," Stone interjected, as he stood, stretched, and walked to the kitchen.

Delgado resumed command of the discussion. "It didn't. We regained fifty-three hostages in 1980, and less than thirty years later we are paying for it with almost six thousand American lives, not including the World Trade Center. One hundred to one. How's that for a shitty ratio? And it's only the beginning."

Six thousand Stephanies and Claires. Jake could hardly listen to Delgado's speech.

"Jake? May I call you Jake? How about I throw some facts at you."

The phony-bonhomie routine, Jake thought with distaste. "No. Don't throw facts at me. I'll tell you when I'm ready for that," he said, his mind now totally clear, the lingering effect of the drug finally gone. "Right now I want you to explain yourself. Who authorized you to do what you did? You *kidnapped* us, for God's sake."

"They must've known it was the only way to make us sit through their little history lesson," Miranda added, with biting sarcasm.

"Is kidnapping any worse than killing a foreign national in his own country? Removing an intelligence target that could've provided invaluable leads? Our only mistake was not abducting you sooner."

Jake wasn't satisfied. "Why couldn't you just talk to me? Tell me what was going on and ask for my cooperation, the way you are now?"

Delgado shook his head. "The game has changed entirely, for a number of reasons. We all agree now that events have presented an opportunity—"

"If you already knew about Ashraf El Biali," Jake interrupted, looking to Sam Stone, "and you didn't want me involved, why did you come to me in the first place, asking me questions, telling me that the bombing was 'special' or whatever?"

Stone waved off Delgado before he could cut in. "We were looking for a potential third participant. If there was a second bomber, why not a third? It turned out to be a false lead. It was just El Biali and the dead bomber. We're—"

"Everything will become clear if you let me continue," Delgado said. "There's a lot you need to know."

Jake crossed his arms over his chest, looked at Miranda. She nodded, though she was staring at Delgado with overt skepticism. "Okay, go ahead."

"All right, here are some more facts. Number one . . ." Delgado touched his right index finger with the left one, "in the State Department's most recent report on 'Patterns of Global Terrorism,' Iran was called 'the most active state sponsor of terrorism.' They spend approximately seventy-five million bucks annually for terrorist-related activities. It's in their national budget."

"Really?"

"Really. Hezbollah is a major recipient." Delgado went on. "Number two, and this is one we're reading a lot about in the papers these days, even being knee-deep in oil Iran is engaged in a major nuclear effort. Despite concerted worldwide pressure, they're on the brink of realizing the dream of the Fundamentalist Islamic bomb."

Jake nodded. The press was having a field day with that one.

"Three: Iran already has the capability of reaching Turkey and Israel with its missiles. We—the CIA—have been able to confirm reports that Iran could launch a ballistic missile capable of reaching the U.S. very soon."

Stone interrupted. "And they might not even need these missiles. By paying a few thousand dollars, people are smuggled daily through Mexico into the U.S. For a country with national budget line-items for the support of terrorist activities, how hard do you think it'd be for Iran to get nuclear explosives smuggled into our territory?"

Delgado looked irritably at Stone. "Will you let me finish?" He turned to Jake. "Finally, number four: All attempts at constructive engagement have failed. The Europeans tried it and what they got, which ain't bad, is some lucrative oil and industrial turnkey contracts. In the meantime, the Iranian mullahs have shut down more than fifty newspapers, confiscated satellite dishes, prohibited public demonstrations, imprisoned and killed dissidents, intellectuals and students. And all of this, mind you, happened mostly during the two terms of their supposedly reformist president. And now with this hard-line president . . ."

Jake nodded again, impatient for Delgado to get to the point.

"And now I ask you this: If you saw what I just described—a theocratic totalitarian country that still calls us the Great Satan, that supports fundamental Islamic terrorism worldwide, that has struck against America several times, that's building a nuclear bomb and will have the capability to hit us; if you saw this, and you saw an American policy that clearly isn't working, would you do something about it?"

The room fell silent, all eyes on Jake and Miranda. Most of the hostility had drained from Miranda's body language.

"I'm beginning to get the picture. You're not officially CIA here, are you?" Jake was actually starting to like these people.

"Not today."

Jake nodded. "It explains why we're talking to two Americans, an Israeli, and a Frenchman. I think I understand the two Americans and the Israeli being here," he said. "But why a Frenchman?"

"Let me add to your understanding of why *I* am here," the Israeli offered. "The Mossad used to be an efficient, effective organization. We weren't always kosher," he smiled, "in our methods of action, but we got things done. We live in a tough neighborhood. When you live in a tough neighborhood, you don't apologize when you're pushed—you push back twice as hard, and you show the other guy that you'll hurt him badly if he messes with you. But due to outside pressure, and also its desperate need for peace, Israel has forgotten the lesson it learned over the past half-century: that outreach, negotiation and compromise, which civilized people see as the only ways to resolve conflicts, are seen by Arab leaders as lack of resolve. Weakness that can and should be exploited."

"Come on, Danny. Israel's been hitting back very hard," said Gerard Duvivier.

The Israeli sipped from the glass of water that Stone had placed before him. "Not even close to what it takes. This government is trying once more to revive a peace process from a position of weakness. It won't work. Power gets respect in the Middle East, nothing else. Do you remember the suicide bomber who blew himself up at that discotheque, killing all those teenagers? The only daughter of my best friend was there. She lost both her arms. One right under the elbow, and the other was blown out at the shoulder. She's blind in one eye and her face isn't a face anymore. She's sixteen. Can you imagine that?"

Jake shook his head but at the same time thought, does this guy know about *my* family?

"She's happy to be alive, or should be," Barzilai continued, looking even more serious than before. In fact, he looked stricken, bereft. "Her boyfriend was killed."

Jake saw the other men around the table looking down and away. "Sorry to hear that," he said.

"The police found out that the bomber had prayed in a nearby mosque just prior to the attack. This information was leaked by someone in the department who's not, shall we say, sentimental about the so-called Peace Process." He snorted. "An angry crowd of Israelis surrounded the mosque and started throwing bricks and rocks. The men inside shouted slogans and threw stones back.

"When I arrived on the scene, the Israeli Police had surrounded the building in order to protect those inside. I speak Arabic, and I heard one of the men talking while he was escorted to safety. He was boasting to another one next to him, saying, 'Didn't I tell you there was no danger? Youssouf is in Heaven with his virgins, we have done Allah's will by helping him, and these pathetic dogs can't hurt us.'

"That man was shot the following day. His killer was unknown, and a note was left on him saying . . ." The Israeli's blue eyes looked upward, toward the ceiling, as he strained to get the words exactly right. "We will hurt those who hurt us. We will kill those who kill us.'" He looked again at Jake. "There was no proof of my involvement in the killing. The Mossad sacked me anyway."

The room fell silent. Again, all eyes were on the outsiders.

"Are you aware that I also lost my daughter?"

"That's why I thought you should hear the story of my . . . friend's daughter. Because it's so similar."

Jake understood that he wasn't expected to answer. He breathed deeply. "And you think dealing with Iran's the solution to everything?"

"It's the key to keeping the U.S. and Israel safe, for sure. America's the Great Satan, but we in Israel are Little Satan. I'm not kidding, that's what they call us: Satan Junior! It's actually sort of humorous, don't you think?" He smiled, then sobered again. "Seriously, Iran will have nuclear warheads that can reach us in a matter of months. Nukes to sneak into the U.S., too. Isn't that something to worry about? Never mind that Iran's been sponsoring 'ordinary' terrorism against Israel for decades. Make no mistake, Mr. Burke. These guys are our mortal enemies." Barzilai paused.

After a moment, he looked pointedly at Jake and added with what seemed to carry special significance, "They're yours, too."

CHAPTER NINE

Jake was about to respond when Delgado stood up from the table with a yawn that was so wide and resonant, it seemed staged.

"I need to stretch my legs," he said. "Gerard, why don't you tell our guests a little bit about yourself and your reason for being here?"

"But of course."

Delgado opened the door and stepped outside. Though Jake couldn't see out the door from where he sat, he heard children playing. Delgado closed the door behind him.

"I'm a little less emotional about this than Danny," Gerard began, "for obvious reasons. France isn't suffering the same level of violence on a day-to-day basis as the Israelis. Not yet, at least."

"Not yet?"

"France is dealing with a population that is almost ten percent Muslim, mostly Arabs, most living in ghettoes, with values that are not Western values. Worse, if you look at our poor and our criminals, it's not proportionate—much more than ten percent are Arabs or their descendants. It's a demographic timebomb that's ready to explode. If you add fundamentalism and terrorism to that . . ." Gerard gave a Gallic shrug. "And what are our security agencies doing to fight terrorism? Very little, I'm afraid. The government of my country is pursuing a strategy of 'constructive engagement'—meaning let's do business with the Muslim countries, let's . . . lick their asses, if the lady will forgive my putting it that way, and everything will be all right. They are beholden to the Muslim vote and France's commercial interests in the Arab world. All told, it's the closest a nation can get to sticking its collective head in the sand. And this, after we've had our own little taste of big-time terrorism."

Jake motioned that he didn't know what Gerard referred to.

"It was when the GIA, the Algerian fundamentalist terrorist organization, hijacked an Air France jet with the objective of blowing it up over Paris."

"Really?" This was news to Jake. He liked Gerard's manner, as well. The man was packing as much information into his carefully crafted sentences as Delgado had thrown at them earlier, but it didn't feel like a lecture.

"As you can see, the attack on your World Trade Center was not a new idea. In our case, disaster was averted because French counter-terrorist forces stormed the plane on the tarmac in Marseille. The terrorists had already killed three passengers. A few months later they beheaded four Catholic priests to avenge the four terrorists killed in Marseille."

Jake shook his head. Something else he didn't know.

"Luckily for us we were able to stop the attack. And it wasn't pure luck because we work closely with the Algerian authorities that are fighting these fundamentalists. It is one of the cruelest civil conflicts the region has ever seen. The terrorists have killed tens of thousands of civilians. It's been relatively quiet in the last few years due to the fact that the Algerian government is no pussycat, either. Because of that, we French are enjoying a respite from terrorism right now. They're too busy fighting for survival at home."

Jake nodded.

Gerard acknowledged the nod and continued. "I find that the issue of terrorism can only be controlled by facing up to it early on and opposing it by force. *Killing it at its source, while it's still weak.*" Gerard shook his head. "This is the war the West is facing. I'm sure you know that the rule of law, the standards of civilization as we know it, do not apply everywhere in the Middle East. Hundreds of thousands of people have disappeared over the past decades in the Middle East and North Africa. We're not talking about one or two kidnapped people, the type of news that makes headlines in our countries. It's *hundreds* of *thousands*. The rules are different in many Arab countries—and we're dealing with the most extreme elements inside these countries."

The door opened. Delgado re-entered the room, his clothes smelling of cigarette smoke. He resumed his seat.

"Okay," said Miranda, who had been quiet for some time. "I get why you're involved. Now what do you want from us?"

Gerard looked at Delgado.

"What we're all trying to say," Gerard told them, "is that civilized methods of combating these people do not work. Our governments operate under constraints that prevent us from fighting this war effectively."

"So?"

"*We* will do it. We can operate outside Congressional guidelines, outside limitations imposed by the Israeli or French legal systems, and we can win this war. It cannot be done any other way."

As if having rehearsed, the four men leaned back in their chairs at the same time and waited for a reaction.

Jake took a deep breath, released it. Nodded. "I get your point. I agree with it. And I can give you another reason why this war can't be won the way the U.S. is currently fighting it." He'd been thinking about this since 9/11.

"Yes?" Gerard said hesitantly.

"One aspect of the liberty that Americans hold so dear is economic— free enterprise."

"Of course," Gerard said. Stone nodded. The other two men listened carefully.

"We believe in free enterprise because it's a basic right. But also because it's the best way to achieve excellence. It rewards initiative and creativity. It rewards *drive*. In the war against terror, though, the U.S. is like a country with a centralized economy—our military initiatives require wide consensus and must run a gauntlet of checks and balances. A terrorist network, on the other hand, operates loosely, with nothing exactly resembling a chain of command. Just look at the structure of Al Qaeda—we could call them *terrorism entrepreneurs.*"

Sam Stone chuckled. Miranda jumped back into the conversation. "He's right. They've got a low overhead, and only minimal training necessary for many separate operations to be effective."

"Now *you* guys," Jake continued, "are like a start-up operating out of someone's garage. I like that. In fact, I'm convinced it's the only way to go about it."

Stone was looking at Delgado. Jake saw an I-told-you-so glint in Stone's smile. For his part, Delgado maintained a poker face.

"So you've been thinking about this too," Barzilai said. "That's good."

"It's all I've been thinking about," Jake replied, as if that wasn't obvious. "So how, exactly, do you propose to win this war?"

Stone responded. "Jake, I'm sorry to have to put it like this to you, but I'm sure you'll understand. If we answer that question, we're taking a big risk, and so are you. I would need to reveal to you elements of our plans, and you can see how risky that would be for us. The risk for you, of course, is this: If you decided *not* to participate, and we had the slightest reason to suspect that you weren't keeping our little secret, we'd have no choice but to . . . silence you. Is that clear?"

Jake had heard the threat loud and clear but was undeterred. How could he express the exhilaration he was feeling, or the euphoria of having found these men? Or of regaining the hope to strike back after the disaster that was Ashraf Ismail's death—and Isabelle's? Of course he was in, as committed as he would ever be.

"Clear enough for me. But my question can wait a little longer." He turned to look at Miranda, who was deep in thought. All eyes fell on Jake's lieutenant. Though unspoken, the offer was on the table for her to leave.

"I'm with Jake to the end," she said decisively. "Anything you tell him, I want to hear. This is his war, and I'll follow his lead, but don't even think about shutting me out."

"Are you absolutely sure, Miranda?" Jake frowned.

The answer was plain in those gunmetal eyes, but she replied anyway. "I'm sure."

Jake was honestly surprised. He wondered, without a trace of ego, if she might be in love with him. The thought unsettled him in ways he preferred not to dissect. His wife had been laid to rest just weeks ago; how could he possibly feel attracted to someone else? But in that moment he couldn't deny that his affection for Miranda was strong. Casting the troubling inner conflict aside, he looked around the room. "Okay, then. So? What's the next step?"

Gerard spoke as diplomatically as before. "Jake, the four of us need to speak in private briefly. May I ask you to give us some time? Would you mind coming back here in half an hour?"

"Not at all. One thing, though. Where are we?"

The men laughed, all except Delgado. Standing, Danny Barzilai stepped to the door and opened it wide. "Welcome to Brooklyn," he said.

Jake and Miranda sat down at a kosher pizzeria on Kings Highway. He ordered a slice of margherita and a cup of coffee. Miranda chose a calzone and Diet Coke.

"Well," he said, once they'd settled in, "what do you think?"

"They're brave men," Miranda said. "Takes a lot of guts to do what they're doing. And with those resumes, I think they've got the stuff to pull it off."

"Why are you doing this, Miranda? Honestly."

She looked surprised at the boldness of his question, but must've seen that he had to know because she answered without hesitation. "I told you before that I'm fully aware of the . . . *gravity* of the problems our world's facing. The chance to do something about that . . . is very compelling. But . . ."

Here it comes. Jake prepared for a difficult moment as Miranda wrestled with something big.

"I do care about you. I see a man about to embark on something way out of his depth with more courage than smarts, maybe."

Jake chuckled. Miranda could always be counted on to be blunt.

"But I'm inspired by that," she went on. "I really am. And I don't want you to do it alone. You're already . . . so alone."

Jake nodded. This wasn't easy for either of them, so he breathed a sigh of relief when the server, a young Latino, appeared with their food.

On the street, mothers with long dresses moved hastily past the restaurant window. So did dozens of children and men with skullcaps, white shirts and black suits. There was an air of expectant urgency all around. Jake asked the kid what was going on.

"They have some kind of holy day starting this evening. My boss told me what it was? But like, I forgot, man." He laughed. "They have to prepare everything so that by dark dinner is ready, the house is clean, and the children are showered and dressed in their best clothes to begin the day. You know their day starts at nightfall, right?"

Jake looked at the young mothers and their children. He saw grace, harmony even, in their hectic pace. He felt sure that the result of the little caucus would be an invitation to join. He knew, too, that he would accept it. What they wanted him for was less clear, though he suspected it had to do with both his near-fanatical motivation and his financial resources—a rare combination. Jake slid down in the chair and crossed his feet. He inhaled deeply, stretched his arms, and surveyed his surroundings in a leisurely fashion. In this anonymous little pizza joint just north of Coney Island, he saw beauty all around him. He felt at peace.

They returned to the house after exactly thirty minutes. The door was open as before. The men were still as they were, as if they'd never moved. As Jake sat down, he tried in vain to read their expressions.

Finally, Gerard spoke. "There were two reasons why I asked for time to discuss this privately. The first is that we wanted to give your friend a chance to reconsider." He met Miranda's level stare and smiled ruefully. "We might've known that was unnecessary. But the other reason is that this is the first time we are bringing laypeople like you into our organization. You are not part of the intelligence community, and we've never had any contact with you before. Frankly, we're worried, as I'm sure you can understand. Worried that you will make a mistake. And one can make a mistake in so many ways—by being overly cautious, by being reckless, by cracking under pressure. Or simply by being stupid. There are literally thousands of ways in which you can cause damage. Does this make sense to you?"

"Sure."

"So I proposed to my colleagues, and they were kind enough to agree, that I take you two with me on our first field operation. I will have the ability to observe you in action and report to the rest. We'll decide on the next steps afterward. Does this also sound reasonable to you?"

"It does." *Hell, yes.*

"By the way, in case you're wondering how we decide things here, it's pretty simple. This is as close a family as you'll ever see. In the past, we have gone through some very difficult times together, and there's no better glue than that. You're now being promoted from strangers to distant cousins. Go to hell and back with us a few times, and you'll be part of the family as well."

Jake nodded. "You still haven't told us *how* you do what you do."

Sam Stone spoke up. "Mind if I take it from here, Gerard?"

Gerard tipped his head.

Stone breathed in deeply, exhaled. "It's impossible for the West to fight Islamic terrorism effectively. It'll never be the Marines who pluck a terrorist from whatever supportive local environment he's taking shelter in. The only ones who can effectively control the terrorists are the governments of their own countries, the countries they came from in the first place. As we know, some of these governments often support them with money and resources, as well as training grounds and hiding places. Others are authoritarian regimes so fragile that they feel they can't afford to fight them, or will fight only if their own rule is at stake. So what we have is support for terrorists or the turning of a blind eye. In most of these countries, the government and the population, while overtly against the slaughter of civilians, are happy—deep down in their hearts—to see the West suffer. We intend to attack the infrastructure of these countries and make them root out any terrorist presence within their borders. We're not looking to replace rulers or change regimes, like what was done in Iraq, but to force existing governments to behave. And we won't wait to be attacked first, either." He paused to let his words sink in. "Any questions so far?"

"At least one," Jake said, remembering his experience in Cairo. Remembering Isabelle Said. "How do you intend to limit what I think you guys call 'collateral damage'? How will you prevent the deaths of innocent civilians?"

"As I said, we'll target infrastructure, which can be civilian infrastructure as well as military installations. We'll protect the civilian population to the greatest extent possible. But shit happens." Stone shrugged. "There may be instances in which despite all our efforts to the contrary, a limited number of civilians get hit."

No more innocent lives would be taken, if it depended on him. Jake actually felt confident that he could make a difference here. "How advanced are you in the planning of all this? Or is it just an idea at this stage?"

"We have access to assets on the ground in certain countries. People willing to help us for a variety of reasons, ranging from sheer greed to a shared belief that this evil has to be contained lest it lead to mankind's destruction. We have a specific first target in mind, which we're ready to strike, and additional targets at an advanced planning stage."

Jake had little patience for this kind of conversation in the world of business—the abstractions and generalizations that took the place of necessary information—and he couldn't take it in this context, either. "Look, you're being evasive because you still don't know if I'm committed. That's understandable. But we won't make much progress this way. I don't know what to say to put your mind at ease and make this productive, but let me come at this from another angle. Why don't you tell me exactly why you want me on board."

"We didn't choose you, remember," Stone said. "You chose yourself. At first, we were pissed off by what you did, to say the least. All hell broke loose when you came out of left field and single-handedly destroyed the Ashraf Ismail lead. This lead was important to the CIA and vital, absolutely vital, to us. It's textbook stuff: They tell us to plan for the unforeseen, but in ten lifetimes we couldn't have prepared for what you did. It was a bloody disaster. Literally.

"But I've always been taught that if you're given lemons you make lemonade. So I came up with this idea and ran it past my colleague here." Stone tilted his head in the direction of Delgado. "In order to do what you had done, I told him, you had to be extraordinarily determined and resourceful. The sheer speed with which you moved from locating an incomplete police report to killing the man who murdered your family, halfway around the world . . . well, frankly, it blew us away."

The corners of Delgado's mouth turned down at this point, Jake noticed. The man was damned if he'd admit to being blown away by anyone.

Stone continued. "And most importantly, you have a lot of money. So I said, 'Why don't we consider bringing him in? We can use him. And we can use his money.'"

So it was the money. That was fine by Jake. But what happened next shocked him.

Gerard pulled an elaborate portfolio from a briefcase and passed it across the table to him. Jake took a look. Inside were the statements—dated that *same* day—of his personal banking and brokerage accounts. The folder also contained a detailed description of his last trading operation that included the profit calculation, and his $3.4 million cut, to the exact dollar. Finally, a special section on Jake's dealings with SBS, including a reference to his last meeting with Suter.

Jake felt simultaneously flabbergasted and furious at the aggressive invasion of his privacy. At the same time he thought, these people are for real. "So you want my money."

"Correct," Delgado replied.

"What can I say?" Stone shrugged. "Depending on the amount of risk you're willing to take, though, we want you as well."

Jake let the silence hang for a few seconds. "Okay. But there's something *I* want."

"Which is?" Stone's voice sounded guarded.

"Whoever was behind my wife's death. The one who sent Ashraf Ismail. I want him. I help you, you help me."

Stone looked at Gerard, who nodded, clasped his hands and said nothing. His expression said something like, *I'm willing to consider it.*

The television in the next room caught Jake's eye—the word 'Highest' again on the CNN banner. "Why's the terror alert at the highest level?"

"As usual," Gerard said, "Homeland Security is being vague with the public, and we're not yet prepared to fill you in on everything. But the essence of it is this: A terrorist organization supported by Iran is preparing a series of linked attacks on U.S. soil for some time during the next week. If successful, they'll make 9/11 look like your Boston Tea Party. Which is precisely why we need to move quickly."

"How quickly?"

"Our first field operation begins tomorrow." Gerard glanced at the financial portfolios, then back to Jake. "Are you still with us?"

That would be the field operation Gerard had mentioned earlier, a trip that would include Jake and Miranda. Why in the world would these guys want two non-professionals in the middle of the action, Jake wondered. *We'll only be dead weight for them.*

Then it hit him: By making them complicit in the group's actions, by incriminating them both, these men would be buying their loyalty. For good.

As if reading his mind, Gerard said, "You'll be breaking the law. You'll be uncomfortable. You'll run risks, but in the end you'll have done something about these animals."

The dealmaker in Jake took over. "I need your answer first. Will you help me find whoever sent Ashraf Ismail?"

"Yes," said Barzilai.

"Yes," said the other three.

"Well, then." Jake turned to Gerard. "What time tomorrow?"

There was quite a bit of information about Jake Burke on the Internet; a man of his wealth and social conscience didn't go through life without leaving a mark. Rifaat found financial articles about Burke's hedge fund and business philosophy. Burke was on the board of several charitable foundations and community groups. Rifaat even found his wedding announcement. Burke's personal loss in the FAO Schwarz bombing, of course, was mentioned several times in the coverage of that momentous day.

Yes, once Rifaat's agent succeeded in bribing the right Cairo detective and obtained the two simple words Rifaat needed—Burke's name—the rest had been easy.

Satisfied, Rifaat sat back and gazed at his computer screen. Finding Burke's home address would also be easy. Or perhaps they would take him at the office. Rifaat would make that decision based on which option would be more unsettling to his enemy. Perhaps they would take his whore as well, to punish her for her complicity.

Rifaat sent for Saajid, a favored choice for this type of assignment. Saajid was as cruel as a dog that you had kicked too many times. And meticulous. An excellent combination.

When Saajid arrived, the muscular young man presented himself before Rifaat with the proper deference, eyes on the floor. Saajid's head and face were as perfectly hairless as a snake's.

"My friend, you are going to pay the Great Satan a visit," Rifaat told him. He saw a flash of excitement in the young man's eyes that he attributed to zeal for service rather than relish for the destination.

"I live to serve," Saajid said.

CHAPTER TEN

When Jake Burke, Miranda Connelly and Gerard Duvivier landed at Mehrabad Airport, Tehran, they carried exquisitely forged passports in the names of René Lecomte, Karen Davenport and Desmond O'Hara, and visas for a two-week stay. Jake remembered smiling when he first saw the two-week stamp on the passport. By coincidence, that had been exactly the length of time he had told his partners he would be away for. To everyone who needed to know, Jake Burke had officially taken a two-week break to climb Mount Kilimanjaro. He would be trekking at altitudes above 18,000 feet, he had told them. The looks they gave him were a mix of admiration and worry that their leader had gone mad. As for Miranda, with her boss out of town, she was supposedly taking a much-needed vacation.

Jake and Gerard wore long-sleeved shirts with the cuffs rolled back, Jake's light blue and Gerard's black. No neckties in Iran, as ties were symbols of Western values—not a good idea if one wanted to disappear into the Tehran crowd. As long as they didn't speak, Gerard had explained, both men could pass for Azeris, the twenty-five percent of the Iranian population that is fair-skinned, speaks a mixture of Turkish and Farsi, and is concentrated in the northwest part of the country, mainly in its capital city. Miranda would be cloaked in the overcoat

called a "manteau" and scarf, but wouldn't have to don a veil or suf-
focating *burka* to walk the streets unchallenged.

"Do I have to walk behind you, or something?" she asked Gerard.

"No, in that regard Iran is not as restrictive as some Islamic societies."

"Gotta give 'em credit for that," she acknowledged with a smile.

They were part of a group tour organized by Victoria and Albert
Tours, a well-established operator with offices in London. After spending the first days in Tehran, the tour would briefly visit Shiraz, Isfahan,
the Caspian coast, Yazd, and the major historical sites of Bam, Persepo-
lis, and Pasargadae. Of course, Jake and Miranda would not be seeing
those places.

The modern Azadi Grand Hotel, a black monolith towering over its
surroundings, had been called the Hyatt before the revolution. It stood
beside Chamran Highway at the Evin crossroad, quite far from the center of Tehran. The tour group milled around the lobby while their guide
went through the check-in procedures. The group comprised English
pensioners, for the most part: men with gray hair and gray clothing, and
women who wore flowery dresses and spoke in chirping voices. Gerard
had told Jake that one of the advantages of a large hotel was that most
did not follow the standard routine of holding their guests' passports for
eventual police inspections. Instead, they photocopied the first pages of
the passport and returned it. This was crucial, as the trio would need to
leave Iran hastily.

Upon arrival, they climbed the stairs to the second floor and entered
the hotel's Internet café. Gerard sent an email to his "father" in London,
telling him that he had arrived safely.

"That should set things in motion," he whispered to Jake.

Jake's room faced the Alborz mountains. Through the grimy glass of
his window he could see the cable car that took tourists up to Mount
Toshal, their guide had said. He was tired, guessed it was the tension.
The trip from London on British Air hadn't been so bad.

On the other hand, he hadn't exactly been energized by his first
glimpse of Tehran, either. Even though he had read about it, and despite
his Cairo experience, he hadn't been prepared for the overcrowded,
smog-choked city of ten million that the guide had briefly led the group

through before they settled in at the Azadi. Not even a hint of old Persia and its glories. The only interesting things Jake had seen were the *jub*, the open-air canals lined with trees. They had been built to distribute drinking water brought into town from the mountains by additional underground canals called *qanats*. The jub, which ran along most of Tehran's main streets, might once have served their purpose. Now, the water in them was clearly undrinkable.

Jake had just managed to fall asleep when Gerard knocked at his door.

"Let's go. They're waiting for us."

They joined Miranda outside the hotel and got into the first of a long line of taxis, an old Renault.

"*Khahesh mikonam, Arg,*" Gerard said to the driver before sitting back.

"Where are we going?" Jake had been given no information by Gerard. The passivity he was experiencing felt alien to him.

"To the bazaar. We passed by it with the guide, remember? I want to see it again. You will enjoy it. It's an incredible place."

Adjusting her floral-patterned head-scarf, Miranda piped up, "And we're going there because?"

"The bazaar is the heart of Tehran, and for that matter all of Iran. Over seventy percent of the country's wholesale trade is done there. And almost a third of the imported goods are traded there. It's very impressive. You'll see." Though his tone was friendly, Gerard's eyes said, *Shut up until we get there.*

Jake couldn't resist a follow-up question and added, "It'd be nice to know what we're expected to do."

Gerard seemed not to hear, though he gritted his teeth. As soon as they stepped from the taxi, he gripped Jake's upper arm and spoke softly but sternly into his ear.

"This is not your company, where you can demand answers. Is that clear? I will give you information as I see fit. *I* am the boss—I thought we made that evident to you before we left. Your first question was not appropriate. We have to assume that the drivers who service these hotels speak many languages and probably report to the authorities."

"Okay."

"Your last observation was just plain stupid. This is serious business, Jake. One *faux pas* and we're dead, do you understand that?"

Jake resented Gerard's tone. But the man was right. "Sorry, Gerard. I guess I'm tired and not thinking straight."

Gerard released Jake's arm. He evidently imparted the same message to Miranda next, whispering intently into her ear. She nodded contritely. When that was done, he resumed the genial tour.

"So. You see these tiny stalls? Almost all of them front for big businesses all over Iran. Don't be fooled by their humble appearance. These people are very, very powerful. For instance, they paralyzed the country's economy when they closed down in support of the Khomeini revolution in '79."

"They did, huh?"

"The bazaar is like a city unto itself. It has its own schools, restaurants, mosques, you name it. Not to mention the financial aspects. At one time the bazaar manages to act as stock exchange, banking sector and the main commodities market of the entire country."

Jake looked at the stalls. Openings no wider than ten feet led into small rooms of different sizes. The largest one looked to be about three hundred square feet in area. He was having trouble imagining that behind these little shops manned by one or two salesmen were actual corporations. Colorful banners bearing Farsi inscriptions hung everywhere—not to mention pictures of a glowering Ayatollah Khomeini, still hanging after all these years. The women were dressed in robes of plaid or black, and the faces of some were covered by veils. Others were unveiled, though, and to Jake's surprise some had an inch or two of hair exposed at their foreheads. The men were dressed like him, in Western-style informal clothing. Almost all wore long-sleeve shirts.

The bazaar had a spectrum of colors all its own that ranged from brown and ochre at one end, to turquoise at the other. And black and white, of course. The scent of spices and barbecued lamb wafted into Jake's nostrils wherever they went. Anywhere he looked, smiling salesmen eagerly tried to engage them. Jake saw tin utensils, beautifully crafted with arabesques and Farsi inscriptions. Down an alley he saw rows of stores displaying silver objects and necklaces of gold. He realized that the shops were grouped by type of product, and he suspected that the alleys were probably named accordingly. Again, it was something like Cairo, though not identical.

He turned to Gerard. "You know where we're going, right?"

"Yes." Gerard kept on walking.

No idle chitchat with *this* guy, Jake thought.

They walked for almost half an hour. Gerard stopped a few times to ask the price of things and, Jake could see, to make sure that they weren't being followed. Finally they entered a carpet store.

Rugs were everywhere, from welcome-mat-sized carpets—prayer rugs, maybe—that had been laid out for inspection by customers, to a tightly rolled carpet that must've been twenty-five feet long. A sort of log of woven fabric, only the brown underside visible. The place smelled like a stable.

A large olive-skinned man with a wide white smile stood up when they walked in. His eyes weren't smiling. On the contrary, they were darting from Gerard to Jake and Miranda to the entrance behind them and back. The man relaxed after Gerard said a few things to him in Farsi. It sounded to Jake as if he and Miranda were being introduced.

The man's eyes caught up with the rest of his smiling face when he spoke to the Americans in slightly accented English. "I am Reza. Welcome to my humble place. May peace be with you."

"Thanks. May peace be with you, too." Jake had learned to respond in kind from a travel guide to the region that Gerard had given him. The book was written by a M.T. Faramarzi and printed in Iran.

Reza went to the back of the store and returned with coffee and cookies. Jake sipped at his coffee and nibbled a cookie, a small cube made with filo dough, pistachios and honey.

"That's delicious, thank you," he told Reza. Actually, like baklava, it was too sweet for him. Miranda nibbled hers with trepidation at first, but quickly gained an enthusiasm that was shared by Gerard. Of course—he had grown up on French pastries. He said something to Reza that Jake didn't understand.

When Gerard noticed Jake's inquiring look, he explained. "I said, '*Dast-e shoma dard nakoneh.*' The exact translation is, 'May your hands not be tired.' It's what a guest is expected to say after eating. Actually, if you don't mind, I'll talk to Reza in Farsi. Things will move faster this way."

The two men spoke for about ten minutes. Then Reza handed Gerard a brown envelope and directed them to the front of the room, where the merchandise was on display. When they left the store, Gerard also carried a carpet about two feet by four feet. Folded into quarters rather than rolled, it was tucked under his arm. He looked like the typical tourist with a local souvenir. They flagged down a taxi and returned to the center of the city.

Sitting in a café a short while later, at a table by a high window looking out onto a beautiful if slightly shaggy garden, Gerard finally spoke directly to his charges, albeit in hushed tones. And only after they had ordered mint tea and more too-sweet pastries from a counter at one end of the room: baklava, the real thing this time.

"A girl could get fat awfully fast here," Miranda joked.

"Yes, it's like Paris that way."

"You seem to be living proof that a guy can eat good food and stay fit. I've never seen someone your age—you must be in your late fifties, right?—in such great shape. The way you move, the way you lift heavy stuff . . . it's like you're thirty years old." Jake saw that she meant it and felt a surprising pang of jealousy. Gerard was certainly the star of this show, guiding them like two children in an unfamiliar land, but why should Jake care?

"Thanks. You're kind to say that. And by the way, I'm past sixty-five."

Jake looked carefully at Gerard to make sure that the Frenchman wasn't pulling their leg. He shook his head. "Amazing."

Miranda was also amazed, but Jake was pleased in spite of himself that Gerard was way too old for her.

Men and women in groups and alone sat at tables nearby, either silently reading their newspapers or arguing passionately about one thing or another. Old men, professors from the nearby university perhaps, wore berets and gripped elegant canes. Café Naderi had been a magnet for artists and intellectuals for decades, according to Gerard. It was one of his favorite places in the city.

"I was stationed in Tehran for a few years, ostensibly as an advisor to the French oil company, Total S.A."

"I know them. They're huge. The world's fourth largest oil and gas company."

Gerard nodded. He tamped his mouth with a paper napkin. "During my stay here in 1988, Total, together with Russia's Gazprom and Indonesia's Petronas, signed a major contract with the National Iranian Oil Co. Total S.A. agreed to invest two billion dollars in this project. You know what the expected profit of Total was when the contract was signed? One and a quarter *billion* dollars. And the prices have gone up since. They are making a bloody fortune. Does this help to explain why my country is always trying to block sanctions against Iran?"

"Very much so."

Gerard sipped his tea. He offered Jake and Miranda a baklava from the plate before them. "No? Anyway, during that stay, my Farsi became quite good. I actually had a great deal of fun here and made some good friends." The tone of Gerard's voice changed as he reminisced.

"Did you spend all your time in Tehran?" Miranda asked.

"Most, but not all. I also spent some time in Bandar Abbas."

Jake chimed in. "Isn't that a port to the south of here?"

"Very good, you've done your homework. It's also the location of one of nine oil refineries in Iran. Produces gasoline, jet fuels, kerosene, solvents, gas oil. . . . Hey, hey—I see your eyes glazing over. You want to pay attention to all this. It's essential for a complete understanding of what we're doing."

"Sorry, go ahead."

"As I was saying, Iran has nine refineries where they refine over one million barrels per day of crude oil. Bandar Abbas is an average-sized refinery. They refine a little over a hundred thousand barrels per day. We're going there."

"Really? When?"

"In three hours."

Jake arched an eyebrow at Miranda. He was beginning to get used to these small surprises. "Good thing I didn't unpack."

"Well, get busy as soon as we return to the hotel room. We won't be taking suitcases along. Use the small duffel bags we gave you and try to fit two days' of clothing inside. We have to leave the hotel unnoticed. It won't work if they see us lugging suitcases through the lobby. Also make sure you don't leave anything behind that could identify you. You won't be coming back for those things."

"What are we going to do in Bandar Abbas?" Miranda asked. Jake nodded and awaited Gerard's response attentively. He was feeling slightly annoyed again, and a bit anxious.

Gerard signaled for their waiter, a positively ancient specimen like all his coworkers. "You'll learn when we get there. Look, I can see that you hate this, that you want more information. What I'm doing is telling you only what's strictly necessary for each next step. This way, if something goes wrong, you will know less and reveal less. Because trust me, if they catch you, you'll reveal everything you know and then some."

Jake felt something shift inside him. Gerard wasn't joking.

Before they paid their tab and headed back to the hotel, Gerard asked if they had any last questions. "It will be a while until we're out of other people's earshot again."

"What were we doing in the bazaar?" Miranda asked, echoing Jake's own thoughts.

Gerard laughed. "Nothing very mysterious. The distances in Iran are often enormous—as I told you yesterday, it's a big country. So Reza got us all the airline tickets we might need during our stay, and everything we'll need to leave the country afterwards. Actually, because last-minute reservations are so hard to get, we need to follow our schedule to perfection. We'll have only that one chance to leave. Otherwise . . ."

Jake didn't need him to fill in the blank. "Got it."

"He also gave us these." Gerard pulled official-looking documents from the breast pocket of his shirt. "These are letters given by the *komiteh* allowing us to travel around the country. The komiteh is the headquarters of the *Pasdaran*, or Revolutionary Guards. Pasdaran is the plural of Pasdar, which means literally 'Guardian—*dar*, of the Pass—*pas*.' Actually, the Iranians claim that the word 'pass,' like 'mountain pass' in English, comes from the Farsi 'pas.'"

"Interesting," said Jake, uninterested.

"Webster's says differently, of course. They say it's from the Latin *passare*."

"Uh, huh." Jake considered saying, *So the linguistics lesson is essential too, huh?* before remembering that this was a man you didn't want to annoy.

"Anyway, the Pasdaran are in charge of enforcing Islamic law. If you see SUVs with darkened windows and men dressed in camouflage uniforms, that's them. They can stop anyone on the street merely to check their clothing, or to make sure that a couple walking together is married. They can go into any house to see if the Shariah is being followed. If they confront you at any time, even if they start pushing you around, stay calm and be polite. They're usually ignorant bastards on power trips. Don't give them a reason to hurt or arrest you."

"And who was that Reza?"

Gerard smiled apologetically. "Sorry, that's information you do not need to know."

They flew to Bandar Abbas on a very old Boeing 727. Jake wondered where Iran Air got their spare parts, what with the trade boycott and all. Though the airport didn't seem large, Jake spotted a sign in English proclaiming Bandar Abbas International Airport. As they walked into the terminal, he saw a single non-domestic flight posted, to the United Arab Emirates.

I guess that makes the airport international, he thought with a smile. He had read that the city had become the main Iranian port since the war with Iraq. Bandar Abbas now handled over half of all the country's international cargo.

Gerard directed the taxi driver to drop them off at a small park across from a bustling shopping strip. They walked into the park and sat on a vacant bench.

"Did you notice a cyber café across the street when we entered the park?" Gerard's tone was sober. Beyond sober, really. Almost solemn.

Nearby, couples walked together in the sunshine. Jake assumed they were married.

"I noticed you looking at it," Jake said. "I'm surprised that such a thing still exists, here in the land of Khomeini."

Gerard ignored the digression. "From that humble cyber café," he said instead, "you'll be sending an email that will change the world."

CHAPTER ELEVEN

Gerard rested his right ankle on his left knee, twisted the heel of his shoe, and removed a tightly folded piece of paper from inside it. "Read this carefully. You will need to think hard before you press the SEND button. Once the email is gone, an irreversible chain of events will begin that may eventually rid the world of fundamentalist Islamic terrorism."

Jake was dumbfounded. "What does it say?"

"Read it for yourself. I don't want to be accused of misrepresenting anything."

"What if I refuse to send the email?"

Gerard shrugged. "Then I'll do it. But you'll have failed to convince us that you're on the same page as we are, and our relationship will be terminated. By the way, you should ask me all your questions now. Once inside, I won't be speaking to you. I don't want anyone to hear your accent."

"Okay. Tell me exactly what I need to do in there."

"I'll get us a computer when we walk in. Take this card." Gerard showed him something that looked like a Visa card. With one thumb he pushed into the middle of it, dislodging the card's circular center, a disk approximately two inches in diameter. Then he pressed the middle of the disk and dislodged its center. "What do you think this is?"

"A disk with a hole in it."

Gerard showed him the disk's other side, and Jake realized it was actually a tiny CD. "Every day, twenty new email addresses are automatically
created in a variety of portals worldwide. This is done automatically
from a central computer in London. When I insert it in a computer's CD
reader, this little optical disk directs that computer to log on to one of
the addresses. All I have to do is to type in a password. If Delgado, for
example, needs to check for emails, all he needs to do is insert his own
disk wherever he is, and after typing his password he'll be logged on to
the same address. It's impossible to trace these addresses because, as I
said, they change every day."

"That's impressive," Miranda noted.

"Yes it is. One day, you'll meet the real genius of us all, an Englishman. We call him Big Ben. His programs generate all the codes of our
operation." Gerard continued his instructions. "You'll insert this disk
into the computer's CD-ROM reader. When prompted, you'll type the
word 'dustbuster.' After a moment, a single email will pop up. In it will
be a short text and a list of Internet addresses. You will prepare to send
a new email and copy and paste the list of addresses to the space that
says 'To:'. Then you will copy and paste the text to the body of the
new email. It will be the text of the page you're holding. Where it says
'Subject,' you will write: 'Warning—ONC Bomb—This Is Not a Hoax.'
Then you'll pause, think hard, and hit SEND."

"What's an ONC bomb?"

"ONC stands for *Octanitrocubane*. The world's most powerful non-
nuclear explosive. This particular bomb is very large with a blast that's
the equivalent of a small nuclear explosion. Despite being enormously
powerful, it's totally non-toxic, turning into simple carbon dioxide and
nitrogen after the explosion."

"It'll kill you, but it won't pollute, right?" Jake said with a smirk, as
he tried to take it all in.

Gerard continued. "Finally, you'll look for the file of sent emails and
erase what you sent from that file. This will make the job of locating us
just a bit harder. They'll always be able to retrieve the email from the
hard disk, but it will be too late by then. Then we leave. Fairly simple."

"Simple?" Jake now held the paper with care, as if holding a live grenade. "Will this whole thing become clearer when I read the text you want me to send? If not, I can tell you right now that I'm not sending anything. You can do it."

Gerard was silent for a few moments. "Read the text. We want an end to Iran's support of terrorism."

"That's simple enough."

"Just read it."

Jake looked at the page he was now holding. The air was hot and dry but fragrant with a delicious scent that emanated from an orange tree just behind the bench on which they sat. Birds were chirping. Somewhere children laughed, but he couldn't see them. The scene was surreal. What was he doing here?

He angled the page so Miranda could see it and started reading.

To the Iranian government, the Iranian and international press and the foreign governments that are the recipients of this message:

This document should be taken with the utmost seriousness. The warning within it is based on a genuine capability to strike, the first example of which will manifest itself in thirty hours.

STOP TERRORISM OR PERISH

Iranians are a unique people with an exceptional history. Twenty-five hundred years ago, Cyrus the Great presided over a Golden Age remembered for tolerance and enlightenment. Sadly, in the last decades, under a leadership that is inept, corrupt, and therefore self-destructive, Iran has become a radical backwater, its progress stunted, its people stifled. Under this leadership, Iran has embarked on a risky and aggressive course, accumulating long-range missiles, developing nuclear weapons, and promoting and supporting international terrorism.

We bear no ill will against Iran and only wish peace upon its people. Yet in order to live in peace, one must let others live in peace. As such, we will force the existing Iranian leadership to respect international norms.

In order to prove our ability to do so, we are taking the following action:

Tomorrow at 20:00 hours, on the island of Qeshm, a major blast will take place. We will be exploding a one-kiloton non-nuclear device. We urge not only the government of Iran, but those of the neighboring countries of Oman and the United Arab Emirates, and international observers to whom we are giving these 30 hours to travel to the region, to ready the necessary equipment to measure the destructive power of such an explosion. Nothing can be done to avoid it. Anyone within a one-mile radius of the explosion's center will be in grave jeopardy. We have chosen to detonate the device in a part of the island that is uninhabited. As a result, no one should be harmed by the event itself. Yet whoever approaches ground zero does so at his own risk. Since we cannot disclose the exact location of the site, we urge all inhabitants of the island to travel to Qeshm's more-populated areas or away from the island altogether.

A warning: Any attempt to locate and dismantle the explosive device will cause its immediate detonation.

During the twenty-four hours following the explosion we will inform you of our specific demands.

"Is this for real? Do you really have this capability?"

Shifting on the bench, Gerard nodded. "This is just the first stage. We have *matériel*—he pronounced the word in French—far more powerful than that. Do you remember the reports a few years ago about suitcase bombs, those nuclear devices weighing around sixty pounds that everyone was speculating Osama bin Laden had acquired?"

"Yes, but he hadn't, or we would've been hit. I'm sure those things never really existed. It's probably impossible to make a nuclear bomb that small." Jake looked at Gerard's smiling eyes. "Or am I wrong, as usual?"

"They did, in fact, exist—and have for a long time. America was actually the first to manufacture them, in the '60s. The lightest one you built was called the Davy Crockett. It was a small rocket, around two meters tall with a cyclindrical bomb at its tip. Very, very portable."

"Shit."

"That's right. Now I'll tell you a little story, which is no State secret. In March of 1995, in Miami, two Lithuanians of Russian extraction offered Soviet-made shoulder-to-air missiles capable of shooting down jet planes to a man they thought was part of a Colombian drug cartel. In actuality this man was an undercover agent.

"This agent said he was interested in the missiles. The big surprise came when the Lithuanians said that they'd have something special to offer, once the missile transaction went through successfully. Would this man like to buy portable nuclear bombs?

"U.S. Customs set up a fake company to buy forty Stinger-type Russian missiles. They eventually paid fifty thousand dollars to the Lithuanians. Why? Because these men clearly knew what they were doing, from the sophisticated financial structure of the transaction to the back-up documentation that they were showing. In fact, they claimed to be backed by the Russian defense minister of the time, Pavel Grachev, who was known to be highly corrupt."

Gerard continued. "The most important reason, though, was something else altogether. During a meeting held in London, the two Lithuanians telephoned the Section of Geopolitics and Security of the Russian Academy of Sciences, the shadow broker for the missiles . . . and the nukes. The full conversation was recorded."

"When was that again?"

"In 1995. The whole thing took almost two years, and then Customs dropped it."

"Why?"

"The feeling was that even if they were able to find out who the other conspirators in Russia or Lithuania were, and warned those countries' governments, they would get nowhere. The connections were so high up that the guilty individuals would be forewarned and would cover their tracks. So your country chose to go public and warn Russia in general terms. That's when Delgado and Sam Stone stepped in."

"What do you mean?" Miranda interjected.

"They did what the American government was unable to do. U.S. national security policy forbids any sting operation that might involve the entry of nuclear material into the country. So Delgado and Stone bought the bombs."

"What?" Jake was stunned.

"You heard me."

"How many bombs?"

"Do you remember General Lebed? Alexander Lebed?"

Jake tried to recall. "Wasn't he a Russian war-hero? A candidate to succeed Yeltsin?"

"That's right. Chechnya and Moldova wars. He became the head of the National Security Council under Yeltsin. Lebed was given instructions by the Russian president to account for 132 suitcase bombs. In a very private meeting, he told your Congressman Weldon, the chairman of the House Sub-Committee on National Security, that he had found only forty-eight."

"You bought the rest?"

"Most of them. A few are still out there. Now, these things have a limited shelf life. Once that period of time has expired, the bombs become dangerous to those who are holding them—unless one is able to refurbish them. We did that. We had access to the necessary material and to technicians who could do the job. Whether those who have the other bombs were able to do the same, we don't know. If they had working bombs, I think we would have heard from them by now."

Jake was dumbstruck. "Are you telling me that you're planning to explode nuclear weapons?"

"No, not really," Gerard answered slowly, as if afraid of Jake's reaction. "We do have the capability but have no intention of using it."

Jake wasn't sure he believed Gerard's organization had nuclear weapons. If they did, though, he certainly didn't believe the Frenchman's professed restraint. The park before them remained as placid and benign as ever. "This whole thing is absolutely mind-boggling."

"Well, it gets better. We will be in Qeshm. Close enough to see what happens, yet far enough away to be out of danger. And what you will see tomorrow will be spectacular. ONC has obviously just a fraction of the destructive power of a nuclear reaction, but this is a huge amount of ONC."

"Why do we need to be there?" Miranda asked, still dubious.

"Because the bombs have been in place for years and the system has never been tested. There's a slight danger that the remote detonator is shot. If that's the case, we will need to rearm it manually."

"Which bombs? The nuclear or the ONC ones?"

"All of them were installed a while ago. We need to be able to rearm this first one, manually if necessary. We haven't tested these detonators for a while. Are you up for it?"

Miranda nodded but Jake wasn't ready to commit. "How big is this bomb, exactly?"

"This bomb is equivalent to a one-kiloton bomb. The same size as a suitcase nuclear bomb. The nuclear bomb your country dropped on Hiroshima was sixteen times more powerful. But this device is still devastating. A one-kiloton bomb is still the equivalent of one thousand tons of TNT. Detonated in downtown New York, this bomb would probably kill 100,000 people instantly. If it was nuclear, its radiation would affect 700,000 more and make an enormous area uninhabitable for a long, long time. But as I said before, an ONC bomb is clean, leaving no radiation behind. Its only drawback is the difficulty in planting this huge amount of explosives without getting noticed." Gerard stared sternly at Jake. "You haven't answered my question."

"Yes. If needed, I'm up for it. I'll go with you to Qeshm."

"Good. Does that mean that you're ready to send that email?"

"Just one more question. What will our next demands be?"

"We want the immediate surrender of two major terrorists and the shutdown of terrorist structures that Iran has been hosting."

"Any demand on their nuclear efforts?"

"No. This was debated extensively, as you can imagine. We decided that we need to keep our focus. Remember the 'Highest Alert' warning? We need to stop them now. That's our priority and we'll stick to it. We'll deal with the nuclear issue as soon as we've been able to neutralize this threat. In the meantime, your government and the Israelis are very much on top of Iran's nuclear efforts. I would be very surprised if Israel didn't try to do something on its own about this. Soon. Having said that, there are those, myself included, who worry that Israel might not be capable of doing it."

"Why?"

"Iran is far from Israel. The straight line distance from Tel Aviv to Bushehr—that's their main reactor—is over a thousand miles, which means that if the Israelis want to bomb the nuclear facilities, their aircraft will require refueling midway. On top of that, the nuclear sites are spread all over Iran. Several of them are underground and many are deep inside densely populated areas. The best Israel can do is delay Iran's nuclear project by a few years. If it wants to fully destroy that country's chance of becoming a nuclear power, it'll have to go in with troops. And that's a tall order these days, with America's troubles in Iraq on everyone's mind. But that's only me. Most disagree and believe that an attack by Israel is not a question of if, but when." Gerard shook his head. "But we've got a job to do. Let me ask the question again: Are you ready to send that email?"

Qeshm was not downtown New York. An explosion in an uninhabited area couldn't do much damage, Jake knew.

He had no doubts, no second thoughts. He was ready. Let them be warned.

And so Jake sat at a PC in the shabbiest cyber café he'd ever visited—pastry crumbs were everywhere, and the mouse of his computer was sticky to the touch with what seemed to be fruit juice. The desk before him was dappled with coffee rings, also sticky. Jake followed the instructions shared with him by Gerard, who sat silently at a nearby computer. Miranda was positioned just outside, an unobtrusive sentry.

Palms ever so damp, Jake inserted the disk, as instructed. A web page popped up, electronically requesting a password. He typed "dustbuster."

An email did indeed await. His heart now distinctly pounding—could the bearded college student seated near him hear it as he typed?—Jake double-clicked on it. The text that sprang up was the demand and warning Jake had read in the park, this time in Farsi as well as English. A list of unfamiliar Internet addresses was attached. Jake highlighted and then copied the list, then pasted it into the "To:" field of a new email form.

He copied and pasted the text to the body of the new message. Under "Subject:" Jake typed the following, in upper-case letters:

WARNING—ONC BOMB—THIS IS NOT A HOAX

Gerard had told him to think hard, but Jake didn't need to think. He only proofread the message to ascertain that all was in order. Then, with a bit of a flourish, he hit SEND.

He cleaned the file of sent emails and turned to look at Gerard, not far away, who nodded subtly.

History was happening.

As agreed, Gerard left the café first. Miranda joined him and they crossed the park. Jake followed shortly thereafter. Soon they were in what looked like an abandoned part of town: neglected buildings and empty streets.

Gerard and Miranda lingered in a copse of trees, allowing Jake to catch up. "This whole quarter is slated for demolition," Gerard explained. "New high-rises."

A black SUV was cruising toward them, two men inside.

Gerard slowed his pace and looked around. "Pasdaran. Walk naturally and ignore them."

The car screeched to a halt ahead of them. It was a Nissan Pathfinder, Jake found himself thinking, trying to control his fear. *It's probably called something different here in Iran. Yes, and the windows are tinted.*

"Let me do the talking," Gerard whispered.

Two men emerged from the SUV, cocky and aggressive. One of them walked toward Jake, barking orders. Jake looked to Gerard and said nothing. The other scrutinized Miranda disdainfully. She remained composed, but Jake could tell she was rattled.

Gerard stepped between the Pasdar and Jake, speaking rapidly but softly. The man tried to push him aside. Pulling out the laissez-passer letters given by the *komiteh*, Gerard stood his ground, humbly but firmly.

It didn't work. The Pasdar read the letters, pocketed them and continued pushing.

Now both Pasdaran were on Gerard, shouting and shoving. The one closest to Gerard reached for his gun. Jake froze. Gerard raised both hands, as if surrendering, still talking without pause.

And then, so fast that Jake doubted it had even happened, he jabbed the man's eyes, ripping open his eyeballs. The man punched blindly, howling in pain, clear liquid mixed with blood pouring from his eye sockets. Miranda gasped as if shot.

In a quick, dance-like move that seemed part of the first jab, Gerard stepped aside and forward, reaching for the second guard. He inserted his thumbs between the side teeth and the cheeks of the stunned man and, in a brutally short outward action, ripped his cheeks open, knocking the man down at the same time with a head butt.

The savagery and swiftness of the scene shocked Jake. Yet he was able to register the first guard screaming and staggering blindly. Reacting without thinking, Jake tripped him. Gerard moved swiftly toward the fallen man and kicked his trachea—there was a sickening snap as the man's windpipe shattered. The Pasdar brought his hands to his neck, gasping for air, unable to emit a sound, his blind eyes desperate with the realization that he was going to choke to death.

Gerard then walked calmly to the second man, who was curled up on the sidewalk, moaning, trying to hold his face together. Stomping on his temple with the heel of his shoe, Gerard crushed the man's skull.

He then bent down, wiped his hands on the dead Pasdar's shirt, and removed the letters from his pocket.

Shocked by the display of savagery they had just witnessed, Jake and Miranda shared a fleeting look of horror.

As they walked hurriedly away, Jake noticed that Gerard wasn't even breathing heavily.

"It had to be done," the Frenchman said. "He ignored the letters. They wanted to take us to the station anyway. We would've been killed there."

Jake said nothing and kept following. It wasn't the fact of the men's deaths so much as the brutality of Gerard's methods that left him feeling distinctly queasy. It took something to kill a man that way, bare-handed, that Jake hoped he never found within himself.

Within minutes, just past an abandoned warehouse, they reached the coastline. Gerard motioned to a speedboat tied to a rotten dock, a dark-haired man in shirtsleeves at the helm. They would be smuggled into Qeshm. After a short ride at full speed, they were dropped on a barren stretch of the mountainous island.

Qeshm was large, approximately five-hundred square miles in size, Gerard explained. It had a sprinkling of small villages and had become in recent years a fast-growing duty-free zone. There was still plenty of space where one could disappear, though.

Gerard told them that the Iranians would likely keep their navy vessels well away from the island until the scheduled time of the blast. After the bombing, it would take at least two hours for the military bureaucracy to agree to deploy a protective cordon around the island. By then, Jake, Miranda and Gerard would have made it safely away.

CHAPTER TWELVE

They slept outdoors on a deserted beach, its sand as white as sugar, two miles from the explosion site. The area was totally bare. Not a speck of green in sight.

Gerard had prepared well. They had water and food. They had a large, thin white cloth that they used for protection against the sun the following day. Sunscreen lotion, even. The white cloth was especially useful when they had to hide from the countless military helicopters that began flying over Qeshm early in the morning. The tension was enormous that day, the heat beneath the shroud almost unbearable.

"Where are you from originally?" Jake asked Gerard mid-afternoon. "I initially pegged you as Middle Eastern, but apparently you're French."

"I'm from Paris. My family is from the south, Marseille. We've been there forever. I guess that's the origin of my looks. You're not the first to mistake me for an Arab. It's quite helpful, sometimes."

"So, no Middle East, huh?"

"Well, yes and no."

The year was 1958 and Gerard Duvivier, son of one of the scientists sent by France to assist Israel in its nuclear program, was having fun.

Gerard, 17, and his friend Ahmed sat in the desert some two miles from the outskirts of Dimona, a small town in Israel's south, with no other light but that from the almost-full moon and the small campfire before them. Gerard had gathered dry branches and set little stones around them while Ahmed was mixing flour and water in a small copper bucket. They then set an old brass plate on the stones and lit the fire. Ahmed placed the dough he had just finished kneading on the plate. And that was it. Perfection. Gerard loved everything about this exact moment: the cool air; the soft sand; the flames' shifting golden light illuminating his friend's face and white *burnoose*, his hooded cloak; the profound silence made deeper by the staccato crackling of the fire; and the smell, ah, the *très magnifique* smell of pita bread being prepared.

They lay back, the fire between them, and exhaled loudly at the same time. Looking at each other, Gerard and Ahmed laughed. It was a perfectly choreographed move and they were getting good at it. Ritual connects, Gerard thought. It brings everybody to a place of no difference. He had lately started looking for powerful phrases with which to impress his classroom friends back in Paris in his self-titled series of "Letters from the Middle East."

Now the two friends would wait until the pita was ready. Ahmed would tear a piece for Gerard and say, "*Bon abetit*"—Ahmed had trouble pronouncing the sound of the letter "P." Gerard would then say, "*Shukran,*" thank you in Arabic. The warmth, softness, and wholesome taste of freshly baked bread would then take over and overwhelm his senses for a moment. Perfection.

Ahmed was tall for his age. He had a strong chin, unusually wide nostrils that made him look to Gerard like a boxer, a muscular body, and a deep tan. He too, was seventeen, and already a shepherd, a grown man, which was a source of no little discomfort for Gerard. Rachel was the reason. Gerard was her boyfriend but Rachel had grown up with Ahmed, her best friend. Prior to moving to Beer Sheva, Rachel's parents had been members of kibbutz Sdeh Boker, some twenty miles away, and Ahmed's tribe often camped close by.

Both Rachel and Ahmed would be joining the army soon—Ahmed was a Bedouin. Bedouins had, soon after the creation of Israel, volunteered to

serve in the country's army despite being Arabs and not under the obligation to do so. Army matters were all Rachel and Ahmed talked about,
often explaining to Gerard that it was security issues and then walking out
of his earshot. Gerard had never been comfortable with the easy familiar-
ity the two shared—which was gradually enhanced as time passed by the
complicity of those with a common destiny.

Later that night Rachel showed up at their campsite. She was tall, slim,
her olive skin beautifully tanned. Gerard adored her brown eyes, which
suggested middle-eastern mystery and contradicted her plain down-to-
earth approach to things. One thousand and one nights of dreams and
desire, Gerard had once told Rachel, your eyes are Scheherazade eyes.

"And you are my Prince Omar, is that right?" Rachel had given him
a patient motherly look and kissed him on the lips, once more making
him feel childish.

"How did you find us? Could you smell the pita?" Gerard asked now
as Rachel approached their campfire. He was enormously happy to see
her, but played it cool in front of his friend.

"Your mother told me you'd be here." She kissed Gerard on the left
cheek and stood beside Ahmed. Gerard could see she was eager to talk
to her friend alone.

"*Ahlan*, Ahmed." Hi, Ahmed.

"*Ahlan*." A wide smile.

Rachel didn't sit down, yet her eyes moved in silence from Gerard to
Ahmed and back.

"Is . . . everything okay?" Gerard finally asked.

"I got my *Tsav*," she blurted, grinning.

"What's that?" Gerard asked.

"It's the order to present myself for initial interviews at the Beer Sheva
army base."

"When do you have to show up?" Ahmed straightened himself.

"In two weeks." As she answered, Rachel half-turned her back to Gerard, who recognized the first pangs of his usual feeling of being left out.

"So you've made up your mind?" Ahmed asked.

Rachel nodded. "Yes. *Chel Modiin*."

Gerard understood. Rachel was going to apply for membership in the army intelligence services. "So my girlfriend will be a spy. Very impressive."

Rachel shrugged. "It's interesting, and you get to know a little more of what's really going on. Anyway," she said, looking sternly at him, "what I'll be doing won't be romantic, unless you get your jollies from assembling and interpreting information."

He shifted uncomfortably by the fire. "What do you think, Ahmed?" This said to deflect Rachel's attention. He didn't need an argument now.

"Good." Ahmed wasn't big on talking.

He gave it one more shot. "What about you? What will you do?" This was the first time that Gerard had been admitted to a conversation about Rachel and Ahmed's secret future and he wanted to make full use of the opportunity.

"I'll be a tracker," Ahmed said, "like my father."

"Really? Why?" Gerard wasn't sure he understood the word "tracker." He was studying Arabic at school, but still he had trouble understanding Ahmed at times. Ahmed always spoke to him in Arabic, and often explained in Hebrew what Gerard didn't understand. Due to Gerard's limited knowledge of both languages, the simpler their communication the better, and that was usually the case.

Rachel explained in French, which Ahmed barely understood, to Gerard's infinite satisfaction. "The Bedouins are by far the best trackers in Israel. They'll know who passed by a wadi and when, even in situations in which a non-Bedouin won't see a single footprint. These days, with terrorists infiltrating from Gaza and Jordan all the time, Bedouin trackers are doing a magnificent job of stopping attacks on Israel before they even begin. Ahmed's father is one of the best." Rachel's face looked beautiful by firelight. "But we shouldn't be talking army matters with you. You're not an Israeli . . . yet." She smiled.

Gerard laughed weakly.

"By the way," Rachel changed the subject, "what's the latest? Do you know when you're leaving?"

France was embroiled in a nasty conflict in Algeria, facing a fierce terrorist campaign waged by the Front de Libération Nationale, or FLN,
against the French local administration and the over one million French
civilians, many of whom had lived in Algeria for generations—since
Napoleon's invasion in 1808. Lately the FLN had been mounting an
average of *eight hundred* terrorist attacks per month. And those attacks
were particularly cruel, involving ritual murders and mutilations of
captured French soldiers. The same treatment was meted out to ethni-
cally French Algerians, regardless of age or gender, and to suspected
Muslim collaborators.

According to widespread reports, the French army had responded by
applying the internationally condemned principle of collective responsibility to communities suspected of cooperating with the FLN. Entire
villages were attacked by every means possible, including indiscriminate
aerial bombardment. Detailed stories of French atrocities, including
extensive use of torture against Muslim rebels, had been filtering back
to Paris for some time now.

Gerard pitied the poor soldiers who were there, fighting an inglorious
war. He dreaded the moment when he would have to join them. For a
moment he thought that it wouldn't be bad to be an Israeli, like Rachel
and Ahmed, to take part in building from scratch a country that had
been created only ten years before—a country seven years *younger* than
he was. It wouldn't be bad to own these moments around the fire, and
this perfect sky, and the ideal future these long-suffering people were
trying to build.

Gerard shrugged. "Father tells me there's a good chance they'll extend
his stay for another year, but he hasn't heard anything yet. If that doesn't
happen, we'll be leaving in six months. I might have to leave anyway."

"Is it because you'll be enlisting in the army in France?"

"Yes, of course."

"But you could be sent to Algeria." As often happened, Rachel was a
step ahead of him.

Gerard nodded. "I'm not exactly happy about it, but it's a war that
needs to be fought. You should understand that better than anyone."

"Actually, not. Israel's not colonizing anyone. We have a small Arab minority and they are citizens with full rights."

"We need to leave there," Gerard agreed, "but we can't back down to guerilla attacks."

"Nobody's supporting you," Rachel said. "Even America is against you. It's a new era. There's no place for colonies anymore."

"You think I don't know that?" Gerard added a branch to the fire, balancing it precariously on top of a dying ember and a piece of what was now charcoal.

This was getting too serious. Everything was too serious now. Gerard wanted to see Rachel laughing. He wanted to see the dimples that even her softest smile revealed.

Several months later, on the day before Rachel left for her first posting in the army and two weeks before his own departure back to France, Gerard went with his girlfriend to the new supermarket in Beer Sheva, the first sign of modern life there.

"I love it," she said, moving through the aisles with him in her dun-colored uniform. "The colors, the rustling of the paper bags, the banging of carts against the counters, the *bing-bong* of the cash registers, the dry cold. It's all so unlike our corner *makolet*, so much bigger."

Gerard was reminded of how insular this young country was. His apparently sophisticated girlfriend was impressed with a supermarket. In fact, the place was nothing more than a large grocery store, far smaller than the *supermarchés* that had recently appeared in Paris. Her enthusiasm for something so unremarkable made her even more endearing to him.

"I'll miss you, you know," he told her.

She moved ahead of him to the cashiers. Gerard was holding his only purchase: freshly baked baklava, the sweet nutty desert that he had learned to love since his father's posting to the Middle East.

"Rachel!" he said too loudly. "I said I'll miss you."

She continued talking with the cashier, her back to him. After paying, she started walking out.

He held her arm. "What about us?"

She finally turned to him, her eyes floating in twin pools of tears. "Please stay here and let me go. I hate good-byes."

Gerard's heart sank; he wasn't prepared for such a sudden separation. "Will I see you again?"

She caressed his face. "I love you. I'll miss you more than you can imagine. But I don't know if we'll see each other again." Rachel tried to smile. She gave him a soft kiss on the lips and left.

They wrote to each other faithfully until Gerard enlisted in the French Army and was dispatched to North Africa. He lost touch with Rachel at the same time that he lost his innocence in the hell that Algeria had become.

During his years in the French colony, Gerard lived a life of rage, fear and shame. The rebels' ambushes and night raids targeted all aspects of normal economic life, mainly the French-owned farms and small industries, and the country's transportation and communications services.

His first posting in Algiers was in a unit guarding a secondary phone exchange on the outskirts of town. His commander once sent him and a fellow soldier to town to retrieve rations from the main distribution center. They returned five hours later to find the operators of the exchange, as well as all the soldiers of Gerard's unit, dead. With the exception of his closest buddy, Paul Robert, the soldiers had been killed in battle. Paul and the employees had apparently surrendered, only to have their throats cut.

Gerard threw up when he saw the scene. Paul had been tortured before his death. His badly bruised body, the barely recognizable face with a sunken eye and the nose cut off, and Paul's urine-stained pants would remain forever ingrained in Gerard's memory. He tried, without success, to block his mind from imagining the horror that his friend had felt.

The guerrillas always disappeared amid the population in the mountainous countryside after the attacks. Gerard found himself hating all non-Frenchmen he came across. It didn't help to know that many Muslims, mainly officials of the colonial regime or civilians who refused to support the revolution, were also being targeted. His hate was fueled by raw all-pervading fear. A fear that was in every military encampment, in every army patrol, in every police post.

He found himself fully supporting his country's army as it commenced moving a large section of the rural population in Algeria, including entire communities, to camps under military supervision to prevent them from assisting the Muslim insurgents. The *regroupement* program forcibly removed over two million people, mostly from the mountainous areas, and resettled them in the flatlands, where many were unable to make a living. Thousands died of disease and starvation as a result. A vast number of villages was destroyed, orchards and crops included.

The war effort against the Muslim uprising became increasingly daunting. By the end of the fifties, France had 400,000 soldiers in Algeria, half its standing army. The French public didn't support the effort anymore. A massive campaign led by the likes of Jean-Paul Sartre, Simone de Beauvoir, Marguerite Duras, Françoise Sagan and Simone Signoret defended *"Le Droit d'Insoumission dans la Guerre d'Algérie"*—the right to be insubordinate with respect to the war in Algeria. Having assumed the leadership of the country with a promise to pacify the colony, De Gaulle realized by September, 1959, that it was impossible to continue controlling it. He called for self-determination from the Algerian people. Every Frenchman knew that self-determination was nothing more than a code word for independence.

Because of his knowledge of Arabic, Gerard was transferred to an intelligence unit. An increasingly frustrated French army performed torture of unspeakable cruelty, but Gerard told himself that he wasn't a part of the torture process *per se*. As intelligence, his role was to provide the questions, that was all. His conscience was not assuaged. He was having more and more trouble falling asleep at night, more and more trouble waking up each day. More and more trouble thinking clearly. The breaking point came on the same day that a cease-fire was announced by a French government more frightened of the spread of public disorder into France than of the Algerian rebels themselves.

It was March 19, 1962, the day before Gerard became twenty-one years old. He hadn't slept at all the previous night. He walked in to witness the first interrogation of the day. In a dark and airless room sat a bound young man dressed in a dirty white *gallabiya*, his face partially covered by a long beard. As he waited for the other interrogators to arrive, Gerard started a conversation in Arabic, or tried to. The man wouldn't respond, clearly in a state of absolute panic. Gerard pulled a chocolate bar from his pocket.

"It's okay, relax. Have some chocolate."

"*Non, merci,*" said the Arab.

Gerard impatiently unwrapped the bar and bit into it. He hadn't had anything to eat that day. He massaged his face and as he felt the stubble, realized he had forgotten to shave. Fuck. Too many sleepless nights—he wasn't functioning anymore.

"*Bon abetit,*" said the Arab. The same words Gerard had heard many times around a campfire, years earlier, in Israel.

Gerard looked at the man, dumbfounded. "Ahmed? Is that you?" He tried to imagine the full face behind the beard.

The prisoner gazed at him, mystified.

"What are you doing here, Ahmed?" Gerard moved closer.

"My name is not Ahmed."

"Don't lie to me, I know you too well. Why did you leave Israel and come here? And the beard? Since when have you become that religious?" In Arabic it came out as "Since when have you become so fearful of Allah?"

The man was trembling. Yet, bucked up by the mention of Allah, he gave his answer with arrogance. "I don't know what you're talking about."

Gerard flipped. "Don't lie to me, you two-faced sonofabitch. You're all lying bastards." Gerard punched him in the mouth, and then grabbed him by the hair, pulling his head back, looking to break his neck, his face an inch from the Arab's face. He suddenly smelled urine and looked down. Out of fear the man had wet himself. Gerard looked up again at the man's face.

It wasn't Ahmed. He could see that now. He looked away, his nostrils filled with the urine stench, his mind flooded with images of Robert's body, the face replaced by that of the shaking Arab.

Gerard left the room, banging the door behind him, rubbing the fist that still stung from the blow he had administered, confused to the point of madness, overcome with rage and a simultaneous feeling of deep shame.

Four months later, De Gaulle pronounced Algeria independent. Over one million non-Muslims left the country, accompanied by a significant number of Muslims who had been loyal to the colonial government. They also moved to France and joined the poorest and most alienated sector of its population.

Gerard went back to France a vastly changed man. Gone was the idealistic teenager. In his place was a hardheaded soldier who believed that over a million of his fellow compatriots had been let down by their government. He blamed France's leaders and a left-wing campaign that he believed had been coordinated, or at least influenced, by the Soviet Union.

Gerard had watched the rebels' pretense of talking peace while destroying all possibility of conciliation. It was a known fact that at the beginning of the conflict, their leader, Ben Bella, had already given orders to kill all *interlocuteurs valables*, the representatives of the Muslim communities who were ready to discuss reforms and accommodations with the French. Gerard had seen all the failed attempts at compromise by Charles de Gaulle. He had seen the rebels killing fellow Muslims who had supported a negotiated settlement, even after the French were already leaving.

Gerard left convinced that conflicts in the Middle East could only be solved from positions of strength. The willingness to negotiate was seen by Arabs as weakness. He now believed that a viable long-term peace would only be possible if both sides were convinced there was no chance of winning through violence or intimidation.

His enlightened friends in Paris asserted that he had misunderstood what actually took place in Algeria. Even if he wasn't wrong, they argued, he had no right to generalize his conclusion to the whole Middle East. They accused him of having become a radical—a racist. Gerard told his friends that sometimes one has to be present, to feel something on one's own skin, in order to understand.

And so he joined the SDECE—External Documentation and Counter-espionage Service, France's equivalent of the CIA—determined to transform his experience in the Middle East into an active role in his country's affairs in the region.

Jake found sunset over the island of Qeshm a blessing—a relief, at long last, from the broiling heat and from the helicopters that had circled all afternoon. He let the darkness embrace him, the sound of waves against the Qeshm shore. He saw that Miranda, however dogged her determination might be, was wilting and grateful for respite. As the minutes dragged by, tension began to mount again. Gerard had insisted that they be ready to set out toward the bomb at 8:05. He said that if it hadn't exploded by then, they'd have to rearm it. The last thing Jake wanted to do was get close to a one-kiloton bomb ready to explode.

At exactly 8:00 P.M., it happened.

The flash lit the beach more brightly than had the brutal midday sun. A terrible burning sphere materialized that was crimson and violet and roiling madly within. Just like a nuclear explosion, a mushroom followed, its towering stem made of earth that rose into the sky with the explosion.

"My God!" Miranda gasped.

Ten seconds later they heard the roar—the carnivorous sound of mass-annihilation. Then a flash-flood of air drowned the tranquil breeze that had gently swept the sand only seconds before. And the heat: Once, as a boy, Jake had stood by the open door of the furnace at school, while the janitor fed coal to the hungry fire inside. The heat now felt like that, only it surrounded him completely.

Terror seized him at first. His proximity to the ominous mushroom, the sheer force of the blast, the knowledge of the destruction that such an explosion could wreak: All of it overwhelmed him. He lost his balance and crumpled to the ground, the event on the horizon riveting him to the sand where he fell. He felt awe, and that feeling humbled him.

Finally, the experience transformed Jake. Something the well-groomed doctor said at the hospital came back to him: *The main thing that causes trauma is powerlessness, helplessness. Impotence.* On his knees in the sand, his hair flying back from his face, his eyelids at half-mast in deference to the cosmic brightness, Jake was cleansed. At last he possessed the power to strike at the root of evil.

"Let's go. They're waiting for us." The voice seemed to come from very far away.

Jake slowly turned to face Gerard Duvivier. "What? Who?"

"They're picking us up. We have a short interval now during which to leave the island. Give me your shoes. We can't leave anything behind." Gerard put Jake's shoes into the open maw of a black rubber bag. He had already finished packing everything else. Miranda stood ready, though she was withdrawn and contemplative.

"Where are we going?" Jake asked Gerard.

"See that orange light coming at us?" Gerard switched on a small battery-powered lantern and attached it to the top of the rubber bag. "I'll push the bag. You two just swim next to me."

Jake picked up the bag and began walking toward the surf. "Are you all right with this?" he asked Miranda.

"I'm a good swimmer," she responded gamely.

Jake smiled and nodded. He was fully keyed-up now. "I'll push the bag."

They swam vigorously, Jake in continued awe of the older man's fitness. True to her word, Miranda swam with a smooth stroke and had no trouble keeping up.

Midway, Jake looked back. The area of the blast was still lit by the heat of the explosion. He swam faster.

They clambered onto the small inflatable dinghy, Gerard making a victory sign to its single occupant. The man was sitting at the stern, holding the tiller of the tiny outboard engine, smiling broadly. "We're using a smaller boat and a quieter engine to leave the island," Gerard explained to his partners. "The speedboat we used on the way in would be too easily detectable."

It took them a short while to decide on the best load distribution, and then they sailed away. Gerard said they needed to go west, but because they were on the east side of Qeshm, they would have to circle the island.

Within less than ten minutes, as they reached the pointed end of the island and turned, the pilot spoke to Gerard in Farsi, the words coming rapidly, the tone urgent. He was pointing beyond the little boat's bow. Jake, who was facing aft, toward the pilot, turned around. A huge black area loomed right in front of them, as if there were no stars in that particular part of the sky. Gerard pulled a set of binoculars from their rubber bag. When he was done, Jake reached for them. The image of what had to be a navy ship filled his eyes. It was sailing toward the island, and they hadn't seen it—the peninsula had blocked their view.

"What do you think?" he asked Gerard.

"I don't know. This isn't my area of expertise, and between us, Ardreshir here is no genius."

If both crafts stayed their course, the dinghy would hit the ship smack in the middle of its starboard side in a matter of minutes. Jake saw the silhouette of a helicopter parked on the vessel's stern. Judging by the size of a standard navy helicopter and estimating how many of them would equal the length of the ship, he guessed that it was at least a 300-foot vessel. The outline was clear against the starry sky; they were looking at a frigate, Jake was almost sure. His father had been a sailor during WWII and he was now thankful for the old man's passion for everything Navy. He was also thankful for his own years sailing. The same outline revealed, most ominously, the frigate's surveillance, gunnery and navigation radars. Luckily, these were mounted on an unusually short mast. Jake guessed that this was done to enable the frigate to pass under low bridges.

Gerard said something in Farsi and they made a sudden sharp turn. Jake was happy to be in an inflatable; any other boat would have capsized. Miranda looked a little green around the gills but flashed a thumbs-up when she noticed Jake watching her.

"What are we doing?" Jake asked Gerard.

"Getting the hell away from here."

"No, no. Go straight."

"Why?"

"That's our only chance. We have to stay in the radar's shadow."

"What do you know about that?"

"A lot," Jake said confidently. "Trust me. This is a frigate, and I know its width. This ship's mast is unusually low. That means there's a big area that the radar doesn't cover, because the ship itself blocks its radio waves. Radar won't get anything that's right next to the ship. There are no searchlights on, so we haven't been spotted yet. There's more than an off chance that we're actually too close to be detected by the radar. We've got to stay there, or move even closer. Turn around. *Now.*"

Jake felt his anxiety rise as the two men deliberated. Finally, the pilot turned the tiller and they were again headed toward the frigate.

"Let's give it another minute and then have him turn off the engine. Our only hope is to sail right past them unnoticed."

Gerard translated. Soon, with the engines off, they saw a mountain of steel glide by. Its wake was huge and their little boat was thrown like a rag. Minutes later, the frigate disappeared behind the island. The four of them remained silent for much longer.

"Okay," said Jake. "Let's go." And off they went, into the moonlit night.

Miranda smiled radiantly, her admiration making Jake feel a little self-conscious. But he was pleased to have proven useful after two days as Gerard's baggage.

A few hours after the escape from Qeshm, Jake sat in an Internet café at the Seeb International Airport in Oman. In Arabic and English, a voice announced that the international flight on which they had booked passage was now boarding. Jake took one last look at the document on the screen before him:

TO THE IRANIAN LEADERSHIP AND ALL THOSE INTERESTED IN PEACE AND STABILITY IN THE REGION:

The next explosion will destroy the oil refinery of Bandar Abbas. Like the previous one, any attempt to locate or dismantle the explosive device will cause its immediate detonation.

We urge the immediate evacuation of the area. No one should remain within a five mile radius of the refinery after 18:00 hours today.

We have credible evidence that the popular Islamic Jihad, an affiliate of Al Qaeda based in Iran, is planning to launch a series of attacks on American soil. Iran has the power to stop them.

Our demands are as follows:

1) Popular Islamic Jihad's leaders, Saleem Al Midhar and Sadeq Al Assad, both presently in Tehran, must be arrested before 13:00 hours today and flown to the Hague by 18:00 hours to await trial by the International Criminal Court. Their arrest and deportation shall be videotaped and broadcast promptly on Iranian TV.

2) Attached to this email is a list of organizations and individuals. We demand the closure by 18:00 hours today of the offices of the organizations listed and the arrest and deportation of these individuals within 14 days from the date and time of this message. This also shall be videotaped and promptly broadcast on Iranian TV.

We will *not* detonate the device if the above demands are complied with.

Do not doubt our determination. Iran's support of terrorism will cease, or your country will be unrecognizable by the time we are finished. Other devices are in position throughout Iran. We will continue to detonate them until your government's illegal activities cease once and for all. Stop terrorism or perish.

Jake hit SEND.

After signing off of the computer, he hurried to catch British Airways' 00:15 flight to London.

CHAPTER THIRTEEN

Later that morning, Jake and Miranda stood with Gerard in front of the entrance to the Hammersmith tube station. Newsmen in aprons hawked Fleet Street tabloids. Pedestrians hurried past into the Underground. Jake could hear an endless series of electronic *dings* as riders inserted their tube tickets into the turnstiles and walked through. Naturally, the weather was cold and damp. It wasn't quite raining, though, and for this Jake was grateful.

None of the stated demands had been met by the mullahs. It was 3:20 in Iran—two hours and forty minutes before the scheduled explosion. Gerard emerged from a public phone booth: the classic glass box, its panes divided by bright red mullions. Only now the phone booths were equipped with Internet access and plastered inside with phone-sex ads.

The arrests had not been made. Most ominously, the Iranians had not evacuated the refinery. Around eighty percent of the workers hadn't shown up, tipped off by the barrage of Internet messages and telephone calls that the group's communiqué had triggered. That left twenty percent inside.

"You're not going to proceed with the explosion, are you?" Miranda asked Gerard.

"*Mais oui.* Of course we are."

Jake tried to control his frustration. "We talked about this. I will not be a party to the murder of innocent people. Not if we can possibly avoid it." Jake had held a trump card all along. It was now time to play it.

"What do you propose?" Gerard asked, clearly humoring them.

"Are you one hundred percent sure that all the workers at the refinery are informed of what's going on?"

Gerard sighed. "Apparently, most of those inside heard but simply didn't believe the rumors of the explosion in Qeshm and of the threat against the refinery. Apparently they didn't believe the Internet messages, either. The Iranian press hasn't published anything, of course. Jake, this is a waste of time. We have to do this—you know that. The bomb will go off as planned, and that's that."

Miranda shot Jake a look that meant, *You're not going to sign off on this, are you?* and Jake nodded curtly. Damn right he wasn't. "Gerard. Unless the workers are warned directly and given a last chance to escape, we will not detonate the bomb."

Gerard gazed at Jake in silent challenge, testing his resolve.

"Otherwise I walk—and my money walks with me," Jake said.

Gerard stared into Jake's eyes for a long moment. Finally he turned back to the phone booth and closed its glass-paneled door behind him.

Once, many years ago, Gerard had been in this position, had struggled with precisely Jake's current dilemma. Almost twenty years after Algeria, he lived in Iraq—in al-Tuweitha, on the Tigris River twelve miles southeast of Baghdad, head of security for the French scientists assisting the Iraqis with their nuclear program.

A country virtually without oil resources of its own, France had panicked during the Arab oil embargo of 1973. It was then that the French government decided to take aggressive steps to guarantee its supplies by striking strategic agreements with producers. The main one involved the transfer of nuclear know-how to Iraq in exchange for secure oil deliveries. As part of this agreement France agreed to supply Iraq with a reactor that they baptized Osirak in honor of the acquiring country, in addition to a small research reactor called Isis.

Gerard arrived on the scene in 1975, his main mission to collect information for SDECE on Iraq's efforts to bypass French controls. At first France had pledged to supply Iraq only with low-grade uranium unsuitable for military purposes. Via subsequent threats of cutting oil deliveries, though, Iraq had been able to force France to agree to supply high-grade uranium—material that could be used for the creation of nuclear bombs.

During the summer of 1980, the small French science community at al-Tuweitha gathered to commemorate Bastille Day. That meant many bottles of wine, many odes to liberty, many patriotic songs . . . and a royal hangover. Gerard rose late the following morning, his head exploding, closed the windows of his al-Tuweitha apartment and turned off the light he had left burning the night before. Five-hundred yards away stood a rectangular building covered by a white concrete dome, a few inches thick, fifty feet in diameter and forty-feet tall at its center. The Osirak reactor.

Gerard had had too much to drink, which was happening a lot lately. The more he knew about the project, the more worried he got. The more he informed his superiors of Iraq's real intentions and got no response, the more he drank.

He needed to be distracted from his thoughts. He turned on the radio. Instead of music, the implications of Osirak were being analyzed by Winston Churchill, grandson of the British prime minister, who was a journalist and a Member of Parliament:

"Time is running out. Few who know Israel can imagine that she can permit a situation to come about in which Iraq, which has a self-proclaimed state of belligerence with Israel, has a nuclear weapon sitting in one corner of a hangar with a Soviet-supplied TU22 Blinder strike bomber."

". . . ready to take off," Gerard added out loud.

He thought about what would happen to those working at al-Tuweitha if Israel were to bomb the facility. Could he make sure that the French contingent would be safe? There was no chance of convincing his government to send everyone home to France, unless he was able to secure good intelligence on the attack and its timing.

He decided to speak to the Israelis. He still had a contact with a Mossad operative from four years before, the difficult days of around-the-clock work preparing for the Israeli raid against the hijackers of an Air France flight holding their hostages at Entebbe, Uganda. Via a physicist leaving on vacation, he sent a letter in code.

A few days later, Gerard was leaving the complex on his way to town, after a meeting inside a flat nondescript structure about 2500-feet square, incongruously surrounded with flowers and low green hedges. It was the oldest building in the complex, having been built as a research facility by the Soviets in 1968.

He passed the Osirak reactor and continued walking toward the exit, past a fuel-fabrication site supplied by Italy that was used, Gerard was certain, to assemble uranium blocks employed in the manufacture of plutonium. Typically, the Iraqis claimed that it was a training facility for their personnel. Gerard reached a concrete wall and the innermost gate of the complex. He saluted the guard briskly and continued to the second gate, the only opening in a highly sophisticated electric fence.

Once out of the complex he stepped into his car and drove for two miles past the vast array of anti-aircraft batteries and surface-to-air missile sites surrounding the facility. He was stopped at several armed checkpoints on his way to Baghdad.

As soon as he passed through the last checkpoint, eight miles from the Iraqi capital, he started to sense that he was being tailed. Traffic was still somewhat thin, yet Gerard couldn't identify a specific car that might be following him. It was just a feeling. But he had learned to trust his feelings.

As he entered the city, he thought he had seen the same white Volkswagen Passat three times. But he couldn't be sure; there were too many of them. Brazil had recently shipped twenty-thousand white Passats to Iraq, all of them with red upholstery. All kinds of explanations for the strange sale had been suggested during the Bastille Day party, the most macabre one being that it was easy to wash the white exterior and blood stains wouldn't show too much on the red seats.

Once he left his car, he was absolutely sure. But without any concrete sign, he wasn't ready to bolt for the French embassy.

He went into a pastry shop he knew well, one of the best in Baghdad. He chose a table deep inside, close to the rear exit, and sat with his back against the wall. He ordered a baklava and a Turkish coffee and waited. Just a few sips of the strong thick coffee quickly put his nerves on edge.

The French government had received special permission from Saddam Hussein himself for the members of Gerard's team to carry weapons. But Gerard was off duty, in need of a break. He didn't relish a day-trip to the city with a gun under his arm and another strapped to his calf, so he'd left his sidearms in a drawer at home when setting out for his meeting earlier. Now he felt stupid. Something very serious was about to happen, and he wasn't ready.

Two men entered the shop and looked around, glancing at him, a flicker of interest in the eyes of one of them—a darker-skinned man who looked North African. The men sat at a table between Gerard and the front exit, next to a *narguila*, or water-pipe. They called the waiter, who brought them an assortment of tobaccos in a box. The waiter half-filled their narguila bottle. Gerard liked his filled with *Arak*, the traditional Arab anisette drink. Because the men were clearly on the job, he guessed they had ordered water in theirs.

There were many combinations of tobaccos and mixtures of tobacco and spices or fruits. The men were creating one of their own. The waiter covered the container with a small perforated-aluminum sheet. Someone turned on the radio, and the sound of a *pessteh* by Abu Aziz flooded the place. Gerard observed all with the detachment his training had given him and waited coolly for the men to make their next move.

The waiter placed a piece of burning coal on top of the aluminum foil. The first man sucked on the pipe. As soon as the man exhaled and Gerard was able to get a whiff of the smell, he knew where they were from. The smell of this specific combination of tobacco and fruits was identical to that of many cafes in Algiers. These men were Algerians. What could that possibly mean?

He didn't like not understanding things, especially if those things were as threatening as these two men. All would be clearer if they were Iraqi. He would know that the letter to his Mossad contact had been intercepted and would rehearse the explanation he had prepared.

Time went by and nothing happened. Gerard started to doubt his instincts, since the men didn't seem at all preoccupied with him. He called out to the waiter, asking for the check. The waiter brought it and walked to the entrance, where he lit a cigarette. The men didn't move. Gerard paid and left a one-dinar tip. He then stood up and started walking toward the front exit.

As he got close to the men, midway in the store, the darker Algerian stood up and turned toward him. The man put his hands behind his neck as if yawning, thereby letting his jacket open. A holstered gun showed. He said quietly in French, "I advise you to return to your table."

The waiter saw Gerard hesitating and asked from the door, "Would you like anything else?"

The distance to the door was at least five yards. Three, maybe four, seconds. More than enough time for the man to draw his gun and fire several shots into his back.

"May I have another baklava? And another Turkish coffee. Very hot, please." Gerard would have to use the back exit. He returned to his table. He decided to wait for his pastry—might as well enjoy it while he allowed time for the tension to subside and the men's alertness to wane.

After a few minutes he saw a silhouette of a third person against the outside light at the entrance to the café. One of the men nodded in silent welcome. Now Gerard was up against not two, but three, operatives. Still, he confirmed to himself that he would be able to turn the table, crouch, and using it as a shield, lunge toward the exit, past the curtain of beads that served as the back door.

The third operative entered, face hidden by the glare of the outside light, and walked directly toward him, one arm at hip level, the other extended forward. Gerard began to duck, but then the face in shadow caught the light from the flickering fluorescent fixture.

He couldn't believe his eyes.

"Rachel?"

It made total sense. Nobody better for the job. Gerard knew exactly what he had to do.

He smiled broadly.

Rachel didn't. She was angry, very angry.

"How does it feel, helping the people who will destroy us?" She spoke to him in French.

"Why do you say that? I'm in charge of the security of my country-men."

She was still slim and her face was the same, the beautiful olive skin still smooth, not a wrinkle to be seen.

"You still have Scheherazade's eyes, you know."

Still standing, Rachel smiled, guardedly. "I'm sorry. I rehearsed what to say so many times, but I couldn't control myself when I saw you. Really, do you have any idea what is being built there?"

"Of course I do. That's why I contacted the Mossad. I also know you will strike against this facility, and when that happens I want to protect our people."

"What makes you think that we will attack al-Tuweitha?"

"Look, Rachel, I'm not playing games with you. Show me the same respect."

She was silent.

"Anyway, I told you what my initial intentions were." He was ready for the plunge. "Now let me tell you what my intentions *are* after see-ing you."

She lifted her eyebrows inquisitively and sat down.

"If there's one thing I learned in Algeria . . . And by the way, what are you doing with these Algerians?" He pointed with his chin at the two men, who were still sitting at their table, smoking quietly.

"Algerian Jews. They left for Israel as children, in '62. They have perfect covers—both are construction workers. That enables them to circulate freely in this country without raising suspicions."

"Right."

"I needed them—I was sent in from Israel to meet you, and I know nothing about this place. You were saying that there was something you learned in Algeria?"

She is much more composed than I am, Gerard thought. He nodded. "The only thing that counts with Arabs is power. Nuclear capability is the ultimate power. And if you saw what I've seen in this country over the last five years, you'd agree with me that Saddam Hussein is the last person on Earth who should have this power. I knew this all along, but I needed to see you to clear my head."

"What do you mean?"

"I mean that I know this facility has to be destroyed." He inhaled deeply. "And I will help you do it. But there's one condition: I want my people safe. Can you assure me of that?"

"I think I can."

"Good. So what are the next steps?"

"We'll get you a list of questions we need answered: exact location of the radioactive material we have to avoid bombing, et cetera." Rachel looked Gerard in the eye. "This could be risky for you, you know."

"I know," he answered nonchalantly. He found himself posturing for her, as if he were seventeen again. "Are we done with business for now?"

She nodded.

"Then tell me about your life these last twenty-odd years. I see you're still doing intelligence work. Children?"

"No," she answered, clearly uncomfortable. "How about you?"

Gerard shook his head. "Married once, quick divorce. Apparently I'm not as easy to live with as I thought."

Rachel laughed. "I could've told you that."

"How about you? Married?" He held his breath.

"No. I'm not easy, either."

"Have you been in touch with Ahmed?"

Rachel smiled. "All the time. He has a huge family. Eleven children. Seven boys. He's a tour guide now."

"A tour guide?"

Rachel shrugged. "It's hard to make a living as a tracker."

They spoke for another hour, until well after Rachel had signaled to the Algerians that they could leave. Finally she looked at her watch and got up abruptly. "I need to go."

"Will I see you again?" Once again the sudden separation. It was as if the twenty-two years had not passed.

But this time the answer was different. "Yes, you will." She put her hand over his hand. "You'll see me a lot."

Iraq attacked Iran two months later, starting a war that would last eight years and would kill close to a million people. Within two weeks, Iran twice attacked al-Tuweitha by air, causing very limited damage. As a result, the al-Tuweitha facility was reinforced by the Iraqis. More significantly, modifications were made to the research reactor, allowing it to start producing plutonium.

In subsequent meetings with Rachel, Gerard gave her complete information on the operation of the facility, from full descriptions of each part of the complex to exact schedules of work. He was assured that the planned Israeli attack would minimize any risk to the scientists and their family. And the wait was on. Months went by.

"The Osirak reactor is going hot in three weeks," Gerard told Rachel over tea and pastries at the shop where they had first reunited.

She nodded. "Yes, you told us that already."

"Once it's hot, any attack will involve extensive dispersal of radiation."

Her face showed no expression.

During the first week of June, a barrage of explosions broke the quiet of a Sunday afternoon. Today is the day, Gerard thought, his heart beating wildly. Thank God it's Sunday, so none of us are at the reactor.

He ran to the window of his apartment. The sky was full of small black and gray clouds—the explosions he'd heard were the sound of anti-aircraft artillery. Yet he saw no attacking plane. Is this only an exercise, he wondered.

No more than a minute later, he saw them. Eight planes. All F-16s. He watched while each one swooped over the reactor and dropped two bombs on the dome. He felt the explosions as the ground shook under him. It was all very precise. The planes approached at exactly the same angle, performed exactly the same maneuvers and flew away. It took less than two minutes. The ineffective AA fire went on for fifteen minutes longer. And it was over.

The following day he was told that the attack had destroyed the reactor completely, while missing the stored uranium and thereby avoiding radiation dispersion. Unfortunately, a young electrician had chosen to go to work early Sunday afternoon, the single French casualty of the air raid.

Four months later, France's foreign trade minister visited Baghdad and confirmed his government's decision to rebuild the reactor. This time, though, France refused to offer 93-percent-enriched uranium. The fuel delivered would be unsuitable for the production of uranium bombs. France also demanded the return of the twelve kilograms of enriched uranium, unless the two countries were able to reach an agreement allowing for France's complete control of the project to prevent it from being used for military objectives.

A few months after that, in part because it had failed to provide any warning of Israel's surprise attack, the SDECE ceased to exist. In the largest ever shake-up of French intelligence agencies, it was merged into the newly formed General Directorate of External Security: the DGSE.

In Paris, walking to Gerard's favorite wine bar on the Ile St. Louis, Rachel stopped, put her hands around his neck, looked at him earnestly, and smiled. "And who said that one man can't make a difference?" Her face showed respect. "You've saved countless lives. Our operation couldn't have succeeded without you."

Gerard kissed her on the forehead. He started to whistle and continued walking, one hand on her shoulder, the other in his pocket, his shoulders back and his head held high.

Gerard came out of the London phone booth, slamming its door behind him. As he rejoined Jake and Miranda, he reserved a frosty look for each of them. "All right. I passed your demand along," he said gruffly.

He had been on the phone for almost thirty minutes—so long that Jake had bought a London *Times* from a nearby vendor.

WHO ARE THEY? the front-page banner headline asked. A subhead at the bottom of the page said, *U.S. Denounces Terrorist Threat against Iran.* Beneath that, an article began,

> Unnamed United States officials denounced the threat against
> Iran even as others accused the Islamic republic of being a major

supporter of terrorist activities against the United States and in the Middle East.

"The country is a source of concern for those who are looking for peace and stability in the region, and its pursuit of a nuclear strike capability is unacceptable, but we will never condone any form of terrorism," said the American president's national security adviser . . .

Jake was still reading when Gerard returned. "What's the verdict?"

"Our Iranian contacts will distribute pamphlets in the refinery, with copies of foreign newspapers that reported the Qeshm blast. It will be taken care of in the next two hours. There will be no need to postpone the explosion."

Jake nodded. "Thanks."

Miranda hugged the unflappable Frenchman. He looked embarrassed for a moment but quickly regained his poise.

"Now they are able to smuggle the leaflets in, even with the heightened security around the refinery, but once their people start distributing them, they will get arrested, never to be heard from again. They wanted us to know that."

"There's nothing we can do about that," Miranda said. "It's a choice between them and the much larger number of innocent workers."

Twenty minutes later, they sat in the restaurant of the St. Martin's Lane hotel, at a table in back, eating lunch.

"Now I owe you one," Jake said. "And I'm willing to pay up. What do you need from me?"

Gerard didn't hesitate to answer. "Twelve million dollars."

"May I ask what it's for?"

"We run an expensive operation. Very expensive. We have supporters in several countries who do it for the cause, like Reza. The majority, though, are in it for the money. And these people need to be paid." Gerard shrugged. "It's that simple."

"Understood. I can do that." Jake had just agreed to part with $12 million, not a penny of which he would ever see again. He felt nothing.

He tasted a forkful of the chef's salad brought to the table by their waiter, recoiled, and wondered how the British could manage to ruin so simple a meal.

"I hope you can tell me now," Jake said, laying down his fork and patting his mouth with a napkin, "because I'm curious. How did you do it? How did you station these devices?"

"In 1997," Gerard said, "Delgado and Stone started buying the nuclear explosives. On seven August, 1998, Al Qaeda attacked your embassies in Nairobi and Dar-es-Salaam. Over 250 people died, mostly Africans. Delgado and Sam believed, correctly, that several Arab countries were supporting these terrorists in one way or another. Actually, they included Pakistan at that time, which isn't Arab, in that group. Pakistan's Inter Service Intelligence, until 9/11 and the Musharaf about-face, was very close to bin Laden."

"Pakistan?"

"Yes. And if you ask me, I still don't know if they really changed or if Musharaf isn't just playing both sides. Anyway, Delgado and Sam decided to place the nuclear devices in strategic locations throughout the Arabian Peninsula and Pakistan. I was invited to join the group. They wanted my knowledge of the infrastructure projects going on in the region."

"And the non-nuclear bombs?"

"In 2000, octanitrocubane—ONC—was synthesized at the University of Chicago. It solved a big problem for us. We needed an explosive potent enough to allow us to create deterrence at a nuclear level, without actually needing to use a nuclear weapon. It's still not perfect—this Qeshm explosion alone necessitated six trucks full of ONC. Qeshm is an island, and not so well-patrolled, but you can imagine how hard it was to get the stuff to Iran's mainland and to place it at the other targets. Not to mention the enormous cost of the material itself."

Miranda interrupted. "I'm assuming the CIA funded the purchase of this material—and of the nukes, right?"

Gerard nodded. Jake smiled wryly.

"And now you need my $12 million. So I take it that the CIA's no longer a part of this?"

Gerard hesitated. "The CIA financed our group at the beginning. Recently, they withdrew funding. That's one reason we brought you aboard. Now the CIA's relationship to us is strictly one of plausible deniability."

Jake nodded. This was about what he had expected. "How did you station the weapons?"

"We bought a series of small companies with infrastructure maintenance contracts in the countries we were targeting—from forklift operating to road paving to toilet cleaning. Anything that would get us inside our targets. All we needed was a team we could trust to install the bombs with their individual systems for remote detonation. Danny took care of that. Israel has an endless supply of agents who can pass for Arabs. Some of them *are* Arabs. Over the years, they've absorbed over half a million Arab Jews."

"Who did you buy the infrastructure companies from?"

No answer. Jake could tell that he had caught Gerard off guard. There was something there.

"C'mon, level with me. Who did you buy them from?"

Gerard shook his head. "It's irrelevant. What do you care?"

"I care because you're so reluctant to answer my question. Unless you can honestly tell me that I'm endangering you by knowing, I want to know."

Gerard breathed deeply. "His name is Abdel Aziz Rifaat."

"Who's he?"

More hesitation. Then, "A wealthy Egyptian. Part of his business was doing maintenance on government installations throughout the Middle East. He was bright and gutsy, a rising star."

"Okay." Jake still wondered why that gave Gerard pause.

"He was also DGSE's best asset in the region, and I was his main handler. He provided us with an unending source of information. Whenever we needed to find out something about the local activities of an American company, for example, he was there. In exchange for all this information, we made sure he got the best construction contracts with the French companies doing business in the Middle East. That's how he became rich."

Gerard spread butter on a roll and ate it.

Jake waited patiently. He'd become accustomed to the Frenchman's conversational rhythm, but this was different.

"For many, it was a foregone conclusion that in a few years Rifaat's construction empire would rival that of the bin Ladens. And it *was* going to happen. The construction jobs the French companies gave him made certain of that."

Jake wondered where the hell Gerard was going with this. He glanced over at Miranda and saw her listening attentively, as if she knew Gerard was about to reveal something important.

"Eventually, I asked him if he would consider selling the old maintenance business. Obviously I didn't tell him that the buyer would be our anti-terror organization. He agreed."

Big deal, Jake thought. No need for all the mystery. Then a thought came to him out of nowhere. "Hold it. Why did you say that this Rifaat *was* doing all this? Is he dead?"

Gerard smiled. "I thought I had gotten away with it." He leaned closer, eyes drifting from Jake's to Miranda's and back. "I'm going to tell you something that I'd planned to withhold until later. It will be a challenge for you to keep your focus after I say this."

"Go on."

"Rifaat isn't a construction mogul anymore. Soon after he sold the maintenance operation to us, he announced his decision to retire and sell the rest of his companies."

"Uh, huh."

"And he disappeared."

"What do you mean, 'disappeared?'"

"He's gone underground. We haven't seen him since." There was a pregnant pause. "Rifaat is now a master terrorist. He's the administrative brain, most likely the real boss, of the Popular Islamic Jihad and—in the terminology that Rifaat himself would use—its franchisees, all the terrorist groups that are its offshoots. He rose to the top in five years. Easy to accomplish with his kind of cash and his shrewdness."

"How did that happen?"

"We can only speculate. But it now appears that Rifaat had been very religious for many years, only he kept it well-hidden. We believe he turned fully on the 20th of February, 1998, when bin Laden and several others issued their famous *fatwa* establishing a World Islamic Front for Jihad against Jews and Crusaders. 'Crusaders' is their code word for Christians."

"Yet he continued to cooperate with the DGSE."

"By then he was already an enemy, using our money to prepare his next step." Gerard shook his head. "I didn't see it."

The waiter approached their table somewhat gingerly. Jake raised his hand. The waiter drifted away. English discretion, Jake thought.

"What do you mean you didn't see it?" Miranda asked.

"Because I was his handler, we were close. I should have seen it coming," Gerard repeated. "When we bought his maintenance company, the sonofabitch had been working against the West for years. He conned me for that long."

Jake inhaled deeply. "That's a biggie."

"It's bigger."

"What?"

"The Popular Islamic Jihad is the group that sponsored Ashraf Ismail's trip to the States. To Boston, and then to the toy store in New York City."

Jake felt his scalp tingle. "What are you telling me?" He sensed Miranda's eyes on him, gauging his reaction.

"The man you're looking for—the man ultimately responsible for the deaths of your wife and daughter—is Abdel Aziz Rifaat."

CHAPTER FOURTEEN

The day after the Qeshm explosion, as the world tried to adjust to the knowledge that an anti-terrorist organization had detonated a one-kiloton bomb and might have deployed many more, Abdel Aziz Rifaat was in Paris for a coordination meeting with the Algerian GIA—the Armed Islamic Group.

France was the only country outside the Middle East where Rifaat felt safe. He had a solid base of support in the local Arab community and excellent forged papers identifying him as a recent immigrant from Algeria. His current contact in French intelligence would also keep him apprised of any danger. When told about the threat of a one-kiloton bomb in Iran, he didn't believe it—the world was filled with lunatics. And a bomb of this size? A joke.

The following morning, he sat with Jasim, his second-in-command. He remained outwardly calm when told of the bomb blast at Qeshm and the threat that followed it: to detonate another bomb, a device planted somewhere in the Bandar Abbas refinery, where Rifaat once had been in charge of maintenance.

His mind instantly flashed to a particular day soon after he'd sold his company, when he ran into the deputy manager of MMS—one of his first employees—on the streets of Cairo.

"I'm on holiday. Unplanned," the man had said, significantly.

"What's going on?"

"All workers have been removed from the maintenance sites and given two weeks paid vacation."

"That's unusual."

The man nodded. "We were told that a team from the head office would be coming in to perform job quality audits."

Something important was happening at those sites. Rifaat wanted to know exactly what it was.

He searched for the two DGSE men. He located one of them. But even under torture the man wouldn't disclose anything. When his interrogators paused for a cigarette and left him alone, the man killed himself. Rifaat dispatched a team to look for the second Frenchman, but the agent had vanished.

Now, at last a clear connection was being suggested—between the mysterious buyer who, with the assistance of the DGSE agents, had arranged to pay him far too much for his maintenance company and the curious temporary removal of MMS employees; and the threatened presence now of another bomb at Bandar Abbas. It seemed likely that the unknown buyer had purchased MMS precisely so as to gain access to the Iranian refinery, making today's threatened explosion possible.

"Why didn't you call me when the bomb went off last night?" Rifaat shouted at his second-in-command, even though he knew he was being unfair. After all, he had turned off his cell phone at the gentlemen's club where he'd met the GIA chief.

"I couldn't get through," Jasim said, clearly miserable to have disappointed his leader.

"You could have called Khalil."

"I did. He said you didn't want to be disturbed." True, his bodyguard had come into the private room just when Rifaat had convinced a comely blonde dancer to give him oral sex for $200 euros. Rifaat had sent him away.

"And when I came back here?" He was shouting now.

"I tried, but you told me to shut up," the lieutenant replied, his voice shaking. True again. Rifaat had been drunk when he returned to the hotel. And concentrating fully on his upcoming sexual challenge with the French stripper, who'd come back with him for only another $200. She'd gotten a bargain, as it turned out—this time Rifaat had been unable to consummate.

"You fucking incompetent son of a goat!" he cried, slapping Jasim's face. "Get out!"

Rifaat showered for an unusually long time. He wanted to forget the woman. All women. By the time he finished dressing, he was calm and purposeful again.

He called Jasim back in and favored his lieutenant with a benevolent half-smile.

"Tell me, my friend, have we heard from Saajid?"

"Yes. Burke is still out of the country. When he returns, Saajid will welcome him home."

Rifaat nodded. That was satisfactory. "It's imperative that we find my old acquaintance from DGSE—Gerard Duvivier. This is now a top priority. Can you do that for me?"

"I will not fail you, sir," Jasim promised. Again, Rifaat was content with the answer. Jasim had been a bureaucrat before entering Rifaat's service, but the man was clever and resourceful. He had not earned his place without proving again and again that he was a true scimitar of jihad.

"Excellent. Now, we must not let the infidels' challenge go unanswered. We will accelerate the American campaign."

Jasim looked uncomfortable. If he had one flaw, in Rifaat's estimation, it was his conservative nature. But that was why he did not lead.

"Accelerate . . . how much?" Jasim asked, swallowing.

"The Wave must break. Immediately."

Jasim nodded, resigned. "Those cells are still in training and reconnaissance . . ."

"They know what to do. Give the order."

Jasim knew better than to question Rifaat's judgment. They discussed the particulars and he hurried off to execute the most serious attack on American soil since September 11th.

Rifaat's breakfast tasted unusually delicious, despite the inability of the French to approximate Egyptian cuisine. He was in good spirits. In a fight, an enemy's strike invariably left him vulnerable to a counterpunch. Hit hard enough, he wouldn't get another chance.

CHAPTER FIFTEEN

Jake said nothing after Gerard's revelation. His world had shrunk to a tiny point of light. He was flabbergasted.

He was ecstatic.

Abdel Aziz Rifaat. Jake committed the name to memory.

"We're looking for him, too," Gerard said. "Jake? Do you hear me?" His voice grew quieter. "Rifaat's the only vulnerability in our plan. He sent people into several of the sites, asking questions and trying to find out what we did there."

Jake struggled to focus on what felt like insignificant details, a visual image of this Rifaat assembling and clarifying in his mind. "Did he find anything out?"

"We don't know. We learned about a few instances of his people snooping around. What about the times we didn't hear of? We used local labor to do a lot of the jobs, except placement of the bombs themselves. That went to the Israelis. That and the regular maintenance that the bombs undergo. We just performed an update on all sites. Will Rifaat put two and two together? Who knows. But when bombs start exploding where his former company does maintenance, he'll figure it out soon enough. The plan will only be relatively safe when this man is gone."

"That explains a lot," Miranda remarked.

"It does, doesn't it?" Gerard smiled wearily. "Don't feel bad, but killing Ashraf really wasn't the best idea. We needed him to locate Rifaat."

Jake didn't need that thrown in his face once more. "But how can you be certain that Ashraf would've taken you to Rifaat?"

Gerard nodded. "That we know for sure. Rifaat used to tell me about his army buddy who ended up killing Sadat—Hamza El Biali, who turned out be Ashraf's brother."

Hamza El Biali. *Pharaoh is dead*, Jake thought.

Gerard continued. "And this dovetails with something else. Old information, but good. From the Guantanamo interrogations. Ashraf was protected by someone high up in the organization."

Jake's eyes floated back to the newspaper. Under the *WHO ARE THEY?* headline was a picture of the Bandar Abbas refinery. Clearly a huge facility. He tried to visualize what was happening there. He lifted his eyes from the newspaper to look at Gerard. "Let's go back to the bombs. How did you know they wouldn't be found and deactivated in the first place?"

"The nuclear devices are all encased in thick lead boxes, so that no radiation can leak and be detected. The only thing outside the box is a thin wire that serves as the antenna for the radio signal. This system is the same for both the ONC and nuclear bombs. It's like the ones embedded in the windscreens of luxury cars. And they're all well hidden. In the Bandar Abbas refinery the bomb is an ONC one. It's much smaller than the one in Qeshm, but the explosion will be magnified by the content of the tank where it's hidden. The bomb is in the bottom of a very large jet fuel tank. There's a false bottom over the bomb. Even if the tank gets cleaned, the bomb can't be found."

Miranda didn't look sold. "What if it is? Found."

"That's our biggest risk. They'll explode if anyone tampers with them in any way, or even tries to move them. It would be a disaster, we know. But we can't allow these bombs to fall into the wrong hands."

"Rifaat," Jake enunciated, giving the name the significance it deserved.

"Or anyone else. But yes, mainly Rifaat."

Jake sensed something. "What else?"

"That's it."

"What else?"

"As long as you promise not to start worrying too much."

"I won't worry if you stop treating me like a fucking child. Tell the whole story, for Christ's sake." The waiter turned in response to Jake's raised voice and then turned away discreetly.

"Ease off, Jake," Miranda said. "Gerard's on our side."

Gerard sighed, ran his fingers through his hair. "Rifaat is a deadly enemy. Just as we are chasing him, he's chasing us. You've met four of us. One of these days, we'll introduce you to Big Ben. That makes five. We once were six. Andre Dahan was my second-in-command. He also dealt with Rifaat. He's dead. You see this?" Gerard looked around, stuck thumb and index finger into his mouth and pulled from a molar what looked like a tooth crown. "There's potassium cyanide in here."

"You're kidding," Jake said, though clearly Gerard was not. Miranda leaned closer to examine the capsule.

Gerard shook his head and continued. "Andre was found dead in the trunk of a car in Riyadh. An autopsy showed that he had died of cyanide poisoning. Someone got him, got the disk and was trying to get the code. Remember the disk?" Gerard again looked around. He patted his chest and pulled the wallet partially out of the pocket of his blazer. "I gave you a code to get started. That was for communication only. There's one code for communication and one code to start the detonation procedure. Any one of us can detonate any one of the bombs."

"No two signatures, huh?"

"Not feasible. We had to trust each other completely. And we do."

Miranda sat back, face a little paler than a few moments before. "How do you know Rifaat's the one who got to him?"

"No disk was found. His body showed signs of extensive torture. He probably used the cyanide when he couldn't withstand it any longer. But no bomb went off. So he didn't give the code away."

Miranda shivered. "Maybe he did. Maybe Rifaat is waiting for the right time to detonate."

"He'll be in for a big disappointment. The codes change every day. And since Andre's disappearance, we all have new disks and code systems."

Jake nodded. "Rifaat might've figured that out, if he tried to blow anything up in the meantime. Next time he won't wait."

"We're assuming that. We're also assuming that if he's searching for anyone, it's me."

"Why?"

"Because I'm the only one left who's been in touch with Rifaat. He doesn't know the others. Shall we get the check?" Gerard signaled to the waiter.

"Wait—if you're the one he's after, then why expose yourself by going to Iran? Why didn't you let the others make the trip?"

Gerard shrugged. "I'm the only one who knows the country, the language. And it's not as though the Popular Islamic Jihad has Interpol working for it. They have limited resources, to say the least. So I was fairly confident I wouldn't be noticed. *Won't* be noticed," Gerard corrected himself.

Miranda was still uneasy. Jake wondered if she was having second thoughts. "But they got your colleague."

"True. But this was a while ago. It happened after a meeting at the French embassy in Saudi Arabia. One of our theories is that Rifaat had a mole in there—which would explain how they were able to find Andre. He generally flew under the radar, stayed hidden from view. That's why I'm even more careful these days."

The waiter brought the check. Both men went for it. For a moment they engaged in a small tug of war. Finally Gerard let go. Jake paid in cash.

"Thank you, sir." The waiter bowed and disappeared.

"How sure are you that the bomb will explode?"

"Fairly. All detonation systems have double redundancy. That means that if the original system fails, there are two others as back-up."

"Mm-hmm."

"Having said that, there are a multitude of things that could go wrong. Don't make me start thinking about them. We did the best we could."

"Right." This was less than completely reassuring.

"The systems themselves are pretty simple. After we insert the disk, we input the detonation code and that brings up a list of locations and the type of bombs. We just double-click on the chosen target. Depending on what time and what day it is, the program gives us a code. It also gives us a phone number. When we are ready, we place a phone call to that number, which is in a house or an apartment that we have rented or bought close to the targets. An answering machine picks it up. If we punch the code during the phone call, the answering machine turns on a powerful radio frequency transmitter. Its signal triggers the bomb's detonation. It's a small variation on what's used in most remote explosions. The advantage is that even if someone enters the apartment or house in question, all they'll see is a telephone, an answering machine, and an old radio, which is where the transmitter is."

Lunch over, they sat in Jake's suite at the Lanesborough. Gerard's body language betrayed the tension he was experiencing. He shifted in his chair and his left eye blinked involuntarily. There was an uncanny contrast between their highly civilized surroundings, from the carved mahogany and the old books to the crystal glasses and whiskey bottle that the butler had just left for them, and the scenes they were watching on TV. The BBC was transmitting jointly with Al Jazeera.

One of the networks had posted a cameraman on a rooftop in the city of Bandar Abbas, with the refinery as a distant background. At a studio in London, three BBC commentators speculated on the power of the Qeshm bomb. A digital display showing the countdown to the announced time of the explosion behind him, the network's anchorman provided background information on recent Iranian history, from the rise to power of the Shah to the present day. BBC's Mideast correspondent filled in additional details on a connection via satellite, his answers delayed by a couple of seconds. The coverage was relaxed, as if in preparation for some sports championship finals.

Suddenly the correspondent's voice grew agitated. "Something's happening at the gates of the refinery," he announced, peering through a pair of what looked like high-powered binoculars.

"Come on, let's get a better shot here," Miranda exhorted the screen, leaning closer to the TV. The camera zoomed toward the gate, but was too far from the action to reveal any significant detail.

"It looks like some people are massed against the gates," the reporter said. "They are trying to leave the refinery and, and . . . apparently they are being prevented from doing so. There is a struggle in progress."

Jake realized he was literally on the edge of his seat. The TV images of the refinery were blurry, but he could now discern the gist of the action.

The reporter was shouting. "They've broken through! They've broken through! It looks like hundreds of people are leaving, running away. The guards, too."

Jake was ecstatic. He stood up and shared a joyous high-five with Miranda. But Gerard merely gazed at Jake's upraised palm.

"Don't you get it?" Jake said. "If enough civilians were killed, the whole thing would backfire on us." Jake almost stopped at his unintentional use of the word "us." He saw that Gerard had noticed it too. "This is great! It looks like the guards were under instructions to keep the workers from leaving. This'll look horrible for the Iranian regime."

Gerard said nothing. He wasn't denying, though, that Jake's analysis was correct.

But less than an hour later, when the time came for the explosion, nothing happened.

One minute, two minutes went by. Nothing. Three minutes. Gerard buried his head in his hands and muttered in French. The BBC anchorman started to speculate that the "terrorists" had bluffed and lost. That the Iranian regime hadn't blinked and would emerge from the episode significantly strengthened. The correspondent in Iran agreed, albeit cautiously at first. After five minutes Jake could hear the disappointment in their voices. They'd wanted action. With considerable awkwardness, they started to wrap up the program.

And then, "Oh, my God! Oh, my God! There it is!"

The correspondent's voice, hoarse with emotion, was drowned out by the roar of the blast. The image became grainy and disappeared momentarily. Then it was replaced by shots from another news camera positioned elsewhere. The second camera showed the shockwave of a series of explosions blowing the walls from buildings, bending towers and flattening storage tanks. Jake realized that on top of the tank's jet fuel, the crude oil and the finished products, as well as the other byproducts of the refinery, had magnified the explosion and multiplied the heat emanating from the fireball.

"Let's pray no one gets hurt," Miranda said, watching pensively.

A second correspondent was on camera now, a woman. Though clearly British, her head was covered per local custom. But then her scarf was whipped off by the searing wind, and her mousy hair blew crazily across her face.

"It's very hot and windy here," she reported stoically. "It smells of sulfur. This is what hell . . ." The sound dropped out. Then, after a last silent take of the woman's frightened face, the image went grainy for an instant before the transmission returned to the London BBC studios.

As Miranda paced, both men sat quietly. Jake saw that Gerard was dumbfounded. And so was he, as he tried in vain to comprehend the destructive power they had helped unleash.

It was time for the group to step forward and identify itself. An hour later, from an Internet café on Leicester Square, Miranda released a third document. Jake, of course, gave it a quick perusal before it went out.

This is a declaration by STOP to the world, the statement began. We are an international anti-terrorism organization called Suspend Terrorism Or Perish—STOP.

The acronym had been Delgado's idea. Jake found it corny but hadn't objected. He needed to choose his battles, and this was a minor issue. The document warned of the destruction of the Iranian refinery of Tabriz, to take place within twenty-four hours. Like the last one, this communiqué urged the compliance with the previous demands and the immediate and full evacuation of the facility.

Less than two hours later, they saw on CNN's Breaking News that an organization calling itself the Iranian Liberation Front had released a manifesto:

Peace be upon you. We are the Iranian Liberation Front.

Fellow Iranians,

The events of 1978–1979 were the inevitable consequence of a monarchy beholden to foreign interests and disconnected from the people. Its many genuine achievements notwithstanding, and despite its propaganda to the contrary, that regime promoted decadence and corruption.

We believed that with the Islamic Revolution of 1979 we were getting independence and honest government.

Instead, what we have is a country ruled by mullahs whose religious training is no substitute for managerial aptitude. We have incompetence in every sector of the government. We have theft and we have impunity. Their use of religion as a cover for their activities has only denigrated Islam.

We have a country where the rule of law, a cornerstone of Islam and stressed so eloquently throughout the Koran, does not exist.

We have nepotism and favoritism in the job market. We have no freedom of expression; strangers tell us what to watch or listen to and which clothes to wear.

We live during one of the darkest chapters in Iranian history, second only to the Arab conquest. We are subjugated by a seventh-century Arab mentality that, once again, totally ignores the identity of the Iranian nation and by doing that, suffocates it.

Yet we have no doubt that this Islamic Republic will inevitably be considered a transitional period in the annals of Iranian history. The dark ages will not last indefinitely. The day will come when there is a democratic Iran, with a new constitution that establishes religion as a private matter for each citizen, completely free from governmental interference.

A referendum was organized soon after the revolution in 1979. By a landslide, the Iranian people chose an Islamic theocratic republic. This republic has now been in effect for over twenty-five years and certainly has had a chance to prove itself.

We demand that a new referendum be organized so that the Iranian people may voice their opinion on the fruits of the

Islamic Republic by voting for or against it, thus answering the question, "Do you want a new government?" Such a referendum shall be held in an environment of total freedom.

In this referendum, the people will be able to vote for or against the removal of the tyrants and their replacement by a democratically elected government without a supreme leader, a Council of Guardians, an Expediency Council, or an Assembly of Experts.

"Who are these people?" Jake asked Gerard. "Are we in touch with them?"

"Reza once mentioned them to me, but no. My guess is that either he is part of this Iranian Liberation Front or he knows them well. At the time I let it pass. It didn't seem to me that we should get involved in their internal politics. The others agreed."

Sparked by the ILF's manifesto, widespread rioting commenced. Over two hundred protesters were hurt and twenty-three killed in Tehran's Azadi Square alone. In a televised address, the recently elected Iranian president, Mullah Aznaveh, urged calm. He rejected the demands of the Iranian Liberation Front and accused the United States and Israel of supporting the Iranian Liberation Front and STOP.

"We are not Chile," he declared, "and Ayatollah Khamenei is not Allende. Nor will you bring this regime down like you brought down Mossadegh. This is not 1953."

He said that Iran wanted peaceful relations with all nations in the world with the exception of Israel, and that it deplored and condemned all terrorist acts against civilians.

The government of Iran announced that no concessions would be made to terrorists. It informed its people that it was evacuating the refinery as a precaution. There was no reason to worry, however, since the devices, if indeed they existed, would be disabled shortly.

To Jake's horror, the Tabriz refinery exploded before the scheduled time, the result of an Iranian effort to defuse the bomb, the first that they'd managed to find. Close to one hundred perished, most of them the technicians sent in by the government to neutralize the bomb.

Shaving and getting dressed in his London hotel suite the following day, Jake watched the riots that had engulfed Tehran on CNN. Chaos appeared to reign throughout the city. Images of overturned cars and widespread looting, of the same street kiosk being burned down, repeated every half-hour. CNN appeared to have a formula that determined how frequently violence should be depicted. A dearth of footage merely yielded repetition of the same images.

Jake had no patience for that. He switched to another channel. There, the hand-held images were initially subdued: crowds milling around, young Iranian men throwing rocks and bottles at passing cars, protesters confronting police, some men attempting to set a car on fire; then the lynching of a policeman who had shot at the crowd, his face a blur of fear and blood. Several men were dragging him around, hitting him with their fists, with wooden bats and metal pipes. With stones. After a while the policeman was inert. They hung him upside down, blood covering his open eyes and dripping from his hair. A man approached with a knife and slit his throat. Then everyone started dancing.

Hypnotized, Jake sat on the edge of the unmade double bed, in the dim room the curtains of which he hadn't yet opened. His mind was a jumble of thoughts and emotions. He wondered if the policeman was already dead when his throat was cut. He wondered at the courage of the cameraman willing to stay so close to the violence, to the blood lust. He wondered at the network's willingness to air the gruesome scene. He felt faint.

He tried to imagine what regular Iranians—not the crazies—must be feeling. Was it elation? Fear? Now flames licked the walls of a five-story office building, shooting from its windows. The British-accented voice-over explained that the building housed the neighborhood offices of the Komiteh.

Jake paced his hotel room. He sat down, lowered his head and covered his ears. He stayed like that for a while, with his elbows propped on his knees and his head heavy against his hands. He thought of its weight. How much did the dead policeman's head weigh? Who was the man's family? Did he have a young daughter waiting for him at home?

Jake turned off the TV. He lay on the sofa and covered his eyes with his forearm. For the second time in three days he was stunned by the violence he had helped unleash. He thought of a saying that he realized he should've remembered during the Bandar Abbas refinery explosion, a quote from the *Bhagavad Gita*. Oppenheimer, the leading physicist of the Manhattan Project, had said it when he saw the first nuclear explosion.

I am become Death, the shatterer of worlds. Jake couldn't begin to imagine his feelings if STOP were to ever explode one of the suitcase nuclear bombs.

A knock at the door roused him from his bleak meditation. It was Miranda, looking very summery in a white sundress. She handed him a grease-stained bag. He peeked in and saw two bacon sandwiches.

"They call them 'sarnies' here," she said. "Hope you're not worried about your cholesterol."

"Not today," Jake said, and let her in.

"Have you been watching this?" He indicated the TV. She nodded somberly and plopped down on his bed. He joined her and they dug into the sandwiches. Jake tasted olive oil and brown sauce.

"Not bad."

Miranda smiled, licking grease off her fingers. "Thought it might cheer you up."

Jake watched a few seconds of chaotic imagery on the news and immediately wished he hadn't. It was killing his already meager appetite.

Miranda noticed his expression and touched his arm. Her fingertips felt electric on his skin. "Remember the big picture, Jake," she said quietly. "It's not easy to take responsibility for other human lives, but it's a beautiful and courageous thing."

Jake was still struggling with his guilt. "It's just the cost. If your actions lead to even one innocent life being lost . . . how can that not haunt you?"

They were sitting so close together on the bed that when Jake met her gaze, an involuntary thrill rippled through his body. The swirl of emotions he saw in her eyes was too personal for him to bear and he quickly looked away.

"I'm very proud of you," she told him, voice slightly husky. The scent of lilac soap emanated faintly from her skin.

Jake stood up abruptly. "I'm going for a walk. I'm sorry."

He hurried from the room.

CHAPTER SIXTEEN

Ghazi Al Ghamdi followed the tourists along the railing, aimlessly snapping pictures with his intentionally obtrusive camera. Far below, the Colorado River buffeted the vast concrete expanse of the Mansfield Dam, twenty minutes from downtown Austin, Texas.

Ghazi fought the trembling in his hands, trying to affect the casual bovine curiosity he'd observed in American tourists and had been practicing in Texas shopping malls since joining the Austin cell three months earlier.

Two other members of the mission team of four, Badr and Rana, were quarreling loudly just behind him. Ghazi discreetly observed them the way the others did, amateur photographers and travelers stretching their legs, on their way into or out of Austin.

Garbed as he was in a University of Texas baseball cap and Tommy Hilfiger windbreaker, Ghazi could pass for an American until he spoke. Even then, he could manage simple phrases with a convincing Midwestern twang.

To complete this vital aspect of the operation, he'd been chosen specifically for his light coloring and Western looks. He didn't have the military or field experience some holy warriors did, so he was honored beyond words to have been given the assignment.

Badr and Rana were arguing in Farsi, looking for all the world like a pair of bickering exchange students. They were young and attractive, which made them an even better diversion.

Ghazi and the last team member, Gholam, walked briskly toward the spot at the edge of the dam wall they had designated after their hurried final recon the day before. No one knew exactly why their mission had been rushed into execution, but they'd had to scramble to finalize strategy. Badr theorized that another, larger, strike was in the works and Popular Islamic Jihad wanted to hit the dam before security was beefed up.

As it was, creating a distraction for video surveillance was the only major challenge. There was no daily bomb detection sweep, and if a device was powerful enough, even a charge dropped in the water next to the wall would bring a gravity dam down. Between what he was carrying and the explosives Gholam had on him, Ghazi had no worries.

The signal came—Badr slapped Rana. She fell silent and he began berating her more loudly than ever.

Such a thing would attract little notice in many countries. In America, land of false chivalry, people paid attention. Several moved now to intervene. What happened next, Ghazi didn't see. He was busy completing his simple but essential task.

As he reached the edge of the wall, Ghazi carefully placed his heavy camera bag over the top and let it drop. Gholam, next to him, did the same. They hurried back to his car, got in, and drove away.

The bombing had been modeled after an attack on the Peluca dam in Croatia in the early nineties and was inspired, at least conceptually, by the "Upkeep," a bomb developed by the British during WWII, which was used effectively to breach two German dams in the Ruhr industrial heartland, the Moehne and the Eder. These bombs had been delivered by the 617 air squadron, later named Dam Raiders.

Their imitators here were two much smaller and hand-delivered charges, but the huge power of the modern explosives would be deployed directly against one single point of the lakeside wall, and the vast pressure applied by the water against that weakened point of the structure would be enough to destroy the dam.

As he and Gholam merged into unsuspecting interstate traffic—Badr and Rana would join them later—Ghazi felt quiet exultation. He checked his watch. In nine hours, just after dawn, Allah's righteous fury would be felt.

Afraid of his feelings, with the images of the Iranian riots swirling in his head, Jake left his London hotel and hit the street. He couldn't be alone, he knew that much. He needed company. Not Gerard, though. Jake needed to be among people whose lives were normal. People who worried, at most, about where to eat that evening, what movie to see. He found himself half-walking, half-running into Hyde Park. Toward Speaker's Corner.

The morning was a rare sunny London morning. Fluffy white clouds tinged with silver and gray scudded across a mostly blue sky. The greenery of the London parks put New York's to shame. And flowers—flowers were everywhere, including many that seemed exotic—lush and tropical. Jake let his nostrils fill with the scent of them, with the odors of tree leaves and mown grass. Couples were walking, children were playing, dogs gamboled with one another. A young blond woman on horseback, her equestrian outfit perfect, cantered past him on a bridle path near the asphalt trail he followed. He noticed her rosy Renoir cheeks.

There were Muslim families too, all of them dressed in dark colors. Some of the women had their faces covered. They were talking quietly with their children. The smiles he could see were sweet and exuded peace. All of this only increased his anguish.

When he reached Speaker's Corner everything changed. Jake had seen most of the speakers before. Each stood on top of his version of a soapbox—a chair, a ladder, crates precariously piled up. Each had his own accusations and dire warnings. One urged a proletarian revolt. How . . . quaint, Jake thought. Another cautioned that the end was near, that his audience should repent before it was too late. A third speaker urged the listeners not to drink milk: "Cow's milk is for calves, not people!" she cried, raising her clenched fists toward the heavens.

Jake stood amongst a small crowd of tourists mostly, and listened politely though he had heard these speakers before. After all, he deeply admired the centuries-old tradition, this very literal example of freedom of speech.

But he realized too, that although the freedom to speak is essential, the hard part is being free to listen. The hard part is having the time, the open mind, to actually *hear* something new and different, maybe radically different.

Standing in Hyde Park, Jake realized that if he wasn't careful he might lose that freedom. Another risk of joining this war on terror, and summoning the single-mindedness to win it, was that he could become the kind of person who only likes words that express better what he already believes in. He might one day look back and not even know when it had happened, when he had lost the ability to explore new ideas, to appreciate new worldviews. Of course he was unwilling to seriously consider communist revolution, Judgment Day, or a dairy-free diet. He was too old for that. But his mind was still open to valid questioning, to revisiting long-held assumptions. And he would keep it that way. He would fight these fanatics, but he wouldn't become one of them. Most importantly, he would keep his mind open to increase his effectiveness, but never to sap his determination.

That bombs had to be detonated, property destroyed, and lives lost—including the lives of innocent people—was a terrible thing. But a *necessary* thing, necessary to the continued existence of free expression and scientific inquiry, to the imperfect but essential liberty, equality and democracy of the West. Jake accepted that these values might not be desired or even appropriate in other places. But these people were attacking him, in his home! He resolved to do everything in his power to limit collateral damage and thereby limit the loss of human life—even if that meant additional risk to him. He had to persevere, though, in the fight against the invading forces of intolerance, whatever the cost.

These were people for whom everything was black or white: friend or enemy, faithful or infidel, House of Islam or House of War. Nothing in between. Neither doubts nor hesitation, much less other viewpoints, could affect them. Hatred energized them endlessly.

Worst of all, they were more tenacious than he was. In poverty, one learns to concentrate. In the struggle to feed and dress and shelter oneself, to subsist, focus is essential. That is why poor societies breed more narrow-minded people, and more fanatics. Not only don't they have the education, they have no desire, no time, no energy for open-mindedness, for new philosophies. Intellectual exercise is not only useless, it's dangerous. Doubts can threaten survival.

If there was to be any chance of victory, Jake would need to match that resolve. There were going to be casualties; he had to accept that. He was fighting for civilization, for intellectual and cultural survival. For physical survival.

The only thing that would separate Jake from his opponents was his unwillingness to knowingly hurt the innocent. Whatever the cause, whatever the stake, he refused to lower himself to the level of an intrinsically wrong action.

Jake nodded to himself, clenching his fists inside his pockets. With a new confidence in his stride, his purposefulness regained, he walked back to his hotel.

Jake was secretly pleased that Miranda was still in his room when he returned. She looked at him curiously. "Sorry about the disappearing act," he said sheepishly.

"Nothing to apologize for."

"I feel a lot better," he said, and meant it. She smiled as if that were the best news in the world.

"I'm glad."

They didn't discuss the moment of sexual tension they had shared. Instead, they joined Gerard in the hotel bar and discussed unfolding events. After the last explosion, and while the riots raged in Tehran and stirrings were starting to be felt in other Muslim countries, the Arab League convened in Cairo. The meeting had ended less than an hour earlier. Considerable skepticism greeted Egypt's foreign minister when he declared that the event had been scheduled long before. The joint resolution, issued at the end of the meeting, had of course condemned the bombings. Additionally, in a somewhat surprising development, the Arab League pointed a finger at the United States and Israel, accusing both countries of supporting the deadly campaign. It was a big departure from the generally lukewarm and vague declarations these meetings usually yielded.

The president of the United States addressed his nation on TV and, by extension, the world.

"Terrorism is an act of violence specifically targeting the civilian population of a sovereign state," he intoned, obviously reading from a teleprompter but giving each word the full presidential gravitas.

"We do not support terrorism in any form, for any cause, against any State. We consider any act of terrorism, by definition, to be despicable. The allegations of the Arab League are frivolous. Both the United States and our allies in Israel view the bombings in Iran as deplorable acts of terrorism."

Gerard scoffed openly at the screen. "No, he doesn't. Or does he think that anyone believes he's not happy with the riots in Iran?"

Jake paid the president a backhanded compliment. "He's gotta say that. And he's good at saying even things that he doesn't believe."

"All right, boys, can we hear what he has to say?" Miranda was serious.

The president stared into the camera, seemingly with real emotion in his eyes. "Our world faces major challenges in these perilous times. The many conflicts that divide us—of politics, philosophy and religion—must be compromised at a negotiating table. The United States is committed to diplomacy."

Gerard laughed out loud. "Yes, sure! The only reason he's playing nice is because he can't find a military way to force Iran to stop developing its nuclear bomb, and he's looking for help anywhere he can find it. What bullshit!"

"C'mon, Gerard. As if you in France are angels. What about Algeria and your other colonies? And the Ivory Coast just now? Didn't your troops open fire on a crowd of protesters in Abidjan?" Miranda said in exasperation.

"They were protesting our presence there. As if France wanted to control a fucked-up country like that. They had killed nine of our soldiers, who were there on a peace-keeping mission. The troops were rattled," Gerard answered defensively.

"I rest my case. Now, will you kindly let me listen to the TV?"

Gerard didn't respond.

The president wrapped it up with the customary "God Bless America" and the pundits took the stage. Interestingly, a few think-tankers from both left and right criticized the president for pandering to the Arab nations with his condemnation of STOP. Their reasons varied, but in essence the sentiment was that what distinguished STOP from other terrorists was their conviction to minimize civilian casualties. That statement gave Jake a thrill of pride. His comrades in arms weren't callous men, by any means, but that particular value was something he'd emphasized and enforced.

Dawn broke quietly at Mansfield Dam. Today's visitors were still in bed or, for the early risers, pouring their first cup of coffee. The only personnel on duty were dam security, unsuspectingly going through the routine of another day.

When the bombs went off, instantly pulverizing a small portion of the wall on the lake side of the dam, the rest of it shuddered and cracked. The power of the Colorado River surged into the fissures, widening them, and larger chunks toppled away. In less than fifteen minutes, the dam was breached.

The mighty river blasted unchecked into sleeping Texas valleys. Sweeping toward cities that might never be the same.

CHAPTER SEVENTEEN

As the Mansfield dam fell, Gerard and the Americans were having an unremarkable lunch at their London hotel. "Did you see the oil futures?" Jake asked Gerard, signaling the waiter for a coffee refill. "The markets are nervous. I don't like that."

"Well, we expected this, didn't we?" As always, Gerard munched on a pastry. He dabbed at his mouth with his napkin. "Besides, what do you care?"

"I care a lot. In '73, when OPEC switched off supply, around thirty percent of the U.S. oil consumed was imported and the other seventy percent was locally produced. As you may remember, we went crazy then. Today, more than half of the oil we consume is imported—a lot of it from countries in the Middle East or others that might join the Arabs in an embargo. You're in a little better shape in Europe now than you were back then because you can get Russian oil, but you'd still be in deep shit if there was an embargo. If prices continue to rise, I don't think it'd take long for us to become public enemy numero uno at home as well as in the Muslim world. Get the picture?"

Gerard frowned, considering. "Yes. We will make a very convenient scapegoat."

"Don't get depressed yet. It's not so bad. The West has been preparing for this. There are reserves of crude sufficient to cover four months of the imported oil needs of America, the EU, and our friends, ready to be shipped to the refineries. OPEC produces less than half of the world's oil. The hard-line members of OPEC, those who might go for an embargo, produce an even smaller percentage. You're talking over a year of zero supply from these people before the reserves in the West are fully used. A full year without income—these countries would implode, and they know that. I don't see them going for an embargo. Unless . . ."

"Unless what?"

"Well, they might bluff. Prices would go up at the very beginning of an embargo. Gasoline prices would skyrocket. They're already pushing the limit consumers can accept. Americans would start panicking. And politicians hate that, as we all know. If there are fears of an embargo, things could become very complicated for us."

"When he's right, he's right," Miranda said, lifting her water glass in a mock toast. Jake found the fluidity in the movement and the twinkle in her smile irresistibly sexy. He marveled that he could even make such an observation, but there it was.

He had never seriously considered cheating on Stephanie when she was alive, though like most married men he hadn't lost his appreciation for the feminine. And since her death he couldn't remember entertaining even one carnal thought . . . until leaving for Egypt with Miranda.

Miranda had always impressed him with her intellect, her competence and, yes, her beauty, but Jake had never felt sexual chemistry between them. Strangely enough, it had been positively crackling of late.

He wondered how that was possible, given the stubborn immediacy of his grief. Whenever he wasn't occupied, Stephanie or Claire would enter his thoughts and Jake would feel a lance of pain that seemed as real as a cold scalpel incising his chest.

After lunch, Jake returned to his suite. Automatically turning the living room TV on as he entered, he walked to the bedroom and started undressing. With all the negative speculation they had just engaged in, he was looking forward to an invigorating shower.

Initially, he didn't pay attention to the TV. And then isolated expressions began penetrating his consciousness: "widespread destruction," "hundreds of houses," "countless dead," "towns swept away."

Holding his shirt, Jake rushed back to the living room. As if to confirm his thoughts in the park, CNN was showing horrifying scenes of flooding. It was early morning in the U.S. A banner crawling across the bottom of the screen said, *In a communiqué from South Lebanon, Popular Islamic Jihad claims responsibility.* Fourteen concrete dams located in as many regions of the United States had been blown up. The operators were unable to trigger emergency response measures in time. Spillways and drawdown works were activated too late. Already casualties were in the hundreds, with the number expected to grow. Jake put his shirt on as if in a trance and sat down, thunderstruck.

Miranda joined him and they watched the carnage in grave silence. It wasn't long before Gerard called. They spent the next hour discussing alternatives and watching the number of injured, missing, and dead mount. They were interrupted frequently by calls on Gerard's cell. Despite having attached a scrambler to his phone, the Frenchman would engage in conversations so deeply encoded that even Jake couldn't make any sense of them. He continued to watch the news, mesmerized. Less than five percent of the inhabitants living downstream from the dams had received warning phone calls in time. The most successful operator had been in Texas, the Lower Colorado River Authority, whose Mansfield and Wirtz dams were hit. They had an automated phone calling system capable of placing hundreds of calls at once. Many residents had been able to evacuate just minutes ahead of the torrent.

Jake was glued to images eerily reminiscent of New Orleans after Hurricane Katrina: a bedraggled elderly woman stranded on the roof of her home; throngs of refugees filing into a stadium; lost children wandering the streets; exhausted faces; tears; and inexorably, the haunting sight of bodies being swept along with debris by unmerciful floodwaters.

Fortunately the response to this disaster had been swift and organized, for the most part.

"This is the first time ever that Rifaat has claimed responsibility for any of his terrorist acts," Gerard informed them. "Did you see that he did it from South Lebanon?"

"Why is that important?"

"For those of us in the business, it's equivalent to a direct message from the Iranians. The south of Lebanon is Hezbollah country. And who are the main backers of Hezbollah? The Iranians."

"Don't the Syrians control Lebanon?"

"Not as much as they did in the past, and the main financial backers of Hezbollah are the Iranians. Rifaat is telling us, in effect, that we didn't succeed in scaring his backers, the Iranians."

"You know what? I think you're right. Either he hasn't heard from the mullahs, or they told him to go ahead and strike—urged him to."

"I guess we didn't impress these lunatics enough." Gerard spoke quietly, struggling to control his anger.

"You're fucking right." Jake was trembling with outrage. "Rifaat exploded the dams before dawn to catch most people sleeping. It was timed to kill as many as possible. I feel like blowing up half of Iran." He paused, seeing Miranda's dismayed expression. "But that's not what I think we should do."

"No?"

"I'd stay the course. Maybe accelerate the pace of our campaign but not its intensity. The initiative has to be seen as ours. They can't even hope to influence us. We have to be like Fate. Unstoppable. Inevitable."

"I see. The others want to become much more aggressive. For the first time the suitcase nuclear bombs were mentioned."

"What, are they crazy?" Miranda said, in horror.

"This is out of the question, Gerard," Jake added. "Nobody's seriously thinking about doing this, right? This line can't be crossed. Ever!"

"Look, let's not kid ourselves. The nuclear bombs were installed for a reason. We all hope that there will never be the need to use them, but they are there. We can cause significant damage with conventional explosives in situations like Bandar Abbas, where the refinery products multiplied the effect of the bomb. In other places, it will be harder. We need to be able to impress the Iranians . . . and scare them. Otherwise this whole thing is an exercise in futile destruction. Gerard's gaze shifted to the ceiling. "But we can leave this discussion for another time. Right now, I think you might be right."

"I know he's right," Miranda said. "They're hoping we'll overreact, do something rash and get ourselves caught."

The Frenchman nodded slowly, thinking with his eyes shut. "Yes, it makes sense. A controlled response. That's exactly what we should do."

After one last phone call, Gerard gave Jake a thumbs-up. "Agreed. It will be done as you suggested."

Jake felt a surge of pride. As they went outside to an Internet café, he felt good to be taking action.

The statement they released tersely announced the planned destruction of a third refinery. The refinery at Abadan was Iran's largest: at 400,000 barrels a day, almost four times as large as Tabriz. If it was destroyed, Iran would be at half its past refining capacity; the economic consequences would be devastating. This time STOP was giving the Iranian authorities only until the following morning at ten, Tehran time, to accept its demands.

Within an hour Iran declared that it wasn't going to wait for a new bombing. The country was cutting its crude oil production and sales by 500,000 barrels a day, effective immediately. It urged the Great Satan to curb its terrorists if it wanted to avoid a full oil embargo. Minutes later, in scattered interviews, the oil ministers of the other non-moderate Arab countries followed suit, jointly matching the production cut. Clearly, this had been rehearsed. Crude oil futures climbed by $3.56 per barrel in the next hour and by an additional $7.28 by the close of the trading session.

From research he had conducted during the takeover of an oil company his fund had invested in, Jake remembered that the disruption in world oil supply during the Iraqi invasion of Kuwait had resulted in a loss of more than four million barrels a day—four times the current announced cut. The markets were overreacting. If he was trading now, he'd be going short, selling oil futures. And getting ready to rake in the profits when oil prices dropped.

But the market analysts were gripped by their traditional herd instincts, and the media always jumped on anything potentially scary. He started to worry about the growing hysteria of the newscasts in Europe and America. There were warnings of a full oil embargo if the attacks continued, of a recession, of a return to the stagflation of the Carter years.

He also started to worry about America's official reaction. While expressing outrage at the dam explosions, the State Department once more condemned the "terrorist" activities of STOP. Would STOP be hunted down, not by the Muslim countries it was threatening to attack further, but by the democracies of the West that it hoped to assist?

Half an hour after watching the explosion at Abadan on his hotel room's television, Jake met Miranda and Gerard for breakfast. The Frenchman had refused to accept his invitation to join them at the Conservatory, the great Crystal Palace of a restaurant on the first floor of the Lanesborough. He had insisted on meeting in Jake's room. Jake ascribed it to the tension they both felt. Several days had passed since the Qeshm bombing and he hadn't had a single good night's sleep. Similar pressures might be getting to Gerard. But now Jake started to wonder. Did Gerard know something that he didn't?

"Yes, we have some problems," Gerard answered when Jake asked. "I won't lie to you."

They sat in the living area of Jake's hotel suite, Jake leaning back in the couch while Gerard perched on the edge of a chair facing him. Miranda sat in a chair by the window, staring at the gray weather with an apathy Jake had never seen in her.

He ordered coffee, juice, and omelets for Miranda and himself, and an assortment of pastries for Gerard. For once Gerard didn't touch his food. They had turned off the TV, which was filled with the images of the explosion at Abadan and endless analyses of what would be next.

"What's going on?" Jake asked.

"They're coming after us."

Jake felt his neck stiffen. "Who's 'they'?"

"We were not as . . . *undetected* as we thought."

"Sorry?" Miranda emerged from her melancholy in a hurry.

"It's Paris. The DGSE. The Americans and the Israelis either know nothing or are pretending not to know."

"Tell us what happened."

"Nothing too dramatic. Right before I went to sleep yesterday, I got a call on my DGSE cell asking point blank which city I was in. I told them I was in London. Within fifteen minutes I got another call with an invitation from our station chief here in London to join him for a nightcap at Claridge's. We've known each other for many years. He had a simple message: 'Stop it, and stop it now. We are aware of your activities and they run counter to France's interests. If you don't stop you will be arrested and we won't be able to help you.' This came just a few hours after Iran's announcement of its production cut." Gerard shook his head. "There's a difference between being pragmatic and being cowardly. Anyway . . . of course I said I didn't know what he was talking about. Gerard paused, then changed the subject." His smile was a sad one. "We actually had a very nice chat after that."

"What do you plan to do?" Jake asked.

"I have no illusions. It's only a matter of time before they bring me in. That's why I don't want you seen with me, why I have to make sure I'm not being followed every time I come to your rooms."

"I understand." Jake was impressed at seeing not even a flicker of doubt in Gerard's eyes. The man wouldn't even consider stopping their efforts to save his own skin.

Gerard talked right past Jake. "We don't know how much the DGSE knows. Frankly, I have no idea where we screwed up. I'm expecting a phone call from either Delgado or Danny in a few minutes. They're preparing a new safe house in New York and also reviewing everything to locate the source of the leak. That is, if it was a leak at all. I was planning to discuss the whole thing with you after their call. If they agree, I will be flying out today on American's 10:00 A.M. flight to New York. You two should leave on a different one, and a later one. American has a flight at noon that will get you to JFK at 2:30, New York time. But don't sit together or acknowledge each other until you leave the terminal. Once you reach the ground transportation area, you may travel together from there."

"Got it."

"I suggest we meet in New York late in the afternoon, say 4:30. I'll give you a number to call, and we'll give you directions then. If there's no answer, or if you don't recognize the voice, hang up and get out of wherever you are. They can trace a call very quickly these days. You'll be contacted later. Who knows? We might all get arrested today. In that case, we need the two of you to be safe."

Jake was amazed at Gerard's composure. *Sangfroid*, the word that he had first read in Alexandre Dumas' *Les Trois Mousquetaires* as a kid, came to him.

Gerard's mind was awhirl with bleak thoughts as he entered the tube station. He had one stop to make before returning to the States—the French embassy. As he approached the platform he had the disconnected realization that this stop was hit in the 2005 bombings.

He had scarcely pushed the thought aside when two men appeared on either side of him. He felt a gun barrel press each of his kidneys.

"We'll see you to the embassy, Mr. Duvivier," promised a soft hiss in his ear. Gerard couldn't quite place the accent—it was a mélange of Middle Eastern flavors—but he knew what it meant.

With a sad half-smile, he nodded. Looked as though he'd be taking that car ride, after all. But the embassy had never been the intended destination.

As he led his escorts back up the escalator to the street, Gerard wondered if Jake had been found too. He dearly hoped not.

CHAPTER EIGHTEEN

Seated several rows apart, Jake and Miranda took the noon flight to JFK. Upon arrival, Jake walked a gauntlet of expectant faces, delighted cries and signs with strange names held by bored drivers. As always, the main airport of the richest city of the richest country in the world looked like shit.

He found a bank of public phones outside JFK's arrival gate. As he walked over, instinct told him to obscure his face with a handkerchief, as if he had a cold. He didn't want to be filmed by a security camera.

He called the number Gerard had given him. The phone rang once, twice . . .

Three rings.

Four. This was taking too long.

At what must've been the eight or ninth ring somebody picked up. It took Jake a few moments to recognize the breathless voice.

"It's okay," Danny said. He gave Jake his instructions to meet them in an hour on a street corner in Queens.

"Is everything all right?" Jake asked. "You don't sound well."

"Repeat the address to me. I want to make sure you have it right."

Jake did so.

"See you there."

"I have a question."

"Not now." Barzilai hung up.

Jake's cell suddenly vibrated. He looked at the display and saw that he had a text message. From Miranda.

B CAREFUL. MAN TAILING U.

Jake surreptitiously scanned the busy terminal for suspicious faces. Nothing jumped out at him. But he didn't see Miranda, either.

He quickly typed out a response and sent it to her phone.

PLAN B. SPLIT UP. CALL YOU FROM THE ROAD.

Then he merged into the foot-traffic and lost himself in the middle of a crowd of high school boys, athletes on their way to one tournament or another. When they passed the escalator to ground transportation, he darted onto it just in front of a family of tourists.

He slouched against the handrail, keeping his entire six-foot-three frame shielded behind the family's corpulent patriarch. It would've taken an extremely close tail to track his sudden movement from the phones to the teenagers to the escalator.

Jake hurried to the cab stand. A yellow taxi pulled up immediately. He got in and directed the driver.

As he settled back in the mottled upholstery, Jake contemplated how dangerous the world had become. The dam attacks only further convinced him, if that was possible, of the necessity of STOP. He wondered how helpless he would feel right now if he'd never gotten involved. Though he was in more danger now, he had the consolation of fighting back.

The rendezvous point was at the northern tip of Long Island City, the Queens neighborhood closest to Manhattan. JFK airport was in the southeastern corner of that borough. Jake would have to cross Queens entirely. He looked at his watch. One hour. They needed to make good time.

Jake noticed the driver's eyes on him and felt a stirring of what he hoped was paranoia. The man was young, neatly groomed and of Arabic descent.

"Tell me, sir, what awaits you in Queens?" the man asked.

"My family." Jake's lie was facile enough, but his unease only grew. Was there more than casual interest in the driver's tone?

"Ah, your wife and children are waiting for you," the man said, with a private smile.

Jake looked at the passing suburban sprawl and tried to quell his rising alarm. Was he crazy, or did he detect a mocking lilt in those words? As if . . . as if the man knew where Jake's wife and child really were.

He felt a panic attack coming on. The details of the cab were becoming too vivid. He focused on the driver's posted credentials.

The face in the picture was dark-skinned and older.

"Let's stop off at the first mini-mart we pass," Jake said, keeping his voice light and unconcerned. "I'd kill for a sandwich right now."

The driver eyed him in the rearview mirror. A shark's grin. "Would you?"

He took the next exit. The ramp looped around through barren scrub, slicing toward a gas station at the summit of a hill several hundred yards farther.

Jake noticed two other drivers leaving the highway after them. Nondescript sedans, like rental cars. At least three men in each.

Jake surreptitiously dialed Stone's number on his cell phone. A secretary's voice came faintly from the receiver. The moment Jake lifted the phone to his ear and said, "Tell Stone that Jake Burke's in trouble," the cab driver violently pulled off the road. The phone bounced from Jake's grip. As he fumbled around for it, he heard car doors opening.

The woman's voice floated tinny from the phone. Asking a question. He snatched it and repeated, "It's Jake Burke. I'm in—"

Both doors were torn open and two burly men dragged him from the taxi. One almost casually slapped the phone from his grasp.

Jake was hustled into a sedan. The convoy took off again.

Two men—obviously someone's muscle—flanked him in the backseat. A man in the front passenger seat turned around to face him. Young, shaven head and intense eyes.

"My name is Saajid, Mr. Burke. We've been waiting quite a while for you," he said pleasantly. "I've had ample introduction to your sinful nation."

"I hope you've enjoyed yourself," Jake said. His panic had subsided, and he now felt a kind of subdued acceptance. End of the line, he thought. He just hoped Miranda and Gerard had gotten away.

"Yes, very," Saajid said. "But unfortunately for you it's given me time to consider how to conduct our business. To give my creativity free reign, as you people say."

Jake stared out the window. They were back on the thruway now, heading toward Manhattan. He'd have to climb over one of the men on either side of him to get to the door, assuming he could unlock it to jump out. There was no escape.

Saajid snapped his fingers in Jake's face, startling him. "Mr. Burke. You will want to pay attention. We were discussing how I'm going to torture you."

Jake felt the inevitable stab of fear, did his best to conceal it to deny this bastard the satisfaction.

"Now, as I was saying. You gave me time to consider my options. To prepare. So you see, your foreign dalliances have not worked in your favor."

Jake nodded, resigned. "Unless I tell you what you want to know."

Saajid seemed surprised, even disappointed. "Well, of course. If you cooperate, it will be easier."

"Good to know." Jake took some pleasure in denying his captor the anticipation.

They traveled in silence for a few more minutes before exiting. The cab had peeled off from the group at some point, so the two remaining cars pulled into a storage facility right off the highway. Rows of dingy aluminum cubes as far as the eye could see.

"Many preparations have been made," Saajid said. "You should be honored."

Jake was starting to panic again, and knew the cold sweat running down his forehead was giving him away. If only he had a cyanide tooth.

The other sedan stopped first, at a cube on the end of a row several hundred yards from any fence line. The three men inside got out. All had semiautomatic weapons slung over their shoulders. Two kept Jake's car covered while the third opened the cube's padlock.

The driver of Jake's car got out and opened a passenger door for the thug beside him, who carefully climbed out and positioned himself beside the door. The other roughly herded Jake out. The second his foot hit gravel, the first man seized him by the arm. The driver took the other.

They were taking great care to prevent Jake from running away. He realized that they fully expected him to do something desperate to hasten his own death. A less painful death. It was a chilling reminder of what awaited him in that storage space.

Jake was hustled into the cube. The drivers and two gunmen remained outside while Saajid and two thugs strapped Jake into a dentist's chair.

"The chair was obtained from a medical supply house. It's useful here because you can be reclined at a convenient angle, properly restrained and kept motionless for surgery. Because, of course, we won't be putting you under."

The single bulb overhead illuminated a nearly empty room but for a carpenter's table and some unidentifiable boxes.

The two thugs stepped back, one taking a post by the door and the other within easy reach of Jake. That one watched him with avid clinical interest. Looking forward to an interesting show, Jake thought sickly.

"It is customary with amputation," Saajid said, opening what revealed itself to be a case for surgical instruments, "to start with things you can live without. An incentive to cooperate, you see. When you've lost so much that you can have no hope of resuming your life, then only a stop to the pain will motivate you. Which is persuasive enough, if your agony is sufficient."

Saajid removed a polished scalpel, twirled it before Jake with a flourish. "That's why I'm going to take an eye to begin with. One piece at a time, to give you time to consider things. First your eyelid—easily detached with a sharp instrument. The real bother will come in working the scalpel around the entire perimeter of the eyeball without driving it too deep. We can't risk damaging your brain this soon."

Jake felt the chill of exquisite horror Saajid intended. Bone-deep.

"So maybe we should start with the questions instead," Jake offered. He wasn't really baiting his torturer now, he was half-hoping he could tell the man what he wanted to know and live with it. Or, more accurately, face death with a clear conscience and both eyes.

All three men in the cube laughed at that.

"Very well, Mr. Burke," Saajid said magnanimously. "Tell me, who are your colleagues in STOP?"

"I'm a free agent," Jake lied, with instinctive courage. Why not? "I just wanted to avenge my family. I did that. It's over, I swear."

"I would love to believe that," Saajid said, though it was clear he wouldn't, "but I think I will repeat the question once your eyelid is gone."

Saajid dropped Jake's chair back to an almost prone position. The thug moved in to clamp his hands on Jake's forehead and neck, steadying him against the headrest. Jake gave in to white-hot panic then, begging and pleading in a stream of desperate words. But he didn't tell Saajid about Gerard, Stone, and the others. He would give his eyelid willingly for them.

Saajid bent over Jake, scalpel poised.

"Mr. Burke, you must stop struggling. We do not have the means to fully immobilize your head. If you jerk around too much, my work will be sloppy. You don't want that, do you?"

Jake couldn't will himself still. He kept begging, appealing to Saajid's humanity—if he had any—and making a futile effort to turn his head away. But the big man was leaning on him. Hard.

Saajid carefully brought the blade down. Jake felt the ultra-sharp edge kiss his skin just above the corner of his eye. A sharp, clean sting . . . He cast his mind to Stephanie, laughing at one of his bad jokes. Imagined his daughter's four-year-old silhouette dashing down the hall in her witch costume on Halloween evening.

Automatic gunfire roared, and the knife left Jake's bleeding skin.

He glimpsed Barzilai behind a brilliant muzzle flash. Heard bodies hitting the floor.

Dazed and in shock, he watched as Saajid slid down the wall, mouth spouting blood. Staring at Jake, not the men who'd shot him, the scalpel clutched tightly in his hand.

Jake felt hands loosening his bonds but was only marginally aware of it. He was in a weird, traumatized limbo. Blinking blood from his left eye.

"Do I still have my eyelid?" he asked vaguely, after the shooting died down.

"You're gonna be just fine." Stone's voice.

As if given leave to let go, Jake blacked out.

CHAPTER NINETEEN

When Jake regained consciousness, he was stretched out on the rear set of a full-sized van. They were moving at highway speed. Miranda's face hovered over his, concern etched on features that seemed positively angelic at this moment. He felt a squeeze of his hand and realized she'd been clutching it tightly.

Jake reflexively touched the corner of his eye and found a thick bandage taped there.

"It'll need a couple of stitches," Miranda explained tenderly. "You've been out about ten minutes."

"How'd you find me?" Jake asked, weakly.

Barzilai leaned over him from the next seat. "You owe your life to this woman. She followed your cab and called us."

Jake looked at Miranda in wonder. "How?"

"I'd staked out ground transportation. Caught a cab right after you did and told the driver to follow you. When they switched cars, I called the number Gerard gave us."

"We hauled ass," Barzilai said. "Thank God we weren't far away."

"We had to convince this one not to go in after you all by herself," Stone added, with a smile.

Miranda nodded, dead serious. "It was the most excruciating ten minutes of my life, waiting outside that storage place . . . not knowing what they were doing to you in there."

"You don't want to know, either," Jake said, just as seriously. Knowing would only make it worse.

He was horrified by how close he'd come to agonizing death. If it had taken STOP even ten more minutes to make their move . . . At best, he'd have been permanently scarred.

Mulling that, Jake fell silent. The men gave him some space to recover. But Miranda stayed with him, hanging onto him as if afraid that he'd slip away forever if she didn't.

Delgado was driving, eyes hidden behind sunglasses. He pulled over behind the decaying structure of an abandoned building in a derelict part of Long Island City and let the engine idle.

The men were stealing glances out the windows as if fearful of being arrested at any moment.

Jake noted that the intrepid Frenchman was conspicuously absent. "Where's Gerard? What happened?" he asked.

Delgado showed no sympathy for what Jake had just endured. "You want to know what happened? You fucked up. *That's* what happened."

"We all fucked up," the Israeli said. "We didn't need to accept what he was demanding. It was as much our fault as it was Jake and Miranda's." He stared at Delgado. "And this attitude will get us nowhere. For God's sake, the man was being tortured half an hour ago."

"What are you talking about?" Jake's anger gave way to confusion. "*What* fuck-up?"

There was a funereal pause. Stone finally spoke, his face ashen. "We've been going over all that's happened to figure out what went wrong." He sounded weary and spent. "We finally figured it out. It could only have been one thing, and we were able to get corroboration."

"Yes?"

"Remember when you demanded that someone inform the workers still inside Bandar Abbas of the upcoming explosion? Our Iranian friends sent their people in with leaflets—copies of foreign newspapers reporting the Qeshm blast. Remember how they warned us that these people would be arrested and never heard from again?"

"Of course I remember."

"Well, they were arrested. And then savagely tortured, of course. They informed on Gerard, who was their contact. The mullahs demanded a solution from the French government."

"How do you know that?"

Danny Barzilai explained. "We still have intelligence assets in Iran from before Khomeini."

Stone continued. "Under Iranian pressure, the French called Gerard in and gave him a warning. Gerard—actually, all of us—decided to ignore it. We went ahead with the Abadan explosion. Then he was called for a meeting at the embassy . . ." Stone's voice trailed off.

"And?" Jake asked softly, dreading the answer. Miranda covered her mouth, aghast.

"Gerard is dead," Barzilai said. He spoke gently, clearly aware of the guilt that would now crush Jake.

"*Hijo de puta!*" Delgado lunged at Jake and had to be pulled off by Stone.

"What's wrong with you!" Miranda exclaimed, humbling Delgado with her smoldering gaze. "He hasn't suffered enough?"

After the four men were settled down again in the van that now seemed very cramped, Danny said, "The body was found not far from the French embassy in London. One policeman recognized the almond smell coming from Gerard's mouth."

"Almond smell?"

"Cyanide smells like almonds. Gerard killed himself. The French say he never made it to the embassy."

"Why would he do that?" But Jake knew the answer.

"Captured. There's no other explanation."

"By whom?" Jake asked, even though it was obvious.

Stone's eyes went from Barzilai to Delgado and back. The two men nodded. Stone continued. "We have one enemy we haven't told you about. We wanted to, but Gerard was against it."

"Gerard told us about Rifaat." Jake didn't know what else to say. He didn't even know what to think. He sat quietly, half turned to the back of the van, looking at the three faces, on each one a different degree of accusation—the faces of men who had been building deterrence against evil only to see it all destroyed by a bungling amateur.

"Yes, and that did him real good." Delgado almost spat the words.

Jake gazed unseeingly out the window. He'd found meaning in his life after being orphaned by it. As a result of his tragedy he had received the ultimate blessing: clarity, in the form of a well-defined enemy, an evil worth dying against.

Now it seemed as if he caused damage to the struggle he intended to support every time he did what he thought was right. It had happened when he killed Ashraf. It was happening now.

"How did Rifaat find Gerard?" Miranda asked.

"We don't know for sure," Stone said. "But the only possible explanation is that he has a source among the French. It's either in their embassy in London, or in the Quai d'Orsay, or—more likely—inside the DGSE."

It really didn't matter now. Jake could never forgive himself. The best chance of defeating Islamic fundamentalism had now been compromised. He'd been given the information that the men would be arrested and he hadn't thought it through. The Great Jake Burke had lost his touch.

Worse, he knew he didn't have the stomach for this. His close encounter with Saajid had proven that. He envied men who could stand up to that kind of extremity, but he wasn't one of them. He would've cracked, maybe once he'd lost his whole eye, maybe sooner. This game was crazy, best played by madmen and zealots. Not middle-aged businessmen. Before his accusers, all but drowning in shame, Jake saw in his mind's eye a scene from some old movie—was it *The Dreyfus Affair*? A general was ripping his stripes away.

In a formal tone betrayed by the slightest quiver in his voice, Jake said, "I'm sorry about that. Deeply sorry. It's clear that I'm out of my depth here—I'm making too many mistakes. It's time for me to go. I'll still support you financially, but I'm out of here. Get in touch when you need the money. It'll be there." He nodded and reached for the van's door.

"Not so fast," Delgado snapped. "Let go of that handle, please. We need to talk some more."

Jake ignored the demand, and the door clicked open. Fuck Delgado. He'd had enough. "If you're concerned about secrecy, don't be. You have my word of honor that I'll never reveal anything." A faint smile crossed his lips. "And no, I haven't forgotten your explanation of the consequences if I speak too much."

"It's not that. Not that at all." Barzilai's hand touched his left arm, placating. "Just listen. You owe it to us. And please let go of the door. This might be a long conversation."

Jake sat back. For a fleeting moment he felt as if he belonged inside the circle again.

Stone cleared his throat. "I admire your attitude: no attempt to pass the buck. Good for you. But we do the same. And it really was our fault. We're the professionals and we made a bad decision. A very bad decision."

Jake kept his silence.

"We accepted your demand and imposed it on our Iranian friends because we needed the money, plain and simple. Between the bribe money we have to offer constantly, the cost of securing octanitrocubane, and the bad terms we accepted in order to secure the Middle East maintenance contracts, we are bleeding profusely. We've reached the end of our financial rope. As a result, some of our companies are on the verge of going bankrupt. We can't let that happen. It would mean that several of our bombs might cease being operational. Worse still, other maintenance companies hired to replace our own could decide to replace a storage tank, for example, and a bomb could explode by accident."

"But I told you that you can count on my money," Jake interrupted. "So money's not an issue any more."

"We understand. But we have to prepare for another situation. Now, I won't say we have absolute consensus here," he stole a glance at Delgado, "but the majority agrees that we have no choice."

"No choice?"

"We believe there's a strong possibility, maybe even a certainty, that the DGSE will actively try to neutralize us."

Jake agreed. He recalled Gerard's description of his meeting with the French intelligence station chief in London, at Claridge's Hotel.

Jake had a pounding headache. He massaged his temples and gazed at Stone. "You said you're sure that the DGSE will try to stop you."

"Yes. And we have to prepare for the eventuality that we all get arrested."

Jake swallowed hard. "How real is this possibility?"

"It's real. The connection among the four of us is quite official. The cover story is that we cooperate in the fight against fundamentalist terrorism. The extra-curricular bombing activity wasn't known. Or so we thought." He paused. Nobody broke the silence.

After a while, Stone spoke again. "Anyway, now that they have Gerard identified, the intelligence agencies of not only France but the U.S. as well will target Danny, Ramon and me. We have to assume that if he has a mole inside the DGSE, Rifaat might come after us too. If that happens, we've arranged for our optical disks to be destroyed. Big Ben isn't officially connected to us, but we've been in contact with him too often. So there's a good chance they'll get him too. He'll never talk, though, and the codes are all in place."

"And the rest of the system? The maintenance companies?"

"To our knowledge no one besides Rifaat knows that we control the maintenance companies. They're safe."

"I'm sorry," Jake said, "but I'm having trouble following you. If you'll soon be arrested—or *worse*, as I well know—why don't you just run away?"

"If we do that, any chance of ever leading a normal life again is gone," Stone said. "Besides, we'd be found eventually. This thing is too high-profile. And we have work to do. We prefer to run the risk of a trial than to spend the rest of our lives on the run, having lost our homes, our families, everything. Who knows, we might be acquitted. After all, it's not like we're criminals. We've been fighting to defend the West against terrorism, for God's sake."

"Sure." Jake knew that his facial expression was showing disbelief.

"What do you mean, 'sure'? What don't you understand?" said Delgado.

"It's not a matter of understanding. I just don't believe you'll get arrested, period. Gerard was killed by Rifaat, not by the French. *You* said that, and I agree. As far as the DGSE, all we know is that they contacted Gerard and told him to cease and desist. That's all."

"It doesn't matter," Stone said quietly. "Whatever happens, happens."

Jake again gazed at the bleak scene outside. He felt enervated. What would prevent Rifaat's men from finding him again? He was doomed. "Just tell me what you want from me, all right? I'm feeling worse by the minute." And he was.

"I'm sorry, Jake." Stone had grown impatient and raised his voice. "But you're not getting what this is about. You're the only one in a position to take over leadership of the organization if we're knocked out. And that's a distinct possibility, since the CIA has discontinued supporting—much less protecting—us, and once these agencies together decide to find us there's no escaping. It's the only alternative we have and it's not even a great solution. Rifaat's only going to want you all the more after today. As long as he's alive, you aren't—"

"Why can't you listen?" Delgado interrupted, patently trying to regain the offensive in what looked an awful lot to Jake like a pissing contest. "If we go down, you're the only one left. He's making this perfectly clear, but you're so caught up in your own guilt that it's not registering!"

"Who the hell do you think you're talking to?" Jake shot back. "I'm not a child. Of course I get the point. Of course I know what you're asking of me. To make decisions that might mean the death or maiming of innocents. To go to jail or wind up dead, when the best thing for me to do right now is to disappear. Find a quiet island somewhere and change my name. But you're asking me for everything, and patronizing me at the same time, you asshole. Why don't you go fuck yourself?"

Delgado didn't answer. Ever so slightly, he shook his head, as if to say *I told you so* to his colleagues. Stone grew livid but said nothing. Barzilai looked away in embarrassed silence.

Jake opened his door and stepped onto the cracked Long Island City asphalt. Miranda followed. Through it all she had listened soberly but said nothing.

Jake walked quickly away from the van before spinning around.

"You'll have the money you need," he said. "Apart from that, forget about me."

CHAPTER TWENTY

Jake walked away from the van. He'd have to get his eye stitched up as soon as possible. He wondered if Rifaat's killers would be waiting for him at home. He might not want to risk going back there. Miranda walked silently by his side.

"Hey!" It was Barzilai behind them, jogging to catch up. When he came abreast of them, he slowed to a brisk walk and touched Jake's shoulder. "Look, you're right. That is what we're asking of you. We know it's a lot. Ideally, you should have a lot more time to decide. But this is an emergency and things are happening fast."

Jake liked the Israeli. He looked at him but said nothing.

Barzilai continued. "We're not unanimous. And all of us have doubts, mainly because of your inexperience and the fact that Rifaat is after you. You're not fully prepared, but at least you'll be conservative. You won't cause unnecessary destruction. Honestly? We wish we had other options. But we don't. When, *if*, the three of us get arrested, you and Miranda are the only ones no agency has a file on. You're totally under the radar, unless they chat with Rifaat. But you've shown that you have the maturity and intelligence to carry on. You'll also have the money." Barzilai stopped walking. "Will you please stop and talk to me?"

Jake continued walking.

He heard Barzilai's voice from a few yards back, the sentences coming fast, urgent. "You've got to be able to leave personalities aside. We're all on the same side. This war we're waging is too crucial for you to allow Ramon to turn you off."

Jake stopped walking, turned and said quietly, "I need to think. I'll be back in a few minutes."

Jake walked for a few blocks with his mind blank, allowing his anger to subside. He felt better out of the van. Ever since his days as an engineering student, he'd liked to go for a walk when he had a problem to solve.

"You're awfully quiet," he said to Miranda.

She smiled ruefully. "This has always been your show, Jake. It's a decision you have to make, but I'll back your play either way. There's certainly an argument to be made for walking away here. Having said that . . ."

Jake knew where she was going. "Sounds like you think I should continue."

Miranda shrugged, maintaining a credible poker face. He chuckled. "Okay, let me talk this through. Please feel free to interject if you feel the need."

"You got it."

"Let's see," he began, "Gerard told us, and Sam Stone confirmed it, that STOP's money originally came from the CIA. Even though Stone said that the Agency had abandoned them, it's possible—likely—that Central Intelligence continues supporting the effort tacitly."

Miranda nodded. "Behind closed doors? Very plausible."

"Now, if that's true, should we get involved in an effort that's known by the CIA and could one day be scrutinized by some congressman seeking higher office or leaked to a journalist looking for fame and a better salary? Of course not." Jake stopped walking, his shoulders sagging. A feeling of emptiness had crept in.

"But it really doesn't matter," Miranda said. "We're already in. We've been a party to the destruction of three oil refineries. You're financing these guys."

"Yes, and I endangered them at the same time. I've made myself a fugitive, hunted by one of the world's most ruthless terrorists."

"Which means you've already gotten to him," Miranda pointed out.

"And this undertaking is the most important thing I'll ever do in my life."

Jake straightened his shoulders. The emptiness was gone. Miranda saw it. She broke into an easy, almost girlish, smile.

"Why do I feel like you just won a negotiation?" Jake asked, amused.

"I didn't," Miranda said simply.

"I'm glad you're here," Jake said.

"Damn right you are."

They turned and walked back to the van.

"What do you have for me?" he asked Delgado nonchalantly, as if seated in a boardroom negotiation session. "I want no more secrets."

Though clearly reluctant, Delgado nodded to Stone.

"First of all, welcome." Stone seemed relieved and almost happy that Jake had been able to bend Delgado's will. "I'm really glad that we'll all be on the same page."

"I second that," said Barzilai.

"We shouldn't stay here too long, or we'll attract attention. But Danny has the authorization," Stone looked for an okay from Delgado, who nodded again, "to tell you everything you want to know."

"Thanks. That does feel better. What's the next step?"

Stone pulled an index card from his coat pocket. "Here are the wiring instructions. Gerard told us that you agreed to send twelve million dollars in. We're assuming that if you're satisfied with the information Danny gives you, you're prepared to do so immediately."

"Correct." Jake glanced at the paper and slid it into his wallet.

Delgado opened the van's sliding door. He extended his hand to Jake. "Sorry if I pissed you off, man. Sometimes I have trouble controlling myself. No hard feelings, right?"

Jake shook his hand. "None."

With the other hand, Delgado pulled out a small envelope and offered it to Jake. "There's a disk in the envelope, inside a plastic pouch. If you find yourself in danger, just press the top right corner of the pouch. It releases an acid that erases the disk. Remember this basic rule: 'When in doubt, do without.' If you feel threatened in any way, destroy the disk. We can always get you a new one. Danny will tell you everything else you need to know."

"Hold it. There's one more thing we need to discuss."

"What's that?"

"Rifaat."

"Don't worry about Rifaat right now," Barzilai said. "He's my top priority, too. I'll tell you why when we have more time. But the safest place you can be right now is with us."

Jake nodded. He trusted the Israeli. "Okay. What's the next step?"

"The next step? Get you patched up. And you have an email to send." With that, Delgado left the van.

Sam Stone extended his hand. He was smiling warmly. "Once again, welcome back. I don't regret bringing you in. And don't be too hard on yourself. That's the nature of this business. Risk and pain and lives lost. You do the best you can." Now he too stepped down from the van and walked to a green Taurus parked down the street.

They drove off to Manhattan, Barzilai, Jake and Miranda in the van following the government-issue Ford, Jake thinking about the next move in the mortal chess game they were playing with Iran.

At the entrance to the Triborough Bridge both vehicles followed the sign directing them toward Manhattan. They found themselves stuck in bumper-to-bumper traffic approaching what appeared to be some sort of checkpoint. Both the Taurus and the van, three cars behind it, were boxed in. They were already on the bridge. There was no way out.

When the Taurus pulled in at the checkpoint, agents in navy windbreakers proclaiming FBI emerged from a car parked by the roadblock. Holding automatic rifles, they surrounded Stone and Delgado. Three Feds barked orders, motioning with their guns for the two men to get out. There seemed to be some kind of stalemate—neither Stone nor Delgado was leaving the car.

"They're trying to give us time to escape," Miranda said.

One heavyset agent thrust his hand into the Taurus and pulled Stone from inside, slamming him viciously against the body of the car. He shoved his gun against Stone's neck. Then Delgado emerged, hands raised. The two CIA men were forced to stand spread-eagled against their vehicle.

"This is it," Barzilai said. "We're toast. You've got to get out of the van."

Jake started to open the door when he saw that other federal agents were walking in their direction, checking the cars between their van and the green Taurus. One of them, his weapon at the ready, was looking fiercely at the line of cars on their side of the road. Getting out of the van unnoticed would be impossible.

"Can't be done," Jake said quietly.

"Is there any way for you to hide in here?" Barzilai looked out. "No, you can't," he answered himself. "They're checking inside all the cars. Hold the top right corner of the disk pouch. If we get caught, we've got to destroy our disks."

The FBI agents reached their van. Jake saw the one at his side press his earpiece with his forefinger and shout to his colleague on Danny's side, "Okay, we got them."

It took a second for Jake to realize that the agent wasn't talking about them. He was saying that the identity of the two men in the Taurus had been confirmed and that the roadblock would soon be lifted. Still dazed, Jake watched Barzilai slowly drive their van past a gun-toting Fed.

"They were obviously looking for Ramon and Stone," Barzilai said, his voice somber.

"And I don't think they're looking for us," Miranda put in. "Or we surely would've been arrested, too."

"I won't wait to find out," Barzilai said.

When they reached the Manhattan side of the East River, Danny turned left onto FDR Drive and then onto the Queensborough Bridge, headed back toward Queens.

"Where are we going?" Jake wanted to know.

"Back to JFK," Barzilai said. "We're flying to Switzerland. From there, to Israel."

Few flights had made Danny Barzilai so anxious, so uncertain of his future, short-term and long. The last he could remember was when he was 22, sitting amid dozens of fellow soldiers in the dark recesses of an enormous plane.

The day was July 4, 1976, and while his mother was watching the bicentennial fireworks in New York City, Danny was slouched against one interior wall of a C-130 Hercules—the Israelis had nicknamed the enormous, low-slung American-made planes "Hippos"—flying south toward Kampala Airport in Entebbe, Uganda.

Uganda was a faraway place. Its ruler, Idi Amin, was a sworn enemy of Israel. An unholy alliance between Uganda, Libya, German terrorists and various Palestinian groups had created the most serious challenge ever to Israel's policy of refusing to negotiate with terrorists. A week before, on June 27th, a group of Arabs and Germans had hijacked Air France Flight 139 en route from Tel Aviv to Paris and flown it to Uganda via Libya. After releasing all non-Jewish passengers, the hijackers threatened to kill the 105 remaining men, women, and children. For days, the same old story dominated virtually every Israeli news report: the story of Jews singled out to die.

Within a few days of the hijacking, the planning team in Danny's unit was told to begin rehearsing an attack on the airport. Though any rescue mission seemed like the longest of long shots, the team wasn't completely ignorant in its preparations. In better times, an Israeli company had actually built an addition to the Kampala Airport in Entebbe. And when the Palestinian Liberation Organization began using Uganda as its center of operations in Africa, the Mossad started assembling a small network in that country.

The group brainstormed, sharing their wildest flights of fancy with one another in hopes of eventually arriving at a daring but workable strategy. No suggestion was rejected out of hand. Someone had the crazy idea of airlifting a black Mercedes limousine like the one used by Idi Amin as a ploy to fool the airport guards. C-130s—the Hippos—were chosen for the mission because they were the quietest of the large aircraft, despite their bulk. Still, the group was worried that the eleven Uganda Air Force MiGs parked at the airport could easily destroy the planes, which would be flying in without a jetfighter escort.

Things on the political front were getting complicated, at least according to the news being leaked to the press. The Israeli cabinet was divided about what to do. Many cabinet ministers favored meeting the demands of the hijackers: to release fifty-two incarcerated terrorists—forty in Israeli prisons and twelve in European countries—as well as two Germans who had been arrested after trying to use a shoulder-mounted missile to shoot down an El Al jet taking off from Kenya. And time was running out—the hijackers had presented Israel with a June 30th deadline. The Israeli cabinet issued a statement indicating that it was considering the option of negotiating. The terrorists extended their deadline to July 3rd.

With information received from the CIA, the French Direction de la Surveillance du Territoire, Scotland Yard, and the security branch of the Royal Canadian Mounted Police, the Mossad had at last assembled a fairly clear picture of the situation on the ground at Entebbe. Mossad agents had interviewed the freed non-Jewish hostages as they arrived at Orly in Paris. The interviews were supervised by a French agent, a man in his mid-thirties with experience in the Middle East. His name: Gerard Duvivier. Kampala Airport was being guarded by a small contingent of Ugandan soldiers. No significant change in the set-up of the airport's facilities was reported—the plans of the building, supplied by the Israeli construction company, were still accurate. One big worry: According to those who had been released, the terrorists were showing signs of preparing to kill hostages.

Danny's team had been briefed on precisely where the terrorists and hostages might be positioned within the airport. One freed hostage, a man by the name of Michel Cojot, seemed to have perfect recall regarding not only where the terrorists were, but even where they had planted explosive charges. Danny prayed that he wasn't faking it. The group was heartened when part of the information Cojot gave was subsequently confirmed through several debriefings of other released hostages, conducted under hypnosis to counteract the normal amnesia following shock.

As the sound of the Hippo's four Allison T56-A-7 turboprop engines lulled him to sleep, Danny reverted to a nightmare he hadn't had since he was ten.

Nazi stormtroopers were running after him, but he was faster, able to reach his school's main building and start climbing the stairs to the first floor. He reached the landing as he heard the orders yelled curtly, the dogs' echoing barks and the pounding of the boots as they hit the steps on the way up. He climbed to the second floor and they were still behind him. Third floor: The yelling got louder. When he reached the fourth and last floor, gasping for air, Danny realized that he had nowhere to run. Nowhere to hide. So he stood there, listening to the short, guttural, diabolical shouts getting closer: "*Hier! Hier! Er ist hier!*"

Just as he had twelve years before, Danny woke up in absolute panic. He looked around the cavernous fuselage of the C-130, which was thirty meters long and spacious enough to have a small helicopter transported within it. Young men like him, most of them sound asleep, looked not merely contented, but so relaxed that they might've been embarking on a vacation.

His group had already gone on many daring missions, but nothing like this. Nothing like flying thousands of miles to the middle of Africa on a defenseless plane that smelled of petroleum and sweat, hoping to land undetected in an airport full of Ugandan soldiers and Arab and German terrorists.

Hoping not to be shot down on approach to the landing strip.

Hoping not to be shot at when exiting the plane via its broad aft ramp.

Hoping not to be shot dead while taking care of business.

Danny tried to block out the roar of the airplane's engines, the barely audible chatter of his fellow soldiers. He knew that three other C-130 planes carried reinforcements. They would be flying in circles a few miles from Entebbe, far enough to be out of radar reach but only minutes away, ready to land right after his Hippo. A group of fifty paratroopers would be waiting for instructions on a boat in the middle of Lake Victoria, a short distance from the airport. Danny also knew that if something went awry there was no way that any of these men would make it in time to avert a bloodbath. The hours went by too slowly.

Finally, Jonathan Netanyahu, the commander of the mission, called everyone to attention.

"*Boker tov, chevreh.*" Good morning, comrades. Yoni, as everyone called him, was in an ebullient mood. Some of the men had been sleeping inside the two Land Rovers aboard the cargo plane or sprawled over their hoods. Yoni had been reading inside the big Mercedes—in the end, they had decided to bring the vehicles, to try to fake the arrival at the terminal of Amin and his entourage. The other men were half-asleep against the fuselage walls. Danny prayed he wasn't the only one petrified by the prospect of their mission. Yoni was almost singing. Danny resented the man's relaxed confidence.

The noise level inside the Hippo went up. Everyone was awake now. Danny felt dizzy with fear. He tried to think about something else, had to think about something else. He was going crazy—something really bad was going to happen, he knew it.

You're freaking out, he told himself. *Relax, you've done this before. No, I haven't. Nothing like this.* His mind wouldn't go where he needed it to go. *There's something wrong here.* Panic was taking hold. Trying to control himself, he started humming quietly. *Sleep, pretty darling, do not cry*, the words waltzed in his mind, a*nd I will sing a lullaby.* That helped. He remembered the last time he'd heard that Beatles song. He was in Tel Aviv with Judith. He had just told her he was leaving for a few days. Some top-secret training exercise, he explained. They were in a restaurant on the water on Hayarkon Street, somewhere north of Jabotinsky Boulevard. The song was playing on crappy loudspeakers, or maybe it was the overall noise level of the place. A breeze was coming in off the ocean. It felt good. The weather was hot, and sitting in the shade didn't help much. But the breeze was cool and smelled of sea. He liked the smell of the sea. Judith looked great. He hated having to leave.

Danny realized that while his mind wandered, Yoni had been outlining the steps of the attack plan. "Is all clear?" he asked in conclusion.

Every head nodded.

He had missed the whole presentation! He was more tired than he thought. But Danny didn't say anything. He knew what needed to be done and was pretty sure that Yoni wouldn't have changed anything at the last moment.

The Hippo was tossing fiercely in turbulence, bucking like a wild horse, dropping like an anvil before stabilizing again. That was okay, Danny said to himself. They had expected atmospheric disturbances.

According to Israeli intelligence, the airport crew at Entebbe was expecting the arrival of a British Airways VC-10 for refueling on its way from London to Mauritius. They had planned to arrive earlier, to identify themselves as that flight if necessary, and to leave well before the VC-10 actually touched down. They were comfortable that while being tracked by radar they would not be identified. Once they landed, though, it would be impossible for the Ugandans and the hijackers not to notice the difference between the huge hulking C-130 and a small VC-10. That was one of the risks they had been unable to eliminate. Their hope for no reaction, or at least for a delayed one, would have to be based on the Hippo's camouflage as a commercial plane and the general inertia of the small staff at the control tower due to the late hour.

Everyone was on alert now. The only sounds Danny heard over the drone of the engines were of ammunition clips clicking into place, of ammo vests rustling as they were donned, and a few tentative coughs. He and several others were costumed as Ugandan soldiers. Someone applied make-up, black as night, to Danny's face.

He was having a hard time controlling his anxiety. And he couldn't see even a semblance of the terror he was feeling in any other faces. The silence was agonizing. Still, when Yoni spoke again, Danny wasn't interested. It was all empty pep talk as far as he was concerned.

"I believe in Israel . . . I believe with all my heart in our ability to carry out any military mission entrusted to us, and I believe in you . . . Let's do it together, and do it the best we can, because it must be done . . ."

Danny spotted the airport as the plane banked right in preparation for landing. The main runway was fully lit. The plane then turned left, aligning itself with the straight row of yellowish lights. Aside from the deafening roar of the engines, absolute silence enveloped the cabin. All lights were off, but Danny couldn't imagine that they would land undetected.

The cabin bounced as the wheels touched the Entebbe tarmac. The aircraft shuddered as it decelerated. With the plane still moving, a group of soldiers jumped to the ground and started placing light signs to enable the three other C-130s to land in case the control tower switched off the lights around the airport. The plane stopped at the chosen place, close to the old terminal. The two Land Rovers and the Mercedes that had been stowed in its belly were driven down the ramp at the rear of the plane.

Next to the cool of the Hippo's cabin, the Ugandan air felt almost unbelievably hot and humid. During one of their briefings back in Israel, the commandos had been told that Entebbe literally sat astride the equator. Danny felt sweat trickling through his make-up.

With a fellow soldier by the name of Giora and four others, Danny moved swiftly, quickly squeezing into the back of the Mercedes and slamming the doors behind them. Yoni sat in the front next to the driver, an officer named Amitsur.

As they drove along the tarmac toward the terminal, Danny made out two Ugandan soldiers standing guard, one to the left and the other to the right of the runway, about two hundred yards from the terminal building. The Mercedes approached them. The guard to the right motioned them to stop.

At least our little ruse got us close to the terminal, Danny thought. Not bad.

"Slow down a little," Yoni said to Amitsur. "Don't frighten the guard. Let him think we're going to identify ourselves."

They drew near. When they pulled up beside the guard, Yoni fired his silenced weapon. So did Giora, behind Yoni on the right side of the car. Danny saw the body fall backwards. The man didn't look dead; he still held his rifle. But his body was unmistakably limp.

Danny heard shots. Their cover had been blown. The other guard reappeared to his left. Danny shot him cleanly in the forehead. Then he heard a deafening discharge of gunshots. The Israelis on the Land Rovers were also shooting at someone. Danny wasn't sure who.

Amitsur drove the Mercedes forward at breakneck speed. In a flurry of flailing arms and fumbling hands, all the men inside the car but the driver removed their Ugandan army shirts, and then used them to clean their faces as best they could. They couldn't afford to draw any friendly fire. Danny felt slightly cooler and less encumbered in his Israeli Army-issue T-shirt.

If the terrorists had heard the shooting, and he was sure it was impossible for them not to have heard, they would start killing the hostages immediately.

Yoni yelled to the driver, "Faster, faster!"

They stopped beside the control tower.

"Out, out! Run! *Run!*"

Danny found himself running ahead of everyone. He was the first to reach the terminal. He turned to look for Yoni, expecting instructions.

But Yoni had stayed behind, at the corner of the control tower, protected by it. That hadn't been part of the plan, had it? He was shouting instructions at the soldiers from the Land Rovers. He looked up, saw Danny, and yelled something Danny didn't understand. Yoni gestured toward the terminal. *Go, go,* he was mouthing.

Danny resumed moving forward. Then he stopped, unsure of what to do. He realized that Yoni had indeed made last-minute changes to the plan back in the C-130, when Danny wasn't paying attention. The other soldiers had now halted and stood around Danny, who couldn't bring himself to move.

Somebody said something to him. Danny didn't understand. Yoni looked at him, shook his head, and started running toward the terminal, toward him.

He finally heard, "In, go in! What's the matter with you?" Then shots.

Yoni made a half-turn, a grimace on his face, and fell.

"Yoni's hit!" someone cried.

Danny's heart sank. He had forced Yoni to expose himself.

He started to run back to pull Yoni out of the line of fire, but Giora blocked his way, shouting, "*Kadima, kadima!*" Yoni had given clear instructions that the hostages were priority; the wounded would only be tended to once the hostages were free.

Kampala was a typical Third World airport, more like a bus station in some far corner of Israel than Jerusalem's Ben Gurion International Airport. The nauseating yellowish glow of flickering sulfur-bulb lights illuminated the terminal's bland exterior, a shrieking halo of jungle insects swarming around each one. The façade was constructed of anonymous concrete and glass, fairly recently built but decaying nonetheless due to lack of proper maintenance.

Danny turned and entered the building. And immediately heard the stutter of semiautomatic gunfire. They were being shot at from farther inside. One terrorist became plainly visible when a glass panel disintegrated. An Israeli unloaded half a magazine in his direction. The man went down hard.

They entered the airport's main hall, which smelled of cordite and perspiration, shouting as rehearsed in Hebrew, English and French, "Everybody on the floor! We're here to rescue you. Don't stand up."

Almost all the hostages—over a hundred of them—lay on mattresses spread out on the terminal floor. Looking up, Danny saw a woman with a gun in one hand and a grenade in another. A man stood nearby, his silhouette stark against the reflecting glass of a window behind him, his Kalashnikov pointing at them. At Danny. Danny didn't have time to aim back. In a split second, his mind coldly told him that he was going to be hit.

And then both terrorists fell—the man first, his face disappearing as several bullets passed through. The woman actually looked surprised as a hail of bullets lifted her, then slammed her lifeless body against the wall behind.

Ilan, an Israeli commando, had shot from Danny's right, killing the man and emptying the rest of his ammo clip into the woman. Danny hadn't moved. Ilan slapped Danny's chest with the back of his hand. "Let's go!"

Danny hadn't had time to react or even to fear death. Now he didn't have time to rejoice at being alive. He realized that the two dead were the German terrorists Wilfried Boese and Gabriele something—he couldn't remember. He had heard Ilan call her the Nazi Bitch. They had been made to memorize the dossiers of each terrorist, but Danny had never been good with names. Nazi Bitch was close enough.

Farther into the lounge, two Palestinian terrorists, Fayez Abdul-Rahim Jaber and Abed el Latif, were able to open fire, Jaber with an automatic rifle and Latif with a pistol. Jaber shot an elderly woman. Danny saw her slump over another woman, bleeding copiously.

Danny rolled into a firing position behind a row of seats. His volley felled Latif and drove Jaber to ground at a check-in counter.

Other commandos moved in, triangulating Jaber. Huddled behind the counter as bullets chewed through it, the terrorist didn't have a chance. He started firing indiscriminately. Danny saw a small girl hit by the spray of bullets.

Jaber was grazed but kept shooting. He was sure to hit another hostage any second. Then Giora bravely rushed the madman. His gun barked, the coup de grace. Jaber sprawled to the floor.

Children walked around in a daze. Some blankets had caught fire and smoke began to fill the lounge. There was screaming, but no more shots.

Danny and his comrades ascended a stairway to the second floor looking for other terrorists. There were two others minimum, at least according to their intelligence—and their intelligence had been impeccable so far. They found two armed men hiding under a couch.

Both were shot point blank, no questions asked.

And then the terminal fell silent. Everyone, commandos and hostages alike, felt it at the same time. It was over.

The shooting had taken less than two minutes.

As he walked back down to the first floor, Danny looked outside just in time to see an explosion of flame, a conflagration in the equatorial night. Demolitions experts were destroying the Ugandan Air Force's Russian MiGs.

In Hebrew, French, and English the commandos began telling the hostages to move calmly out of the terminal. "You are going into the big plane outside the terminal. Please take your belongings." The hostages started streaming toward another C-130 that had flown in just for this purpose, past the young soldiers now protecting them. Danny watched them move past. Many were crying.

And then he saw two soldiers walking up the same ramp, carrying Yoni's dead body on a stretcher.

In the end it was his father's connections that landed Danny Barzilai the job that would define his life. It had all come from a casual conversation during the leave Danny's team was granted after Entebbe. They were walking to the *makolet*, the small grocery store down the street from where they lived. Haim Barzilai had asked him what his plans were when he left the army.

Danny said that he didn't know yet.

"There's time," he said.

"What do you mean, 'time'? If you don't send in your applications you won't get into a university. Your cousin Amos, who you should call once in a while, by the way, told me that the Hebrew University's deadline for applications is less than two months from now."

Danny had no patience for Amos, that tight-assed jerk. "Who says I'm going to study after the army?"

His father stopped walking. "What? Have you gone crazy?"

Danny had planned to get to the applications in the next few days. He had answered as he did just to spite his father, so the man would stop comparing him to Amos.

But now he realized that he really didn't want to attend university. "There's absolutely nothing that attracts me to Hebrew U., or any other school, for that matter. I have bigger plans."

"And they are?" A patronizing half-smile, almost a smirk, dominated his father's face.

"I'll let you know in due time." Defiantly.

Danny's father looked hard into his son's eyes and said, "You're behaving very strangely, Danny. This isn't you." He turned around without another word and walked back home.

Danny turned the other way and walked toward the makolet. He wanted to buy *halva*, he told himself. He really needed to eat a nice sweet piece of halva.

For Danny, the days that followed the Entebbe operation were grueling. By failing to pay attention when he should have, Danny had killed Yoni. Exhaustion was no excuse. Nor was fear. Still, the nation was exhilarated and he was one of their heroes. He was one of the commandos at Entebbe. That meant his father's pride, his friends' respect and pretty much any girl he wanted. Reluctantly, he accepted all that. And the more he did, the worse he felt.

Over the next weeks his parents probed him quietly, trying to figure out his state of mind. He found it strange to be treated with such concern, as if he was mentally unbalanced. At moments he wanted to tell them how bad he felt—how undeserving to be called a hero their son really was. He couldn't, though. He couldn't bear the thought of his father's disappointment, of his mother's unconvincing attempts to tell him that he was being too hard on himself.

He started longing for a place where he would be left alone, where privacy was respected, where the ability to fake it was an asset. A place where few questions were asked. He thought about the remarkable intelligence work that had made Entebbe possible. He thought about the faceless allies his team had counted on to get the job done.

Danny started reading about the Mossad. What he found out made him want to read more. The organization seemed haunted by phantoms, men with the lowest of profiles—unknown people living in an unknown world. Maybe there he would be given one more chance to perform.

So he told his parents one evening that he wanted to work in Israel's secret service. Did they have any contacts? Danny suspected that his father did, from his army days. He looked at the wrinkled face, now inscrutable. His father didn't answer. But when he was quietly transferred from the Sayeret Matkal to a training course for Mossad candidates, he knew he had guessed right.

What followed seemed to last no more than an instant: his first tailing exercises, where he learned that it was much harder to follow than to find out that one was being followed; his first *slik,* secret compartment, not found by his fellow candidates; his first interrogation; his first mission abroad, to photograph a meeting between an East German cultural attaché and a Palestinian college professor at a street corner in Istanbul.

His first wife, first child, first affair. His divorce.

No more than an instant, and he was looking into the mirror and no longer seeing a tall, radiant young man. At the climax of his life Danny still had his long blond hair, but in his early fifties he was slightly balding.

Thanks to too much desert sun, he now had leathery skin. Dark puffy pouches under his eyes.

No more than an instant after his entry into the Mossad training facility, it seemed, he had found himself standing in the living room of his ex-wife's home, preparing to tell her of the death of their sixteen-year-old son, blown to pieces by a suicide bomber at a discotheque in Tel Aviv. The boy's girlfriend, the only daughter of Danny's best friend, had lost both her arms and was unspeakably disfigured in the blast, but lucky enough—if you could call it that—to survive.

So when Sam Stone, his American colleague of so many assignments, invited him on a mission some weeks later, one that Stone said would be the most vital Danny would ever know, that would help him avenge his child and spare other fathers the same fate, the decision was easy. It was also a mission—and here Sam was absolutely clear and bluntly honest—that Danny probably wouldn't survive.

Danny had never been so sure of the agreement he'd made with Sam Stone as he was at this very moment.

"I'm sorry about your son," Jake said. "Why didn't you tell us before?"

"Given your loss, I thought it would hit too close to home. Wanted to spare you that."

"Thanks." Jake gave Barzilai's shoulder a brief squeeze. The Israeli's faint smile carried more empathy than ninety percent of the condolences Jake had received since the FAO Schwarz bombing.

He looked back at the road. They'd barely moved since Barzilai's account of his days as a young commando. "I can't believe this traffic." Jake pounded the dashboard before him in frustration. They sat in a bumper-to-bumper tie-up on the way to JFK.

Barzilai pulled out his cellular phone and turned on its Internet feature. He sent a message to Big Ben, to one of the changing email addresses, using his phone's voice-recognition software. Once connected, the Israeli said curtly in a somber voice, "Paragraphs One and One-A are under discussion, and Paragraph Two is deleted." After a moment of silence, he added, "Paragraph Three is now One, and the new Paragraph One-A is the one that followed Two in the first draft. Negotiations are continuing as planned."

If, against all odds, this message was intercepted, it would appear to be no more than an instruction sent by a lawyer drafting a contract. To Jake, though, it was obvious: One and One-A were Delgado and Stone, Two was Gerard. Three had been Barzilai, who now was One. *Discussion* meant *arrest*, and *deletion* had to mean *death*. Of course, *first draft* was Jake's trip with Gerard to Iran.

Jake understood. He was now One-A, STOP's new second-in-command.

Barzilai's second phone call was to buy an economy roundtrip ticket to Switzerland. He suggested that Jake and Miranda travel as they always had. First class.

"Once at the airport, we might be unable to communicate," Barzilai said. "They could be looking for me, too."

Jake called his travel agent to order tickets and was quiet after that. The image of the violent arrest on the Triborough Bridge burned in his mind. He tried hard to grasp the situation.

In contrast to the stalled traffic they now sat in, STOP seemed to be unraveling at a staggering pace.

CHAPTER TWENTY-ONE

When word reached him that Saajid and his team had been killed, their mission a failure, the emotion Rifaat felt most keenly—handily dominating anger and frustration—was surprise. He was genuinely shocked at this turn of events. The team had apparently slipped up somewhere, allowed their communications to be intercepted. But the report Rifaat received was that it wasn't the FBI who raided their cell. It had to be Jake Burke's friends and comrades in arms. STOP.

Rifaat had been pleased to capture Duvivier, but his pleasure had turned to frustration when the Frenchman confessed nothing before committing suicide. Remembering the fruitless death of Andre Dahan, the first French agent they had apprehended, Rifaat had specifically given instructions to pry Duvivier's jaws open immediately upon capture for the extraction of any suspicious teeth. His men claimed that they'd had no time to do that. The Frenchman had killed himself instantly, they said.

Rifaat was now left with no way to get to the buyers of his companies or any other lead to STOP. He told his men to look for anyone in the French agents' immediate circle who might be connected to STOP in any way. A long shot, at best.

Nonetheless, all indications were that STOP was in disarray. Ironically, the harder Rifaat hit America, the more STOP's allies turned on them.

Today Rifaat met Jasim in a public place, the garden courtyard of a Byzantine palace. Many sites older than this still stood in Lebanon. Rifaat had always been compelled by the power of ancient architecture. It suggested the permanence of civilizations greater than the behemoth child, the United States. And proving that nation's mortality had become Rifaat's obsession.

These thoughts led easily to his business with Jasim, who was as averse to risk as always.

"It's too soon," he was saying. "We were lucky with the dams. But this . . . They haven't amassed enough explosives and will have to rush the acquisition. The transactions will be detected and they'll be arrested."

Rifaat inhaled the scent of red oleander. "My friend, you should know as well as I that it was Allah's mantle that kept our heroes safe before, and it will again. The martyrs will complete their holy duty. Give the order."

Jasim nodded, either convinced or realizing that argument was worse than futile. It was very likely hazardous to his health.

"And the Iranians approve?" he asked.

"Of course. They are eager to punish the West for permitting these outrageous affronts on holy soil."

Rifaat meandered through the garden, enjoying the flowers. Jasim followed obediently.

"Any news from France on the dead agents' contacts?" Rifaat asked.

"Nothing specific yet, but apparently there's a woman. Israeli . . . We'll know more soon."

"That's good." Not all was lost. Rifaat felt better. "I want to know where Burke is. We will avenge poor Ashraf and Saajid. His name must mark him for death anywhere he goes. But I want first to interrogate him—personally. Find him."

"I will spread the word. The faithful will obey."

Rifaat dismissed Jasim with a wave. He would stay here for a few minutes before driving back. This place reminded him what he was fighting for.

"God is great," he murmured to himself.

Barzilai decided to stop off at a hospital and wait out the traffic for a little while. Meanwhile the emergency room doctor stitched up Jake's eye. His got-in-a-fight story was accepted without comment, despite the fact there was no swelling or bruising around the cut. New York hospitals were always very busy.

When the van finally reached the Van Wyck Expressway, traffic began moving more swiftly. Barzilai darted among the usual late-afternoon parade of taxis, limos, SUVs and delivery trucks heading for the airport.

"I need to get rid of the van," he told Jake, "so I'll be dropping you off close to the departures level of Swiss Air. I'll meet you there as soon as I can. Wait for me before security. If they don't delay us there too much, there's a good chance we'll make the 6:30 flight to Zurich."

Jake looked at his watch; 5:15 P.M. At least another fifteen to twenty minutes to reach Kennedy. This was an international flight out of JFK, and Barzilai still had to ditch the car and walk back to the departures terminal before they both went through security. The man was an optimist.

"Gerard told us that he was confident you could handle the disk," Barzilai continued, sounding totally calm and in control. Only the Israeli's white knuckles as he gripped the van's steering wheel betrayed the tension he was probably feeling. "He said you went through the whole procedure twice. Can you? I mean, handle it?"

"I can." Jake could. The consequences were enormous but the procedure was simple enough.

"Be careful, my friend."

Jake smiled. "Yes, sir."

"We've got a few minutes. Let me answer any questions you have now. If I make it in time and things are quiet at the gate we can talk more there. What do you want to know?"

"Just a small question," Miranda said. "If they get you, what does Jake do then?"

"As you can imagine, we've been planning this for a very long time. Every single step is programmed on the disk. The program will offer them to you in sequence. You have discretion to delay or cancel each individual explosion. You can also scroll down the target list and initiate an action that was planned for later just by clicking on it. Obviously, you can't create any new targets. And you'll have to enter the code each time you access the program. Ah, and you can always change the texts of the communiqués."

"What if something doesn't work?" Jake asked.

"Contact Big Ben. You do it the same way as when you send the emails, only on the 'To:' line you type 'Big Ben.' Capitalize the *B's*, with a space between the words. To check for his answer, just click where it says Inbox after you've inserted the disk. Very simple and user-friendly."

Jake didn't like it. "Too simple. No redundancy."

"I forgot you're an engineer." Barzilai smiled. "Okay, let's say you have to destroy the disk. In that case, you'll be contacted by Big Ben. He knows that once the process has begun, he's supposed to get an update from us at least once a day. That's why I left him a message just now. If the update doesn't happen for two days, he'll try to personally contact One—that's me, or One-A—that's you. If he can't do that, the game's over. He'll publish the location of all bombs and deliver the codes for disarming the devices to the American ambassador in London."

"Tell me about the CIA's involvement in STOP."

"You sure know how to change subjects fast." Barzilai seemed surprised. That had been exactly Jake's intention. "All right, then. On that Christmas Day in 1991 when the Soviet Union disintegrated, its nuclear weapons were in the hands of four different—now independent—countries: Russia, Belarus, Ukraine and Kazakhstan. The other three besides Russia are now free of nuclear weapons. And Russia's inventory seems to be more secure now."

"That's not what the papers say," said Miranda, with a note of cynicism.

"I didn't say secure. I said *more* secure. There's still a huge quantity of weapons-grade nuclear material being transported and stored with very little safety. Not to mention the potential bribery of security guards and nuclear workers." Barzilai shook his head. "Anyway, it was even worse a few years ago. The Russian *Mafiya* and the radical Muslim elements in the four republics, especially Kazakhstan, were a source of enormous concern."

A fire engine, its siren at full blast, sped past them, momentarily drowning out Danny's voice.

He went on. "Sam Nunn of Georgia and Senator Richard Lugar of Indiana got Congress to pass the Soviet Nuclear Threat Reduction Act, also called the Nunn-Lugar Act and the Cooperative Threat Reduction program—they refer to it as CTR—"

Jake interrupted. "Let's cut to the chase, shall we?"

"C'mon. Bear with me. I wrote a full internal Mossad report about this. You won't let me show off a bit?"

Jake laughed without feeling much humor. "We don't have time."

"Seriously, you need to understand the context. We'll have more time if you stop interrupting. Anyway, the idea was for the U.S. to provide assistance for dealing safely with the Soviet nuclear weaponry. The first 400 million dollars were transferred from the Department of Defense to these programs right away. Perfectly reasonable idea, right?"

Jake realized that Danny was actually waiting for him to either agree or disagree. He nodded dutifully and said yes.

Barzilai continued. "The only problem is that governments have to negotiate these agreements and that takes time. Just to give you an idea, it took three years to negotiate the process of tagging the nuclear inventory with the former Soviet republics and the Russians especially, who continue to play hardball today. Don't misunderstand me. Even though there are those who criticize CTR as a bungling Pentagon bureaucracy, I think it was the best your government could come up with. Over time, it deactivated thousands of nuclear warheads, over a thousand ballistic missiles including submarine-based ones, their silos and launchers, over a hundred strategic bombers, tens of strategic missile submarines. All in all, important quantities of very deadly hardware. Yet there are those who say that it was all bullshit, that these were just a small fraction of the whole thing."

"Was it?"

"What?"

"A small fraction?"

"Yes. But better than nothing. If you'll let me continue . . . By mid-'95, some people at the CIA saw that the CTR program was bogged down. It had only been able to spend 176 million dollars of the 1.6 *billion* that Congress had authorized. They saw what was really happening on the ground during those still-chaotic times—especially with the suitcase nuclear bombs—and knew that something had to be done. It took them over a year to put a plan together and get the necessary approvals, but by early '97 they went out to the market and tried to buy every suitcase nuclear bomb that was being offered, to keep them from falling into the hands of terrorists. Totally illegal activity, and the few people in on this absolutely top-secret operation knew that they were risking their careers, to say the least."

"How long was the CIA involved?"

"Until a new director was put in place. He went ballistic, no pun intended, when he heard about it. Actually, in typical bureaucratic behavior, he didn't *want* to hear about it. As the ones in charge of the operation, Ramon and Sam were informed that the issue would be taboo from then on. They were told to make this thing disappear, to find a way to dispose of the bombs safely, and erase all traces of them. By that time America was already under attack by terrorists who were supported, to varying degrees, by several Islamic regimes."

"Uh, huh." Jake noticed that they were passing the entrance to Atlantic Avenue, just a couple of miles from JFK.

"So with the help of Big Ben and Gerard," Barzilai went on, "and with mine too, I should say, they obeyed their director's orders and made the suitcase nukes disappear—by placing them where they are today. Later on, when that CIA director was replaced by the present one, the Agency realized the strategic value of what had been done, and they even added additional targets, placing ONC bombs in those." Barzilai was now smiling dryly.

Miranda spoke up. "And with characteristic American behavior on security matters, things flip-flopped once more. I guess with Delgado and Stone arrested we have a pretty clear picture of the CIA's position on STOP now, don't we?"

"Oh, no, they'd already dropped them a while ago. Sam and Ramon have been rogue agents for some time. The only reason they hadn't been arrested is because they knew too much and could—would—embarrass the Agency in a major way if they were to talk. But I guess the situation's become too hot. The Agency can't turn a blind eye anymore to what we were doing. With the French putting on pressure, and—this is me just guessing now—threatening to go public, they had no choice. They were informed by the French, who got it from the Iranians, that Gerard was deeply involved in the explosions. And it's well known to the main agencies involved that Sam and Ramon were working with Gerard, as a team, in terrorism-related matters. They simply had to do it. They had to arrest Sam and Ramon."

Jake nodded. "Yeah, makes sense."

"And now they want to quash this before it gets out of hand," Miranda added.

"Where does that leave you, Danny?" Jake asked.

"I was never an official member of the team. Don't forget, I'm no longer with the Mossad. So I'm not sure. If they do know about me, three possibilities exist. One, the CIA's enlisted the FBI, who's already looking for me here. The second possibility is that the CIA's informed the Mossad that they want to question me and has asked for access to me discreetly before arresting me here or putting out an Interpol search, which could make this whole mess public. If that's the case, the Mossad would let me know. I've been fired, but I still know too much about this operation and others. I'm sure they'd prefer for this interrogation to take place in Israel. The third possibility is that they want to talk to Ramon and Sam before they do anything else."

"Which do you think is the most probable?"

Barzilai had turned slightly left in the final approach to the airport. "It's either one or three. I don't think the CIA has talked to the Mossad about this yet. I haven't heard from them."

"So it's fifty-fifty that they're looking for you. And there's no place more obvious than the airport," Miranda said.

"Right."

"You know what?" Jake was thinking clearly now. "We'll go ahead and board. A man and a woman won't draw undue attention, but three extremely late passengers running to catch the same flight just might. If they get you, they might stop us too, just to see if there's a connection between the three of us. And these days everything's videotaped. If you make the flight, great—we'll see you when you get on the plane. They board first-class passengers before anyone else. If you don't make it, I'll wait for a call or a message from you at my hotel. We'll be at the Baur Au Lac. You know it?"

"Who doesn't? And you're right, that makes sense," Barzilai said, his smile tense. They were on the outside lane facing the entrance to Terminal 4. The sign above the entrance to the building said, *Singapore Airlines*. "Go ahead. Swiss Air—"

". . . is here too," Jake finished, stepping out of the van. "See you soon. Be quick. And good luck, my friend."

Hasim Khafar sipped the weak American coffee and gazed at the façade of Jake Burke's home half a block away. He could probably draw that building from memory and get every detail.

Since Saajid's untimely death, Hasim and another Saudi-born jihadist had been posted at Burke's residence. When their enemy returned home, Hasim's orders were to kill him by any means necessary. Even if it meant giving his own life in the process.

This wasn't a sacrifice Hasim was afraid to make. Saajid had been like a brother to him. If Hasim's last act was sending Saajid's killer to hell, he could think of worse ways to leave this earth.

Hasim glanced at the passersby, shaking his head. He couldn't get used to all the scandalously clad women walking the street. To his eye, their short skirts and open-necked blouses were like whore's garb.

He glanced over and saw Abdul dozing in the passenger seat. The big man's knees were pressing the dash. Hasim pitied him for that. Yes, Abdul could tear a phone book in half with his bare hands, but he never seemed comfortable in a world built for smaller people. Hasim's most conservative estimate was that his partner stood six-foot-nine and weighed three-hundred pounds. Still, Abdul was obviously comfortable enough to sleep on the job.

Hasim considered rebuking his associate but wasn't foolish enough to provoke the giant, and he also couldn't blame Abdul for his boredom. This mission had been dull to the extreme.

Jake Burke had never returned. If he needed anything from home, he must've used envoys who passed in and out with the residents, unrecognized.

It was time to take a chance.

Hasim opened his car door. Abdul startled awake with a guilty expression.

"I will be right back," Hasim said simply. Abdul grunted in assent.

Hasim approached the building. The doorman was in his sixties, a spry and energetic fellow with old-fashioned cap and gloves. He greeted Hasim with a pleasant but practiced smile.

"Good evening, sir."

"Good evening," Hasim said, pleased that his excruciating English lessons were being put to good use. "I am looking for Jacob Burke. Do you know when he will be back?"

"I'm sorry, I don't," the doorman said at once. "Mr. Burke is overseas on business. Wish I could be of more help."

Hasim smiled affably. He had a cherubic face that was difficult to mistrust. Pulling a hundred-dollar bill from his wallet, he folded it in half and used it to brush imaginary lint from his lapel. At eye level, there was no way the doorman could fail to see its denomination.

"Do you know where he went by any chance?"

"Well . . ." The doorman hesitated, thinking. He was either searching his memory or deciding whether to accept the bribe. "I can tell you this," he finally offered. "The concierge called the car service to run him to JFK, an Iran Air flight. So he was heading to the Middle East."

Beaming, Hasim shook the man's hand and passed him the bill. "Thank you, my friend."

"You didn't hear it from me," the doorman added, making the money vanish with all the speed of a Vegas magician.

Hasim nodded. "And no one asked you about it, either."

"No sir," the doorman said.

Though he could barely contain his excitement, Hasim hurried around the block before returning to the car. It would be foolish to give the doorman a description of his vehicle, or Abdul.

"What was that all about?" Abdul asked when Hasim slid behind the wheel and started the car.

"Burke went to Iran," Hasim said, letting some self-satisfaction creep into his voice. "Americans are so corrupt. The doorman told me for one-hundred dollars."

Abdul's blocky features betrayed consternation. "Maybe we should stay here. What if we miss him?"

"It will be easier to track him over there," Hasim said as he pulled into traffic. "And anything is better than sitting in the car, day after day—am I right?"

Abdul nodded. "This is true."

Hasim drove purposefully. The trail might be cold, but at least there was a trail. He was confident they could still carry out Rifaat's death sentence and avenge Saajid. The next step was clear. They were going to John F. Kennedy International Airport.

Little did Hasim know, his quarry was also there. But not for long—they'd had no problem making the flight to Zurich. Jake was disappointed to find that the first-class section of this plane was located to the left as one boarded, while both business and economy were to the right. He wouldn't know if Barzilai was on the flight until after takeoff. And if he really wanted to play it safe, he shouldn't even go to the back of the plane to check. *Damn.* Another sleepless night.

And it was. Jake was exhausted as he followed the other first-class passengers off the plane in Zurich. To his ultimate frustration, there was no line at passport control, so he had no chance to look back while waiting. He'd have to wait even longer to find out if Barzilai had made it out of the U.S.

"It'll be all right," Miranda said, noting his frown. "Danny knows how to take care of himself."

Jake almost said, "So did Gerard," but didn't want to sting Miranda with such a comment. Her familiar presence beside him on the plane had been his sole comfort overnight. He found the small sounds she made, dreaming fitfully, very endearing. Like having some semblance of a family back.

The border policeman waved Jake in after a perfunctory look at his passport. Jake milled around next to the baggage carousel as if waiting for his suitcase. It took considerable effort not to react when he saw Danny, who made a beeline to the men's room, purposely fail to acknowledge them.

Jake joined Barzilai in the restroom. While they washed their faces at adjacent sinks, the Israeli said almost inaudibly, "I'm not sure I'm not being followed. I'll meet you at the Baur Au Lac in a while. Let me leave the bathroom first."

The taxi ride from the airport took less than twenty minutes. As the diesel Mercedes pulled into the elegant driveway, two bellmen materialized, one holding the taxi door for Miranda and the other rushing to the trunk of the car to retrieve their luggage. Of course, they had none. No Swiss Francs, either.

"*Ich habe kein Gepäck. Können Sie das Taxi für mich bezahlen?*" I have no bags. Can you pay the taxi for me? Jake turned then, and walked swiftly into the hotel lobby.

"*Kein Problem, Herr Burke.*" Nothing was a problem at the Baur Au Lac.

They had agreed to meet at Zurich's most famous hotel, and the one where Jake was best known, for one single reason: its absolute discretion. Barzilai would be immediately directed to Jake, just as a multitude of other private clients had been in the past. The hotel staff was known internationally for its prodigious selective memory. They remembered the minutest detail of a client's preferences yet instantly forgot that client's actions—which banker he or she met in its meeting rooms or restaurants.

Jake had stayed in the hotel countless times, mostly on business, though he had spent many memorable days and nights here with Stephanie. His wife had loved Zurich. The city's orderliness, elegance, and service had pleased her. Along with the shopping, Jake thought, with a smile cut short by pain.

Before he was led to his usual suite, Jake bid a temporary farewell to Miranda at her own door. After so much time together, parting even briefly felt oddly difficult.

In Jake's rooms, the view overlooking Lake Zurich was nothing short of spectacular. The living room, with a large couch and several reading chairs, was immaculate and welcoming. He recognized on the bookshelf a book he had finished reading during his last trip and left behind. He resisted looking at the bedroom. After the sleepless flight, the king-sized bed might be too appealing.

As soon as the bellman left the suite, Jake went down to the lobby. It was so quiet there that he could hear the ticking of the beautiful clock by the stairway. No sign of Barzilai. He described the Israeli to the two receptionists, who he'd known for many years and trusted completely. He walked to the main restaurant, one of his favorite places in all of Zurich. For years, it had been the meeting place of choice for the city's elite and the occasional celebrity. Jake didn't care about that. He decided not to eat yet and wait for Barzilai.

He walked to the lounge, its imposing skylight bathing the room in morning sunlight. He sat close to the great fireplace, which was not in use at the moment. In winter, Jake loved to have a cigar and cognac while looking at the flames. Now a white-jacketed waiter rushed to his side, took his order, and returned in less than a minute with fresh coffee.

Miranda joined him and they spent a few moments like vacationers, actually avoiding the subject of their harrowing circumstances. It would've been perfect if Jake hadn't been so anxious to see the Israeli. He needed badly to be reassured that all was well.

CHAPTER TWENTY-TWO

A very long half-hour passed before the main receptionist entered the room with Barzilai right behind. His stubble and the disheveled blond hair only amplified his look of extreme concern.

"Did you see?" Barzilai asked as soon as the receptionist was out of earshot. His eyes were bloodshot.

"What?"

"Pictures of Ramon, Sam and Gerard were on every TV screen I passed. The captions under the photos even identify STOP."

Jake was stunned. "It must've happened in the last half hour. What about you or me?"

"No. I think the French and the Americans decided to go public, to show that they'll fight terrorism of any kind. It looks like my ex-colleagues in Israel are covering for me and not supplying any identification. It'll take a while for the Americans to find a picture of me in their archives, if they have one at all. And it looks like no one but Rifaat knows you're with us. Yet."

"And Big Ben?"

"Big Ben's another story altogether. He's actually quite famous in the UK, but as one of the young geniuses responsible for creating the first Internet search engine, which was later taken over by a software giant.

The trickery of his colleagues kept him from making any kind of a profit on the patent. He's now forty years old and still brilliant, but basically alone. Ben has money now, all perfectly hidden, but that's because we pay him royally. Don't misunderstand . . . his heart's in the right place, but he's much more cynical since he got screwed. He's now into amassing real money. For us it's worth it, though. As you know, Big Ben has set up our entire communication structure and an almost perfect system of remotely detonating the bombs. Bottom line? No agency knows about him, unless we've been followed. And if they arrest him, he won't talk."

"How can you be sure?" Miranda asked, ever wary.

"He's famous enough and outspoken enough that they won't begin to question him without the presence of a lawyer. They'd need proof to do anything to him. And they don't have it—that's for sure."

They walked to the almost-empty restaurant. It was a little before ten in the morning.

"What do we do now?" Jake asked, once the waiter had left with their order.

"We keep hitting them. Even though I don't think that'll get us any-where." Despite his obvious concern, the Israeli was surprisingly cool.

Jake was aghast. "What are you saying?"

"We do as planned. You heard what Ramon said. We have an email to send."

"But you don't believe it'll get us anywhere."

"Right."

"And we've been doing all this bombing for what? Talk to me, Danny."

"The truth? I've had serious doubts about the course of action we were planning to take in Iran since the beginning. I made that clear to the rest. But it was Ramon's operation."

"Not anymore. You're One now, and I'm One-A. Not because we wanted it that way, but because Stone and Delgado are out. We'd better be sure of what we're doing. What are your doubts?"

"In contrast to many Arab countries, who really are artificial assem-blages of different tribes, Iran is a true nation with a tradition of uniting against foreign attackers and suspending internal conflicts until those attackers have been defeated."

"And the riots we've been seeing?"

"Forget the riots. They'll be quashed soon. I don't think we'll get the Iranian theocracy to cave. It's actually the other way around—the way things stand now, we're propping up their leadership. I told you, when attacked they unite, even if it's behind leaders they don't like."

"The people seem to be getting fed up with the mullahs," Miranda observed.

"Yes, but it'll take them years to get rid of these guys. In the meantime, they continue to progress in their nuclear program and their support of terrorism."

"What do you propose we do?"

"I need to think." Barzilai looked tired.

Jake leaned back and closed his eyes for a moment. He then opened them and leaned forward. "Okay, let's go over this step by step, shall we? You know, just applying logic to the situation."

Barzilai nodded, almost imperceptibly.

"Let's review where we stand in our little game with the mullahs. I'll describe our actions, you describe the Iranians' reactions. This should help us clarify what our next steps should be."

"Uh, huh." Barzilai wasn't showing much enthusiasm.

"Just humor me. Like we humored you on the way to the airport, remember? By the way, I happen to agree with you. I don't like the way this is going at all. That's why I think we have to stop and review this whole thing. Hey, it beats blindly obeying Delgado's instructions."

"All right."

"I'll start. Our first move was to detonate the bomb in Qeshm."

"They didn't respond," Barzilai said.

"We next threatened to destroy the first refinery—Bandar Abbas—and presented our demands."

"They rejected them."

"Not really. They didn't believe we could do it. If you'll remember, they ignored us and didn't even evacuate the refinery."

"Right." Barzilai sat up straight. Now he was paying attention.

"Next we blew up Bandar Abbas, identified ourselves and threatened to destroy the second refinery—Tabriz." Jake spoke slowly, sipping his coffee. "We warned them that we had the ability to strike a third time and that they'd better take us seriously. And what happened?"

"They tried to disarm the bomb in Tabriz—which caused the deaths of close to a hundred of their own people and, more to the point, the destruction of the refinery. Next they gave the okay for Rifaat's massive attack on the American dams. And they made sure that your government knew it was them. Which means that they suspected the U.S. was behind the explosions."

Jake nodded. "I agree. What we did then was to ignore the attacks on America and maintain the same pressure. We threatened the third refinery—Abadan."

"They probably reached the conclusion that they hadn't succeeded in scaring the U.S. government. They drastically cut the production of oil." Barzilai went for his coffee.

"We blew Abadan up," Jake continued.

"They put pressure on the French, who were probably scared shitless of losing their contracts and of the effect of rising oil prices." Barzilai was talking fast now.

"How were the Iranians able to pressure the French?" Jake asked, obviously knowing the answer.

"They got results out of torturing Reza and others, and found out that Gerard was involved. Gerard was DGSE. All Iran had to do was show their findings to the French government."

"That worked," Miranda said.

"Yes. They've gotten the French to cooperate fully, killed an operative of STOP and hit the U.S., just in case. They probably feel that they've been able to stop the whole thing." Barzilai sounded like his old self. "On top of that, your law-abiding and naïve government arrested Stone and Delgado, instead of just looking the other way. Could they be any stupider?"

"No choice," Miranda said. "All the French had to do was to threaten to expose the whole thing. The scandal would've been enormous. A covert CIA program. America installing massive bombs inside the infra-structure of countries it isn't at war with."

"Anyway, Jake added, "after Gerard's death and the arrests, the Iranians probably believe there's no need for any concession to STOP."

"Right. At this moment, the mullahs are sure that they're winning." Barzilai sounded angry. "We have to change that. *Now*."

"How?"

"With a massive attack." Barzilai clenched his fists. "You remember those old movies where you had two teenagers driving a car at high speed toward each other? If no one changed course, they would crash and die. And the one who veered off would lose and be the chicken. There was one with James Dean, wasn't there?"

"*Rebel Without a Cause*."

"Iran is playing a game of chicken with the West now. The mullahs believe that STOP is really a proxy for one or a combination of Western countries. And they think they're winning. From Iran's point of view, the West has ceased its support of STOP and even started to arrest STOP's members. And you know what? They *are* winning. Unless something very dramatic happens, Iran will continue its present course of action, while waiting for the West to finish off STOP."

"You mentioned a massive attack . . ." Jake was uncomfortable with the idea. He would hear Barzilai out, but at some point the constant escalation of violence had to end. He wondered if there was a way to end it.

"We've got to do it," Barzilai continued. It has to be decisive and so big that we won't ever need to bomb anything else again. We have twelve other targets in Iran. We should blow up at least eight of them."

Jake was nodding silently, meaning that he was thinking, not agreeing just yet. Miranda was definitely not in accord with Barzilai's reasoning but had kept quiet so far.

"There's one big advantage to this strategy," Jake acknowledged. When we turn to the other countries, and they see the destruction in Iran, they should cave fairly fast."

"But? You don't sound convinced."

"I'm not. These mullahs are crazy."

Barzilai nodded vigorously. "You're absolutely right on that one. Take Yazdi, the head of Iran's Expediency Council. On top of being extremely corrupt, the guy's a madman. A while ago, he declared that an all-out nuclear attack on Israel would destroy it altogether, with less than catastrophic damage to the Muslim world. The man is willing to accept nuclear retaliation from Israel—which will be massive, and he knows that. Believe me, our limited attacks aren't making much of an impression on him."

"Okay," Jake said. "Let's use your own logic. What you're saying is that a massive attack isn't sufficient. As long as the mullahs are there, Iran will stay the course."

"No," Barzilai replied, "what I'm saying is that Yazdi and his group won't budge. I think the rest of the mullahs might knuckle under if faced with an overwhelming attack."

"Understood. One more thing . . . did you say, 'corrupt?' I tend to imagine these mullahs as being radically religious, uncaring about anything material—"

"Ha!" Barzilai sipped his coffee. "Iran's leaders are running the country as a business that everyone with any importance is part-owner of. You've got five-hundred or so mullahs occupying political positions. All of them, *all of them,* are shareholders in some 'privatized' corporation, or else trustees of the major revolutionary foundations. As the head of Iran's Expediency Council, Yazdi's in a perfect position for that. And he has the main players in the country's power structure in bed with him. Yazdi and his clique are major shareholders in over a hundred companies. These people are too entrenched. And incredibly greedy."

"I didn't know that." The seed of an idea was taking shape in Jake's mind. Miranda looked excited—she could always tell when Jake was on to something.

"Yazdi's involved in . . . I should say, 'controls'—most of the foreign investment in the Iranian oil industry. You must've read about a deal where Japan invested billions of dollars in Iranian gas and oil. Yazdi's group made a fortune. It's an open secret. We know that, and the majority of the Iranian people know that. They just can't prove it. Irrefutable proof might trigger a revolution. Iranians are fed up with all the graft and thievery. That's why they elected this hard-line president who ran on an anti-corruption campaign. But apart from some publicity stunts, he's getting nowhere. These corrupt mullahs will only let go if they're personally attacked."

Personally attacked. The outline of the idea was becoming sharper. "One more thing. The riots."

"What do you mean?" Barzilai drank avidly from the now-cold coffee.

"When the Iranian Liberation Front issued its communiqué—that's what sparked the riots."

"You're right. It wasn't our attacks that sparked them, it was internal opposition that got the people to rise up."

"And that's another reason why the massive attack might not be the solution, because our attack would be an external attack. We might need to do something different, in the end. Something much more daring, if we're going to change Iran's course of action."

Miranda nodded vigorously. "Exactly!"

"But what?" asked Barzilai.

"I don't know." Jake shook his head. "But one thing I do know is that the Armageddon you're talking about is too much. Too much destruction. Too much blood. We won't win that way, and I don't want to try. We need something that'll stop the people from uniting behind these mullahs. And we have to get to Yazdi and his crowd. It's a tall order." Jake smiled, his idea now perfectly clear. "But I think I have a plan. It's a one-two punch that'll only require a last limited attack and will get us what we want. But I need to do some checking before I tell you about it. Just a couple of phone calls, maybe a short meeting. Why don't we take a break while I do that? We could meet in two hours in my suite."

Barzilai's blue eyes squinted curiously but he asked nothing. "Okay, done deal. I have things to do in Zurich, too. That's why we stopped here on the way to Israel." The Israeli got up. "I'll see you in two hours."

After Barzilai left, Jake and Miranda went back to his suite to discuss the new plan.

"I like it," she said, when he was done. "But it's too risky for you to do it alone and you know it. There might be dangers that you won't see. You need someone with you to talk things through. You've got to let me come with you."

"No way, not again," Jake said, adamant. "I can't put you in that position. Too dangerous."

"Jake," Miranda said passionately, "what you said to Danny down there . . . you hit the bulls-eye. This is the answer! But you can't do it without me."

Jake turned to the window. The thought of risking Miranda's life again devastated him. "No," he said softly. "I'm sorry . . . I can't lose you, too."

She was suddenly beside him, her hand on the small of his back. He turned to look at her. The emotion in her eyes had softened the gray to an almost silvery sheen. She looked fragile and beautiful.

"You never will," she said, and suddenly he was pressing her soft lips to his. She yielded instantly to the kiss, and then said, with supreme effort, "Wait, if it's too soon . . ."

"No," he whispered. "Now, before it's too late."

He slid his arm around her body and brought her to him. He smelled her hair and felt the pressure of her breasts against his chest.

"You have no idea how much I want you," he said.

He kissed Miranda again. She clasped her fingers behind his neck and held his mouth against hers. She was shivering. He kissed the nape of her neck.

He undressed her slowly under the soft light streaming from the bedroom. The sweater, her skirt, and finally Miranda's flesh-toned bra and panties dropped to the floor. He heard her breath quicken. Her eyes were on him, giving. Only the thinnest gold chain remained about her neck. And her wristwatch.

Jake didn't take his own clothes off. Instead, he lifted her in his arms, carried her into the half-dark bedroom, and gently laid her on the bed. Only then did he undress. When he returned to the bed, she pulled him onto her, biting his lips, urging him to take her. He didn't. Not yet.

Unhurriedly but intensely he explored her body. At times gently and at times roughly, he touched, opened, kissed, bit, and savored her until she lay spent and motionless, her slightly slanted eyes closed, coal-black tendrils of hair framing her head, full lips parted, breathless, cries of happiness and despair alternating like night and day between her sobs.

He ran his fingers through her hair again and again as he waited for the tempest of her feelings to subside. He kissed her and she kissed him back, her lips inviting. Then she turned to him and rubbed her crotch against his body. There was a desperation in the way she clung to him, anguish in the heat of her breath, anger in the way she scratched him.

"I can't take this anymore. I want you in me," she said, biting his shoulder.

Finally, he pushed her legs apart and entered her urgently. The only sound in the room was the rustling of the sheets. He lost track of time. They were sweating. Jake was gasping, Miranda moaning. And then they came, furiously, together, her contractions swallowing him, her legs firmly around his buttocks, holding him there inside her.

By the time they finished making love, the two hours were almost up. They shared a quick shower, during which Jake's grief for his wife and guilt at what he'd just done flared inexorably. Miranda saw it in his eyes and was going to say something when he gently pressed his fingertip to her lips.

"This wasn't a mistake," he told her. "If Stephanie's looking down on me, I know in my heart that she understands."

Miranda nodded, and for the rest of their all-too-brief shower they were giddy as schoolchildren.

When they went downstairs, the trusted main receptionist walked from behind the counter and gave Jake a sealed envelope. "This is from the gentleman that came to meet you this morning. His instructions were very explicit. I was supposed to keep this envelope on me until I could deliver it to you personally."

A handwritten message inside the envelope said:

Sorry, I have to leave. Unexpected developments. Meet me in
Israel. Do not fly directly in—there should be no record of your

entering the country. Make your way to Sharm-el-Sheikh, in Egypt. Go to the Pyramisa Resort Hotel. Someone will meet you there.

They would have to work fast to set Jake's plan in motion. First he called New York and woke up his banker and friend, Ted Suter.

He began by thanking Ted for his help in Egypt. Thanking and apologizing profusely. It was long overdue, and they both knew it, but Suter was an old friend and a businessman to boot. When he said that all was forgiven, Jake took him at his word.

"What are you doing now?" Suter asked.

Jake sidestepped the question. "Can UBS arrange a meeting with Nasrullah Yazdi, head of Iran's Expediency Council?"

"The Middle East? Oh, no. You aren't planning on doing anything crazy again, are you?"

"No, I just want to make some money. Can you get me that meeting?"

"No, I can't. Certainly not for an American. The best I could do is arrange for you to see his representative in Switzerland."

"I'll take that. But there's one more thing. We can't use my real name."

"Have you lost your mind? Whose name would you have me use?"

"An alias. After the Egypt fiasco, you'll have to vouch for me as a new player. I know this is a big request, and I wouldn't ask if it wasn't terribly important. I'll owe you big-time. I really want to do this deal and there are Islamic extremists who want Jake Burke dead."

That seemed to do it. They worked out the details of Jake's and Miranda's new identities, and Suter called the head of UBS's private banking, who arranged a meeting for "Walt Landis" and "Roberta Pierce-Reynolds" with one Abbas Zuhayli at Banhoffstrasse 40. Zuhayli was a confidant of Yazdi and had been the Yazdi family's Switzerland-based asset manager for many years.

Twenty minutes later Jake and Miranda were walking on one of the world's great shopping streets, the Banhoffstrasse. Jake knew it well. Most Swiss banks had private clients who invested in his main hedge fund, and those banks' offices lined this beautiful street. He felt at home taking a walk from the Baur Au Lac, away from the lake, down Banhoffstrasse.

They joked about the temptation to hold hands, but it felt a little strained. There was no time to discuss the parameters of their new relationship, if that was what it was, and Jake was certain the situation felt as surreal to Miranda as it did to him.

The first thing they did was to stop at Grieder to buy appropriate clothing. He had little trouble finding a conservative dark blue suit. Fortunately, Miranda had a prototypical build and they could buy off the rack. There wasn't time for tailoring, or even more than a cursory check of the fit.

"How do I look?" she asked, resplendent even without shoes in a charcoal suit.

"Magnificent," Jake replied, quite honestly.

Next they hastily chose a pair of versatile heels to complete her ensemble. Equipped at last, they set out for Banhoffstrasse 40.

Along the way they passed the beautiful building that housed the offices of Credit Suisse. Jake noticed that even the Swiss had been forced to do some cost-cutting. The building had been partially transformed into a shopping arcade. He saw an electronics shop. He went in and bought a DDR-3000 voice-activated digital recorder.

They reached the entrance of a non-descript office building and rang the button next to a sign that read, WCT—World Commodity Traders. Once buzzed in, they took a slow elevator to the third floor, where a receptionist was waiting to usher them into a meeting room that was bare of anything except for a writing pad and pen.

Two minutes later, a short chubby man, the roundness of his smiling face actually enhanced by a goatee, walked in with his hand extended. "Welcome, Mr. Landis., Ms. Pierce-Reynolds. Mr. Landis, I've heard good things about you."

"All lies," Jake smiled back.

"Can't be. A recommendation this enthusiastic from SBS is hard to come by."

After the initial pleasantries and the de rigueur offer of coffee, Zuhayli grew serious. "So what can I do for you?"

"I have an idea about how to help Iran recover some of its losses if the explosions continue."

"Yes?"

"With each destruction of a refinery, the overall refining capacity of the world diminishes and the price of refined oil products like gasoline goes up. On behalf of Iran, I can buy 'call options,' the right to buy these products in the future for a price that's fixed now. That way, your country will recover part of the cost of rebuilding its refineries because these options would go up in value after each explosion. I can structure it for you efficiently . . . and very discreetly."

"And how exactly would you execute that?"

"I represent a consortium of private investors. Bold men. We have a large discretionary fund for aggressive investments. You remember when George Soros made over a billion dollars betting against the British pound? We did the same thing at the same time, shadowing his transaction. We made a little less than Soros. Just a little. That was, in fact, our first major deal."

"That was in the '80s, right?"

"'92. Anyway, we've handled a high volume of transactions of this type. To add a few more is easy and unnoticeable." Jake winked. "I could do this for Iran as a country and, very discreetly and unknown to anyone, for individuals who would profit in parallel from the structure. Like we profited from Soros' big bet."

Zuhayli was clearly interested but also skeptical. "I was told that you're a top businessman of the utmost reliability. But as you can imagine, one has to be careful these days. Why don't you show me something?"

"All right," Jake said. "I'll do that. I'll do a sample transaction on your behalf, and I'll even fund it myself. If there's a new explosion, there will be profit made. Where do you want it sent?"

Zuhayli was impressed. "You'll do that? What if it doesn't work and there's a loss?"

"There won't be. But if there is, I'll eat it. I'm not structuring this as a one-time transaction. Iran has money that it could invest better. I'm trying to build a long-term relationship with you, and I want to show you what we can do. The only thing I'll ask for is a meeting—with you present, of course—with Mr. Yazdi and his team. I want to give a presentation on the transaction itself, as well as all the other things we can do for them. That is, if you're happy with the first transaction. If you say no, no problem. I have other countries in mind, but I'm talking to you first and exclusively."

The Iranian paused and closed his eyes, thinking. Then nodded. "You know, everything in life is timing. And you came at the right time."

"Why is that?"

"It's the recent events. We could use some good news. I'll explain later." Zuhayli smiled and touched his arm. "I'll see what I can do. I'm pretty sure it can be arranged. I have very close contact with Mullah Yazdi," he said proudly. "There's nothing I do here that he isn't aware of, in real time, as it happens. Let's meet here at my offices again tomorrow, same time. I'll have your answer then."

"I cannot stay," Jake said, deciding that since Barzilai was expecting them, either he or Miranda had to go on to Egypt. "But Roberta will be here tomorrow. If the answer's positive, she can start working with you on the terms of the contract covering our future relationship with your firm . . . predicated, of course, on your being happy with this first sample transaction."

Jake and Miranda left the offices of Abbas Zuhayli with a recording of the conversation and the wiring instructions to Green Leaf Limited's account at Bank Hochsteiner. Green Leaf Limited was Yazdi's British Virgin Islands holding company. Step one of the plan was in place.

"It went great," Jake said, giving her a quick hug once they were around the corner. "I just wish he hadn't asked us to stay one more day."

"I can handle it," she said confidently. "Meet you in Israel the day after tomorrow."

As they rushed back, they passed Spruengli, Jake's favorite coffee-house-cum-patisserie, on Paradeplatz. It made him think of Gerard and his sweet tooth. A sad thought, but Jake tried to focus on the future. He hoped that maybe, just maybe, he'd found a way to get the job done without the carnage. What he had set in motion was bold, dangerous, maybe fatal, but he had not a flicker of doubt.

Marty Rosenzweig went in for his morning coffee at Dunkin Donuts. The Hispanic girl behind the counter gave him a break when he came up twenty cents short. "Much obliged, little lady," Marty said with a tip of his Patriots cap.

He noticed something strange on the way out. Marty was observant—guys like him, retired and one bounce from homeless, tended to notice things; not much else to do but look around. A guy was counting the steps to Faneuil Hall from the Government Center T-stop. Marty could tell that by his deliberate movements and silently moving lips. Though his wardrobe was new L.L. Bean, he was obviously of Middle Eastern descent.

Just then, the man turned his head and caught Marty's eye. Marty glanced away, stirring his coffee.

When Marty looked back, the guy was gone.

CHAPTER TWENTY-THREE

Jake felt self-conscious and jittery as he entered Cairo International Airport. Even though it seemed like an eternity, he had been here only seven days earlier. While still in Zurich, he'd considered calling Mike Iqbal, Isabelle Said's nephew, to offer his heartfelt thanks—and his most sincere apologies for the death of Mike's aunt. He assumed that the young Egyptian was able to escape any fallout from the gun battle outside Ashraf's house. But he decided not to run the risk. Some zealous police investigator might've tapped Mike's phone.

Jake stood in the sole immigration line, his thoughts a continuous loop of probabilities. He was trying to convince himself that the Egyptian police had no records on him. That even if they did, they were unlikely to interface with the immigration authorities. That even if they did share information, immigration probably wasn't organized enough. All wishful thinking, he knew. As the minutes passed, he questioned the wisdom of blindly accepting Barzilai's instruction to enter Israel via Egypt. When his turn came to hand his passport to the unshaven immigration official, he hoped that he wasn't telegraphing his anxiety.

"Visa?" the official said in a clipped tone.

Visa. He had forgotten. His travel agent had arranged everything last time.

Jake shook his head, narrowing his eyes to indicate a lack of comprehension.

"Visa. Visa," the man said, his pointer stabbing Jake's passport.

Jake shook his head again. "I don't know."

The official settled back in his chair and started leafing through Jake's passport. With the passport open to one of the pages, he lifted his eyes and stared at Jake for what seemed like a very long time. He resumed flipping through the document. Jake heard grumbling. He looked back. The line behind him was growing.

"Last visit. Where visa out?"

The officer was pointing to his first visa. Jake was in trouble. Naturally, his passport hadn't been stamped when he was flown to the U.S. in Malouf's plane. He didn't know what to say, so once more he made the uncomprehending face.

The officer stood up. He opened a door behind him and exited the booth. He signaled Jake to accompany him.

Jake tasted fear. He followed the official to a small windowless room, where he was shown in and a thick glass door closed behind him. He had a choice of three filthy chairs, all oozing dirty yellow foam from torn armrests.

An armed guard loitered nearby, a cigarette dangling from his lips.

More than an hour later, Jake's imagination had exhausted all possible scenarios and their probable outcomes. Whatever logic he applied, the conclusion was the same: He was going to be arrested.

The scruffy immigration officer walked in, a half-smile on his lips. He lit a cigarette and offered one to Jake.

"No, thanks." Jake smiled as widely as he could manage.

"No visa come in," the man said, shaking his head.

Jake shook his head, too.

"No visa go out." The man was smiling. He looked like a cat holding a mouse by its tail.

"Sorry," Jake said.

"Bad."

Jake said nothing.

"Very bad."

The guard walked in, and the two Egyptians spoke briefly. The guard looked tersely, maybe threateningly, at Jake. Then he left the room.

"Prison, yes?" The immigration officer's smile had grown cold.

"Why?"

He shrugged. "No visa in. No visa out."

"I want to speak to the American consul."

"No problem. Tomorrow."

"Today?"

"No today." The man ended each phrase with a long silence, as if expecting Jake to say something.

Jake didn't know what, though. But then it dawned on him. Of course, why hadn't he thought of it before? He pulled out his wallet and offered it to the Egyptian. "Money?"

The man stood up angrily. "What?"

"To buy visa. How much?" Jake rubbed his pointer and middle finger with his thumb.

The man pulled out a crumpled piece of paper and wrote on it the number 25.

"Dollars?" asked Jake.

The man nodded.

Jake pulled out a hundred-dollar bill and handed it to the immigration official, signaling that he didn't want anything back.

The Egyptian looked at it and said, "No visa out."

Jake gave him another hundred-dollar bill.

The man gave Jake a warm if slightly sticky handshake. "Welcome to Egypt."

Jake made it to Sharm El Sheikh on Egyptair's last flight. Flight 227 took off at half past midnight and landed on time at 1:25 in the morning.

He phoned Miranda from the airport and told her about his close call. She promised to bypass Egypt on her way into Israel and told him that she hadn't heard from Zuhayli. She'd spent the day getting a suit tailored for the Yazdi meeting and, she added wistfully, missing him.

Jake never checked in at the Pyramisa Resort Hotel. Immediately after passing the wide-open and unmanned security gate of the hotel, his taxi was stopped by an older Arab man dressed in a white *galabyia*. The man was tall, dark and bulky, with a flat nose like a boxer's. He appeared to be in his mid-sixties. He said something to the driver, looked into the back of the car and nodded to Jake, signaling him to open his window.

"You know Danny?" he asked.

"Yes."

"I've been waiting for you. Come with me."

Jake paid the taxi and followed him.

Once they were at a safe distance from the taxi and its driver, the Arab handed Jake a brochure. "I work for an Israeli company called Neot Hakikar. We are the biggest company in Israel offering desert tours."

"You don't look Israeli." Did Jake have the right man? What with exhaustion, jet lag, and the stress of his run-in at Egyptian customs, he wasn't sure all of a sudden. Had he really been asked if he knew Danny, or something that only sounded like that?

"I am a Bedouin," the man said simply. "If we are stopped by the Egyptians, you are a tourist and I am taking you on a private tour of the Sinai desert. If they ask you where you've been, you answer that you've been to the Ein Hudra Oasis. Tell them you were impressed by the wells and springs and all that greenery in the middle of the desert. After that, we went to the canyon of Wadi Talla and visited the beautiful pools of crystal water. If they ask which pool you visited, you answer Kalat el-Azrak. Repeat after me: Ein Hudra, Wadi Talla and Kalat el-Azrak."

It was the right man. "Ein Hudra, Wadi Talla and Kalat . . ." Jake repeated.

"El-Azrak."

"El-Azrak."

And that was it. Jake didn't hear another word from the man for the next two hours.

They drove north in an open jeep. The desert air was cool, crisp. Jake looked up. The sky was clear and extraordinarily beautiful. A blanket of stars—he was reminded of Qeshm—and a sharp crescent moon rising behind his right shoulder. If he had seen a picture of this in print, he never would've believed it was real, so many and vivid were the stars.

"It's cold," he said, an hour or so into the trip. His energy was starting to wane.

The Bedouin guide stopped the four-wheeler. He went to the back and returned with a dusty crumpled windbreaker. Within minutes, lulled by the jeep's abrupt movements, Jake fell asleep.

He woke up with a sudden jolt. "Where are we?"

"We drove through Wadi Gibi," the Bedouin answered reluctantly, then continued, as if by rote. "Wadi is 'valley' in Arabic. We passed the Ras Abu Gallum Nature Reserve—great snorkeling in the coral reef. We are approaching Nuweiba. Look to your right. That's the Red Sea."

"Are you really a tour guide?" Jake asked.

"Yes. Why?"

"You don't like to talk. Tour guides like to talk."

The man laughed. "You're right. I don't get many tips. But this is part-time only."

"How do you know Danny?"

"He used to work for a friend of mine."

"Uh, huh." Jake decided to stop asking questions and soon fell asleep again.

He awakened to the Bedouin speaking again. "We are crossing into Israel. No need for passports on this path."

Jake roused himself. "Is it that easy?"

"No. But it's not impossible. Actually, terrorists use routes like these. Most are caught. Some aren't."

More silence. Ten minutes later, they were on a narrow paved road. The jeep went faster.

Jake started to shiver, cold air penetrating his clothes, the loaned windbreaker. Freezing his hands and face.

The Bedouin guide looked at him. "We'll be stopping in a few minutes."

They swerved off the paved road and onto a dirt one. After a short while, Jake's companion turned the engine off. Jake could see a few tremulous points of light on the horizon. They seemed to be a few miles away from a city.

The Bedouin lifted two duffel bags from the back of the jeep and walked away from the dirt road. He seemed to be looking for a specific spot. When satisfied, he opened the bags and started removing things.

"Gather some wood, please. There are dry branches everywhere. See?" The man was arranging small rocks in a circle.

When Jake came back with his arms full of sticks, his Bedouin guide was mixing water and flour in a small copper pail.

"Why don't you set the branches over there," he said to Jake, pointing to the ring of stone.

The Bedouin set an old brass plate on the stones and lit a fire. When the plate was hot, he placed the dough he had just finished kneading on it.

"Have some bread," he said minutes later. The man's voice was somewhat hoarse.

Jake, who had been lying on his back gazing at the stars and enjoying the absence of the freezing wind, looked at him. The Bedouin's eyes were moist.

"Are you okay?"

"Yes," the man answered softly, his voice raspy.

"Are you sure? What happened?"

"Today I found out that a friend of mine died."

"Sorry to hear that."

For the first time the Bedouin spoke without being asked. "I wanted to stop exactly on this spot for a reason. We used to come here as kids, almost fifty years ago. I hadn't seen him for many years, but he was very, very close to my heart." His teeth shone unusually white under the light of the stars.

The hushed desert breeze enveloped them once more. Jake listened to the delicate scratching and the muted thuds as the pile of wood rearranged itself, the occasional sharp crackling followed by a burst of sparks. His heart was heavy. He didn't know this man but shared the immense feeling of sadness emanating from the quiet Bedouin.

The sun was rising when the Bedouin pulled out a cell phone and spoke briefly into it, in what Jake figured was Hebrew. Then they drove into a tiny village on a hill a few miles outside Jerusalem. Back in tourguide mode, Jake's companion explained that Beit Zayit had once been a typical agricultural cooperative, a *moshav*, but was now a trendy suburb of Israel's capital.

They approached a small stucco house framed by cypresses. Outside stood a tall slim woman, her lined and tanned face framed by long silver hair that glinted in the light of early morning. Jake immediately noticed her striking eyes. They conveyed an uncanny sense of mystery and sadness. This is as beautiful as a woman in her sixties could ever be, he thought.

"This is Rachel. She used to be Danny's boss."

"Hello, Jake." Her handshake felt warm but rough. "Sorry for the mess outside. I was gardening yesterday and never tidied up. Coffee?"

"Yes, thanks. I need it."

"You have some time before Danny arrives. Do you want to rest a bit? How about a shower? I can lend you some of my husband's clothes."

He showered, lay on the bed in the room she led him to, and was instantly asleep. He was awakened by Barzilai's voice. Danny and Rachel were talking in the living room. Jake looked at his watch. He had slept for forty minutes. He felt reenergized. He put on the borrowed clothes. Then he opened the bedroom door and walked down a short hallway and into the living room of Rachel's house.

The room was furnished simply but with sophistication. Tall art books, the words on their spines written in Hebrew, French, and English, filled a low bookcase along one wall.

"Danny."

"Good to see you, Jake. I'm happy you made it safely. But where's Miranda?"

Jake looked at Rachel and back at Barzilai.

"You can speak freely. Rachel is aware of the whole operation. She's retired from the Mossad and has no obligation to tell them anything."

Jake filled him in on the details of the plan and why Miranda had stayed behind. Barzilai bombarded him with questions, trying to identify the plan's weak points. It took a while to satisfy him.

Rachel told Jake, "Ahmed said good-bye. He didn't want to wake you." She was looking intently at his clothes.

"Nice guy."

"Very nice," Barzilai said. "Jake, there's something you should know. Rachel is Gerard's wife. His widow."

Suddenly, many things made sense. Jake looked at Rachel. Her expression was set, but she was blinking repeatedly, fighting tears.

"An unbelievable man, your husband. In a very short time, I grew to respect him a great deal. A really unbelievable man." Jake was at a loss for words.

Rachel nodded, silently. Blinking faster.

"Jake was the last one to see him alive," Barzilai told her. "Do you want to talk to him about it?"

"We'll have many opportunities to do that. The two of you have a lot to take care of now."

Brave woman, Jake thought.

"Okay," Barzilai said, turning to Jake. "How did your meeting go?"

"Very well. After you left—" Jake began.

Barzilai's cell phone rang. The Israeli looked down at the display.

"Just a moment," he said to Jake. "Hello? No, wrong number." He hung up and told Rachel, "He's here."

"Another visitor," Rachel said.

"You'll finally meet Big Ben," Barzilai explained to Jake.

"How come?"

"He's bringing us new disks. With the arrests of Ramon and Sam, we can't be too careful."

A minute or so later, Jake heard the crushing sound of tires on gravel and the sound of a car door opening and slamming shut—all a little too fast. Danny walked to the front door and opened it.

A man strode into the house. He was tall and wide and red. He wore a white T-shirt that made the freckles on his arms seem to glow. He had thin harsh eyes: blue, bold, focused. His lips were fleshy and pressed tightly against each other. His nickname was accurate, Jake thought. The man was big. And angry.

Big Ben walked straight to Rachel. For the longest time she disappeared in his embrace. In the giant's arms, she finally cried. Big Ben had tears in his eyes. With his own vision blurred by tears, Jake saw that Barzilai was crying too.

Jake remembered Gerard's words a few days ago, in the small house in Brooklyn. *This is as close a family as you'll ever see. In the past, we have gone through some very difficult times together, and there's no better glue than that.*

He also had said, *Go to hell and back with us a few times, and you'll be part of the family.* Jake was getting there.

Big Ben hugged Barzilai and extended his hand to Jake. "Pleasure to finally meet you, lad."

"Same here."

"Let's get down to business, shall we?" Barzilai rubbed his temples. "You have something for us, I believe."

"I do." Big Ben extracted two credit cards from his wallet. "The method is the same. The only change is a small one in the code system. It's a bit inelegant and cumbersome, but it's safe and it'll serve as a Band-Aid until I have more time to give you a different system."

"Coffee, B.B.?" asked Rachel, who had pulled herself together.

"Sure."

After she had left the room, Barzilai explained to Jake, "She and Gerard were romantically involved, on and off, for most of their lives. When Rachel retired from the Mossad four years ago they got married, secretly. Our group knew about it, but no one else. Certainly not the Mossad, and not the DGSE. Neither one would've been happy."

Jake nodded and returned to the subject at hand. "Why doesn't she get a disk?"

"She's very ambivalent about STOP. She doesn't believe in it, so she won't help." Barzilai sighed. "Still, she won't fight it because, as she's said more than once, she can't suggest a better alternative."

"Back to the code," Big Ben said. "You will first send an email to *NoToTerror*—that's one word—at aol.com. You will receive an auto-reply message. A date and time will be specified in the text of the message. I'll change that every day. Then you will go to a site called *time-anddate*—again, one word—*dot-com*. You'll choose option 'customize countdown.' It asks you to input a date and time. You'll input the date and time from the nototerror return email. This site counts the number of minutes from that date and time, until the moment you ask for the countdown. You'll see the number of minutes it displays. Just add that number to the end of the original codes you were using until now. That's your new code. You'll insert the disk in the computer within thirty seconds from getting the number of minutes. If you let more than thirty seconds pass, by any chance, start over again. Is that clear?"

"Yes, but give us an example, just in case," Barzilai said.

Rachel walked in with coffee. "There's paper on the desk over there." Setting the tray down, she stepped out of the room again.

"Thanks." Big Ben walked over and returned with a blank piece of paper. "Let's say I send you the date 9/11/2001, 08:45, and the site gives you . . . say, two million minutes and the original code is ABC9. Your new code is ABC92000000. You get it, right? This new wrinkle causes the code to change every minute. Before it changed only once a day. It's simple, but enough to throw off a decoder. At least for a few days."

"Are we done with this? May I change the subject?" Jake asked, placing the new disk in his wallet.

Big Ben bowed briefly in his direction.

"Can you help me with a wire transfer? It needs to be untraceable."

"What do you need, exactly?"

"It's a transfer to the Swiss representative of an Iranian official, and I can't have it traced back to me."

Big Ben smiled. "Laundering money, Mr. Burke?"

Jake felt his face flush in anger.

"Just kidding," the big man continued, while scribbling on the same piece of paper he'd used to show them the code example. "Here's where you transfer these funds. From this account the money will go to the account of Hall and Sons on the Isle of Man. The records of that transfer will be erased—I'll take care of that. Hall and Sons is a company officially controlled by Banque Normand Didier of Geneva. Only they don't know that they control Hall and Sons." He winked. "I'll give instructions for the transfer from the Hall and Sons account to your man."

"Any risk in that? Someone had same-day information on all my finances. Everything. Am I still being monitored?"

Barzilai and Big Ben laughed at the same time.

Barzilai put his arm on Jake's shoulder. "Who do you think got that information? You need to have more faith in Big Ben."

"Well, if you really can perform miracles, I need one. If I gave you all the details of a bank account at Bank Hochsteiner, what information could you get from their records?"

"A lot, or nothing. I'd have to check."

"How fast can you do that?"

"Very fast. Now, I just need to know if this bank of yours is part of SWIFT."

"The Society for Worldwide Interbank Financial Telecommunication," Jake explained to Barzilai.

"If it is, I could do something. As you know, lad, SWIFT services thousands of financial institutions in almost two hundred countries. So it's possible, even probable, that Bank Hochsteiner is one of them."

Jake nodded. "What kind of information could you get?"

"Where all the international transfers that this account received via SWIFT came from; the date, value and sender; any special instructions or references. If Hochsteiner uses SWIFT, I'd guess that almost all their international transfers go via their system." Big Ben turned to Barzilai. "SWIFT is very efficient, reliable and user-friendly. Those who use it tend to stick with it."

"What else?" Jake asked.

"If Bank Hochsteiner hasn't spent serious time and money on security, I could probably enter their internal database, including their Know Your Client files. As I'm sure you're aware, all Swiss banks now have an obligation to know exactly who is behind an account. The days of the anonymous numbered accounts are long gone."

"What if they don't use this SWIFT?" Barzilai asked.

"I've almost never heard of a sizeable bank that doesn't."

Now Rachel re-entered the room. "The man with all the answers," she said, smiling in Big Ben's direction. He winked at her and smiled back.

"Jake, your plan has lots of moving parts," Barzilai said, "so let's make sure we're all on the same page here."

Barzilai, Big Ben and Rachel listened in silence as Jake walked them through each step of his plan.

Finally Big Ben nodded. "It could work."

"Are you really prepared to take this risk?" Rachel asked. "The chances of both of you getting killed are enormous."

"I know, but I have to do it. If we succeed, our next attack on Iran will be the last one. If not, this could go on forever, with more destruction and bloodshed than I can take."

"I think you're crazy," Big Ben said. "The odds are extremely slim."

Rachel disagreed. "Despite the odds, sometimes one man can make a difference."

"Then I'll say one more thing." Big Ben turned to Barzilai. "They can't even try it without the cyanide tooth cap."

Barzilai nodded grimly. "I can arrange that."

CHAPTER TWENTY-FOUR

Harvard Square was lively on the weekends and during the evening. The hub of Cambridge, it bustled with college students, street performers and families. Spike-haired teens with punk-band patches on their fraying denim would panhandle on the Red Line steps. In the fall, brilliant maple leaves gathered along the sidewalks.

Now, ten seconds after the detonation of fifty pounds of TNT in a truck parked on Brattle Street, the Square was a surreal picture of devastation.

The pedestrian mall at ground zero was in ruins. Those not dead already soon would be, for an eerie pall of lethal dust hung in the air.

Blocks away, car alarms wailed and a cloud of that dust, carried by the wind, followed a mob of panicked survivors fleeing west. A few suspected the truth—the dust, and the wind itself, were laced with radioactive material. Material that would poison the cells of all living things.

A series of soft beeps reverberated urgently in the small house. Barzilai stopped talking in mid-sentence.

"The hourly news," Big Ben explained to Jake while opening a pack of chewing gum. "The country stops every hour, sometimes every half-hour, to listen to it. Especially in moments of crisis like these."

Rachel hurried toward a credenza at the end of the living room and turned up the volume of an old Zenith World Radio, a positively antique blue-steel box with a round mesh speaker at the center, its dial glowing orange.

"*Hashaa shesh vehinei hahadashot . . .*"

Within a few seconds, Rachel's eyes were wide open, her forehead deeply creased. Barzilai seemed to be in shock too.

"What—" Big Ben started, only to be interrupted by Barzilai's raised hand and angry stare. Jake heard the words "Cambridge" and "Boston."

"Two explosions in the Boston area," Barzilai reported rapidly. "High radiation levels detected. It looks like terrorists detonated dirty bombs. One in Cambridge, in Harvard Square and—"

"*Where?*" Jake couldn't believe it. His alma mater, effectively destroyed. "Oh, my God."

"Many dead, they're saying. Three hundred and twenty-six now, because it's eleven at night there. That's both locations. They're talking more than a thousand over time."

All fell silent as the announcer continued. Big Ben chewed furiously. Barzilai rubbed his face, profound furrows between his closed eyes.

"The other explosion was in Boston," he translated to Jake in clipped words. "At . . . Fan Hall?"

"Faneuil Hall."

"Yes. The city's in a panic, people desperate to evacuate and escape the radiation. It's a stampede. Terrible . . ."

Jake hung his head, wiped the involuntary moisture from his eyes. When would it end? They had to find Rifaat, they had to bend the Iranian mullahs. They had to.

Barzilai kept reporting, though he trailed off at times, perhaps to spare Jake a grisly detail.

"Now they're talking about rioting throughout Iran. ILF issued a new announcement urging all to come out and protest. Their main demand is a referendum on the government."

The old radio's sound was surprisingly crisp. "*Tachazit mezeg haavir . . . meunan chelkit . . . bemishor ha hof . . .*"

"What are they saying now?"

"Now it's the weather forecast." Barzilai shrugged. "They always end the hourly news with that. The world can be falling apart . . . It's always the same."

"Three hundred and twenty-six dead. More to come." Jake felt pain in his jaw. He was clenching his teeth too hard. "They've destroyed Harvard University. It'll be unusable for years, irrespective of how fast they can clean it up." He made a rough calculation in his head. "And a radius of two blocks in Boston. That's billions of dollars worth of real estate. Plus the other costs. They're trying to hit our economy too."

"It's the fear that's most damaging," Big Ben said, pacing the living room from end to end, like a caged lion. "The psychological effects alone—"

"Hold it," Rachel interrupted. "More news."

"It looks like it's the Popular Islamic Jihad. They just issued a communiqué from south Lebanon." Barzilai was speaking while trying to listen to the radio.

"It's Iran, then. They're making a point again," Jake said. But he was thinking *Abdel Aziz Rifaat*. He had to go outside and walk again. To think. "I'll be back in ten minutes."

"Where—" Big Ben started to ask, only to be interrupted again.

"Let him go," Barzilai said. "This is how he solves problems."

Jake stepped out Rachel's front door and into the smell of jasmine and the sounds of twittering birds and braying donkeys. A dry breeze blew. He barely noticed.

By the time he returned about a half-hour later, he had a better idea of what the next steps should be. The others seemed to have a plan, too.

Barzilai spoke first. "We have to strike Iran. But not another soft blow. I say we create a massive attack. It's time to use at least one of the suitcase nuclear bombs. They took it to the next stage; whole areas of Boston are now covered with radiation. Let's give them a bit of the same. Fire with fire."

Jake was dead set against a nuclear attack. "We discussed this before. They can't even think they're influencing us, changing our course of action. We have to be unstoppable, mechanical. Inevitable, like Fate."

"Things have changed," Barzilai argued. "They've upped the ante, big time. This can't be ignored. We—"

"Now more than ever," Jake continued, "if we go ahead with a massive attack, especially a nuclear one, we accomplish two things, both of them bad. One, it'll look like retaliation by the United States. Then, in order to distance itself from our attack, the U.S. government might go on a full offensive against us, possibly targeting you in particular. I can see them putting enormous pressure on the government of Israel to give you up, Danny. Do they have information on Big Ben?"

No one answered.

Jake turned to the red-haired giant. "Your arrest would cripple us." He waited for comments, got none, and continued. "For symbolic purposes, and to make a clear point, they might even decide to send Ramon and Sam to be tried by the International Criminal Court in Holland."

"And what's the second negative?" Big Ben had his arms crossed over his chest. He wasn't buying Jake's reasoning.

"We would destroy any chance of the Iranian people rising up against their government."

"I see your point," Barzilai said, "but I still think we should deal them a major blow. Remember our analysis? Not only do the mullahs think they're winning, they're getting cocky. That's the only way I can interpret Iran giving Rifaat the go-ahead to execute a hit of this enormity."

A heated discussion went on for another half-hour. This time Jake was unable to get the moderation he was looking for. Barzilai and Big Ben were adamant. In the end, they reached a compromise.

Miranda arrived soon thereafter, in Ahmed's company. She had traveled through Jordan without difficulty. Though Jake was delighted to see her, on mutual agreement they refrained from any public display of affection.

Miranda hadn't yet learned of the tragedy in New England. Once informed, she was shaken but resolute. She had a cousin in Somerville, near the Cambridge bomb-site, and tried to call several times but couldn't get through.

Once she'd been brought up to speed on the new developments in Jake's plan, everyone went into Rachel's back yard. Barzilai brought a small case along. One by one he removed a large phone console, a fold-out antenna, three cables, one battery and a laptop.

"Nice," said Jake, to be nice.

He shouldn't have. Big Ben started talking about the equipment with such passion that Jake had to ask, "But is this yours or Danny's?"

"It's Danny's. I told him to get it. I have one in the UK." And he went on talking about the technical marvel that the gadget was.

Still at work on the assembly, Barzilai smiled. Obviously, he'd been here before. Jake lost Big Ben somewhere around the time when he was talking about the foldable, high-gain antenna and its integrated compass coupled with an audible signal-strength indicator that allowed for super-easy satellite tracking.

"Whoa, wait a minute. I have just one question. What does this . . . ap-paratus *do*?"

"Transmission from this machine is untraceable. By the time our email is out, no one can track its source. Not today, not ever."

"Ready," said Barzilai. "Jake, would you like to do the honors?"

Jake went through all the steps, starting with sending the email to NoToTerror@aol.com and retrieving the auto-answer back. In less than three minutes he had access to all screens. When the lists of targets to choose appeared, he did so. He changed the message. The list of recipients was the same as those contacted about the Qeshm detonation. Jake hit SEND.

Back inside, they turned the radio back on. It was now seven-thirty in the morning, an hour and a half after they'd heard the news of the explosions. In less than ten minutes, the broadcast was interrupted for breaking news. Barzilai translated. "STOP has informed Iran that three more refineries in that country will be destroyed by the end of the day. The explosions will take place at 18:00 Iran time—nine hours from now. We repeat . . . three more refineries, those at Arak, Kermanshah and Shiraz, will be destroyed today. Additionally, the group is demanding that all vessels and personnel leave the port of Anzali, a secondary Iranian port on the Caspian Sea. They're also demanding that the area within a twenty-kilometer radius from the port be totally evacuated. They will destroy that port at 18:00 Iran time, exactly a week from today's explosion. STOP has urged the Iranian government to learn from past events in order to prevent unnecessary casualties. It is repeating its now-traditional warning: that any attempt to tamper with the bombs will cause their immediate detonation. Despite the absence of a specific threat, there's concern that STOP might be deploying a nuclear explosive at Anzali. There's no other explanation for their demand to evacuate such a large area around that port."

"Do you know Jerusalem?" Barzilai asked Jake.

"No."

"We have some time until the reactions start flowing in. I'll take you and Miranda around. It will be good to get out a bit."

"I can see you're not afraid of being arrested. What if my country pressures yours to give you up?"

"I'll know about it in time. It's not as though I don't have friends in the Mossad any more." He rested his hand on the doorknob. "What are your plans, Big Ben?"

"I'll be staying here with Rachel. If she'll let me."

Rachel nodded, a sad smile on her lips.

"Rachel is down," Barzilai said, when they were seated in his car. "I'm happy Big Ben is keeping her company. These two will spend the day reminiscing." He turned the engine on. "Are you sure you want to go forward with your plan?"

"Yeah, I am. Especially now. If I don't succeed you'll be blowing that port up—and with a nuclear bomb, for God's sake. I still think this is pure madness."

"And you can't be sure that the wind won't carry the radiation farther than the twenty-kilometer radius," Miranda added.

Danny's eyes were set. "It's decided. You wanted a chance to stop this from happening and you got it. You have seven days until the explosion. Do you still want to go forward?"

Jake and Miranda nodded at the same time.

"Then we have a few things to do. First . . ." Barzilai looked sharply at them. "I need to get both of you to a dentist." He took out a cell phone and spoke into it quietly. "He's expecting you in half an hour," he said, folding the phone and putting it back in his pocket.

"Yes." Jake ignored the allusion to the risk they would soon be taking. "By the way, at some point today, I'll need a computer with Power-Point and a broadband connection. I'll also need a very good printer."

"No problem. Do you both have your passports on you? You'll need them for the dentist."

"I'd like to have the computer as soon as we're done there, if that's okay with you. I'll need a few hours, and the sooner I start, the better. And don't forget, you need to get something else for me." Jake didn't spell it out, even though they were out of anyone's earshot.

"How could I forget? I'll need to talk to the right people, though, and they'll need a slew of authorizations. That is, if they agree, which is by no means certain."

"And if they don't?"

"We'll have to come up with another idea."

"I'm counting on you." Jake had limited time to put his plan into action.

Barzilai stopped the car in front of an old building, its Jerusalem-white stone stained by a dirty brown. "Dr. Shoshani, third floor. He's expecting you."

There were no patients in the reception area when Jake and Miranda arrived. The furniture was old, but the equipment was obviously very modern. The dentist, Dr. Shoshani, had a round belly, a double chin that grew rounder every time he nodded, and an equally round pink face with cheeks that were almost red. The man was a profusion of circles and semi-circles. He spoke in English with a strong French accent.

"You are fully aware of the procedure, right?"

"Yes."

"Then you will sign these forms for me. Please read them carefully. The first one tells me about your motivation for doing this. The second is a description of the procedure, and the third is a release. I need your passport. I will make a copy of it, and you will sign the copy in order to authenticate it, yes?"

Jake sat down to read the forms. According to the first one, his motivation was fear of abduction and extreme torture. Correct. He signed it.

The second form, the description of the procedure, was longer. The dentist would sedate him with a combination of Forane, Fentanyl, Midazolam, Propofol, Zemuron, and Droperidol. Zofran would be used for his recovery. A single person would perform the procedure, including the anesthesia, and this entailed additional risks. Dr. Shoshani would remove most of his upper right, second molar and replace it with a crown. The description of the crown could be found in Appendix A of the form. Jake would probably feel pain for a few days, until his maxilla adjusted to a slightly different position. He might also feel his mandible, but all that would disappear. Okay—Jake signed that form too.

"Where is Appendix A with the crown's description?"

"It's the last document."

Jake started reading the third document, the release. At a certain point, he started to laugh. Miranda looked at him as though he'd finally cracked.

"What is it?" asked the chubby dentist.

"This is almost an exact copy of a typical American release form. According to this, only a madman would go forward with this procedure."

"That's right, only a madman." The dentist stared at him in silence.

Jake signed the form.

"You sure you're up for this?" he asked Miranda. She showed him her form—she had signed it already. Jake had to hand it to her. The woman was tough.

"Come on," she teased. "You forget who you're dealing with?"

Appendix A described the mechanism of the crown. In order to activate it, Jake would have to bite sideways, then grind his teeth no less that twenty times in thirty seconds. He'd hear a cracking sound, which meant that acid had been released inside the crown. After approximately one minute, that acid would create a hole in the crown, allowing its contents to flow into Jake's mouth. He had only that one minute to remove the crown, if he wanted to abort the process. At the end of that minute, he'd feel a strong burning sensation as the acid entered his mouth—a sensation that wouldn't last long. It wouldn't last long because the acid was mixed with liquid cyanide. Death would come swiftly.

"Why do I need to be sedated?"

"Besides the pain? I need your head totally immobilized. I can't run the risk of the slightest movement. Until covered by the crown, the acid receptacle is easily breakable."

"I need to be especially alert during the next few hours."

"Okay. I'll give you additional antidotes for your recovery. You might feel nauseated afterwards, but you'll be alert."

The dentist's prediction was on target. Jake woke up feeling extremely nauseated, but his mind was clear. He noticed extra volume on the right side of his mouth, as if he had a grape seed stuck in the middle of his tooth, stopping him from a full bite.

"Get used to chewing with the left side. You can do it slowly with the right, but try to avoid it."

"You bet your ass I'll avoid it."

He heard laughter. It was Barzilai, standing by his side with Miranda. "I see you're back. We should get going. I have good news."

"What are your plans now?" the Israeli asked when they were back in the car.

"I need to look at what the markets are doing and simulate a series of transactions with gasoline futures. Then we have to prepare a presentation, make several copies and have them ready in case they call me for a meeting in Iran. You told me you had good news for me."

"I do. I got all the necessary approvals. We can go forward with the plan. You'll get the new passport you asked for, *Mr. Landis*. Also, just give me the presentations when they're ready. They'll come back exactly the way you need them."

Back at Rachel's house, the computer, already connected to the Internet, was waiting for Jake in the room he'd slept in hours ago. A color printer was on the table next to it.

Miranda joined him and went to work. The first thing Jake did was check the previous day's closing option prices on NYMEX unleaded-gasoline future contracts. The profit he would be sending the Iranians would be defined by the difference between that price and the price after the explosions. Trading would start in approximately eight hours, at 9:50 A.M., New York time. Roughly half an hour after the explosions.

Due to the destruction of the three refineries, options prices would rise sharply immediately at the opening. Jake was sure of it. He decided to send Abbas Zuhayli, Yazdi's man in Switzerland, about three million dollars in profits. He figured that a free sample of that kind of money would attract anyone's attention.

Barzilai stepped into the room. "Jake, Ben and I will be back in three hours. Will you need us before then?"

"We'll be fine."

"If you need anything, ask Rachel."

"I'd actually prefer to work without interruption. I'll need all the concentration I can muster."

Miranda smirked at that. "Let me know if I hinder your concentration," she said after Barzilai left.

They set to work on his presentation. They would describe "his investor group", their investment strategies, and the mechanics of this transaction. It had to be the best sales job they'd ever done. While they worked, Jake kept hearing the beeps from the radio, announcing the hourly news. An hour later they sounded again. And then a third time.

Rachel walked in a while later, pale once more. "Your president just finished addressing the nation. He says America will fight all kinds of terrorism, including the kind being waged by STOP. Yeah, he actually mentioned STOP. Danny's on his way."

CHAPTER TWENTY-FIVE

"They evacuated ten blocks around Harvard Square," Barzilai reported. "They did the same with Faneuil Hall. Two huge areas contaminated with radiation. Many residents have cleared out on their own. The roads are jammed in all directions." He had walked in with Big Ben a few minutes after Rachel told Jake and Miranda about the president's speech. "And now your president's foolish move. Looks like America is losing the game."

"Which game?" Big Ben asked, his voice unsteady.

"Danny and I were talking about the game of chicken. It's—"

"It doesn't matter," Big Ben interrupted. "What do we do now?"

"Calm down. It's too early to panic." Barzilai remained unruffled.

"I don't want to spend the rest of my life in jail," Big Ben replied. "You yourself said that if the U.S. turned against us it would be impossible to hide. Until now, all they did was arrest Sam and Ramon. Now they're targeting the whole organization."

"But nobody knows about you."

"How sure are you of that?"

"Fairly sure. Don't worry, we'll get you out of here soon."

"How about *now*?"

"Okay, *now*. You'll be on a flight out to London today, you have my word." Barzilai turned to Jake. "When he gets into these moods, there's nothing you can do."

The Englishman sat down, relaxed somewhat after Barzilai's assurance. He turned to Jake. "While you were cooped up here, I got into the internal database of Bank Hochsteiner. Surprisingly lax security for a Swiss bank. About that account you asked me to check: There are several layers of ownership between Green Leaf Limited and the actual beneficiaries, but I got the whole thing. The real owners are Nasrullah Sadr Yazdi; Mirza Sadr, Yazdi's oldest son; and Mahdi Sadr, his youngest. Do these names mean anything to you?"

"Are you kidding? Yazdi's the man I'm trying to get." Jake was ecstatic. "Can you prove this ownership?"

"I have the actual form that discloses the ultimate beneficiaries. It's an official document sent by the bank to the Swiss authorities."

"Great. Now I need you to take care of one more thing for me," Jake said. "You can do it from the UK, but it's better if I give you the details now."

"No problem. What do you need?"

"It's the transfer to Green Leaf Limited I told you about." Jake gave him a typewritten page with Green Leaf's account information. "I'll need the money in their account tomorrow morning, Zurich time."

"Get it to me early and it'll be there within an hour. Anything else?" Big Ben stood up.

"Yes. Let me tell you the most I can hope for, and see how much of it you can do."

Big Ben nodded. "Carry on."

"I'd like to have all the details of this transfer leaked to the world media. I'll give you the calculations of the profit. This is a profit-participation deal, so you'll have the sum that was transferred, when it was transferred, where, et cetera. The ideal scenario would be for you to have all of this reach the media outlets like a press release from Bank Hochsteiner. Can you hack into Hochsteiner's communication systems?"

"That I can."

"Perfect. You get the picture, right? If the thing comes out as something official from Bank Hochsteiner and the media contacts them, they won't be able to deny it because that would be straight-out lying. Swiss banks will keep secrets, but they won't lie. At worst, they might refuse to comment."

"Yes."

Jake pulled out another printed sheet of paper. "Here's what I propose for the text of the press release. It starts with the bank saying that as a result of an internal investigation on accounts of alleged corrupt foreign government officials, they've uncovered an account owned by Green Leaf Limited, which has received several doubtful payments, in particular a recent one of over three million dollars. It discloses the full operation and the profit calculation, ostensibly as something that the account holder had shown the bank, looking to replicate the operation with the bank's help."

"Understood. I'll see what I can do." Big Ben looked at the printed page. "Did you actually buy the options?"

"No, this is a hypothetical operation. We'll make the Iranians believe that we actually executed it, but the profit that we'll be sending them will actually be my own money." Jake smiled at Big Ben's naiveté. "It's not only you. I don't want to go to jail, either. And buying options—betting on new attacks on Iranian refineries—would be a sure-fire way to attract attention."

"When do you want the press release to go out?"

"When we're back from Iran. I'll call you as soon as I'm back to give you the okay to issue the press release. If Miranda or I don't call you within five days after our departure, go ahead and send it out."

"If you're still there, they'll kill you," Barzilai said.

"If we're still there after five days, we're already dead."

Big Ben, Barzilai and Rachel looked at Jake in silence. Big Ben finally stood up gingerly. "Well, I'll be going, then. You look after yourself, lad."

"I will."

Barzilai turned to Rachel. "I need to get some work done with Jake. Do you mind taking B.B. to Lod?" He still referred to Ben Gurion Airport by its old name.

Big Ben stood in silence, awkwardly shifting his weight from one foot to another. He then walked over to Jake and held him by the shoulders.

"Be careful, will you?" The red giant enclosed Jake in his embrace, a bear-hug truly worthy of the name.

"Don't worry," Jake replied. "And you have a safe trip back to London."

Jake turned to Barzilai after they'd left. "Will he perform? He seemed a bit emotional. Actually, he looked downright unsettled."

"This has happened before. He has this hang-up about being outside the UK. He'll be okay as soon as he gets back home."

"I see."

Barzilai shook his head in exasperation. "It's a problem, though. And it's one of the main reasons why he could never play a more important role in STOP, despite his brainpower."

"Give me a second, will you?" Jake walked to the computer in the next room. He brought back a batch of papers and handed them to Barzilai.

Barzilai held the papers carefully, as if holding something explosive. "Good, it's ready."

"Yes. That's the presentation. You have ten sets there. Twelve pages each."

"We're almost done, then. Give me your passports. We'll need them to prepare the new "Walt" and "Roberta" ones. Also, I'll get you back-dated entry visas to Israel, a separate document from the passport. When you fly out, remind them not to stamp the passport, just the stapled document. They're used to doing it because of the Arab boycott, but you never know . . . you could get a distracted immigration officer. You'd get in trouble in Iran with an Israeli stamp in your passport."

"Good thinking." Jake didn't bother telling Barzilai about his close call in Egypt.

"The next step is a complete check-up for both of you. Then the doctor will give you the medication, and you'll be ready to go." The Israeli's face was lightly flushed. "This is exciting. I think you're nuts, but if you pull this off, it could be what it takes to win this. As simple as that."

Jake shrugged. "I don't know about that. But if it works, it'll save many lives."

Barzilai exhaled loudly. "Okay. Let's go. I'll drop you off at the doctor."

"If we have time, I'd like to get a new suit," Jake said. "Zuhayli's seen me in the only one I brought. That wouldn't look right."

"When you're finished at the doctor's, just grab a taxi and tell him to take you to the Malka Mall—'Canyon Malka' in Hebrew. I suggest we meet back here at four."

"Let's make it ten to four. I want to be by the computer when the market opens in New York."

Jake returned to Rachel's house with an attaché case and a carry-on suitcase half-filled with new clothes. Finding a suit hadn't been easy. In the four stores he visited, the sales people told him it was impossible to make the needed alterations in less than two days. An orthodox Jew, who took him to a townhouse outside the mall and literally delivered him to an elderly tailor, had saved the day.

Once back in "his" room, Jake opened the carry-on, put the pills he had received from the physician in a vitamin bottle, and proceeded to remove the tags from his new clothes.

Barzilai walked in carrying an ordinary shopping bag. In it, though, were the ten presentations, each in a tightly sealed plastic envelope. He bowed and extended them to Jake. "Your presentations as ordered, master. Anthrax apprehended on its way to Hezbollah, a strain unquestionably developed in Iran. We deposited it electrostatically on the white areas of each of the pages. We then covered the pages with a thin and undetectable film of plastic adhesive. The powder will stay stuck until touched." Barzilai also gave Jake and Miranda the old and new passports and showed them the Israeli entry stamp on separate documents.

Jake inspected the presentations. They looked perfectly innocuous inside their transparent plastic envelopes. "Thank you, my friend. These documents will receive the attention they deserve."

He sat down at his computer; he still had a few minutes until four. He typed, *www.reuters.co.uk*. The site was inundated with news about Iran. The American president had said once again that America would not tolerate terrorism of any kind. Dire consequences would follow renewed destruction in Iran. For once there was agreement between these two enemies: Iran's president, Mullah Aznaveh, also warned of dire consequences if it were to be attacked again. Another caption on Reuters' home page said that the refineries had been evacuated.

At 4:00 P.M., Jake heard the beeps coming from the radio indicating the hourly news. Rachel had turned it on. He went to Bloomberg to check the opening quotes of unleaded gasoline options.

At 4:15, while Barzilai was teaching Jake how to set up the satellite phone outside, his cell phone rang. As he continued the assembly, Barzilai cradled the phone between his shoulder and ear. All he said, many times, was, "*Ken, eivanti.*"

Rachel translated in response to Jake's inquiring look. "He's saying, 'Yes, understood.' It sounds serious," she added.

After the call, Barzilai turned his cell phone off. "We can't have any more interruptions now," he explained.

"What was that call about?"

"A friend with the Mossad. He said that if the refineries are destroyed, they'll come after me. The threat against the port was the final straw. Everyone understands that we're planning to blow up a nuclear weapon. The American pressure is enormous. Just like we thought."

"And what'll you do?"

"I'll hide. Rachel will drop you two at the King David Hotel."

Jake nodded.

"Since I won't be reachable, I'll call you every hour, starting tomorrow morning at eight. If your Iranian contact calls from Zurich, I'll arrange for us to meet somewhere. We can review the plans before you go."

They walked inside to the computer. Jake inserted his disk and retrieved the phone numbers and codes for the three refineries.

Back outside, Barzilai checked his watch. "Four-thirty. Ready?"

Jake nodded.

Barzilai dialed each number and input a different code each time. Five minutes later it was done. They listened to the radio. New beeps. Breaking news. The three refineries were destroyed.

Barzilai left in a hurry.

Jake went back to his computer. The option prices had hit the maximum allowable price increase. Jake arranged for the wire transfer into the account given to him by Big Ben.

He then loaded his suitcase into the back seat of Rachel's car, but Miranda kept the attaché case with the presentations on her lap. They drove out of the moshav and onto the Tel Aviv-Jerusalem highway. They arrived in Jerusalem in ten minutes. Jake noticed three armored vehicles at the entrance to the city. Soldiers were inspecting a battered old Mercedes. All the other vehicles drove right in.

Miranda asked Rachel, "How do they know who to look for?"

"It's mostly tips. The intelligence is quite good. You'll also notice that the cars from the West Bank and Gaza have different plates."

"And cars belonging to Israeli Arabs?" Jake wanted to know.

Rachel looked at him, surprised. "Why would they have different plates? They're Israeli citizens."

"You've had cases of Israeli Arabs helping terrorists. I've read about it."

"True, but they are very few. We cannot target the Israeli Arab population as a whole because of these few crazies. Can you imagine what this would do to an already-strained relationship between Arabs and Jews in this country?"

Jake looked outside. They were driving along a wide avenue flanked by an enormous and well-kept garden on the right and modern buildings on the left.

"Over there," Rachel said, pointing deep into the gardens, "is where the Knesset, our parliament, is. We have several Arab parliament members." Rachel described the most important sites as they passed them. Jake could sense her love of the city. Most of the buildings were made of off-white stone. Some smooth, some chiseled, some rough. All the color of sand.

They approached the King David, an ornate rectangular building built of the same local sandstone. It had been built in 1931 on King David Street, Rachel explained. At that time, the road was called Julian's Way. Jake wasn't sure if it was the time of day, but the color of the hotel seemed to take on a shade of pink.

Now Jake saw several TV trucks and at least five armored vehicles. Several tall men in dark sunglasses, coiled wires connecting their ears to the backs of their necks, surrounded the hotel.

"Oh, shit," Rachel said. "They moved him here."

"Moved who?"

"Your Secretary of Defense arrived a few hours ago, unannounced. I forgot to tell you, with everything going on at home. Danny said he'd be staying at the David's Citadel, another hotel, but I guess they brought him here at the last minute."

Jake and Miranda exchanged nervous glances. This could spell trouble. Security blocked Rachel's car some fifty yards from the hotel's driveway. Fear of car bombs, they explained. A birdlike, bespectacled door attendant with black dyed hair approached, apologizing for the confusion. Jake should walk to the hotel. Did the lady need help with her luggage?

"No, I can handle it." Jake turned to Rachel. "Thanks for the lift."

She looked deeply into his eyes. "You're doing a great thing, you know?"

"They still have to call us. This could take forever or not happen at all."

"Just the fact that you decided to do it . . ." Rachel got out of the car. "I hope to see you soon. Come back safely."

She hugged both of them in turn. As they started to walk away, he heard her calling him.

"Jake, could you come back here, please?" She was already at the wheel of her car. He went to her side and bent down to talk to her. "No, come inside, both of you. It will only take a minute."

He threw the carry-on in the back seat and got back in the car, holding the attaché case.

Rachel looked him in the eye, then at Miranda. "I shouldn't be telling you this, but you have the right to know. Have you thought about what the secretary of defense is doing here?"

"A little. I think he's issuing an open threat to Iran. If we know that Rifaat is backed by Iran, so does the American defense establishment. It's a warning, and it's public."

"I'm sure that's what the pundits are saying on TV as we speak," Miranda added.

"You're almost correct."

"Almost?"

"Yes, it's not only a warning. America and Israel are going to attack Iran."

Both Americans were caught off guard, to say the least. "When?" Miranda asked.

"Very soon. Weeks. It will be devastating. Your president has decided to go all-out—"

"What?"

"To teach Iran a lesson that will never be forgotten."

"How do you know that?"

"I just know. And now you know. This is what I meant when I said that you're doing a great thing. If it works, it's not only the nuclear explosion at Anzali. You could stop this descent into hell. Save many more people than you probably even imagine."

After going through a long security check and a surprisingly short check-in procedure, Jake left his bags in his hotel room. To maintain protocol, he and Miranda would continue to make separate accommodations. Jake did suggest that she meet him in the bar. Not so much because he wanted a drink, but because he felt antsy. She readily agreed, but indicated she would be down in a few minutes.

Jake rode the elevator downstairs to the bar. A sole businessman sat in one of the booths, nursing a scotch on the rocks. Jake sat down at the bar and ordered a bottle of Beck's.

The TV was on. Sky News was covering what looked like riots all over Iran, which were being crushed mercilessly by the Revolutionary Guard.

The network also showed snippets of Mullah Aznaveh speaking on a local Iranian TV station, declaring that foreigners would never bring Iran to its knees.

Muttering something in Hebrew that sounded like a string of expletives, the bartender switched the station to CNN, which was showing excerpts of an unusual morning address to the nation by the American president. He was preparing the country for an escalation of terrorist attacks. He blamed radicalism on both sides. The caption under the image said that the president had announced that, in a sign of its total rejection of the actions of STOP, America was sending the two members of the group who were U.S. citizens to be tried at the International Criminal Court.

"And make no mistake," the president intoned, giving the camera a steely-eyed, unblinking stare, "any nation that takes part in an attack on the United States will instantly be at war with the United States. And to win that war quickly and decisively, every option will be on the table."

Miranda arrived and they watched the rest of the president's address. Afterwards, talk turned to what lay ahead.

"It'll be a miracle if we pull this off," Jake said, frankly. "There are a million ways to screw up."

"We know our stuff, backwards and forwards," Miranda reminded him. "It's going to be okay."

She followed his thoughts, so they said in unison, "Better than four nines," to echo in an uncertain situation Jake's familiar refrain when he liked the odds of a transaction. They laughed together, and for a moment Jake was sure everything would work out.

Back in his room, they reviewed their preparations one more time. They were ready, he felt positive.

Jake looked outside toward the Old City Walls. The day was approaching its end, and the city had taken on a golden hue. The next morning close to four million dollars would be hitting the account of Green Leaf Limited. An almost infallible mechanism called Greed would set things in motion.

All they had to do now was wait.

Danny stepped onto the street and, as he'd learned in his youth, smoked a cigarette with one hand cupped over the ash to conceal its light. It was reflex, older than his instinct to smoke outside. Many Israelis were still smokers, but Danny had spent enough time in America to step outside before he lit up. Whether or not the house's owner appreciated his courtesy, he'd come to enjoy a contemplative smoke in the late-night air.

He was spending his first night in hiding at a bed-and-breakfast in Beit Zayit, not far from Rachel's. An assumed name and a low profile would keep him anonymous for a single night. After that, he had a number of hideouts lined up. He would never stay in the same place for long. Like the art of an unobserved smoke, eluding notice had become second nature to the former Mossad agent.

Noticing others was equally rote for Danny. He spotted the three men, though they moved like wraiths all in black as they hurried down the street, each man walking some three yards behind the other. It was unusual for men to walk together like that. If they were three friends taking a walk, they should be side by side. And they probably wouldn't move so swiftly and quietly.

Danny stubbed out his cigarette and quietly followed them. He had taken to carrying a Jericho 941 Police Special and was comforted by its weight in his shoulder-holster.

The interlopers ascended a hillside path into cypresses. Directly toward Rachel's little stucco house.

That was all Danny needed to know. He left the trail and ran through the brush, looping around the house.

He was breathless but in position as one of the men stole up to the wall and peered into a side window. The man, wearing a mask now, pulled something from his coat—it was too dark to see what.

And Danny shot him.

Danny remained pressed against the backyard fence, gun drawn. As the intruder fell, hit in the head, Danny rushed silently along the side of the house.

He saw a flash of movement at the front. One of the other men turned the corner and, almost comically, ran straight into Danny's gun sights.

"Hold it," Danny ordered, voice a hiss.

The man was trapped. He put his hands up.

Danny stepped closer. "On the ground!"

The man complied. Just then an exterior light flashed on. Danny glanced over to see Rachel herding the other man from her house. She was disheveled but beautiful in her nightgown, brandishing Israel's latest assault rifle.

"Thanks, Danny," she said. "Must've been your shot that woke me."

"Keep that handy, do you?" Danny chuckled, his weapon pointed at the prisoner.

"You bet I do."

CHAPTER TWENTY-SIX

The piercing sound of the hotel-room phone just a few inches from his ear jarred Jake out of a deep slumber. The night before, without turning down the covers, he had fallen back on the king-sized bed, fully dressed.

"It's 8:00 A.M. This is your wake-up call." It was Barzilai.

"I'm awake," he lied. He fumbled about for his watch. He had slept for only four hours. After leaving the bar, Miranda had snuck into Jake's room and they'd made love for half the night, the emotional coupling of lovers who weren't sure they would get another chance. Reminders of their own mortality hovered over them, heightening every second they shared in a way that was, to Jake's mind, at once beautiful and terribly sad.

But he wouldn't have changed a moment of it.

"I'm happy you're awake," Barzilai said, "because I have news for you. Three men tried to infiltrate Rachel's place in Beit Zayit. I killed one and the others were taken alive."

"What's that?"

"You're sure you're awake? We've got prisoners. Rachel's okay, by the way. Moved to a safe location."

"I don't get it. Why would she be a target? Who even knows about her?"

"The only person that comes to mind is Rifaat himself. Maybe her wedding to Gerard wasn't as secret as they'd hoped and the French knew about it. We're assuming that Rifaat has somebody inside French intelligence. Anyway . . . we hope to find out soon. I suppose you haven't heard anything from your friend in Zurich."

Jake checked his watch again. "It's too early."

"Okay. Look, just to be safe, don't leave the hotel. Right now the King David is probably the safest place in Israel. And will remain so as long as your secretary of defense stays there."

"No problem."

"I'll call you in one hour, okay?"

They spoke every hour through noon. By 12:30, Jake was starting to feel discouraged. If Big Ben had done what he'd promised, Abbas Zuhayli in Zurich had received the funds several hours ago. In Jake's experience, there were two kinds of decision-makers: those who took immediate action when they saw an opportunity, and those who deliberated extensively, looking at all the angles before making a move.

Jake hoped that Yazdi and his team were the first kind. If so, he expected to receive a call immediately after Zuhayli notified them about the money. If not, it would be several days later, if at all. He only had six days left until the Anzali explosion.

He went downstairs to the hotel lobby, walked out to the veranda and sat at a table overlooking the swimming pool. The place was beautiful. A big lawn glowed greenly beneath the cloudless sky. White-clad waiters hurried about, serving beautifully tanned bodies in different positions of relaxation. The air was filled with the shouts and laughter of children. If not for the Hebrew he heard being spoken, he would've doubted that he was in Israel, the country most targeted by terrorists.

He went back inside. Television cameras had been set up at the far right side of the lobby, close to the breakfast room. A slim man with a trim beard, a striped tie over his button-down oxford, was speaking into a microphone that said BBC on it. Jake recognized Noah Chadwick, the well-known professor of international affairs and philosophy, and a frequent guest of the BBC.

"We should agree that fanaticism and irrationality are not a privilege of Middle Eastern people. As a matter of fact, the arrogance of certain Western States that proclaim themselves a universal police force and to have authorization to interfere in the internal political and economic issues of less powerful countries, is more dangerous to international peace and safety than Fundamentalist Islam."

"You don't really mean that, do you, sir?" asked the reporter holding the microphone for him.

"Yes, I do. These countries try to impose not just laws but societal *values* on other countries. When these are rejected, the policy of influence turns suddenly into a policy of war." He was now talking to the camera, his eyes angry, his gestures expansive.

"The so-called war against terrorism is nothing but another chapter in the long sad story of Western paranoid belligerency. Once upon a time, there was the communist monster. When that fell, Western paranoia was thus deprived of its favorite obsession. Luckily for the West, Fundamentalist Islam appeared to fill the role of universal enemy."

"But these people are targeting civilians, women, children—"

"It's understandable. They're fighting against much more powerful enemies. What would you do in their place? What would you do if you wanted to be free? The West is being hypocritical, as always. It would've done the same."

"I don't think so. In a much more extreme situation, I don't remember the French Résistance targeting the wives and children of the Nazi officers who ran the occupation of their country during the Second World War." Chadwick had succeeded in irritating the reporter.

Chadwick waved his hand dismissively. "This whole thing's being blown out of proportion. How many people have the terrorists killed? In this country, Israel, three times as many people die of traffic accidents as in terrorist attacks. In America, approximately *fifty thousand* people die every year from car crashes. Look, fear of destruction is an essential part of Western culture. The cohesion of some societies depends on battling a common enemy. The absence of positive values to be affirmed leads to a desperate and manic search for witches and ghosts, creatures that supply the society with negative values to be hated by everyone."

What an idiot, Jake thought. That's why it's so hard to engage in dialogue, he realized. Some people can always find justification, however veiled and intellectually belaboured, for the killing of thousands of civilians.

He felt a vibration. The cell phone was ringing.

"Mr. Landis? Good afternoon. Zuhayli here. I am calling to confirm receipt . . . receipt of the funds."

"Good. And how are you otherwise?" In contrast to the Iranian's apparent excitement, Jake's voice sounded relaxed. At least he hoped it did.

"I have booked all three of us on Iran Air's Flight IR750 from Athens. It leaves at four in the afternoon and gets us into Tehran a little after eight in the evening. We have a meeting early the following morning."

"We'll be there."

"Excellent. I suggest we meet at three o'clock at the gate. Your tickets have already been paid for."

"You shouldn't have done that."

"Mr. Landis, you have credit with us. A lot of credit. I'll see you tomorrow."

Jake went to Miranda's room and relayed the details of his conversation with Zuhayli. She was thrilled. Jake cautioned her against overconfidence. The ball was rolling, but this was still a highly volatile situation.

When Barzilai called on the hour, Jake told him everything.

"Where are you?" Barzilai asked.

"In the lobby."

"I suggest you go up to your room and pack. I'll call you right back with your flight arrangements. You don't want to be arriving in Athens from Israel—they might be able to check. I'll book you through London."

Barzilai called again as Jake was packing. "You're on an El Al flight that leaves in a little under three hours and gets into London at eight-thirty tonight. You'll stay at the Airport Hilton, right next to Heathrow. Then you'll catch tomorrow's British Airways flight to Greece. It leaves at 7:25 in the morning and gets you to Athens at 13:05, three hours before your flight to Tehran."

"Got it. Thanks."

"Why don't you go downstairs and check out, then look for one of the men in security who's there now. His name is Yossi Segev. You can't miss him. He's six-foot-five, with a shaved head and dark skin—Middle Eastern dark. He's wearing a dark blue suit and a light blue tie. Tell him you're Robert Gordon. He'll arrange for security to bring you and Miranda to me. He thinks you're a member of the American press covering the defense secretary's visit."

"Okay."

"After you leave the hotel, walk one hundred yards to your right. There's a small parking lot there. You'll see a white Mercedes with the logo of the Ministry of Tourism on both side doors. I'm behind the wheel as we speak, awaiting your arrival."

"Trying to impress me, Mr. Barzilai?"

"Just trying to be efficient."

Four agents, walking around him as discreetly as four big men in dark suits and sunglasses can be in an informal country like Israel, accompanied Jake and his assistant to the parking lot.

He saw a white Ministry of Tourism Mercedes, but no Barzilai. The driver was a much older man. Grey hair, glasses and slumped shoulders. The man was signalling him to come closer.

It *was* Barzilai. Jake recognized the eyes behind the heavily rimmed glasses. The stubble of the Israeli's beard was much more pronounced than usual. Everything else and nothing else were the same. His facial expression alone, which seemed to indicate that he was trying to overcome a feeling of constant pain, made Barzilai look very different and much, much older.

"Everything okay, man?" Jake said as soon as he sat in the car. "Don't take this the wrong way, but you look like shit."

"You think so?" Barzilai turned to him, removing his glasses and smiling. Miranda giggled.

Jake was dumbfounded. The Israeli was back to his old look. He had straightened his posture and the tortured look on his face was gone. Barzilai had been able to add twenty years to his age by wearing glasses, turning his blonde hair white, and using the muscles in his body and face.

"You're good. You should be on stage," Miranda remarked.

Barzilai smiled smugly. He turned the key in the ignition, shifted into drive, and pulled out of the parking lot. "Let's talk about your trip, shall we?"

"Go ahead."

"Have you thought about the possibility that this might be a trap? They might've checked you out and discovered that Walt Landis or Roberta Pierce-Reynolds don't exist."

"I thought of that. But there are so many rich Americans looking to do business—with anyone—that my motives seem perfectly reasonable. And they received a recommendation from a major bank they trust." Barzilai started to object but Jake raised his hand. "Let me finish. Besides, if that's what it takes, I'm willing to run the risk."

"What if they saw you with Gerard in Iran or in London? What if they saw you here with Rachel?"

"I don't think that's the case, but like I said, I'm willing to take the risk."

Barzilai shrugged. "It looks like you've thought this through."

"That's all I've been doing," Jake pointed out. "Look, it boils down to a basic question. Purely for argument's sake, let's accept that my country has been screwing up for too long, intervening in too many places, behaving like an empire. In addition, let's assume that we see the light, that we stop doing that, and that our military stops acting as protector to our multinational companies. We'd go back to basics, spend money and energy on fixing our own problems: poverty, crime, education, etc."

"Okay . . ."

"Am I prepared to live in isolation and accept the risk that the same people who did what they did to us—and to *themselves*, in Tanzania, Saudi Arabia, Iraq, and elsewhere—will play nice from now on? Am I prepared to assume that we won't be attacked anymore, that they won't produce weapons of mass destruction and deploy them against us?"

"Well said," Miranda said, nodding in agreement. Barzilai studied their faces, as if getting the measure of them.

"And you're willing to die for that."

"Do I want to die? No, I want to live. And I still have Rifaat to deal with."

"You Americans are crazy, but I love you," Barzilai said, grinning.

Miranda gave his shoulder a squeeze. "We love you too, Danny."

As they drove on, Jake noticed what looked like the carcasses of ruined trucks at different points along the road. "What are these?" he asked Barzilai, pointing.

"The remnants of trucks and buses destroyed by the Arabs during Israel's Independence War. We keep them here as a reminder."

Within a few minutes, they were approaching Ben Gurion Airport. "I want you to memorize a phone number," Barzilai said. "It's one of those prepaid cell phones—bought with cash. I'm hiding, as you know, and this is a good low-tech solution. Call me when you're out of there."

At 3:00 P.M. the following day, Jake and Miranda sat at Athens International Airport's Gate 12.

Abbas Zuhayli walked over. "Happy to see that you made it." He offered his hand and Jake shook it.

"I hope you were able to set aside a few days for your visit," the Iranian said, sitting down beside them.

"Not really. I need to fly to Amsterdam tomorrow night. I have a breakfast meeting the following day." Jake looked at the one-way ticket he'd bought. "It's KLM's Flight KL434, which leaves at 2:25 A.M. and arrives at 6:05 A.M. in Amsterdam."

"Okay. We'll make it work."

"Who are we seeing tomorrow morning?"

Zuhayli smiled, clearly proud of his influence. "Mullah Yazdi himself."

"Excellent."

When they landed at Mehrabad Airport, Jake noticed that Iran looked very different this time. He sensed tension all around. The airport swarmed with uniformed policemen and the cocky-looking Pasdaran.

As luck would have it, Zuhayli had checked them into the Azadi Hotel. Jake hoped he wouldn't be recognized. They had stayed with

Gerard at the Azadi for a brief time only, but it had been just a week ago, and the hotel had the copy of the fake passport with his picture on it.

They all had adjacent rooms on the 11th floor. Zuhayli invited the Americans to his room and asked them to step outside onto the balcony.

"I had my room bugged once. Yazdi has enemies." He closed the sliding glass door between the balcony and the room. Because their rooms were in the rear of the building, their view was of the deserted hotel parking lot.

"I like it better on this side. The front is too noisy," the chubby Iranian said, caressing his goatee. "I have news for you, Mr. Landis."

"News?" Jake raised an eyebrow at Miranda.

"You didn't think I would enter a transaction of this magnitude, let alone on behalf of Mullah Yazdi, without doing my homework first, did you?"

Jake froze.

The Iranian lit a cigar. There was no sign of a smile on the round bewhiskered face now. "No one has heard of you or your investors, let alone conducted business with you in the past."

With enormous effort, Jake spoke calmly. "What are you talking about?"

"Don't even try, Mr. Landis. If that is your name, which I very much doubt. I must tell you that I considered letting my associates here know about this."

Jake realized that the Iranian didn't know who he really was. He kept his relief in check. There was still a play to be made here. If he didn't make the right one, he was dead.

"Of course it isn't my name," Jake said. "I would never do business like this under my real name. The public relations fallout alone could cripple our domestic reputation. With all due respect to you, Mullah Yazdi and all of Iran, your nation couldn't be more unpopular in America if it tried."

The Iranian nodded, puffing on his cigar, conceding the point with a gesture. "I am a man of the world. I understand this. But the mullahs . . . they are not likely to share my cosmopolitan attitude."

Jake realized this had become a shakedown. Still, a much more comfortable position than he'd thought he was in thirty seconds earlier.

"All right. What do you want?"

Zuhayli chuckled. "Three million U.S. dollars in my account before you leave Tehran. Otherwise, you won't leave this city."

"Understood. Let me think about it." Jake was relieved to have a little time. Would he still be able to go forward with the plan? Would he still be seeing Yazdi? He didn't dare ask.

A car door slammed in the hotel parking lot, eleven stories beneath them—the first activity of any kind down there since they'd stepped onto the balcony.

"I also wonder one thing." The Iranian looked at Jake intently. "Why do you need us? You could buy the options for your own account and keep all the money."

Money. The man was blinded by money. "Two things: One, I was trying to build a relationship that would benefit me in the future; and two, if I buy the options for Iran, it's much less likely that anyone will connect it to my capital group. It's just Iran trying to mitigate its losses. I prefer to keep twenty percent of the profit and run no risk of complications."

"You're set to make millions of dollars here. I say you take fifteen percent, not twenty. For the size of the transaction we're looking at, twenty percent profit is a lot of money."

Jake shook his head. "No. Twenty percent is reasonable. I'm not being greedy here."

The Iranian shrugged. "Fair enough."

"I guess now the meeting with Yazdi is history, right?" Jake held his breath.

"Of course not. He's expecting you. Moreover, I *want* it to happen. No, nothing changes. They do not know anything. And if I get my three million, they will never know. On top of that, I make a commission on their profit—it would be a waste to give that up."

"All right. Forgive me, but I'm tired. I'll see you tomorrow." Jake couldn't stand looking at the man for one second longer. He moved toward the glass door leading to the Iranian's hotel room.

"Don't be upset. You'll recover this money very fast. One more bombing and you're in the black again. Between the two of us, Mullah Yazdi needs you. He is under attack internally. He is identified as the main architect of an anti-West nuclear Iran and he's having trouble defending his position after the bombings. The money you bring will help him neutralize the critics. That is why you were called here so fast. Mr. Yazdi is a very cautious man. Usually he takes a long time to decide things."

"What time is our meeting?" Miranda asked.

"Nine. And the protocol is that we get there at least fifteen minutes before the scheduled time. We should leave at eight."

"All right, then. I'll see you tomorrow," Jake said curtly.

Zuhayli handed him a card. "I've noted where the money should go on the back. You might want to give your instructions as soon as possible."

"It's two and a half hours earlier in Europe." Jake looked at his watch. "It's 6:30 P.M. there. The banks are closed."

"America is still open," said Zuhayli.

"I can't send you money from the States," Jake protested. "It would be open to investigation by the tax authorities, and I might be forced to explain the whole thing."

The Iranian threw his cigar out. It fell the eleven stories into an enclosed area littered with garbage and countless cigarette and cigar stubs. A wall separated it from the parking lot and the hotel itself. The area looked as if it had never been cleaned. "Well, I'll be downstairs at eight tomorrow morning," he said. "I will wait for you next to the concierge desk. You can always give your instructions after the meeting with Mr. Yazdi. Have a good night, Mr. Landis. Ms. Pierce-Reynolds."

They left the Iranian's room without answering. Let the sonofabitch sweat.

After breakfast the following morning, Jake withdrew a bottle of water from the mini-bar and opened a small container that said TWINLAB B-100 VITAMIN CAPS.

Each of the supposed vitamin capsules actually contained 250 milligrams of Ciprofloxacin powder and 50 milligrams of Doxycycline, also powdered. The physician in Israel had shown them how to crush the oblong white Cipro tablets and the small round pink Doxycycline tablets, open the vitamin capsules and replace their contents with the powdered antibiotics. During an inspection, it would've been highly suspicious if either of them were found carrying medication to combat anthrax infections.

In the spare bedroom at Rachel's house, Barzilai had told Jake and Miranda more about the anthrax inside the printed presentation packets. It had been developed in Iran and shipped to the Hezbollah—and seized by Israel during an incursion into Lebanon. Barzilai pointed to the poetic justice of this anthrax being in their hands. "Let the Iranians be hoisted on their own petard," he'd said.

"The Iranians have come up with a particularly aggressive strain of *bacillus anthracis*," the Israeli added quietly. "The spores of this strain move very rapidly to the lymph nodes. Once there, they germinate, leading to the release of several toxic substances. A regular anthrax infection comes in two stages: the first usually lasts a few days and the symptoms are like those of the flu; the second stage develops suddenly and results in shortness of breath, fever and shock, due to a lack of bloodflow to the body. This particular strain compresses the first stage into less than a day. The second stage happens a few hours after that."

Barzilai had been deadly serious when he spoke the next words. "Once the presentations are out of the package and start being manipulated, the aerosolized anthrax spores become airborne. They'll enter the lungs of anyone breathing that air. Inhalation anthrax is the deadliest form of anthrax, and there's no way out. You'll be breathing those spores too." He'd paused to look at them gravely. "The vaccination protocol is three subcutaneous injections given two weeks apart. After that, you get three more subcutaneous injections at six, twelve, and eighteen months. We have no time. You won't be vaccinated when you get those spores in your lungs. The antibiotics, especially a dose like you'll be taking, should protect you, though. Now pay attention, Jake. There are no guarantees. Even with the antibiotics, either of you—or both—could die. Is that clear?"

It had been clear then, when he heard Barzilai's warning, and it was clear now. Jake swallowed eight capsules—four times the recommended dosage for regular anthrax treatment. Miranda was certainly doing the same in her room.

"*Alea jacta est*," he whispered to himself. The die is cast. Julius Caesar had said that when crossing the Rubicon. No turning back. Jake put the presentations in his attaché case, looked at the mirror, adjusted his tie carefully, and walked out to the elevators.

CHAPTER TWENTY-SEVEN

Zuhayli, Miranda and Jake arrived at the State Expediency Council offices at 8:40 A.M. They were patted down by a policeman, and then they waited in line to pass through a metal detector.

"This wasn't here the last time I came," Zuhayli said.

A burly armed security guard led them to a small room off the lobby where a watchful woman took their names. She dialed a phone and spoke softly into it. Finally, a harried-looking man came to pick them up. He took them to a meeting room on the second floor, all the while breathlessly talking to Zuhayli in short sentences.

Throughout the building, Jake noticed newly installed security cameras, some with wires still hanging, surveying everything. The place seemed to be on fire. An inordinate number of people struggled to move between offices at a frenetic pace.

"They received a new threat a few minutes ago," Zuhayli explained after they were left alone.

"Wow, I didn't know that," Of course, Jake knew perfectly well. It was part of the plan he himself had put together. "What did they threaten now?"

"The refinery at Isfahan—that's 265,000 barrels of refining capacity—and another target at Bandar Abbas. They already destroyed the refinery, now they're after the port."

"When?" Miranda inquired, with only casual interest.

"Tomorrow evening at eight for the Isfahan refinery, and a week later for the port at Bandar Abbas—they want the whole city evacuated. Bandar Abbas will be a ghost town. Mullah Yazdi may be late for our meeting."

"It's understandable."

Zuhayli made several unsuccessful attempts to initiate a conversation with them. They waited in silence for almost an hour.

Finally, another overweight man with a round face entered the meeting room. He had an uneven white goatee and a bulbous nose and, in contrast to Zuhayli, was at least six-feet-four-inches tall. The man was dressed in a flowing grey robe and a white turban. He looked preoccupied.

Zuhayli stood to attention. "Mrs. Pierce-Reynolds, Mr. Landis, please meet Hojjat-ol-Eslam Yazdi."

Jake stood as well and extended his hand. "Pleasure."

The man shook his hand briskly, then spoke in Farsi. Zuhayli translated. "Very sorry for the delay. We have an emergency." Yazdi waited patiently for the translation.

"No problem," Jake replied.

"I will not be able to sit with you now."

Jake looked at Zuhayli in silence. The room was cold but the man was sweating.

"But I have arranged for a larger meeting this afternoon at three," Yazdi continued, via Zuhayli. "Can you be here?"

Jake heard Zuhayli exhaling in relief.

"Yes, but please bear in mind that I'm scheduled to fly to Amsterdam tonight. My flight leaves a little after two in the morning. I have a breakfast meeting that's related to our discussions and my offer to you. Would you like me to leave a written presentation with you, in case we're unable to meet later?"

Zuhayli began translating. His tone sounded apologetic.

The mullah interrupted. "Okay. Three," he said in English. He said a few clipped words in Farsi to Zuhayli. Then he turned and left the room.

On the way back to their hotel, Zuhayli said something to the driver. A few minutes later they slowly passed a vast complex that looked shuttered, locked up.

"Do you know what this is?" the chubby Iranian asked.

One of the entrances bore a bald eagle emblem: The Great Seal of the United States. "The American embassy?"

"Not anymore. It is now called the U.S. Den of Espionage. We only use it for the training of the Revolutionary Guards. The taxi will turn right and you'll see the southern walls. Look at the murals."

Jake saw a huge image of the Statue of Liberty against a background of the American flag, except the face of Miss Liberty was a threatening skull. Something had been written next to it.

"What does it say?" Miranda asked.

"It says: *You America. Be Angry With Us and Die of This Anger.*"

"And there?"

"*Down with America.*"

"Is the hatred that strong?"

Beside him on the backseat of the taxi, Zuhayli shrugged. "Not anymore. Look, the murals are fading. You were a convenient enemy, that's all."

"Not anymore?" Jake asked.

"To be honest, ordinary people hate America less. But nothing has changed in the government."

The last mural Jake saw was an American flag painted vertically, at the end of each red stripe a realistic drawing of a bomb. The stripes signaled the downward trajectory of bombs dropping from a plane. Over the flag, in English, were the stenciled words: DOWN WITH THE USA.

Zuhayli lowered his voice. "All arranged?" He was making the number three with his fingers, apparently indicating three million dollars.

Jake nodded, unsmiling.

"Today?"

Jake nodded again.

Zuhayli sat back and sighed, content.

"You are a very intelligent man. It has been my pleasure doing business with you."

Jake did not respond. Finally they arrived at the hotel.

"We'll see you in the lobby here at two," Jake said. He was furious that they hadn't had the chance to deliver his presentation to Yazdi. What if the man didn't show up for the second meeting?

"Let's make it earlier," Zuhayli suggested, once more caressing repeatedly a goatee that was a copy of Yazdi's but dyed black. "I'd like to go over the meeting with you. In fact, why don't you come to my room for a minute right now?"

That was troubling. Miranda looked at Jake, and he nodded imperceptibly. "Will Yazdi be at the three o'clock meeting?" Jake asked as soon as they were out on the Iranian's balcony once more. He looked downward at the hotel lot, where a total of three parked cars sat in the hot morning sun, light banking off their windshields. The vast majority of the hotel's guests came via taxi from the airport, it seemed. The enclosed area was as dirty as before.

"He cannot afford not to be. I told you, his faction is under attack by the moderates. The bombings have already cost most of the refining capacity of the country. If Isfahan's refinery is destroyed, there will not be much left at all. And the port at Bandar Abbas means over half of all the international maritime trade of Iran. What you offer is a way to mitigate the bombing's impact."

"Who'll be at the meeting?"

"You know what he told me before leaving? 'Don't be late. My whole faction in the government will be there.' Mullah Yazdi is using you to rally his troops." Zuhayli's eyes danced. The man was excited to be brokering a meeting like this. He was also excited, no doubt, about the millions he expected to receive.

Jake hadn't transferred the three million and had no intention of doing so. He might need it for STOP. Zuhayli would probably ask for details if the conversation went on, so Jake cut it short. "I need to do some work. I'll be in my room if you need me."

"The money?"

"Relax, will you? It's, what—seven-thirty in London? Nothing's open yet."

"London! Not Switzerland? I thought you managed your finances in Zurich. Now we have to wait another hour."

Exactly what Jake had intended by saying London. They needed the extra time. "Sorry, but that's where I have this kind of money available."

"You gave instructions for it to be done at the opening, right?" The Iranian's voice was almost plaintive.

"Yes. Relax."

Two hours later, at 1:00 P.M. in Tehran—9:30 A.M. London time—Zuhayli knocked on Jake's door. "Mr. Burke. Please come to my room immediately."

Standing on the balcony outside his room again, Zuhayli said, "The money hasn't come in yet."

"What's the matter with you?" Jake looked at his wristwatch, stalling for time. "My bank opened half an hour ago. Have you ever been able to get a wire transfer done in less than one hour?"

"I don't believe that you have transferred the money."

Miranda shot a sidelong glance at Jake. "You're crazy. The money is there," she said. "I arranged it myself."

Zuhayli shook his finger at her. "I want you to go back to your room. I want you to call your bank. I want you to get me the reference number of the wire transfer—I can trace it in minutes. If you have not made the transfer, the meeting with Yazdi will not take place and you will be arrested. Don't play with me. If I tell Mullah Yazdi that you are not who you say you are, you are both dead."

Jake looked at his watch. "We have to leave soon."

"I told you. This meeting will not take place unless the money is in my account." The little Iranian was apoplectic, shaking with rage. "This is final." He turned away from Jake and leaned on the balcony's parapet, holding the rail with both hands. "Now go!"

No choice, Jake thought to himself. The man would destroy the whole plan. He was literally considering pushing Zuhayli off the balcony, but he'd never get away with it. Even if he did, Yazdi might refuse to meet with Jake if his middleman was missing.

Miranda subtly nodded to Jake, as if to say, *Give him what he wants.* Jake inwardly gritted his teeth. He'd have to pay up.

"Fair enough. We'll wait until you've confirmed the transfer." He'd said it affably, but was deciding at the same time that the avaricious bastard wouldn't live to enjoy it.

They retired to Miranda's room, arranged the immediate emergency transfer, and obtained a reference number. Then they took it back to Zuhayli along with a little something else.

"Here you go," Jake said, delivering a piece of stationery with the number written on it. And one of his presentations.

"What's this?" Zuhayli asked, flipping through it.

"It's a copy of today's presentation. I thought you might want to review it before our meeting."

Zuhayli flipped some more and returned it to Jake. "Perhaps later. We must settle this matter first."

To minimize the spread of anthrax spores, Jake snuck the proposal back into its folder while Zuhayli was on the phone. He slipped it under his jacket and followed Miranda to the door.

"We've got to leave in half an hour," she said. "Please let us know when you get your confirmation."

"Rest assured, I will," Zuhayli said.

They left him there, huddled expectantly over the telephone.

It was ten after two and Jake was adjusting his tie for the fifth time when Zuhayli reappeared, all smiles.

"We may proceed," he said, beaming.

"Good. We're late," Miranda said tersely, and snatched her attaché case.

In the car, Zuhayli asked for another copy of the presentation. "I seem to have left it in my room," he explained sheepishly. Jake handed him a "clean" copy. No reason to infect the innocent driver.

The harried-looking man from the day before received them at Yazdi's offices and again took them to the small meeting room on the second floor. Once the man had left the room, closing the door behind him, Jake let his body slump and rolled his neck back, forth and sideways, trying to ease his nervousness.

"Do not worry, Mr. Landis, you will do fine," Zuhayli said, with a classic shit-eating grin. He didn't have a care in the world.

That would change in the next couple of hours.

Jake looked at his watch: 3:12. A few minutes later, the same man returned. He took them to the third floor this time. They walked on heavily carpeted hallways to what looked like a corner of the building. The man opened the double doors and motioned the Americans in.

At least twenty turbaned men were seated at a large round table. All had short beards. Most were plump. Each seemed to be accompanied by at least one aide. Jake looked around the office. It was large and decorated with exquisitely inlaid pieces of furniture. Paintings of Khomeini and other mullahs Jake didn't recognize covered the walls. The window glass was heavily tinted and surely reflective when seen from the outside. The feel of the place would've been one of secluded and luxurious security, if not for the anxious faces of those around the table.

Yazdi said something. One of the younger men seated in the outside circle stood up, turned to Jake and said, "At the request of Mullah Yazdi, I will be translating this afternoon."

Zuhayli looked mildly disappointed. Jake nodded. "Very well. I'll start by distributing the presentations. They're written in English, though the graphs are self-explanatory. Please tell them that I'll go over the text slowly while you translate. If they have questions, they should please stop me." Jake took one presentation and walked around the table to Yazdi. "Mullah Yazdi, allow me to give you the first one."

Yazdi took the anthrax-laden presentation. "Thank you," the tall man said, a tight smile on his lips.

Jake wished he had brought more folders. "I wasn't expecting such a large meeting. Would you gentlemen mind sharing the presentations?" Miranda distributed the copies.

He went through his talk in forty-five minutes. Every few minutes a different man would quietly enter the room and whisper in Yazdi's ear. Yazdi would nod and dismiss the messenger.

In one way or another, all the men were handling the presentations. The mullah himself repeatedly licked his thumb to turn the pages before him. In his mind, Jake could see the anthrax spores lodging themselves in the Iranians' lungs. He tried not to think of his own. Or, worst of all, Miranda's. That was too horrible to contemplate.

CHAPTER TWENTY-EIGHT

The mullahs' follow-up questions related to the size of each transaction and the total profit to be made. Some asked detailed questions, a little *too* detailed. Jake suspected that they planned to buy some options personally.

At a certain point, the man who'd escorted them to the room re-entered and whispered something to Yazdi. The mullah looked surprised. He turned slightly to stare at Jake, then he interrupted the meeting to say something in Farsi. The translator said, "Five more minutes."

Zuhayli gave Jake a significant look. Jake started sweating. He looked at his watch: ten after four.

At the end of the five minutes Yazdi clapped his hands. The mullahs stood, passing the presentations to their aides. Jake stood up also, like a college professor at the end of class.

Yazdi spoke directly to him in English. "Wait here, please."

Yazdi beckoned Zuhayli into the hall with him. Jake shared a moment of eye contact with his blackmailer. Now that Zuhayli had the money, there was no reason to protect Jake's secret. Except, of course, the thought that there could be more.

Sure enough, Zuhayli winked at Jake on his way out of the room. Jake knew a second three-million dollar demand couldn't be far behind.

For the moment, he and Miranda were alone in the conference room. She looked at him. They didn't dare speak. The room could be bugged.

Twenty agonizing minutes later, Jake stood, walked to the double doors, and opened them. Two uniformed guards stood outside. They motioned him back in. He tried several more times to leave, showed irritation, asked to speak to Mullah Yazdi. No results. The guards gestured them inside every time. He sat down once more at the conference table and looked at Miranda. He saw determination in her eyes, and was suddenly enveloped by an unexpected calm.

The die had been cast.

Yazdi returned to the conference room a little after seven, this time without the translator. "Sorry for the delay," he said. "That crazy organization has threatened our main port and one of our largest refineries." To Jake's surprise, he spoke in fluent English. But then he realized, of course. He'd encountered it before in negotiations with the Japanese. Translators gave them additional time to think.

"I know. Mr. Zuhayli told me."

Yazdi nodded. If Zuhayli had given them away, Yazdi was showing no indication yet.

Yazdi raised the palms of both hands and massaged his temples, as if fighting a headache. Jake now noticed that the Iranian's eyes were bloodshot. He seemed unfocused.

"I know it might not be the right time, so please forgive me, but I need to ask you. Is your country interested in the transaction?"

Yazdi nodded impatiently, as if terribly weary. "Yes, yes, of course. Can you make one transaction immediately, but ten times bigger than the sample transaction?" Yazdi seemed alert and focused again.

"It can be a hundred times larger." Jake could practically see the mullah calculating almost half a billion dollars. "It would have to be discreetly distributed among several option buyers who would front for us. I have a breakfast meeting tomorrow morning in Amsterdam with the head of another group of investors. They have the capacity to help me structure a transaction worth roughly half of that—approximately two-hundred-million dollars in profit."

"What do you need?"

"As I said, a computer and a phone."

"No money?"

"Not yet. The deal will happen in eight to ten individual transactions. For now I need one of your banks to confirm that they'll open a letter of credit guaranteeing the first transaction. If you can, please use Bank Melli. We know it well. I also need a letter from you authorizing the transaction. The letter should also confirm that my firm's profit participation is twenty percent. I'll advance money for the first transaction because I understand that things are hectic for you and we don't have much time. Please understand, though, that this will have to be the last time I do that."

"Yes," Yazdi nodded. "You will make a parallel transaction in the name of Green Leaf. This one will remain confidential. Understood?"

"Yes, of course. How many options do you want me to buy for Green Leaf?"

"One-fifth of what you'll be doing with Bank Melli."

"Isn't that a bit much?"

The mullah smiled. "One should grab the opportunities when they come." Yazdi sneezed. "I won't shake your hand. I think I am coming down with a cold."

By the time Jake and Miranda made it back to the hotel, it was a little after eight in the evening. Miranda went to her room, and Jake climbed the stairs to the second floor and entered the hotel's Internet café. He sat at a computer, looking for news on the Internet.

It was hard to believe that only a few days had passed since his first visit to the Azadi Grand Hotel with Gerard. The Frenchman had sent an email from this same computer to his "father" in London, telling him that he'd made it safely, setting everything in motion.

The latest threat by STOP was big news. So were the much larger riots on the streets of the major Iranian cities, and the violence with which they were being crushed. In Tehran, the riots were concentrated in the southern part of town, around Bazaar Molavi and along Mostafah Khomeini Avenue. Which explained why he hadn't come across any disturbance during his time in the city.

Jake glanced at his watch frequently, counting the minutes to his flight. The wait was agonizing. What if Yazdi or the other mullahs had gotten worse and someone made the connection to their meeting with him? He expected at any moment to see a team of Revolutionary Guards coming for him.

At ten past ten, two men came looking for him. They had a letter from Yazdi to Walt Landis and a copy of another letter from Bank Melli to its main corresponding bank in the UK.

At 11:00 P.M., moments after Jake returned to his room to pick up his luggage, he heard a knock on his door. It was Abbas Zuhayli asking Jake to come to his room.

As they stood once more on the balcony outside Zuhayli's room, the Iranian said, "I know you are planning to go to the airport soon, but I have bad news, Mr. Landis. You cannot leave tonight."

Jake froze. "Why not?"

"Because I don't want you to. I will need another transfer tomorrow morning. Five million, this time. I think you can afford it." The man's eyes were bloodshot.

"And how will you stop me?"

"This is not a serious question, is it?" Zuhayli sneezed and blew his nose loudly. "I need just one phone call. You know that."

"And if I give you the extra five million, how can I be sure that you'll let me leave tomorrow?"

"You have my word of honor," said the Iranian, without batting an eye.

By this time tomorrow, all the mullahs who'd met with Jake would be very sick or dead. The connection between the meeting and the sudden illnesses would be quickly established.

That Zuhayli would be dying too was no consolation. The sonofabitch was still capable of trapping Jake in Tehran. And not flying out tonight meant death. He had to leave. Now.

He knelt as if to tie his shoe. "Okay," he said softly, "but there's something else I need to say to you."

The Iranian crossed his arms and looked down at him. "What?"

Jake grabbed both of the little man's legs under the knees and stood up abruptly. Zuhayli's knees buckled and his body fell backward. He was suddenly over the parapet, like a flailing Olympic high-jumper.

"*Fuck you,*" Jake said, as he pushed Zuhayli farther into the void.

Jake saw a look of surprise on the Iranian's face, right before the man let out what was more of a whimper than a scream.

As he turned toward the sliding glass door to Zuhayli's room, Jake heard the impact of the body on the deserted parking lot's pavement. He looked down. Zuhayli had fallen in the enclosed area off the parking lot; his body was now framed by garbage and cigarette butts. Jake quickly took his tie off and used it to open the balcony door. He didn't want to leave fingerprints.

Inside the room he snatched the coffee table and put it on the balcony, against the parapet. Because he was short, Zuhayli would've needed a boost to get over the railing and commit suicide.

Jake inspected the suite and made sure that he hadn't left anything behind.

He looked through the peephole, made certain that no one was outside, and walked quickly to Miranda's room.

"We need to go, now."

Miranda saw the urgency in his eyes. Without a word, she closed her small suitcase and followed him.

They went to Jake's room. He retied his tie in the mirror. Then he snatched his luggage and they rushed downstairs to the lobby.

They checked out and asked for a taxi to the airport. All the while, Jake feared that alarms would sound any moment at the discovery of the dead body.

Minutes later, they were on their way.

The concierge told Hasim Khafar that the American businessman he described had just gotten into a taxi bound for the airport. Not two minutes earlier.

Hasim gladly paid for this information. He hurried to rejoin Abdul and the Pasdars assisting them in Tehran. But they weren't at the car. He impatiently scanned the parking lot and saw them returning from the rear of the hotel. Some commotion was going on back there.

"What happened?" Hasim asked.

"Someone found a body," Abdul reported. "An Iranian man."

"Burke's on his way to the airport," Hasim told them. "We'd best make haste if we're to catch him."

They piled into the Pasdaran's SUV and sped off. Hasim was delighted at this fortuitous turn of events. It had been a very frustrating trip thus far. Burke had left few traces of his presence and Hasim had resorted to making inquiries at every hotel in the city. At last, Hasim was only minutes behind his prey.

"He will be slowed by the street rabble," said the Pasdar driving. "Those fools and their protests will serve Allah's purpose, after all."

The Iranian was right. Midway to the airport, when their taxi reached Kheyabun-e Azadi, Jake heard a growing disturbance ahead. Rhythmic chanting punctuated by random shouting. Banging and small explosions. Shots.

Then traffic stopped. The street here was littered with piles of burning tires, remnants of street barricades and smashed windows.

The taxi driver tried to back up, but there was nowhere to go. A crowd had encircled a small Peugeot behind them and was rocking it, lifting its tires off the pavement. The occupants scrambled out of the car right before the mob succeeded in overturning it. This created an opening for the taxi driver to back away.

In absolute panic, he shifted to reverse and accelerated. Jake heard the distinctive thuds of metal against flesh. They had hit two rioters.

Something apparently thrown by the mob landed on Miranda's lap. She blinked, and realized what it was: a Molotov cocktail. Gasoline in a beer bottle with a burning rag cork. Luckily, the bottle hadn't broken.

Miranda snatched it up and cast it out the window. The cocktail shattered against the pavement, exploding in flames. The fire drove back the angry men, giving the taxi the extra seconds needed to escape. The driver slammed into gear and peeled out in a fishtail turn. He gunned the car back down the street.

They rounded a curve and entered a block the mob had already passed through. The street was abandoned. For a moment Jake thought they were out of the woods.

But then a car blew into the next intersection and skidded to a halt, blocking their path. A black Nissan SUV with tinted windows. The siren went on, a forbidding bleat.

Their taxi driver muttered a helpless prayer. Jake felt intense anxiety and the certainty of a fight he doubted he could win.

"Go around them!" he ordered, but the taxi driver shook his head.

"I cannot, Pasdaran!"

The SUV doors flew open and four men jumped out. One was huge, like an NBA center. Two were arrogant young men like the other Pasdars, but the fourth was stout, baby-faced and actually smiling.

All had a hand on a gun, tucked in a waistband or shoulder-holster. The angelic one urgently beckoned Jake and Miranda.

"I'm not getting out of this car," Miranda said, white-faced.

"Do what they say!" the driver pleaded, hands in the air. Jake gestured to the gunmen as if to say, *Easy, we're cooperating*, and moved slowly toward the door. Desperately searching his mind for a plan but with only an instant to think, he came up maddeningly dry.

As Jake's hands curled around the door handle, six screaming young men appeared from nowhere and blind-sided the Pasdaran with makeshift cudgels. In a seemingly suicidal display of rage, they rained wild blows on anyone within reach. It looked like the briefest of respites for Jake and Miranda because the big man shrugged off the two young men who had targeted him and started firing at point blank range.

But in the next instant, the reason for the rioters' heedless courage became clear.

They were only the advance charge.

Like a tidal wave, the mob surged around the SUV and engulfed the four men, swinging bats, bricks, and knives. Some carried actual swords. Others carried what smelled like gasoline-soaked rags.

The big man was chopped down before their eyes, pierced by an anonymous sword. As he sank into the vicious throng, his eyes rolled like a crazed bull's just before the matador's final strike.

The others had managed to get back into the SUV, but the driver's door was caught open. He was pulled back out, firing his sidearm blindly. Jake heard one of the rioters laughing. A boy no older than fifteen plunged a long knife into the Pasdar's back. The man turned brokenly, trying to get a shot off at his assailant. Two more stabbed him, while a third smashed a brick against his head. The Pasdar went limp.

Someone poured the contents of a bottle on him and threw the body back into the SUV. The smell of gasoline was now nauseating. Others spilled several other bottles into the Nissan. The other Pasdar managed to get out of the car and started running away, chased by dozens of men. The stout baby-faced man tried to get out, but the crowd didn't let him. He wasn't smiling now. Someone threw a flaming rag inside the vehicle. The interior of the SUV exploded in a ball of flame. The screams that followed were agonizing.

Only then did the taxi driver's foot find the gas pedal. Though babbling a litany of prayers as tears rushed down his cheeks, he found sufficient composure to pilot the cab around the blaze and get them out of there.

Jake glanced out the back window. The mob swirled around the pyre, a joyously bloodthirsty dance of celebration. A few yards away, a group of men was butchering the Pasdar who'd tried to escape. During the few seconds the killings had taken, the cab had been completely forgotten, once the true object of the people's fear and hatred was vulnerable before them at last.

Jake looked at Miranda. She was in shock.

When KLM's Flight 434 took off, the man in seat 2A of the new Boeing 777 finally relaxed. He was shaken by the riots but in high spirits. They had succeeded in their mission. He closed his eyes and remembered their arrival in Iran, an eternity ago, with Gerard. A lot had changed but it was only the beginning. He was proud and he was tired. He dozed off.

In his dream, his wife was playing Debussy's "Clair de Lune," their piano majestically placed under the shade of a vast oak tree in Central Park. He was holding Claire's small hand, running happily with her, chasing squirrels, his daughter's delighted cries of pleasure blending with the piano's melody. His little Claire. And then she stopped and said, "Daddy, it hurts. I can't breathe, please get me out of here."

Jake opened his eyes. He had one more piece of unfinished business: Abdel Aziz Rifaat.

BOOK III

CHAPTER TWENTY-NINE

Their flight landed early in Amsterdam. Jake was exhausted from the travel and the stress, but didn't notice any signs of anthrax infection. Yet. It was 5:55 in the morning. Miranda had coughed a few times during the flight, each one making Jake's heart skip a beat. But every time she gave him a reassuring smile that lit up her whole face.

"Feeling great," she'd say, and he was able to relax a few minutes longer.

They walked out into the enormous mall that was Schiphol Airport and placed a call to London.

"We're back. All went well. One plus forty," was all he said to a sleepy Big Ben.

All nonstop flights to Tel Aviv left in the afternoon and got them to Israel only at night. With some luck, though, they might be able to connect via Frankfurt, which would get them back in Israel by two-thirty in the afternoon. He hurriedly walked to the ticket counter, bought two one-way tickets to Frankfurt from a laid-back and excruciatingly slow agent, and ran with Miranda to the gate of Lufthansa's Flight 4685. A steward closed the plane's door immediately after they boarded.

Jake and Miranda had a little time to kill in Frankfurt. After buying tickets to Tel Aviv, he noticed clusters of people around the airport's TV monitors and walked over to one of them. The monitor he chose was tuned to the German ZDF-TV.

Big Ben had done his job faster than Jake expected. The caption read, *Taegliche Nachrichten: Iran im Chaos*. News of the Day: Iran in Chaos. Big Ben had issued fake press releases by three Iranian news outlets: *Islamic Republic News Agency—IRNA*, the *Khorasan News* and the *Tehran Times*. In different ways, the three outlets reported that there had been a major disaster during a governmental visit to a chemical plant outside Tehran. Several government members, including Nasrullah Sadr Yazdi, were either suspected dead or very ill. First information seemed to indicate that, in addition to Yazdi, some forty members of the highest echelon of the Iranian government had participated in the visit to the chemical plant.

Next came a correspondent from another German TV station interviewing a member of the Iranian Liberation Front. With a voice electronically disguised, the man, seen only as a dark silhouette against a white background, was saying that there had been a coup. Practically all the hard-line members of the Iranian government either were dead or had disappeared. The correspondent asked the ILF member if he thought there was any foundation to reports that the men had been killed by anthrax. Was the chemical factory really an anthrax plant?

Jake and Miranda stared at each other. It was done. All her fear in the last few hours suddenly released, and she sobbed silently into his shoulder while he held her. Jake closed his eyes, buried his face in her hair, and murmured a mental thanks to the heavens.

After a few moments he would never forget, Jake walked away to call Barzilai's cell.

"All went well," he said. "LH686."

"Got it," the Israeli answered. "When you get here, I'll see you at the Hertz counter in the arrivals hall."

Jake walked to his gate. Lufthansa Flight 686 to Tel Aviv was already boarding.

Four hours later, Barzilai stopped them a few yards from the rental-car area. He had the old man's disguise on, his back even more bent than when Jake had last seen him driving the Ministry of Tourism Mercedes.

"A lot's happened in the few hours since we spoke, my friends," Danny told them.

"Did Big Ben release the statement by Bank Hochsteiner as planned?"

"He did better than that. He also released a compressed sound file of the recording you gave him of your meeting with Zuhayli, copies of all the documents of your transaction, and the details of some other incoming sums of money. By the way, there was over a billion dollars in the Green Leaf account."

"How did the bank react?" Miranda asked.

"The bank's spokesperson stated that the press release wasn't theirs, but when asked whether the transactions took place, she refused to comment. It was clear to everyone that the transactions were real. It made headlines on all the news programs. Until the next bombshell."

"The next bombshell?"

"You know that the Iranian parliament is called the Majlis."

"Yes."

"The number four man and leader of the moderate faction, Mohsen Moin, has gone on national TV, flanked by the head of all armed services and other paramilitary organizations, *including* the Revolutionary Guards. He declared that a major disaster had occurred. He's assuming leadership of the country 'while the Supreme Leader is indisposed.' I think they either arrested or killed the man. Moin is calling for general elections in ninety days."

Jake didn't say anything. He was overwhelmed.

"There's more," Barzilai continued. "Mohsen Moin addressed the community of nations and declared that Iran has made the choice to concentrate on its internal development, and will therefore cut ties with all non-Iranian liberation movements. He also declared that Iran will be reviewing its policy vis-à-vis nuclear energy. He invited the Iranian Liberation Front and several other organizations to join the government in a national meeting. They're being called to chart a joint strategy for the political opening of the country."

"Sounds like a lot of talk. Nothing concrete."

"Let me finish. The new government has also arrested several elements who," he made a gesture that meant quotation marks, "'mistook

Iran's hospitality for a license to damage Iran's reputation.' All these people are being flown to Holland, to face justice at the International Criminal Court. Bottom line, Jake, we won."

Jake fished out the letters from Yazdi and from Bank Melli. "Have Big Ben divulge this too. There will be no remaining doubt about the corruption after that."

Barzilai pocketed the documents. "We prepared a communiqué from STOP informing of the suspension of all bombings. It's waiting for you to send it out. You earned the honor."

Jake hugged Miranda. "That'll be done by this lady here."

"Of course. Silly me," Barzilai smiled.

Jake clapped his hands. "Okay, that's good. That takes care of Iran. Syria's next."

"Good? That's all?"

"*Very* good."

"Very good?"

Jake hugged Barzilai and said, "Un-fucking-believably great, man." He meant it, but as Miranda embraced the Israeli as well, Jake's mind was already on Rifaat. It's him or me, he thought. Next time it'll be poison in my drink or a sniper's bullet. "Now let's get out of here. You're a wanted man and I don't want to call attention to us."

Barzilai laughed. "Don't worry. As of ten minutes ago, I'm not persona non grata anymore. I shouldn't advertise my presence, but I'm off the wanted list here in Israel. At least for the time being."

"You could go back onto that list pretty fast. We'll continue taking the same precautionary steps as before."

"Right you are," Barzilai said, chastened. "What do we do next?"

"Three things. Finalize this Iran deal, begin the process with Syria, and look for Rifaat."

"The third could get easier soon. I told you that of the three guys who attacked Rachel's moshav, we caught two alive. One isn't talking. The other's already admitted that he belongs to the Popular Islamic Jihad."

They issued the warning to Syria. The text was very similar to the opening threat against Iran. It urged Syria's dictator not to delude himself that he could avoid Iran's fate. The first target would be the 135,000-barrel Banias refinery, the country's largest. The only thing different from the first announcement to Iran was that, this time, Jake and Barzilai gave instructions to Syria on how it could communicate with STOP secretly.

Syria didn't respond at first. Jake and Barzilai had to go forward with the destruction of the Banias refinery to prove to them, and to the rest of the world, that STOP's capabilities weren't limited to Iran. Fortunately, the Syrians had taken STOP's warning and evacuated the refinery. There were no casualties. Syria capitulated fast after that. Within hours of the explosion, the country's foreign minister announced in clear terms that his country would be expelling all terrorist organizations. In a speech to the 250-member People's Assembly, Syria's dictator tried to save face by declaring that the actions were not a result of STOP's pressure, since the sovereign nation of Syria would never capitulate to blackmail.

"Over the last several months, under my orders," he declared, "our internal security forces have been in the process of rounding up all rogue elements operating in the country. The present actions are a continuation of this policy."

The media received the declaration with derision. "A perfectly transparent surrender," CNN called it.

For the first time, STOP had scored an unambiguous victory over terrorism.

Using the back channel as per STOP's instructions, Syria passed on the known whereabouts of militants it was "monitoring for the sake of international security." This information included the precise location of the Lebanese seaside villa of Abdel Aziz Rifaat.

At the safe house in Galilee where Rachel was hiding, Jake overheard her and Barzilai arguing in Hebrew. Barzilai was preparing to leave, a look of fatalistic satisfaction on his face.

"Where are you going?" Jake asked.

"We're going in."

Jake turned to Rachel. "Is that true?"

She nodded. "One of the men who came after me in Beit Zayit broke when told that we knew where Rifaat was. He was shocked when he heard the address given to us by Syria. There's no doubt now—the man's reaction was the best possible confirmation of the address. He also told us lots about Rifaat's set-up: the number of guards posted outside, distribution of the rooms, et cetera. But it's crazy. The Mossad hasn't had time to prepare the operation and Danny's group has decided to wing it."

Barzilai shrugged. "We don't have time for preparations. Rifaat already knows that Syria caved. He might try to escape."

"Rifaat is probably surrounded by so much security that this could well be a suicide mission. I've told Danny he's leaving on a rogue mission. They don't have the authorization of the Israeli army to act, and he won't have their protection either."

"Who's going?"

"There's a group of soldiers and reservists that all have a bone to pick with Rifaat, a personal beef of one kind or another. The majority has had loved ones killed or maimed by Rifaat's people. Danny's one of them. They decided long ago to go after him as soon as he was located."

"Well, I also have a personal issue with the man. I'm going too. And Danny, don't even think of telling me not to. This is precisely the reason I got involved with you people in the first place. Either I accompany you or I'm out, and STOP can kiss my money good-bye."

The Israelis' objections were a small hurdle compared to Miranda's. She wept openly when Jake told her, then turned in fury on him.

"Do you have a deathwish, or do you think you're invincible now that you've escaped so many times? Either way, I keep thinking about what Suter's friend said in Egypt. Luck always runs out, Jake!"

"Miranda," he said, taking both her hands in his, "everything I've done has led up to this. I can't rest until Rifaat is dead. And if he somehow escaped and I wasn't there . . . I wouldn't be able to live with myself. This is my only chance to have a normal life again. To close this chapter for good."

She nodded, but her shoulders crumpled. He realized she fully expected him to die.

Jake wasn't sure she was wrong.

CHAPTER THIRTY

Jake piloted the 55-foot Ferretti with Lebanese identification over a calm sea. He kept the boat at thirty knots all the way to the coast north of Tyre. They were stopped twice on the way. First by the Israeli navy in the waters ten miles off Rosh HaNikra, Israel's northernmost sea town. Their trip had been cleared in advance, but in order to proceed toward Lebanon, they still had to endure a shouting match with an overzealous young navy officer and suffer a detailed onboard inspection by the officer and three soldiers who looked no older than fifteen.

The second time, they were ten miles from Tyre. A Lebanese patrol boat approached. Amnon, one of the members of the attack group and a Sayeret Matkal veteran like Barzilai, spoke Lebanese Arabic perfectly. The other men looked suitably colorful and drunk. Amnon was able to convince the soldiers that he was a Lebanese tour-guide taking tourists around.

They docked at the quiet end of the port on the northern tip of Tyre's Natural Preserve. One of them remained in the boat. He would be picking them up after the mission. The others went ashore. To anyone looking on, they were a boisterous group of seven Englishmen led by a hapless guide. They ordered beers at the closest seaside bar, while their guide spoke on a cell phone. Within fifteen minutes, a tour bus approached, driven by a local Mossad operator. They went to the boat and unloaded two large boxes of the kind used to keep frozen fish. The boxes were heavy and each had to be carried by two men.

"Great fishing," Amnon explained to the incurious bar manager, who was only too happy to do any business at all that late on a weekday afternoon.

During the short trip north, toward El Ramel and the center of Tyre, the team removed bullet-proof vests from the large boxes. They also withdrew pistols, automatic rifles, and explosives, and transferred them to individual duffel bags and backpacks, covered by fishing gear. The group checked in at the Rest House, a small thirty-room hotel on Esterahat Street, four miles from Rifaat's isolated seashore villa.

They walked out of their rooms at 3:00 A.M. A sleepy manager, hearing the creaky stairs, came out to offer service. They took him at gunpoint to a bathroom in one of their rooms, where they tied and gagged him. They left the room and hung a "Do Not Disturb" sign on the doorknob. As quietly as possible, the group stepped into a moonless night.

In the tour bus, Barzilai gave everyone a copy of Rifaat's photograph. Jake memorized the bulging frog eyes and the puffy lips. The driver dropped them at a secluded spot in the northern outskirts of Tyre, a mile and a half from Rifaat's villa. They were counting on not being stopped by the police of the sleepy town as they proceeded on foot to the villa. If that happened, they'd be tourists going out for early fishing. Any angler worth his salt knew that this was the best hour to sail out.

They had calculated that once they reached Rifaat's villa the whole operation would take six minutes. With luck, they'd be back at the Ferretti boat twenty minutes after that. A total of twenty-six minutes. It should take a little over an hour to reach Israeli territorial waters.

From the moment they left their rooms, no unnecessary words were exchanged. Communications were curt, and whoever spoke waited for all of the others to signal agreement. They waited, too, as Barzilai translated for Jake. He felt part of a team, a good one. Still, he was nervous, if not downright scared. He started to doubt his decision. His harrowing escape in Tehran had made him cocky. Back in Israel, he'd made the decision to join the assault team on pure adrenaline, never stopping to consider the stakes. What was he doing on a mission like this, among professional soldiers? Like a snake around his body, like smoke under the door, a feeling of dread began to choke him. *Who do I think I am?*

Without the moon to light the way, they had to be careful. They walked silently over a dirt road pockmarked by potholes. Once in a while a dog would bark, only to be silenced by a shout from an angry owner. In the dark, without the use of flashlights, it wasn't hard to fall. It took them fifteen minutes to get safely away from the last houses of the city and another half-hour to cover the remaining mile. It felt longer to Jake.

They finally reached the stretch of pavement that led to Rifaat's non-descript white-stucco house. It had two stories with a second-floor terrace overlooking the water. The only sound was the waves breaking against sand to their left.

Outside the house, they found two sentries fast asleep, one of them sitting on a chair that stood precariously on two legs, its back against a wall. Each sentry was shot cleanly through the forehead with silencer-equipped guns.

Though he'd seen so much of late, even at his own hands, Jake was still struck by the sudden, brutal violence. He now felt an all-consuming fear. It was blind, strength-sapping panic, overwhelming in its intensity. For an instant after the shots there was silence, as the soldiers looked at one another like dancers getting in sync. Then the silence slowly began filling up with sounds: the ocean again; the shifting of sand under the Israelis' feet; the in-and-out of his own breathing; his heart's lub-*dub*, lub-*dub*. A buzzing hum in his head.

They split into two teams as planned. Barzilai and another soldier went into the house while Amnon, Jake and four others stayed behind to defend against Lebanese police or other Popular Islamic Jihad members.

Jake wrestled with his budding panic attack, reciting his favorite things like a mantra. He felt as if he was about to collapse. That couldn't happen. Damn it, this is my chance to end it, he thought.

The plan was for Danny to set explosives against the door of Rifaat's room. They assumed it would be reinforced and locked against intruders.

Danny and his partner Uri silently climbed the stairs to the second floor.

As Uri covered him, Danny crept to the door of the master bedroom. He slipped the explosive charge from his belt and carefully affixed it to the panel closest to the knob.

Danny sensed something—not a movement, but a shape-—from the corner of his eye. He turned his head to see a tall man standing in the hallway outside Uri's range of vision. He was just staring at Danny through the sight of an old machine pistol.

For a second, they made eye contact. The man had the cool gaze of a professional killer.

The pistol roared and Danny felt blazing heat pummel his body.

Rifaat jolted awake at the distinctive report of Khalil's gun. He reflexively reached under his bed and grabbed the AK-47 kept there.

Sitting up in bed, he slammed home the magazine and flipped the safety off.

There was more gunfire outside the room. Lots of it. Keeping his weapon trained on the door, Rifaat picked up his cell phone and dialed.

Ali, his driver, picked up. Scared. Rifaat spoke in a hurried staccato.

"Ali. Bring the car around. Outside my window. Now."

Rifaat moved to the window and peered out. He saw dark shapes out there. Unfamiliar, unfriendly shapes.

He dialed another number. He was calling Zafir, another bodyguard. The man should be down the hall. Zafir didn't pick up. Rifaat threw down the phone in disgust.

He saw his touring car pull up outside. The men he'd seen before raked it with high-caliber ordinance. Ali's shape rocked behind the wheel and went limp.

Rifaat turned away from the window. He must trust Allah for his salvation. Rifaat felt only a moment of doubt before the certainty that Allah was with him brought him comfort again.

After Barzilai left, Jake's heart was racing. He expected the blast in less than a minute.

Instead, shooting suddenly broke out and lights went on all over the house. Jake heard frantic shouting in Arabic and short calm commands in Hebrew. To his dismay, he identified many voices in Arabic, coming from different parts of the second floor. The two Israelis seemed to be greatly outnumbered.

They were surprised by a car barreling up to the side of the house. The other commandos opened fire on it.

Then Jake's group moved silently into the house. There was no one on the ground level. One of the Israelis started up the stairs and was blocked silently by Amnon. That made sense to Jake. They needed a better assessment of the situation, or they might be walking into what could be a well-prepared trap.

The on-and-off staccato shooting grew into a full-fledged fusillade, followed by a long silence.

A series of shouts in Arabic echoed in the house. No Hebrew. Were Danny and the other Israeli dead? Jake heard someone call for Abdel Aziz.

Another voice answered.

"*Alahu Akbar,*" it said.

It had to be Rifaat. The sonofabitch was still alive. The buzzing sound of Jake's panic attack was growing in volume and rising in pitch. Don't let it happen again, Jake told himself. *Stay calm. Stay conscious.*

Don't pass out.

Don't pass out.

Amnon walked silently back to the front door, opened it and banged it shut. Then he shouted something in Arabic.

"*Shurta! Police!*"

Jake understood. Amnon was posing as Lebanese police, trying to lure the terrorists downstairs.

Another voice, which Jake identified as Rifaat's, asked something.

Amnon answered with what sounded like an order.

Jake heard the lurching footsteps of at least two terrorists on their way down. Upstairs, he heard a number of other voices. He counted at least three, plus Rifaat's. Were there more?

As the Arabs came down, Jake made out the legs and their guns, muzzles angled down. When they saw Amnon, they raised their weapons. The Israeli jumped out of range of the erupting AK-47s, just as the terrorists' shots carved holes on the wooden floor where he'd stood. Two other Israelis backed against the sides of the staircase opening sprang out, a spray of bullets pouring from their submachine guns. One of the terrorists spun, his head a shapeless mass of red. The other was blown off his feet, his body arching forward and backward spastically under the impact of the shells. The four Israelis flew up the stairs, jumping over the slumped dead bodies, shooting as they climbed.

Jake's peripheral vision darkened suddenly.

His stomach felt like a fist.

His lips began to move but no words came out. His throat was clenched tight.

Finally he managed to mumble to himself, "While My Guitar Gently Weeps."

His voice rose in volume as Jake mounted the stairs. Anything to keep the panic attack at bay. "Smith and Wollensky!" he cried out as he climbed.

One Israeli looked back at the mad American who was following them up the stairs, holding an Uzi and shouting.

"Häagen Dazs! *Häagen Dazs*! HÄAGEN DAZS!"

When he reached the top, he saw several more collapsed bodies littering the hallway, one of them slumped over the balustrade. He saw Amnon and the others engaged in battle with terrorists holed up in a bedroom. Even though Jake couldn't see the faces of the enemies inside, he counted two sources of fire. Something was wrong. Downstairs, he had heard the voices of four Arabs still alive after the initial shootout. Amnon and his group had trapped two. Where were the other two?

He advanced down the hall and saw Uri, Barzilai's partner, spread-eagle on the floor, eyes gazing sightlessly at the ceiling.

Barzilai, bleeding profusely from shoulder and groin, was lying behind a bullet-mottled marble planter. The vest had protected only his chest.

Suddenly a third shooter leaned out from behind an oak sideboard and squeezed off a burst with an antiquated machine pistol.

Jake rolled beside Barzilai. The stone planter absorbed the fusillade.

"Pinned down," Barzilai said weakly. "Miracle he didn't take you out getting here."

Jake peered around the base of the planter. The broad door near the shooter's position must be the master bedroom. Rifaat.

"You're hurt," Jake said, trying to gauge the Israeli's condition. It wasn't good. It looked as though at least one bullet had perforated an artery. Barzilai was knotting a field tourniquet around his thigh. Jake helped him yank it taut.

"Do something for me," Barzilai said. "Can you draw him out a little?"

"Danny—"

"Trust me, all right?"

Jake did trust him. So he made himself a target, aiming at the hallway and waiting for his enemy to appear.

The cold-eyed man stepped into a firing angle and opened up on Jake. At Jake's feet, Barzilai fired from the floor. But he was shooting at something on the door to the master bedroom. Just in time, Jake realized what it was.

The charge.

He slumped behind the planter.

The door exploded. Debris pounded the floor.

When Jake looked back, he saw Rifaat's bodyguard staggering. He was a bloody mess, a hundred shards of wood stabbing through him. The pistol dropped from his boneless grip.

Barzilai finished him with a shot to the head.

"Go! Get Rifaat!" he urged Jake.

Jake was past second thoughts, hesitation or fear. He charged to the blasted frame of the bedroom door and thrust his gun barrel into the room.

Standing unsteadily was a surprised Abdel Aziz Rifaat, his right arm in tatters, an AK-47 on the floor. He'd caught some shrapnel and was deathly pale.

Jake walked into the room, his weapon pointed at the terrorist's chest.

He looked at his enemy and felt his index finger poised against the trigger of his gun.

Rifaat said something.

Jake didn't shoot.

In those extra instants, emotion fled his body and reason set in. He had the man. The bastard would be far more useful under interrogation.

Rifaat's left hand shot to his mouth. He bit on something, an expression of victory in his smile. Jake sprang toward him, trying to grab the man's arm, but it was too late.

Rifaat fell. His eyes grew enormous, as if trying to escape a face that was now a repulsively gruesome mask, all muscles contracted, lips stretched into a ghoulish grin of pure suffering. Guttural sounds and muffled screams of agony came from the now-closing throat, the sound mixing with flowing mucus. The terrorist clawed his way to Jake's feet in desperation, as if repenting for taking the poison, his eyes begging for help.

Jake stepped back, disgusted. Just as well, he thought. He pointed his Uzi at Rifaat and pulled the trigger. More bullets than he expected tore through the man's neck and head.

For the shortest time, Jake looked at the terrorist's face. So little was left of it. Abdel Aziz Rifaat was now merely a dead piece of flesh. Jake had reached the final destination of his journey, from pain to revenge, and he knew it in his mind but not in his heart.

Like a train sliding on its rails even after all brakes are pulled, the inertia of his hatred continued to carry him forward. He pulled the trigger once more and watched as the bullets punched more holes into Rifaat's corpse. If only it were possible to kill beyond killing.

Finally, he left the room to rejoin the group.

The shooting had stopped long ago. Jake knelt next to Barzilai, who was being tended to by the team medic.

"Did you get Rifaat?" the Israeli asked, voice little more than a whisper.

Jake nodded. "He's dead."

"Keep up the other good work, you promise?" the Israeli said, his voice even weaker.

"Hey, I don't like to do other people's work," Jake answered. "You'll be good to go soon."

"I don't think so." Barzilai looked pale. He was breathing with difficulty, struggling to pull air back into his lungs. "Take care of Rachel. She looks tough but she needs support. Gerard was everything to her."

"You worry too much. You should rest now," Jake said, feeling warmth around his knee. He looked down at a spreading pool of blood. The severed artery in Barzilai's groin was more than a tourniquet could stanch.

Amnon looked at his watch. "Seven minutes. We need to move." His voice was somber. "They'll kill us all if we stay here."

The other Israelis assembled two stretchers and carefully laid Barzilai and the dead soldier on them. All moved swiftly toward the beach.

Two of the large duffel bags contained inflatable dinghies. Minutes later, they were rowing away from shore, with Amnon talking to the Ferretti by radio. Shortly after that they were on the large boat, sailing at full speed toward Israel. Jake looked at his watch. The whole operation had taken twenty-four minutes, two less than planned. He heard a gasp at his side. Danny Barzilai had just died.

And finally Jake cried, thick and anguished tears, the unrestrained sobs growing deeper and more desperate, as his grief—and most of all, his anger—at last surfaced and painted the world red. It was the first time he'd truly wept since the day at the toy store. He sat down and let the release of absolute sorrow wash over him at last.

EPILOGUE

---◆---

FAMED HEDGE FUND MANAGER KILLED IN TEL AVIV

Jacob H. Burke a victim of suicide bombers while visiting Israel's high-tech industry

Jake Burke was dead. The Wall Street Journal said so.

Rachel had arranged for his name to be added to a list of those killed in a suicide bombing at the Hilton Hotel in Tel Aviv.

The only people who knew he was still alive and in hiding were Rachel, Big Ben and Theodore Suter, the trustee in charge of managing the Stephanie Claire Foundation for Victims of Terror. He was also responsible for making Jake's money available for additional funding of STOP, if necessary. Jake looked at the stack of *Herald Tribunes* and *El Pais* piled beside his neatly made bed.

A lot had changed in the days and weeks since he'd left Israel. Early on, rumors began circulating that the change of leadership in Iran had been a coup orchestrated by the CIA. Discredited after consistently failing to predict major events that would shape America's priorities, from the fall of the Soviet Union to September 11th, the Agency was suddenly being lionized by intelligence analysts in the world press as having solved the once intractable issue of Iran by promoting the coup.

As time went by, STOP became synonymous with a successful intelligence operation. The more America's president denied any involvement with STOP, the more the pundits extolled the cleverness of this "new American intelligence posture."

These pundits let out a collective I-told-you-so when the spokesperson for the White House announced that the two ex-CIA agents, Samuel J. Stone and Ramon T. Delgado, would not be sent to the Hague after all. Jake was sure that the only reason for this was that the administration had realized that a trial at the International Criminal Court would expose the CIA's early involvement with STOP. Nevertheless, the decision served as confirmation to the rest of the world that STOP was indeed a CIA operation. Why would the president protect the two men, otherwise? A cover article in *The Economist* presented the convincing theory that the president had the two men arrested because he didn't know the full extent of the CIA's involvement with STOP. He had decided to keep the Americans on U.S. soil after being fully informed.

Having been deposed, the dictator of Syria fled into the night. His whereabouts remained unknown. The new head of the Syrian Baath party, in coordination with the Lebanese army, sent troops back into southern Lebanon to disarm Hezbollah. They didn't bother with the Popular Islamic Jihad. That organization had disintegrated in furious infighting after the death of its leader, Abdel Aziz Rifaat.

But the struggle wasn't over. Far from it.

Pakistan still refused to launch a major purge of the pro-Islamist elements of its intelligence service, the ISI. It also resisted demands that it mount a concerted military operation to eradicate the fundamentalist presence from its northwestern region.

Saudi Arabia, its ossified monarchy paralyzed by fear of an Islamist coup, was still a problem. Jake had decided that the Saudi ruling elite would only change if STOP showed it that not acting meant the destruction of the kingdom's infrastructure.

Jake's silent movie, now longer, still played on. Stephanie was still looking adoringly at Claire in the toy-store entrance. The clean-shaven man with the bulky trench coat coming down the escalator, followed by the flash.

Isabelle Said's wise eyes watching him, blue as the Mediterranean . . .

Ashraf's dead eyes staring blankly, the hammer embedded in his skull . . .

Gerard battling the Pasdaran on the streets of Tehran . . .

A new sun flaring on the shores of Qeshm . . .

Rifaat's body jerking and dancing at the impact of bullet after bullet . . .

Danny Barzilai saying a soundless good-bye . . .

Silent scenes all.

Nothing blocked Jake's sorrow now. Nothing stopped his deep cleansing pain. His vision was now unclouded, his mind clear.

From his desk, Jake could see the Giralda, the most prominent structure in Seville. It had been built by the Almohades, an Islamic dynasty of fanatically strict religious belief. Contemporary fundamentalist Muslims cited their reign, during which Muslim medicine, philosophy, mathematics and literature were the most advanced in the world, as an example of what would come to be as soon as the war against the West was won.

Those same fundamentalist Muslims also reminded their listeners that after defeating the Christians at the end of the 12th century, the bellicose and intolerant Almohade leader Abd al-Mumin, ordered all of the churches and synagogues in southern Spain destroyed.

Looking out his window at the tower, as someone practiced the piano in a nearby apartment, Jake pulled what looked like a credit card from his wallet and deftly removed a small circle from its center. He thought of Jorge Santayana, a Spaniard born several centuries after the Muslims had been driven from his country. During his years as a professor at Harvard, Santayana had once said, "Those who cannot remember the past are condemned to repeat it."

It wouldn't happen this time. Fundamentalist Islam would be stopped. Jake took a long look at the optical disk and inserted it into his computer.

A soft womanly touch caressed his shoulder. He looked up at Miranda and smiled. He was finally at peace.

As the scent of . . . was it orange blossoms . . . wafted into his room on a warm breeze, Jake closed his eyes and listened quietly to the soft piano sound. He had recognized the opening notes of Debussy's "Clair de Lune."

AUTHOR'S NOTE

———◆◆◆———

This story is born of true events. While avoiding legal problems, I stayed as close as possible to real people and real situations. For those attentive to developments in the Middle East, a good part of this book will feel familiar: from the Entebbe Operation, the Osirak bombing, and Operation Spring of Youth, to past and present realities in Egypt, Israel and especially Iran.

Nasrullah Sadr Yazdi is a blend of three powerbrokers in Iran. As his name suggests, Abdel Aziz Rifaat is a combination of easily recognizable players in the macabre business of Middle East terrorism. Hamza and Mohand El Biali are based on two brothers, Khaled and Mohammed Shawqi al-Islambuli; Khaled was the assassin of Egypt's president Anwar Sadat and his brother Mohammed became a close associate of Osama bin Laden in Afghanistan.

The Popular Islamic Jihad is based on the characteristics and modes of operation of several terrorist groups, mainly the Egyptian Islamic Jihad, Al Qaeda and Hezbollah.

The suitcase nuclear bombs are real. Of 132, only forty-eight have been located, leaving a shocking eighty-four bombs still unaccounted for. In the late 1990s, Russian Defense Minister Igor Sergeyev confirmed that the USSR built the bombs. Additionally, Dr. Alexei Yablokov, a past member of the Supreme Soviet and former Science Advisor to President Yeltsin, verified both the existence of the small-sized bombs and Russia's inability to find them.

The U.S. Customs undercover investigation was initiated in 1995 and lasted two years. It did indeed end with the arrest of the two Lithuanians who were peddling suitcase nuclear bombs. In its indictment, the U.S. District Court also named the Russian Academy of Natural Sciences for "conspiring to locate and negotiate the source of weapons of mass destruction."

I am indebted to Georges Fleury and Pierre Miquel, whose writings greatly influenced my understanding of the consequences of the Algerian War for today's Middle East. I extend my gratitude as well to Steven Emerson, whose Investigative Project, a vast intelligence and data-gathering center on militant Islam, has been an invaluable source of information.

Special thanks to Richard Falkenrath, Robert Newman and Bradley Thayer. Their superbly prophetic *America's Achilles' Heel* inspired this book.

I would like to gratefully (and humbly) acknowledge the help of Adam Sexton who was there from the beginning and showed me how to write; Ed Stackler, for his invaluable expertise with the manuscript; to Andrea McKeown, for her painstaking editorial care; to Rebecca O'Meara whose energy lifted us along; and especially to the tireless Ken Atchity, who made this project happen.

—A.K.